Away with the Færies

MADELEINE COOK

First published in 2015 by Madeleine Cook

ISBN 978-1-518-89506-7

The right of Madeleine Cook to be identified as the author of thi work has been asserted in accordance with sections 77 and 78 of the Copyright Designs and Patents Act 1988.

A CIP catalogue record for this book is available from the British Library.

All rights reserved. No part of this book may be reproduced in any material form (including photocopying or storing in any medium by electronic means) without written permission of the copyright holder except in accordance with the provisions of the Copyright, Designs and Patents Act 1988. Applications for the copyright holder's written permission to reproduce any part of this publication should be addressed to the publishers.

Copyright ©2015 Madeleine Cook

Prologue

They were the Wise Ones. Through the hazy light of dawn, eleven pairs of angry eyes stared into one. They stood in their pale gowns, all matching except for the different coloured bands tied loosely around their waists. Above them a dark ochre sky was warped and twisting in on itself, drawing them upwards. Eleven of the Wise Ones now encircled one, their feet no longer touching the ground.

Bælor's wings wavered, and he released a defeated sigh.

'Armænon, you have disgraced us.'

The subject, his dark eyes glowing with the reflection of a scorching sun, said nothing. He kept his hands clasped together, holding Bælor's gaze.

Even Zian, the other culprit in this matter, remained silent and selfish while Armænon received what should have been a shared punishment. Hæthena, her voice soft, was the one to ask.

'Where is the necklace?'

Their wings beat together in unison, fanning out a fine dust from the ground. The Wise Ones, also named the Elana, were protected within an invisible shell that would soon be raising them into a new world, created with the help of a precious emerald stone. It was a stone more powerful than any other on earth, for the Elana's magic had been infused deep into its core.

'Where is the necklace?' Hæthena repeated.

'I cannot say,' said Armænon, unclasping his clammy hands to flex his fingers. Anger pulsed through him. He was being isolated, shunted from his family for wanting a power they were each entitled to. Zian hovered between Raole and Hæthena,

1

Away with the Færies

unable to meet Armænon's eye.

Kreed's expression was dark and threatening. 'We have the Emerald,' he said. 'Do you realise what you have done? It is no longer whole and a shard of the stone is now lost.' Sensing his rising temper, Raole cut in.

'May we come to a decision, Bælor?'

'You have jeopardised our future!' Kreed raged.

Bælor silenced him with a glare before turning slowly to address Armænon.

'You are banished. You will not be joining us in the other world, and will therefore suffer in these lands of the Human for as long as you can endure. Now, we are leaving.'

There was nothing left to say. The Elana continued their ascent and Armænon watched as the distance between him and them grew and grew. Then there was a flash of iridescent green light and he felt the moment when the Elana departed, taking a part of his soul with them – taking his magic. His hands crushed against his chest and he fell, scraping his knees on the hard ground. After a while Armænon gathered himself and rose, lifting his face to a now still, dark sky.

He wandered towards the horizon, his wings fluttering slowly to the rhythm of a nervous heart, the anger having dispelled from him like dust. He needed to find the necklace.

Kreed's words resounded in his mind:

'Do you realise what you have done?'

Chapter One

She waited impatiently outside the house. Curling her numb fingers into a loose fist, Sky knocked again and started to count the seconds, watching her breath appear like ice clouds before they evaporated in the cold January air. She'd counted to eight before hearing the stampede of footsteps as her friends raced down the stairs. Sky braced herself. The door was opened by Fran, flanked by Cassie and Hannah.

'Sorry about that,' said Fran, pulling Sky in by her arm. 'I think we had the music too loud. Were you out there long?'

Sky shrugged out of her coat, shrugging off any bad feelings. As the warmth of central heating enveloped her, she felt her muscles relax.

'Oh don't worry,' she said, smiling, for tonight was Simon Milton's party and she couldn't wait to get ready and go. Hannah and Cassie were already trampling up the stairs, talking and laughing.

'What are you wearing tonight?' asked Fran eagerly, and with her bag over one shoulder Sky followed her up the stairs.

'Well I've got a choice of three outfits.' It had been difficult choosing, so what else could she do but ask a friend's opinion? Fran's purple painted bedroom was cluttered with all sorts; text books and make up, hair appliances, they were spread across every surface. Fran closed the door and Hannah turned the volume up on the hi-fi.

Sky was applying some kohl eyeliner when the tip snapped off. She stared at it for a long moment before releasing a sigh, flopping back in the chair. Typical.

'Does anyone have a black kohl pencil? Mine's decided to break.'

Hannah's response was mumbled, and Sky turned to see her attaching false eyelashes. Fran was cross-legged on the bed, fumbling through her make up bag.

'I've only got brown.'

Sky groaned. 'What about Cass?'

Fran looked at her and shrugged. 'She's just popped into the bathroom.'

Sky made her way across the hallway and saw that the door was ajar. Before entering she paused, unsure as to whether or not she could hear her friend crying. It took only a second more to determine that Cassie was definitely crying. Biting her lip Sky nudged forward so she could poke her head around the door, her heart weighing heavy in her chest.

Cassie sat on the edge of the bath, dabbing her eyes with a tissue stained with blotches of mascara. She took a shaky breath and looked up, her eyes red-rimmed and puffy.

Sky wanted to cry too. She stepped in and shut the door, forgetting about the eyeliner, fixing her concerns on something far more important.

'Do you want to…talk about it, Cass?'

Cassie pursed her lips together, resting her elbow on the sink. 'There isn't much I can think of to say,' she said. 'I just seem to start thinking about it and then I can't stop. Talking about it only makes it more real.'

Sky closed the lid on the toilet and sat down onto it, feeling the buzz of excitement ebb away. For a while she sat quiet. It was tricky finding words to console her friend whose mum had been diagnosed with the 'big C'. It was dreadful. Sky's palms were clammy when she rubbed them together. 'She's having… treatment?'

Cassie nodded. 'She will be.'

'I'm sure it will be f-' Sky stopped herself before finishing the sentence. 'Fine' was a totally over used word, a filler for emotions. 'Technology and treatments these days are amazing, Cassie,' she said instead.

Chapter One

'I know, but I'm still scared. I shouldn't be worrying tonight. She told me to have fun and everything, but I feel bad.' She leaned forward and covered her face. 'This sucks.'

Sky moved next to her friend and put an arm around her hunched shoulders, contemplating what she personally would want to hear.

'Don't cut yourself up about this. It's the weekend of Simon's party. It might even be a good distraction.'

'A welcome distraction,' mumbled Cassie, sitting straight. 'Thank you.' She wiped her eyes with the soggy tissue and chucked it in the bin. 'I should probably redo my make up.'

Sky knew her friend was inspecting her half-made face.

'You know you only have eyeliner on one eye?' Cassie said a few seconds later.

'Totally, and if you've got a black kohl pencil I can finish the other eye.'

A glimmer of pale sunlight shone through the windows of the east wing, highlighting particles of dust that floated through the air.

Sky could hear the murmurs as she drew nearer to room 5E. Bursting in, the door swung shut behind her and, naturally, everybody turned to stare at The Late One.

She walked forward, clutching her bag while scanning the room for a place to sit. Cassie patted the empty seat next to her and Sky hurried over and sat down, unravelling her scarf. She placed her small bag on the table, dreading "the look" Mr Elmsbury would undoubtedly throw at her.

'You're late, Miss Francis,' he said sharply, taking off his glasses. He was known for disliking students with bad punctuality. It was just typical that her first lesson had to be English, and she had to be late.

'I'm sorry,' Sky mumbled, reluctantly meeting her teacher's stern gaze that somehow made her feel like the only one in the room, and not in a good way. She knew the class had their eyes on her too.

She needed to say something, but struggled to think under the pressure of Mr Elmsbury's gaze. The silence filled her ears. 'I missed my alarm!' she blurted out, regretting the words the moment they fell from her mouth.

'Maybe you should set the volume a little louder,' Mr Elmsbury quipped. He put his glasses on and turned back to the board, pen in hand.

'As I was saying, you have the choice of persuasive or descriptive...' he went on, scribbling the key words onto the whiteboard. Sky combed through her black hair and glanced across the room, only to catch sight of Alex and Louis smirking at her. She rolled her eyes.

'Still recovering?' Louis mouthed.

Sky narrowed her eyes at him and mouthed back 'you too?' She couldn't have been the only one still suffering.

The boys looked at each other, and then nodded slowly. Mr Elmsbury huffed.

'What do you think about that?' he enquired, focusing on Sky.

She swallowed hard and stared back without a clue. Of all things, she noticed the flecks of grey at his temples that hadn't been there when she'd started in year 7. Was his hairline receding?

Mr Elmsbury approached her desk and leaned forward – one of his interrogation techniques. Sky stared into dark blue eyes that seemed to engulf her like an ocean.

'Perhaps you would tell me,' he said coolly, but his jaw was set and his left eyebrow twitched. 'No?'

Sky's mind was blank. 'Sorry sir, I don't know,' she admitted, keeping her chin up. In the same way Mr Elmsbury disliked bad punctuality, Sky disliked interrogations. She picked at the lid of her pen, holding her teacher's gaze.

'Pay attention,' he said before walking away. Sky flipped open the text book in front of her, longing for the day to end even though it had barely started.

During morning break, Sky sat with her friends in their usual spot beneath an old tree on the outer school grounds. All the trees were naked; their crooked branches reaching out for leaves that were once attached. Sky gazed out through the fence, at red

Chapter One

brick houses of the neighbourhood, and past them to the plots where people grew their fruit and veg. Cows wandered about on the hillsides minding their own, ignoring the dense charcoal sky that overshadowed them.

'I think the hangover only really hit me today,' Alex said. 'My parents aren't too happy.'

Louis reached forward, yanking Cassie's pink woolly bobble hat from her head.

'Cass, you're still recovering too aren't you?' he teased and Cassie grimaced, sliding a gloved hand down her face.

'Mum told me to have a good time so I did, but maybe I had too much fun. Dad got really annoyed at me. I don't think I'll be allowed to do it again…or at least for a while. Maybe after the mock exams.' She sorted out her hair and gave Louis a threatening look. 'Can I have my hat back please?'

Louis ignored her request, pulling it onto his own head of brown hair. With an exasperated sigh, Cassie stuck out her arm. 'Give.'

'Pink really doesn't suit you,' Sky told him.

'Don't be lame!' Louis exclaimed when she ripped it off of his head.

Sky shrugged, giving him a what-do-you-expect sort of look before returning the hat to its rightful owner.

The group lapsed into a calm silence. Sky sat back and watched the cows, a few mooing at each other, some sitting down. Minutes later, thunder echoed across the hills.

'Wonderful,' she said to herself as the heavens opened above them. Closing her eyes, she felt the first cool drops of winter rain.

Sky walked home beneath dark clouds, the cold air nipping at her nose and cheeks.

She turned left into Margrove Avenue – the final stretch. It wasn't a pleasant place in winter; spindly trees hung over the path, their branches teasing those who walked along it. The odd streetlamp offered a comforting glow to pedestrians and despite the fact it gave Sky the creeps, she'd be damned if she let it show. She walked with firm footsteps and kept her bag close.

Her stomach grumbled, signifying the first real hunger she'd felt since Saturday. There was a newsagent not far from here, but to get there would mean turning and going back. It didn't take long to decide. Sky stopped, rolling her bag off of her shoulder. A moment later she'd retrieved her purse and taken out a handful of change, only then tuning in to the hasty "clip-clip" of heels on concrete.

A collision caused Sky to stumble back, and a shower of coins flew into the air. They tinkled onto the path, scattering. She stared at the iceberg she had hit: tall, dressed in a suit, a head of long brown hair. The lady seemed puzzled and gazed at Sky with questioning eyes.

Sky, her right shoulder throbbing, was unsure how to react. She took a deep breath ready to speak, flinching when the woman blurted out, 'You need to watch where you're going!'

She continued like a wind-up toy and Sky could only stand there stunned.

'My arm is almost out of its socket!' Sky could have laughed at that. 'You must always watch where you're going otherwise things like this happen.'

She had her hands on her hips, and a face contorted with contempt.

'Excuse me!' Sky retorted. 'It works both ways,' she pointed at the woman, then to the ground. '*You* weren't watching where *you* were going. I wasn't even moving,' she finished indignantly. This stranger had a nerve.

The woman glanced down. 'You're r-right,' she stuttered, the colour draining from her face. She clutched her chest. Sky was not amused by this performance.

'Care to help me pick up my change, seeing as you made me drop it all?'

The woman looked up with fear in her eyes, her mouth half open as if she'd witnessed something terrible.

Sky went through a few possibilities. Perhaps she was on her way back from a funeral, or having problems at work. She breathed in

Chapter One

the cold air and it helped clear her mind.

'I'm sorry to have caught you in a rush,' she said, rubbing her shoulder while waiting for a response. Preferably an apology.

But the woman rushed off without a word, keeping her head down. Sky shook her head in disbelief and watched her hurry away and out of sight.

In a fit of pique she knelt down to pick up her change. Spotting a pound coin she reached for it, and in doing so something sharp dug into her knee.

'What now?' she groaned.

A necklace of all things. A delicate gold chain with a dazzling green gemstone. Sky picked it up, captivated by the brilliance of it. It must have belonged to the iceberg.

Some strange notion was telling her to take it.

'It's too late to give it back anyway,' Sky muttered, and slipping it into her jacket pocket picked up her remaining coins from the gritty pavement.

Hooking her bag over her shoulder she set off once more, eager to get home.

Chapter Two

Christian walked beneath an azure sky. Coin jingled in the pouch he carried, and the cobble stone beneath his feet was pleasantly warm from the sun. Færies acknowledged him with a wave or bow which he had hoped would make him feel more integrated. Instead it left him feeling more isolated, and the difference between him and all other færies was clear to see. Christian smiled back regardless as he continued alone through the crowd of people – his people.

He couldn't help but wonder who would become the future queen of Krazonia. What did she look like? How would they meet? He recalled various conversations he'd overheard between his mother and many others, about a possible marriage. Hæthen, a place of snow-covered mountains and icy rivers, was home to Princess Faye. They said she was a beauty, with wings like that of a butterfly. She was intelligent and gracious, with hair the shade of ripe cherries and rich, olive skin.

Perhaps she would be the one.

Eventually he saw the large, brown flag waving at him in the breeze. The market place was teeming. Voices were raised, færies were shouting and laughing; the strong smell of fruit picked fresh from the vine and vegetables from the ground lingered in the air. Many Krazonians made way for the prince so he could get the best each stall had to offer. His protests went unheard. He offered the payment in coin – four lunes to be exact – but it was declined.

'Please!' Christian exclaimed, thrusting the bronze coin into the stall owner's hands. This often happened, much to his frustration. 'I'm just the same as you!' he wanted to shout.

Chapter Two

'No sir. Take them at no cost, for it is the least we can do,' the færie said kindly, offering the lunes back to him.

Christian exhaled in exasperation, feeling the nudges of other færies who only wanted what was best for him. Voices got louder, and all eyes were on him as he refused to take back the money.

'No, I insist,' he replied with a forced smile, before darting away with the bag of fruit and vegetables. The town square was a hive of activity. Taking flight to get away from the crowds, he noticed then his mother settling a dispute.

Of course, Krazonians loved it. They would gather in the square to hear the queen's verdict on various matters. He remembered passing her this morning, hunched over piles of paper in the drawing room, ink pen in hand. She had mentioned a disagreement between two crop owners that needed to be addressed. So that was the cause for so many excited færies.

A while later Christian was in his room when his mother, Anya, appeared in the doorway looking anxious. The long sleeves of her dress were rolled up, always a bad sign.

'I want you to help your sister. She thinks I'm punishing her and will not stop complaining. I've asked her to welcome a new family and help them set up their new home in Morel village,' she said. Her wings were taut.

'She seems unable to grasp the importance of good conduct. I only want her to learn how to deal with these things so she will know in future.' Christian could see Anya was not amused, and it often happened that she was embarrassed by her daughter's erratic behaviour. Rhia was helpful when it suited her.

'If anything I'll make things worse. You know how stubborn she is.'

'I know,' his mother replied, her gaze expectant. 'This family is from Gloryn.'

Christian sighed. 'Morel village?'

'Yes.'

'Okay, I'll go,' he said, following his mother down the corridor. When she went up the staircase he went down, meeting two guards Dill and Rhys at the main doors.

'Good day,' said Dill. Rhys nodded once and stood aside,

allowing Christian to pass.

'I've been given orders to help my sister,' he muttered, but laughed a little when he caught Dill's smirk.

'Best of luck,' the guard said, moving forward to push the door open wide. A gust of warm air met Christian and the sunlight streamed in, glinting off of the guards' metallic armour.

'Thank you,' he said, wings unfurling. 'I don't think she will ever learn.'

'She will, just perhaps not yet.'

'We'll see.'

When Christian reached the village it wasn't difficult to spot her. He slowed down to make a careful landing and made it just in time, as he had to leap forward and catch the planks of wood that fell from his sister's grip.

'Have you not got any rope?'

Rhia scowled at him and resumed her struggle with the four planks of wood. She could hardly hold one. Christian placed a hand on her arm.

'Allow me,' he offered.

'I'm guessing mother told you that I need help. I don't. I can manage,' Rhia said icily, wandering a few steps away to pick up a tangled rope. 'And yes, I have rope.' She looked at him, her grey eyes like flint. Something else was bothering her, but with Rhia in this mood it wasn't even worth asking.

'Presumably you've refused the help of other færies?' Christian asked, watching Rhia awkwardly bind the rope around the wood. The brown waves of her hair blew about in the breeze, disguising her face, but it was apparent that she was not happy. Letting out a huff she threw the frayed rope down.

'You tie it!' she barked, folding her arms.

Birds sang in the large oaks of Morel village, and a færie was playing a flute.

'Cheer up Rhia. Help me with this,' Christian said, tying the knot and bundling the planks into his arms. 'Where are we going?'

Chapter Two

The princess shielded her eyes with one hand and pointed with the other. Following the direction in which his sister was pointing, Christian caught sight of the family who were having the tree house built. Two children sat beneath a tree, laughing together in the shade with their small fragile wings flickering at each funny face they made at each other. Christian's smile faded when he looked back at his sister.

'Is this punishment to you?'

Rhia straightened up. 'I never said it was punishment.' She glanced down and scuffed the ground with her heel. 'But you know what happened the last time I tried to help someone.'

Christian's arms were beginning to tremble and ache. He shifted the wood with his knee.

'I know,' he said quietly, remembering the chaos all too well. The memory was like a poison dart in his chest, spreading a dull pain. 'Look, the sooner we get this done...'

'Yes, I understand. Mother wants a good example to be set,' said Rhia dryly. She led Christian down the hillside to the family.

The parents were Simya and Gray from the lands of Gloryn, Krazonia's ally over in the western region of the kingdom. With the help of Gray and another Krazonian, Christian began work on the tree house while Rhia flew about handing him this and that. Every now and then he'd catch her eye and she would immediately look away, her expression hardening so that no emotion could escape through her eyes.

It took the remainder of the day to complete.

As the sun began to set, one by one the torches were lit around the villages; markets closed and færies were settling down for the night. Christian flew to the ground and ignoring the twinge of a splinter in his finger, admired the work done. The two young ones, who Rhia had mumbled were called Willa and Byron, were flying around the tree, chasing each other in circles while their mother stood below watching them. For a while she conversed quietly with Rhia and Christian could hear her speaking in joyful tones. His sister didn't sound so joyful. To Rhia this would only ever be a duty, not something to be enjoyed.

The sun had nearly vanished, leaving remnants of rose-coloured cloud across a dark blue sky.

Christian's expression was thoughtful as he gazed across at the landscape. Beyond Krazonia's villages, the Ever-Growing Forest, Bluewater Glen and over the hills of plush green grass the scenery began to change: ground grew rough; soft grasses and cobble stolen by the arid earth of Zania. Christian felt that familiar prick of hatred, like a thorn, dig into his heart. Zania was no ally. Tæ was a hard-hearted, cruel færie, and in her desperation to get hold of the Emerald had driven any chances of reconciliation with Krazonia into the ground. Krazonia had always been one step ahead, until the tragedy four years ago. Somewhere something went wrong and Tæ had almost won.

Although Krazonia had retrieved the Emerald, Christian's father had died for it.

'That stone is a curse,' he said quietly.

Christian was drawn out of these thoughts by sudden movement at the edge of his vision and he turned to see Rhia with her arms raised, both hands clutching either side of her head. Her eyes were half shut as if she were in pain. The new family had already withdrawn to their new tree house, so now it was just the two siblings facing each other.

'Rhia, what is it?' Christian asked urgently.

'It's nothing – nothing,' she snapped, screwing her eyes shut.

'How bad is it? What are you seeing?'

'It's...'

Biting his lip, Christian waited. At times like this there was nothing else he could do. The air around them was gradually cooling, the sun now lost behind the distant mountains of the Hæye region. Night had set in. Rhia relaxed her shoulders. She glanced at her brother, eyes shiny in the torchlights' glow.

In one swift movement her wings were open. 'It was nothing. I'm going home.'

'Rhia wait!' But she was up and gone. Christian shook his head, watching her go.

He bid the new family goodnight and ambled up the hillside, deciding to make his way home on foot tonight.

Chapter Two

He woke with a start. A dim light filtered in through the sheer curtains and Christian sat up feeling dazed. His heart was pounding. Slowly he pushed back the bed sheet, his eyes still adjusting to the change from the vivid colours of his dream. Christian walked across the cold floor to the windows and peered out. All was still. Not a wing stirred. Some of the torches continued to flicker brightly, but most were reduced to a faint ember. At the eastern edge of the world, clouds lifted to reveal the faint, jagged outlines of Hæthen's mountain range were silhouetted against the backdrop of a dawn sky.

He thought about his dream.

The Emerald had been taken. Christian ran across the hills, calling and searching for help but there was no one. Struggling for breath he'd forced himself to reduce his run to a walk, continuing to scan the world with alert eyes. When he turned he appeared to be standing in the town square, but it was deserted. He realised then where the stone was located. Soon a loud, bitter laughter began to chase him; the unnerving sound filling his ears. He flung a door open to a færie's hut and was momentarily blinded by a spectrum of bright colours. He thought that through it all a færie with long, dark hair stood, holding the stone. He went to reach for it, and it was then that he awoke.

He walked to the bedroom door and opened it, stepping out tentatively. Glancing left and right down the corridor he spotted Simian, another guard, patrolling. Before they locked eyes Christian pulled back into his room and took a deep breath. What was this uneasy feeling that caused his heart to beat so fast? This night was no different to any other night.

'Go back to sleep,' Christian told himself before returning to bed. He lay on his side and for some time remained awake, listening to his own breathing. He needed to speak to Rhia, or mother. His sister didn't suffer for nothing. The head pains she had were always connected to that glowing green stone.

His sister did not suffer for nothing. So why had she said it?

Chapter Three

Sky closed the front door and leaned against it, the delicious aroma of frying onions stealing through the air. She hadn't made it to the newsagents, so the smell of food sent her taste buds into a frenzy. The house was warm, and Sky unravelled her scarf as she walked into the living room to see her dad, James, standing at the bookcase, stroking his chin while he searched for a particular title. He seemed to be in deep thought, but turned around when Sky fell back onto the leather sofa.

'What are you looking for?' Sky asked, shrugging out of her jacket.

'Graham has asked to borrow the Heath Martin trilogy and I'm wondering where I've put it.' His clear blue eyes clouded over, as though he were trying to recall its whereabouts. Giving up the search, he sat down next to Sky.

'Mum's cooking tonight, as you can tell,' he said with a grin.

Sky smiled back, her fingers already fumbling for the necklace. She drew it out and placed it onto the coffee table. The perfectly chiselled piece of stone gleamed, and Sky could hardly think straight with it sparkling before her. She heard her father speak.

'Wow Sky, where did you get that?'

'Um,' she said when she'd found her voice. 'I discovered it on the way home.'

'Lucky find. If that is real emerald it's extremely precious,' James remarked, standing up. 'You might want to think about handing it into the police though, there could be someone out there looking for it.'

'I will.'

Chapter Three

Sky pushed aside the books and make-up that cluttered her desk to make space for the necklace. She positioned it so the chain shaped an oval - how it would look if somebody was to wear it. Sky sat onto her spongy swivel chair, twiddling her thumbs, debating whether to put it on. It felt sort of wrong. She leant forward to inspect it again, utterly enraptured yet unable to fathom why. Sure, her family had bought her plastic rings, dainty necklace's with pearls and pretty 'diamonds' but they didn't sparkle like this stone.

It was as though she could look into it. Gazing at the stone the size of a twenty pence piece, it seemed to shine from within, its colour deepening at its core. Sky searched for ways to describe it.

'Yes,' she murmured when it clicked, remembering one particular memory from a family holiday:

Standing up in the boat, I look out: the edges of the sea are crystal blue and the sunlight dazzles on its surface, but when the world beneath the ocean falls, the sea deepens into an abyss. It turns from aqua to liquid ink.

This stone had that same affect. In her hands, it felt as though it carried the weight of history. She knew for a fact, judging by its slightly scathed edges that it had one.

Her phone buzzed twice but she didn't check it. She didn't respond to her parents calling up the stairs to say dinner was on the table. Only when James thumped on her bedroom door did Sky untangle her thoughts and drag herself away from the desk, but not before the necklace was hiding safely in her chest of drawers.

Sky breezed past her father in the hallway.

'I think I'd better phone the police, regarding that necklace,' he said.

She paused at the top of the stairs and swallowed, the feeling of guilt causing her heart to beat double time.

'It isn't right, is it?' Only when she said the words aloud did she realise that in fact, she did feel bad. When it wasn't in front of her she could see things clearly. The necklace was not hers and she had taken it. For all she knew that stone could be a hundred years old, a family heirloom! She hadn't even considered its sentimental value.

Sky remembered the woman's pale face and the fear etched into her features. She'd pretty much fled the scene, but why?

'The best thing to do is to inform the police. Someone may well be looking for a lost family treasure. But,' her father said with a shrug, 'if no one claims it, it's yours. Your conscience will be clear.'

Sky nodded.

'I'll give them a ring, and I'll let you know if anybody claims it. Alright darling?'

'I hope they do,' Sky said as she made her way down the stairs, trailing the wooden banister with trembling hands.

Sky clicked the button and her bedside lamp sprang to light. She blinked hard a few times as her eyes adjusted to the change. Sleepily she checked the time: 5.01am. All she could think about were the dreams from which she'd just woken. Strange dreams that felt worryingly real. It took her a few minutes to come out of the world she'd fallen into and she lay passively, her mind skimming over the vivid images affixed there.

Soaring green hills, a warm breeze on her skin and a scorching sun. She had felt something pressing against her back as she wandered through what seemed to be a town square, and a busy one at that. Glancing down she found herself a foot in the air, but this didn't alarm her. She knew what she was doing.

Soon, she was flying among the clouds.

Sky ran her hands through mist, spinning through the wisps of white. Her lungs took in the thin air quickly and it didn't feel enough, but she put it down to the excitement. At that moment she thought of nothing but of the direction she would fly next.

Suddenly the air around her condensed and she couldn't breathe. Clouds vanished. She'd gone too far, to a part of the world where if she looked up the vast blue turned black, and she was being pulled further out into the nothingness by some invisible

Chapter Three

force. Hands gripped her, tugging her back. She screamed but no sound came out. Terrified, Sky squeezed her eyes shut.

When she opened them again she was in her bed lying motionless. Sky gasped for air, clutching her chest in panic. The bedside lamp was still on. Wait.

Sky checked the clock: 5.23am beamed back at her in neon red. She had actually fallen asleep again and reverted to the dreams she'd been contemplating what seemed like only seconds ago. She sat up and leant her back against the cool wall, pondering on the second dream. It had been short, and slightly less eventful. The emerald, larger in her dream, had been the subject. There was no gold chain, only the stone.

She'd cupped the stone in her hands. Somebody wanted it and it she needed to keep it safe. She held it close to her chest as she ran through a small, deserted town to some unknown destination, and after what felt like a long time, stumbled into a little house: a hut. It was uninhabited. Cradling the stone she lowered her head, her black hair cascading down and covering it like a curtain.

She heard a loud bang and jumped.

Sky's eyes felt stingy, as if she hadn't slept at all. With a sigh she switched off the light and snuggled down, hoping to slip back into slumber.

Sleep did a no-show, much to her exasperation. School would be very long and very tedious indeed, Sky thought as she slid sluggishly from bed two hours later.

Chapter Four

Christian tapped lightly on his mother's bedroom door the next morning, hoping to catch her before breakfast.

'Come in.'

He went inside, closing the door behind him. With a bow he wished the queen good morning, attempting a smile. Thankfully she wasn't looking because it was a poor attempt. Thoughts of the stone, his sister and his dreams hung over him like a storm cloud.

'Good morning,' Anya said, turning away from the window. The curtains were tied back, revealing the beautiful sunlit lands of Krazonia. The morning sun was already dazzling and Christian could just see the lake, its surface glittering. His mother's smile was warm and welcoming like the sun. Christian hated the fact that he could very well ruin this cheery mood, and they weren't even half way through the day. Anya was mindful of other færies' feelings, especially her children's, and would inevitably notice her son's unhappy disposition.

'Did you not sleep?' she asked, her features softening in concern.

Christian rubbed his face. 'I didn't really, no. I must speak with you about Rhia,' he said before he could swallow the words back down.

'You wish to talk about Rhia,' Anya said calmly, but in the undertone of her voice laid apprehension. Stretching her pale wings she sat down on the edge of the bed, still in her flowing night dress, and patted the space next to her. 'Sit down.'

Christian complied, placing his hands on his lap. The Emerald was at the other end of the room. He stared at it, watching it glow

Chapter Four

within its glass dome.

'Yesterday, before sun down, Rhia suffered one of her headaches,' he said, looking at his mother for a reaction to his words. She would either nod knowingly or an expression of perplexity would overcome her features, signifying that Rhia had not said a word. It was the latter, and her wings stiffened. She said nothing.

'I am aware of her connection with the Emerald and that four years ago, she found the Elana of Bluewater. We know they gave her this…power, meaning she would always know when the stone was in danger. I believe she saw something yesterday but didn't want to tell me. Either that or she couldn't figure out what she'd seen …I'm not sure which is worse. I dreamt of the Emerald last night, and I can't shift this feeling that something isn't right. Is it possible for you and I to feel things too? Being in such close proximity to the stone?' Christian drew breath.

All was silent for a while, until Anya spoke. 'Your sister said nothing to me.' She shifted away slightly, gazing across the room. Christian got up and walked to the window. He could hear the carpenters chopping wood, a repetitive, blunt sound echoing over the hillside.

'She wouldn't put us in danger like that, would she?' Christian looked at his mother, and she at him. Her expression gave no inner thoughts away.

'No,' she said simply.

It was farfetched, but Christian couldn't help asking.

'What about the Elana?'

At that his mother stood up in sudden anger, an emotion that had never suited her. Her eyes darkened.

'The stone has been in our family for generations. In the times it has been sought and fought over, we have kept it safe. The Wise Ones, before departing, chose us over Hæthen, Gloryn and Zania.' She said the final word without flinching but it still pained Christian. 'We were chosen as its custodian.' He thought resentment had found its way into her voice, and it wasn't surprising. She'd lost her love, the king, over it.

'Why us?' Christian replied, feeling a rush of irritation. It caused a tingly, burning sensation under his skin.

'You are aware of its powers Christian, don't be so naïve. You are also aware of Tæ and for the last ten years of her reign it has been her obsession. She wants its power – your father died for it. Tæ cannot see past her own greed,' Anya finished coldly. She ran her hands down her dress.

'You say that as if I didn't already know!' he snapped.

She sat back down, overlooking his outburst. 'I'll speak to Rhia. It could have just been worry that made you dream about it. It was only a dream, remember that.'

Christian nodded, the frustration subsiding.

'And whether it is possible for us to feel things too, I do not know,' Anya murmured.

Christian wasn't sure whether to stay or go. He passed his weight from foot to foot. 'It wasn't my intention to ruin your day...' he said.

'Please don't worry. Don't worry about any of this. I'm sure all is well,' replied his mother, and by the sounds of it her mind was already on other things. Christian watched her walk towards the window silently, and he knew then it was time to leave.

He did so and clicked the door shut, trapping in the sunlight.

Christian was on his way to town when he collided with a flustered Rhia.

'Rhia, are you okay?'

'I-I don't know!' she stammered, breathless and wide eyed.

'You really don't seem it. What's wrong?' Christian wasn't going to let it go this time.

'Where is mother? There are Zanians here – two – three of them coming to the mansion. They're on their way as we speak.'

In a flurry of movement Rhia went to pass Christian, but he caught her arm.

'You knew this would happen, didn't you?' he fired at her.

'No! I didn't. I didn't see anything,' she exclaimed, sounding close to tears. A mixture of guilt and shock caused Christian to let go of her arm and Rhia seized the chance, flying away, leaving him

Chapter Four

in a dust cloud. He choked it out and raced up the hill towards the mansion.

Reaching the main doors, the atmosphere had already changed. Guards stomped around with serious expressions, checking their armour, murmuring to each other. Rhia was nowhere to be seen and nor was the queen.

Rhys, the young, fresh-faced guard, appeared at the bottom of the stairs.

'Sir,' he bowed quickly, distracted.

'Rhys, does my mother know that Zanians are on their way?'

'Yes,' he answered without hesitation. 'I am to round up the guards. Dill and Gayle will shortly be with your mother. There will be two guarding the stone.'

'Good,' Christian replied, making his way up the spiral staircase. He walked quickly along the second floor corridor and turned left. He could hear Rhia talking in a loud, angry voice. He burst into the room, not bothering to knock.

'...when I want to be here!'

Christian met the wide eyed gaze of his exasperated mother.

'Both of you go to Bluewater. I don't want you here,' she said, and Rhia folded her arms, staring firmly at the floor. 'Simian is downstairs and he will escort you,' Anya continued, sweeping her long, light brown hair up to tie it back. She then began to wring her wrists, looking to Christian. 'Will you go?' she asked.

Not much time had passed between the conversation with his mother this morning, and now.

'Come on, Rhia. We need to leave,' Christian said, feeling his wings twitch. It was as if the frustration had passed on from his sister, to his mother and then to him.

'I need to know what's happening,' she said. 'I can't go.'

'I'm sure mother will inform us.'

'Why not save her the hassle?' Rhia retorted, throwing her head up to glare at Christian, as if he had caused this disorder.

'Enough!' Anya cried. 'You will go!'

Dill and Gayle entered the room, a sign for Christian and his sister to leave. Rhia could not fight mother on this one and begrudgingly she dropped her arms to her sides, pushing past the guards to get out.

'It was the right decision for us to come here,' Christian said, hoping it would be enough to lower the invisible barrier Rhia had raised between the two of them as they flew through Krazonia village. Simian flew behind, more than likely aware of this tense and awkward situation. Rhia beat her wings faster, broadening the distance between them.

'Why will you not speak to me?' Christian's question went unanswered and a wave of anger coursed through him. 'Fine, don't,' he said sharply. Rhia was so difficult. If only she'd opened up about her concerns and problems when they started, they might not have become a mountain too big for anyone to climb and she might not be so bitter about it - bitter and selfish. It was as though she sat at the top, looking down on those who tried to reach her. It was never going to be enough. Christian inhaled deeply and for some time focused on the feel of his long, sturdy wings beating together. The summer air blew warm against him as he flew, his mind lingering on previous thoughts. Not only was Rhia making her own life troublesome, but her family's too.

They headed west. Looking back, Christian could see the mansion had shrunk to the size of a blueberry, and before long it would be out of sight. Soon he and his sulky sister would reach the tranquillity of Bluewater Glen, with its meandering streams surrounded by high rocky walls and tall grass that stirred in the breeze. No færies inhabited it, for it was near the outskirts of Krazonia. Clearly Anya wanted her children out of reach from whatever was going on at home. Christian felt the pressure knots in his shoulders ease, but the anxiety would not recede until he knew what was going on.

He slowed to a hover before landing in the long grass. It swished against his knees.

'Simian, you can go back. Rhia and I will be fine here.'

The guard looked unsure. 'Your mother ordered I escort you.'

'Exactly,' Christian replied with a reassuring smile. 'You've

Chapter Four

done just that, now I want you to go back. You should be there. We're fine.'

'As you can see, all is well,' he heard Rhia say, her words coated in sarcasm. Already she was wandering off, wading through the grass and hitting it with her hands as she went. Christian shook his head at her. 'Don't worry Simian. Please, go.'

The guard bowed and took to the air once again, this time in haste. Tousling his dark hair, Christian closed his wings and trod through the grasses after his sister.

'Rhia, for the sake of the Elana, wait!' he shouted, knowing full well she would hear. She stopped, much to his surprise. He'd expected it to take at least three attempts.

'This situation would be more bearable if you actually spoke to me,' Christian said when he reached her. They stood beside the stream.

Rhia frowned. Christian could see her fighting with emotion. She blinked back the tears that formed in her grey eyes and pressed her lips together, keeping it inside like she always did. After a long moment she looked down, unlocking her gaze from Christian's.

'Do you not understand?' she spoke so quietly her voice almost blended in with the sound of trickling water. 'You know I sense these things, and that I should know when the stone is in danger.'

'Yes.'

'You know I have visions. But yesterday it was as though something was obscuring it completely.' She looked up at him, her expression pained. 'I feel like this is my fault. I hate it.

'I didn't want to come here because every time I do I am reminded of the Elana,' she covered her face with both hands, her voice coming out muffled, 'and what happened four years ago. I hate them too.' Her hands slid from her face. She looked utterly drained, and older than her years. 'You wonder why I don't like helping people. The one time I helped that deluded færie and saw the Elana with my own eyes, here in this place…look what happened to me.'

Christian put a hand on her shoulder but she shook it off.

'I'm relied on for when events like this occur. I didn't ask for it, and now I'm not seeing I feel I must take all of the blame because who else would have known?' She hesitated, eyes glazing over. 'Who else should have known..? I can't necessarily change the future, but I can help us prepare for it.'

Christian gazed at her, no longer angry. Four years ago when his father died there had been another incident. Rhia was blessed, or cursed, by the Elana of Bluewater Glen, giving her this vision. Before he had chance to offer any kind words Rhia had caught onto his gaze, which of course to her would be demeaning.

'Don't look at me in that way,' she said, her tone bordering on contempt, all vulnerability gone as quick as lightning. 'Let's just sit here for a while and then go back.'

Christian raised his hands and sighed. 'Okay.' He wasn't going to push for conversation if she was already on the edge. They patted the grass with their feet and sat down. Christian trailed his fingers through the cool stream, wishing the serenity of this place was enough to pacify him. Sunlight twinkled on the water's surface and butterflies with wings emerald green flitted by. The knots in Christian's shoulders pulled tight again.

He sat with his sister in a tense silence, waiting.

Chapter Five

The following night Sky couldn't sleep. She tossed and she turned, and made a flustered attempt to rearrange the pillows and quilt so she lay in a completely different position. Even then, all she could think about was that stupid necklace.

Sky gripped her quilt and squeezed it in her fists until her fingernails hurt, wishing she'd never picked it up. Any feelings of guilt she'd manage to harbour came back double strength and she wished then that the bed would swallow her up.

'Why?' Sky muttered to herself. Even when she'd tried the old technique of counting sheep, they only turned green.

Another hour passed. Fuming, she threw back the bed covers and sat up. She had no idea of the time and she didn't care. Crossing the room to her chest of drawers, she was all ready to take it out when her hand froze, a cold fear seeping through her.

In its bed of jumpers and shirts the small stone was glowing as if it had a pulse, illuminating the items around it in a bright green hue. Pressing a hand to her mouth Sky stumbled back, horrified.

Cautiously she peered into the drawer, and a small squeak escaped her lips.

'This can't be happening,' Sky whispered, wrapping her arms around herself, trying to keep together. Things like this just. Didn't. Happen. She walked to the window and peeled back the curtains, seeing a moon still in reign high up in the black, cloudless sky. The streetlamps were off – so it was past two in the morning. Sky stared at the moon for a while, waiting for her heart to stop pummelling her ribcage, and for the necklace to stop glowing.

After a few minutes Sky crept back to the drawer, only to see that nothing had changed.

Fighting her fear she picked it up, daring it to be real. She held the chain between her thumb and forefinger and the jewel dangled before her, turning gradually like a mobile above a cot. It continued to glow.

'Right, okay,' she murmured. If she didn't accept the situation for what it was, she would definitely go mad. She had to take it at face value. After shutting it away Sky made the decision to go back to bed and it would be very simple: she would go to sleep, wake up and get ready for school.

As always these things were easier said than done.

With tired eyes Sky scanned the area by the front gates in search of her friend. Cassie always met her here alongside the row of silver birches, but today there was no sign of her pink bobble hat. Perhaps she'd decided it was too cold to wait. Sky continued up the path, detached from the noise and liveliness of the younger years that bustled around her. The image of a glowing stone clung to her mind, refusing to disappear. She couldn't bring herself to share this with any other person, not even her closest friends, but if she could find the lady who dropped it maybe then she'd get some answers.

To add to that, she was greeted by a worried looking Louis at reception. His backpack was half unzipped next to his feet and he held his mobile in a vice-like grip. The rest of the world was a blur when Sky focused on his green eyes. Emerald green, like the-

Stop.

Taking a deep breath, she adjusted the strap on her bag and approached her friend, not sure what to expect. A hundred conversations echoed around them.

'Morning Louis, what's up?'

'Didn't Cass text you? I'm just about to check with reception that her dad has phoned, so that her absence is authorised.'

Chapter Five

Thinking back to the night before, Sky had heard her phone buzz but never got round to checking it, not even a sideways glance to see who'd sent the message.

'I haven't checked my phone,' Sky confessed. Knowing Cassie's situation, she should have her phone at hand all the time. *Why did she ignore it, telling herself she'd "check it later"?*

Silly question.

Cassie's mum wasn't well. All of her close friends knew this and they didn't talk about it much at school. It was easier that way for Cassie to have two separate lives, so to speak. Sky imagined at school she could act as though everything was as it should be. She would focus on each lesson, work hard, and hang out with her friends who made her laugh and helped her forget. At home it would be tough to ignore.

Louis looked down at his phone, his voice distant. 'Hilary has been taken to hospital. Cass texted this morning about it to say she won't be in and her dad would phone.'

Sky nodded. 'You're here to confirm with reception,' she said as the bell rang, cutting their conversation short. The five seconds it rang felt more like a minute.

Louis leaned forward the second Paula the receptionist finished her phone call.

'Excuse me, was that Michael Harrow?'

Paula's look was assessing. 'Yes. Now, you don't want to be late for registration do you?' she told Louis coldly, her words followed by a smile, as if it would soften the harsh tone in which she'd spoken.

Sky raised her eyebrows at the receptionist before turning away. 'I hope Hilary is…alright.' She didn't know what else to say. Did this make her a terrible friend, not knowing?

Louis sighed and zipped up his bag before slinging it over his shoulder haphazardly. 'I hope she is, and Cassie.' He was obviously very concerned, as was Sky. She linked an arm through her friend's and the two of them began their walk to the east wing.

At five o'clock the next morning Sky lay awake. Wrapped up in the quilt she lay as still as a statue, feeling the steady beat of her heart, and listening to an owl hooting from somewhere in the darkness. Soon the streetlamps would flicker back on and the long two hours before Sky had to get up for school would begin. She'd had yet another strange dream that prevented her from going back to sleep, and she couldn't stop thinking about it. Once again, it revolved around the stone attached to the necklace.

The room had felt never ending, like an illusion. If she ran forward the walls would expand. She could never reach an exit. There was no ceiling, only a view of grey, billowing storm clouds moving fast. Sky looked around in despair and when she turned she met her reflection, another illusion. 'You must help me,' she said. Sky stared, perplexed, and the vision jumbled her thoughts.

It took some time to find her voice. 'What can I do?' Sky asked, feeling the ground tremble in her dreams. The mirror image of her held the fragment of emerald.

'You're running out of time,' said the other Sky.

A flash of green light and what felt like an electric shock jolted her awake, and Sky found herself in her bedroom, a matchbox in comparison to the place in her dreams. She'd lain still for a while, staring at the ceiling. No storm clouds, just painted swirls.

Sky pushed back the covers with a sudden urge to check it was still in its place.

It was there, emitting its green glow. Staring at it, Sky contemplated what to do.

The jewel was captivating but also frightening. Slamming the drawer shut, she rushed back to the warmth of her bed, and with trembling hands pulled the quilt up to her chin. She tensed her body, hoping the trembles would stop. It felt like she'd been thrown into an ice cold lake.

Sky closed her eyes, trying to think about it rationally. So it glowed. Maybe there was some hidden battery in it somewhere or maybe it was fibre optic?

'Stop trying to justify it,' she whispered into the dark. 'Why can't I get rid of the thing?'

She was late for school. Having to be physically pushed out the

Chapter Five

door by her exasperated mother, Sky dragged herself through the gates. Miss Redrow was one of the most laidback of all teachers but nine thirty was not acceptable. When Sky had wandered in at that time, her maths teacher could only stare with eyebrows raised. Glancing up at the clock, she told Sky to sit down and that they'd talk at the end of lesson.

Sky nodded and slumped down in her seat in between Louis and Hannah. Both studied her cautiously.

'Is everything alright?' Louis whispered a minute later. Startled, Sky looked at him.

'Yeah, I'm just tired,' *and I found a necklace which has a glowing stone attached to it*, she nearly added, but lost the nerve. It was as though she was harbouring a dreadful secret.

'You look pale. Well, paler than usual.'

'Thanks.'

Nothing Miss Redrow said about quadratics made sense. Well, they made even less sense than they normally did. At the end of lesson Louis and Hannah loitered by the door, but Miss Redrow pointed 'out'. Sky proffered a reassuring smile.

The teacher tapped something into her laptop and closed it shut, proceeding to give Sky her undivided and slightly unnerving attention.

'Sky, why were you late this morning?'

'I just got a really poor night's sleep, that's all. I'm really sorry.'

'Is that all it is?'

'I assure you that's all it is.'

'You're good friends with Cassie.'

Sky nodded, very much aware of her friend's absence in class. 'Yeah.'

'We offer counselling,' Miss Redrow said slowly. Sky stood and listened, waiting for her teacher's inevitable suggestion. 'If you want to talk about it you can speak to Lilly or Patrick. This is an awful thing for Cassie and her family, and it will no doubt have an effect on her close friends.'

'I understand,' said Sky. 'Thank you.'

Miss Redrow scrutinised her for a long moment. Sky turned her head to the large window at the far end of the room; raindrops trailed down it like tears, smearing the landscape.

She heard the chair squeak. Miss Redrow walked to the door and held it open, allowing the noise of other pupils walking and talking to stream in. 'You don't seem your usual self, that's all,' she said. 'I will let you off, but just this once. Off you go.'

Sky forced a smile, slinging her bag over one shoulder. She joined the throng but felt the least part of it. 'Je suis tres fatigué,' she would say, if Madame Roche asked.

Another day over. Sky zipped her coat up to her chin and at the school gates said goodbye to her friends. With her phone in hand she called Cassie, and as she walked home beneath the gloomy winter skies, listened to all her friend had to say: the good and the bad.

That night there were more dreams.

She was running as if in a race for some distant prize. There was a figure sprinting alongside her but the face was just a hazy outline of features. Sky ran with this stranger through a dense forest. In her dream the heavy darkness pressed down on her like two hands and she sensed the trees rose up and up, walling her in. Her wings were tightly closed against her back. A weird feeling, she thought, as her legs ran for her.

A dim pool of light drew them ever closer.

'We're almost there,' it was a smooth male voice that addressed her. The stranger grabbed her hand.

Sky shocked herself awake again. Pulse racing, she checked the time: 3:04am. Why did this keep happening? Rubbing her eyes Sky went across to the chest of drawers, knocking into her standing light along the way. She paused for a second, waiting for the disorientation to pass. 'This sucks,' she muttered. 'I'm not in a forest anymore.'

She plucked it out of the drawer. It was a clear night; the moonlight crept in through the curtains, causing the chain to glisten under its pale gleam. The stone pulsated green, matching the rhythm of Sky's heart: slow and heavy. Her mind drifted elsewhere, back to her dreams. She could feel his touch still, lingering on her left hand.

Drawing back to the present, Sky placed the necklace tentatively

Chapter Five

among her clothes and returned to bed. Fluffing up her pillows she rested her head, releasing a sigh. This couldn't go on forever.

The moment of sleep didn't come. The clock beamed 4:30am and Sky was still awake. Her body felt like it had consumed three energy drinks all in one go. Lying with her head at the end of the pillow, she had one arm dangling off the edge as she drew patterns on the carpet with the tip of her forefinger. In an abrupt movement she turned over, screwing her eyes shut and forcing crazy colours behind them. Her mood had flipped to that of resentment and it stung; malice poured into every thought that entered her brain. She cursed the woman for dropping such a thing and not coming back for it. She cursed herself. She should have just left it. Burying her face in the pillow, Sky let out a muffled cry of desperation. If this continued onto the weekend she'd throw it away. End of.

Chapter Six

Christian had a surprise on his way home. He was passing over Morel village when he caught sight of his friend, Lyra. She and her mother had a crate crammed full of fruit, and were still adding to it. It must have all been freshly picked because Lyra was inspecting each one, from blueberries, to oganberries and apples, wiping them over with a cloth to rid them of the specks of soil that stuck to them. She and her mother were most certainly getting it ready to take to the market, for Lyra's father had a stall there.

Christian hadn't visited in a long time, not since the dark months. A heavy, uncomfortable feeling resided in his stomach at the realisation of how much time had passed. Lyra hadn't deserved the way he left things. She'd been a good friend to him. Christian could picture her: a heart shaped face, full of freckles from the sun, a captivating smile that seemed to lift her brown eyes. She was tall and nimble on her feet as well as in the air.

When she'd expressed her feelings to him however, she made clear that his reaction wasn't what she had expected or wanted. Their fathers had been friends. Moran was King José's life-long friend, fellow soldier and adviser. They'd flown into battles, visited allies and foe, side by side. When Moran had been injured and lost the ability to fly, it had very nearly broken them both. Not even the best færie dust or medicines could help him. And when the king lost his life, Moran lost himself for a while. With a hysterical eleven year old sister and unresponsive mother, Christian threw himself into the Krazonian family's arms struggling to cope with it himself. Lyra supported him.

Chapter Six

Soon after, there grew a strange, unfamiliar feeling between the two færies that Christian was not sure how to deal with. Sometimes he'd catch his friend observing him and she would quickly smile before looking away, as if she felt guilty for doing so.

As the years passed Christian became accustomed to this feeling. She was one of his dearest friends, always one to lift his spirits. Her smile was always brighter when he was around, Moran told him once. Moran and his wife Talaya were forever grateful to him – the son of the Krazonian king had remained friends with their daughter. Talaya had murmured that to him a few summers before over a cup of melrogan juice. Christian wondered why she'd said it. 'Being friends with your daughter has never been an imposition. We get on well,' he'd replied.

A distant, thoughtful smile had lingered on Talaya's lips for quite some time after that.

Snapping back to the present, Christian made the decision to speak to his friend. He headed down, his heart hammering the way a carpenter would hammer wood.

Lyra froze when she saw him, fruit in one hand and cloth in the other. She quickly straightened up, her expression unreadable.

Christian tried a smile, lifting his arms up in hope she would embrace him and not walk away. He hoped his face asked the question.

Lyra's brown eyes looked him up and down. She began to wipe over the fruit as if he wasn't there.

Christian dropped his arms. 'Hello Lyra,' he said, hoping the words would penetrate.

He could see her fighting her conscience in the way she swiped across each fruit, mostly missing the dirt so Talaya had to wipe it again. Lyra shook her head a little and scrunched up her nose. The apple was bruised. Christian wondered if she was too.

He made a silent prayer to the Elana that she would speak to him. Talaya eventually acknowledged his presence with a nod and a 'hello'. Then she flew back into the hut, a place that Christian used to wander into so casually all too often.

Eventually Lyra threw the cloth down to wipe her hands, her eyes cast downwards. Without a word she approached him and allowed herself to be embraced. Christian hugged her tightly and closed his eyes, wanting to apologise but knowing that Lyra had already forgiven him. It was easier to say nothing.

They stood face to face.

'Christian Meldin, how is it?' she asked with a tilt of the head.

How is it?

Over the hot, lambent flame of a candle Lyra had confessed her feelings to him. Christian was all too hasty in confessing that he did not feel the same. At that, her eyes widened. She looked dismayed. Then she pinched the flame and the light went out, hiding her tears. That's how things were left because Christian had flown away, unable to face the fact that he had hurt his friend and, in a way, let her down. But he couldn't help how he felt.

'Are you still here?' Lyra's voice entered his brain, bringing him round.

'Things aren't good,' he blurted out, trying to order his thoughts into line. 'Can we talk?'

Lyra chewed her lip and looked around, at færies getting on with their daily business, at the butterflies and to the sky, anywhere but into Christian's eyes.

'Can we, please?' he repeated.

She combed her hands through the natural waves of her hair and sighed. 'Yes,' she took his hand. 'I've missed you.'

'I've missed you too.'

～

Christian walked with his friend to the edge of Morel woods, choosing to sit in the cool shade of a tree that towered over them. He watched the dancing shadows of leaves against the grass as they swayed in the breeze. Here morel mushrooms sprouted in groups, and if he inhaled deep enough, Christian could smell their earthy aroma. Leaves rustled. The wind was changing, but he ignored it.

'Speak,' Lyra said.

He picked at a blade of grass. He had to say something.

'I didn't mean to react how I did.'

Chapter Six

Lyra smiled as if she knew he would begin with this particular subject. 'Half a year was a long time for me.'

Christian's throat tightened. He pressed a blade of grass between his fingertips. 'I know.'

'But in that time I realised that, though I meant what I said, I might not have dived into it had my parents not pushed me. Well, my mother. You were my closest friend and they could not believe their luck.'

'You say luck? Lyra, our fathers were like brothers. You and I grew up together. My status doesn't come into it…well, it shouldn't have,' Christian replied, his mouth going dry. Is this what Talaya and Moran thought of him? He managed to swallow the words, keeping the thought to himself. The now cold breeze teased his skin, causing a shiver down his arms.

'I hope you don't feel…betrayed,' said Lyra. 'It isn't like that. My father saw you as his own son.'

'What are you saying?'

'Mother knew how I felt, and being so close with you - we spent a lot of time together didn't we?' Lyra reached out her hand but hesitated, as if having second thoughts.

'When you were grieving you reached out to my parents as if they were your own. You can't blame them for thinking about the possibility…' she trailed off, and Christian knew it was so he could say 'what, the possibility of there being an "us"?'

'I was going through a hard time and they welcomed me with open arms,' he said. 'Are you implying that your mother and father kept me close for the reason that they wanted us to be more than friends?' This conversation was heading in the wrong direction all too quickly, and Christian could feel his temper rising.

'Christian, you were dear to them. You still are. When your father…afterwards…' Lyra combed through her hair with slender fingers. 'It's as though he lives through you. My father could see that and he didn't want to let go. I suppose my mother saw it differently. She believed you had feelings for me, and the prospect of her daughter becoming a princess was appealing. They only want what is best for me.'

Christian had a flashback to a few summers previous, visualising that mischievous smile. Talaya had been planning.

'I see,' he muttered.

Lyra's posture stiffened. 'Christian, I meant those words and you know that. You…'

'I apologised for that!' he snapped, standing up and unfolding his strong wings. 'Why are you telling me these things?'

'Sit – please sit back down,' Lyra's voice was thick with tears. The wind blew harder. Christian remained standing but enclosed his wings. He breathed in and out to level his anger, and after a long moment sat back down.

Her lower lip trembled and her brown eyes were pleading.

'You've confused me,' Christian murmured.

'Because you are prince, are people not supposed to take offence to anything you say? Are we not allowed? Your words hurt me. Does that not surprise you?' she was saying, knocking the ground with her fists. 'I am completely aware of your status. Luck is not the word, lucky is. Can you imagine being an ordinary færie, living an ordinary life only having the Princess of Hæthen as your closest friend? I confessed then, and I won't deny it now.'

'Deny it?'

'That I love you.'

The words Christian was about to say got lodged in his throat. With clammy hands he rubbed his face. 'Lyra, please – please don't,' he choked, feeling out of his depth and wanting to laugh and cry at the same time, for he would have to break her heart again.

'I just want you to know,' she whispered. 'Forget about my parents, forget about what my mother had hoped for. You flying by like this has thrown me. I hate the fact you left so suddenly yet I find myself forgiving you now you're here.' Her lips puckered and she fell silent.

Christian shook his head. 'I'm sorry, Lyra.'

'After all of that,' she said quietly, 'we have not yet touched on the subject of your concerns. Let's just change the subject shall we?' But her tone had switched to that of someone who could not have cared less either way.

Christian looked to see his friend staring at him, the glimmer

Chapter Six

of emotion having left her eyes.

He was having second thoughts. Seeing Lyra in this mood, knowing he'd been the one who made her that way, led him down the coward's path. Just like before.

'That was it. I wanted to say how sorry I am.'

'Of course.'

Christian could almost see their friendship disintegrating before him like færie dust into the air. 'I really am sorry. You are still dear to me, you must know that.'

Lyra shook her head.

'Can't we pass this?' he questioned, unable to repress his anger. Their friendship had been life-long and he did not want to let it go, despite all that had happened. 'I will forget what you've told me about your mother's intentions. We've forgiven each other. Why not go back to how it was?'

Her gaze was sorrowful, as was her smile. 'Christian, I wish I could.'

He stood up slowly and when Lyra mumbled a goodbye, he released a half-hearted laugh.

'I'm not saying goodbye, Lyra.' But he couldn't look at her. 'I will see you again, unless you really don't want me to.'

When she didn't respond Christian knew he had to go. With a nod of acceptance, he lifted. She began to cry. Christian flew away, wishing and wishing upon many things: that he didn't have to hurt his friend, that he wouldn't have to face the truth when he returned home and the fact he wished his father had remained on this earth. Four years had passed and it still hurt, so much.

Christian took a breath of humid air. There would be a summer storm.

'Good timing,' he mumbled to himself, just before an unexpected gust of wind blew him off balance. He almost collided with another færie, and for once did something only his sister would do – grunt an apology and keep flying.

Christian slowed down to inspect the world around him. He found storms fascinating, though they didn't happen often. They intrigued him. How within such a short space of time the winds could change, the air becoming thick with the scent of rain to come. The skies would transform from cerulean to a deep violet and with that, thick grey clouds from which heavy warm rain would fall.

Færies could sense it in the atmosphere. Most stopped what they were doing to head into their huts and tree houses.

There was a white flash, soon followed by a deep rumble of thunder. He felt the first drop of rain on his cheek. Christian drew towards the ground and landed, folding in his wings. Some children were in the square running around, excited by the storm.

The rain fell harder, and Christian revelled in it. He walked back to the mansion, temporarily forgetting what awaited him.

Dill and Rhys were at the doors, glancing around warily. They raised their eyebrows and smiled as he approached, dripping wet.

'Sir, if your mother could see you,' Dill chided. Rhys shifted in his armour and smiled again, but there was worry in his green eyes.

Christian stepped inside feeling invigorated from the rain. If he saw mother, he wouldn't be afraid to hear what she told him. He could take it.

With both hands he shoved back his dark hair from his face, flicking drops of water at the guards.

'Sorry.'

Dill wiped down his chest armour and shook his head, his expression settling to that of concern. 'Christian, you are aware of the visit we had this morning?'

'Yes.'

'Good,' and with that Dill turned, signifying the end of that conversation. He was a stubborn guard. He would say no more.

Rhys, forever in his shadow, did the same.

Chapter Seven

She sat at the top of a hill. The sun was blazing. Sky fanned her fingers across the luscious grass that surrounded her, taking it all in. She wasn't alone. Once again his face was indistinguishable but she recognised his touch when he brushed a hand across her shoulder.

Rain began to fall and it brought with it a cool, calming sensation that filled her senses.

She blinked and the world around her altered for a split second into jagged rock and granite. Like a flickering slideshow her mind flipped between the two settings until she felt sick with confusion. Sky couldn't determine where she was going and could only stumble between the two dreams until she awoke, and with a jolt.

The sickness still swelled in Sky's stomach and she blinked hard, retaining the images of blue skies followed by rain and rock, and despair. She slowly disentangled herself from the delusions of her dream world and rubbing her head, moved so her legs stuck out from beneath the quilt. Perching on the edge of the bed she slumped forward, head in her hands.

Her stomach churned as thoughts knocked about her head, making her feel dizzy.

'Ugh,' she muttered.

Standing up, Sky turned to examine herself in the wall mirror. She had on her favourite black hoodie, crumpled from having been slept in, and leggings. She must have fallen asleep fully clothed and her ponytail was sagging; strands of black hair stuck out all over the place. Sky Francis resembled a pale, wide eyed ghost. Then she caught sight of the chest of drawers through the mirror's reflection, and remembering what she said she'd do, stomped across the room and practically fell to the floor, wrenching open the drawer.

'There you are,' she said, pulling out the necklace. The stone glowed furiously and she felt the same fury within her. She went to the window and opened it, throwing the piece of jewellery out into the darkness as though it was garbage.

'Good riddance!' Sky shouted after it before slamming the window shut.

Resting her forehead against the cool window, she watched her breath fog up the glass and gazed into the night. There came a faint, hesitant knock on her door.

'Are you alright in there?' her mum whispered through the wood.

Sky unstuck herself from the window and turned around.

'Yes, totally fine,' she replied with a nervous laugh. 'It was just a moth, you know I hate them.' She could picture her mother's face: eyes downcast as she listened hard to her daughter's meagre excuse for strange behaviour. Sky walked quietly to the door.

'You haven't been yourself lately,' Grace said.

At that, Sky opened it ajar. 'I've had a lot on my mind. I do have GCSE's coming up you know,' she said with a shrug and a complacent smile. 'I'm fine.'

She knew her mum was suspicious.

'You've been tired and grouchy and I've hardly spoken to you this past week. Where's your coursework?'

'I'm not talking to you about this now.'

'Then when will we?'

'We can talk tomorrow?'

Grace was not amused. 'Fine, tomorrow we will talk. Try and get some sleep,' she said before walking away across the dim landing in her polka dot pyjamas.

Sky closed the door and listened to the footsteps recede, waiting for the familiar sound of her parent's bedroom door squeaking shut. As soon as it did, she made her way across the room and bent down to look beneath her bed, grabbing onto a pair of grey

Chapter Seven

plimsolls.

Slipping them on, she tiptoed back to her door. Then as quietly as possible Sky made her way across the hallway, descending the stairs with light footsteps. Taking a breath, she ventured out into the night, not caring that it was late. She had to get away.

Sky hadn't thought about where she was going, but the sound of a noisy car's engine as it roared by jolted her senses, causing her to stop. A streetlamp shone down, bathing her in a pool of amber light. She chewed down on her lip. Had this been a stupid idea? Across the road the pavement was overshadowed by conifers and when she gazed into the darkness her heart almost stopped.

'It's just the wind,' Sky muttered, her legs carrying her forward. For a while she walked with her arms wrapped around herself in an attempt to keep warm.

Eventually she spotted the newsagents and paused to check her hoodie pockets. More often than not she had some fifty or twenty pence pieces sandwiched between the fabrics.

'A-ha!'

Fifty pence gleamed back at her from the palm of her hand. Heading up the hill, Sky could see the shop was still open and soon enough she was at the door. Stepping in, the bell tinkled and she squinted down the aisles, the intense artificial light hurting her eyes.

'Excuse me ma'am...' Sky spun around, coming face to face with a shop worker in a pale red chequered shirt that was two sizes too big. He studied her with eyes enlarged by thick framed glasses.

'We are closing in ten minutes,' he said with a smile.

'Okay,' said Sky. 'I'll be quick.'

Hoping a menthol chewing gum would help clear her head, she went towards the cramped middle aisle but squeaked to a stop at the sight of a familiar face. Kneeling down a few meters away was the woman she'd bumped into a week before!

Sky tightened her ponytail before taking a few steps forward. After buying the gum, she'd wait for the shop to close in hope of speaking to the jewel-dropper. In the process of pulling out one pack of gum half of the selection fell from the shelf, and she watched with despair as they scattered across the floor. *Why?* She wanted to cry. *Why?*

Groaning inwardly, Sky knelt down and started picking them up one by one, knowing the sound would have caught the woman's attention. Looking up, they met each other's gaze and recognition flashed in the strangers' eyes. She said nothing but came over, wearing the same shirt as the boy. Sky realised she worked there.

'Do you have the one you want?' the woman asked politely, avoiding eye contact.

'Yes,' Sky said shortly, standing up.

'Good,' and she walked past, disappearing into a room behind the counter. Approaching the boy worker at the till, Sky waved the pack of chewing gum and almost threw the fifty pence piece at him.

'Thanks,' she said and upon leaving the shop took a deep breath. The cold night air was sharp in her throat. She clawed open the packet of gum and threw one into her mouth.

Time passed. Sky sat cross-legged on the pavement and was gathering tiny bits of gravel together when she heard voices. She'd asked herself a few times why she still waited, like a creep with nothing to do, and finally her reason emerged. Quickly she stood and withdrew into a darker shadow.

'What time are you working tomorrow, Adam?'

'I'm working twelve until close. You?'

'I'm in at eight, lucky me.'

'That sucks. Well, see you tomorrow Elle.'

The shop sign illuminated the immediate area below it a sort of yellowish green, and Sky eyed the woman surreptitiously, waiting for her chance to appear out of the darkness in the least disturbing way possible. Adam crossed the road, whereas Elle started towards where Sky was standing, but the moment they locked eyes she turned on her heels and fired off in the opposite direction.

She rushed after this Elle, who wore a coat with a fur hood. 'Excuse me. I just need to talk to you!'

With no reply, Sky increased her pace. 'Elle, this is not fair,

Chapter Seven

would you please stop?'

Eventually she caught up and grabbed the woman's shoulder, the response being a chilling glare.

'Get off of me,' she hissed.

Sky recoiled. 'Sorry. You know who I am, right?'

Elle hadn't averted her gaze and was breathing steadily, probably contemplating how fast she could run.

'Yes,' she murmured. 'I do know who you are.'

Sky sighed with relief. 'Right, okay.' She took a step back, hoping it would come across as polite, not defensive. 'My name is Sky. Last week we had a collision…' *And you were rude as hell to me.* 'I dropped all of my change, you dropped a necklace. I picked it up and would like to apologise to you now for doing so, because it's caused me nothing but issues,' said Sky. Who would have thought a piece of jewellery could cause "issues"?

Elle's plain brown hair was tied up in a bun and apart from mascara, her face looked clean of makeup. She did however look very tired.

'You don't need to say sorry. If anything it should be me apologising.' Her expression looked pained. 'I shouldn't have rushed off.'

'Unfortunately you did just that.'

'I think we should walk and talk, Sky. I'll start from the beginning.'

∽

They walked slowly and conveniently in the direction of Sky's home. Elle didn't seem to mind.

'Okay,' said Elle. 'About four years ago I went to a car boot sale with my parents. We were browsing when I spotted a necklace in the jewellery section, and to me it stood out amongst everything else.'

'How old were you, if you don't mind me asking?'

'Fourteen. Why?'

That made her eighteen, only two years older than Sky. She looked to be in her mid-twenties. 'I'm curious that's all. I'm sixteen.'

'I see. So this lady catches me looking and invites me over. When I ask to hold it, she is more than happy to show me but advises it would only be worth wearing on special occasions. "It's a special necklace." When I think back, she was pretty desperate to get rid of it.

'I asked how much. It was priced at £10.00, but having already bought some other items I only had £6.50. She didn't even have to consider it. She said it probably wasn't even worth its original price, it was just imitation. Clearly she didn't know the truth. Anyway, I had plans to wear it for my friend's fourteenth birthday that weekend.'

Sky looked down at her feet, watching every step. Her toes were numb and tingly from the cold. 'Did you?'

Elle took a shaky breath. 'Here's the thing. The following night I had these weird dreams. They felt so real, you know? The colours were vivid. I could smell the rain...' Her voice faded as a car drove past, the sound of its engine slicing through the conversation.

'I've had some really weird dreams too,' Sky said when the road was quiet again. 'In one I was flying. It felt-' She shook her head, parts of the dream coming back to her, of white clouds and sunshine followed by a void she was being dragged into. 'It felt very real.'

Her voice came out scratchy, like she needed to clear her throat.

'I presume it's started glowing?' Elle asked.

'Yeah,' said Sky uneasily. 'Does it have some sort of mechanism in it, or is it fibre optic?' It sounded ridiculous aloud.

'No. It's glowing because...' She paused. 'You need to understand that everything I say is true. And you must listen.'

'I'll listen.'

'That tiny piece of emerald on the necklace is connected to an alternate dimension equivalent to this earth, only they aren't humans, they're færies. As in people with wings who fly about and can sprinkle færie dust from the palms of their hands. The reason it glows is because in the other world it is in danger, or soon will be.'

Sky somehow managed to suppress a bout of panic, but when

Chapter Seven

she spoke the strain was evident in her voice. 'My dreams are connected too?'

'Yes, but the dreams I can't explain. I couldn't then. In the other world there's an emerald stone that is extremely powerful. It's protected by a realm called Krazonia, and there is the Elana-'

Sky stopped walking, feeling a balloon of anxiety expanding in her chest. 'Wait.'

'You need to know this.'

'I can't get my head around it, Elle. I wish I'd never taken the thing. Do you want it back?' Her jaw had begun to ache and the swell in her throat would soon lead to tears. It was that or...

Elle shook her head as Sky laughed, but she couldn't help it. Her options were laugh hysterically, or cry hysterically.

Sky's eyes were watering and her chest heaving by the time she'd calmed down. Elle's face was stern, her features carved out of stone.

'I had my chance,' she said, 'now it's someone else's turn. I know it sounds farfetched Sky but the kingdom exists. Laugh it off if you must but you will inevitably end up there. Let me guess, the dreams are recurring and you feel extremely tired due to a sporadic sleeping pattern, and you find yourself waking up in the early hours. Have you tried to get rid of it yet?'

Sky wiped her eyes and nodded once, confirming all of Elle's claims. 'I threw it out my window tonight. It's been driving me mad, which sounds stupid because it's a necklace, but you know.'

Elle smiled dryly. 'I bet when you get home it will be exactly where you first placed it. I tried stamping on it and throwing it away but it always ended up where I first put it. I didn't wear it to my friend's birthday, but when I put it on the strangest thing happened. Well, I fainted but woke up in the other world and I freaked out.'

Sky stared at her. 'You woke up in the other world?'

'When I woke up in Krazonia, I went in search of help. Each realm is ruled by a king and queen. I tried to explain to them what had happened to me but I was threatened with exile. They thought I was some sort of spy. They considered my explanation of coming from the human world and I could see it scared them.

The fact I was there means the portal between our world and theirs remains open. There's still a way for us to get through and it's that necklace. Because of their fears, they turned their backs on me. I knew the emerald was in danger but no one listened.'

'What did you do?' Sky whispered, there not being enough air in her lungs to push the words out at normal volume.

'The princess helped me. Her name is Rhia. She'll be about fifteen now...she said the Elana could help me see what I had to do. Let me tell you I was scared but she led the way through Blue...Bluewater. That was it.'

Sky was dumbfounded, and could no longer feel the cold. She could hardly feel anything.

'The Elana are historic in their world. The Wise Ones they can also be called. It's the same as us having the twelve apostles.'

Sky couldn't speak.

'We reached these caves in Bluewater, and it was lit by fireflies. I swear to you on my life everything I tell you - it really happened to me.

'I heard voices: ancient sounds that echoed all around me. I was so scared, thinking, this isn't my world. I didn't want to be there.' Elle's sentences stopped and started as though the memories were returning in short bursts.

'I felt out of my depth. Rhia told me to explain myself. I – I tried. Then something came over me – an overwhelming fear... and I ran away. I ran and left her.' Elle's eyes shined with tears. 'See? It haunts me even now because I failed. I was too young and I didn't really know what I was doing.' Her hands clutched at the air in frustration.

'There was no way of preparing for it. This light filled the space around me and I heard Rhia calling but I didn't go back to help. Eventually I found my way out. Shortly after there was chaos. Krazonia was under siege. If I'd stayed there I would have known and together Rhia and I could have gone back to the king to warn him,' she paused, covering her eyes. 'The next thing I know I'm back in my bedroom, the necklace dangling around my neck like a dead weight.'

Elle started walking again, briskly, so Sky did the same though

Chapter Seven

her limbs felt heavy and cold like they'd been filled with lead.

'So are you saying I need to put the necklace on and go to this place?' she asked. 'What if I don't want to? I don't want to go to another world! I still can't even comprehend a land of… no. I can't.' It was true. Sky couldn't picture herself wandering through the world she'd dreamed of. Dreams were dreams and they weren't real, especially those within which she had wings.

'Whether you believe in fate or not, I saw my chance to escape from it when we bumped into each other. I don't care how selfish that makes me. It was meant to be you,' said Elle matter-of-factly but Sky wasn't ready to accept that.

'Why was it in your pocket?'

'Funnily enough I'd come from a job interview and planned on throwing it into the river.'

'The nearest river is like, ten miles.'

'Yes, I was going to drive there.'

'You said it's impossible to get rid of it so why even try?'

'When you've had it for four years, you'll try from time to time,' Elle said quietly. 'Sky, if you don't do this you'll only be swamped with these dreams and it will be the only thing on your mind, if it's driving you mad after one week…'

'I get it, I get it,' Sky interrupted, the balloon in her chest continuing to expand. 'We're near my road. I'm going to have to go.'

'I'll walk with you.'

'Do I really have no choice?' Sky asked despairingly.

'Well you do, but I wouldn't want you to go through what I've been through.'

'This isn't fair!' Sky exclaimed, resting against the ice cold metal of the gate leading to her house. 'I don't know what's worse. Elle, I can't do it. Please take it back.'

'I'm sorry, I won't. I can't. You need to believe you'll succeed. At least I've given you some warning. I had none.'

'I won't succeed in anything!'

Elle gazed at her intently. 'Look, when you get to Krazonia, search for Christian or Rhia. From what I can remember, they're usually seen around the square and villages…' she was saying as if Sky had jumped at the chance to accept this ludicrous responsibility. 'If not, then head straight for the mansion. You must try to get through to them. My decisions caused horrific consequences because the Krazonian king was killed-'

'Please stop!' Sky cried, shooting a look to her parents' bedroom window. Through the curtains she could see a light had been flicked on. 'I have to go. Is there anything else I should know?' she said hurriedly.

'Um, that I'm sorry. The sooner you put it on the sooner this will all be over.'

Sky could see through the small window on the front door that the landing light had been switched on. She had about five seconds.

'You'll have a better chance than me. Good luck,' Elle said before darting away. Sky pushed open the gate just as her mother opened the front door.

'Sky, what on earth are you doing out here? Get inside!'

'I'm sorry mum,' she said automatically. 'I needed some fresh air. I know it's late.'

'It's gone midnight and it is freezing.'

'I'll be right in.'

'Now!'

Sky cringed. 'Let me just check one thing,' and she rushed round to the side of the house, kneeling down in search of the necklace. She found no trace of it. Numb to the core and still trying to digest all of the information she'd just been force fed, Sky went quietly inside.

Chapter Eight

The rest of that day was strange for Christian. His mother barely spoke a word, and spent most of the evening in the drawing room with the door shut. Simian stood beside the doorway and advised Christian as he passed that the queen was not to be disturbed.

'She's my mother. If I want to speak to her I will,' Christian argued.

Simian shook his head. 'She said you would say that, but she wishes to see no one.'

That night Christian had another dream in which he was scouring the lands for the lost stone. Once again, the colours were vivid in his mind. He got out of bed and paced the floor, waiting for his pulse to slow and for his wings to stop trembling. It took him longer to get back to sleep this time.

The following morning Christian was told by his mother to return to the serenity and safety of Bluewater, as more Zanian messengers were coming and she didn't want her children to be around when they arrived. But this time Christian felt disinclined to leave.

'Will you tell us what's going on?' he boldly ventured with Rhia standing firmly beside him. For a moment the two siblings were united by the same thoughts. Christian knew his sister was as reluctant as he was to leave.

'Well, mother?' Rhia pressed.

Anya frowned. 'Why are you questioning me? I ask you both to head to Bluewater, returning at midday when there will be a meal waiting for you,' she said as though that made it okay. Christian sighed inwardly. He wasn't going to win.

'Yes, but-' Rhia started but was cut short when the queen raised her hand, her expression stern.

Christian tried a more reasonable approach. 'Surely I will need to deal with this someday, as will Rhia. Why not begin by letting us stay? Zanians are coming to Krazonia and we just want to know why. Also, we can support you,' he beseeched.

'You both must go.'

Rhia stamped her foot. 'What if we don't want to?'

'You will go!' Anya shouted suddenly. Christian watched her pace up and down, her cheeks scarlet, wings tightly enclosed. She was right. He and Rhia being here would only be an added stress so it was time to leave, for her sake.

'Rhia, come. We're better off in Bluewater,' he said. Rhia glared at him pointedly before walking to the large windows. She pushed one open and without a word jumped out. Christian followed, hesitating at the window to look back at his mother. Her hazel eyes were filled with panic, and her attempt to smile formed an expression of confusion. Christian turned back to the window, gripping the frame with one hand, and his mother's face was imprinted in his mind long after he'd flown away.

Christian flew slowly through Bluewater Glen. Rhia, a way ahead, made no attempt to converse with him. *So be it,* he thought, looking around in hope the beauty of this place would reach out and steal away his bad mood. The glen was a secluded valley; a small stream ran through it and butterflies danced amongst the yellow smyrniums. The stream water was so clear that if he stopped to look, tiny fish could be seen swimming within it.

Letting his mind wander, Christian considered the Elana. When he was young his father would tell him tales of the Wise Ones: the Elders of the Earth, and how they were alive at the Beginning. Where they originated from was not known. Such a picture was painted in his mind of these heroic færies – they had created the Færie Kingdom, shaping the lives of those who lived today.

The generation of Christian's great grandfather were the last to ever see them. It seemed that as time went on they were known

Chapter Eight

less and less. Eventually the eleven Elana disappeared completely, closing their wings once and for all to go into hiding. Færies could not understand why. Father told him that a long, long time before his own life on earth, the Wise Ones had agreed to split and cover the four realms of the world. Krazonia, Zania and Gloryn had three, but only two resided in the mountains of Hæthen.

'I thought there were twelve?' An eight year old Christian had asked so innocently, perched on his father's lap. José gazed down at his son, and Christian remembered thinking wondrously how strong his father was, and brave. The king flashed a smile and his son smiled back, waiting for an answer.

'Armænon was left behind in the human world. He had betrayed his Elana. It is believed that he created a necklace with a shard of the Emerald because he wanted to be most powerful, and rule the Kingdom, but he misplaced it in the land of humans and was therefore banished to live and suffer among them forever. That is all we know of him.'

'Where is the human world?'

Father's laugh was husky. 'That is another story all together.'

Christian felt the memory dissolve as a lone cloud drifted over the sun. The Elana are cowards, he thought bitterly, clenching his jaw. They should still be around, offering protection to those who need it. At this rate there would never be peace – for as long as Tæ ruled, Zania would remain the enemy. Without the so called 'Wise' Ones, Christian knew that one day the heartless queen would get a hold of the stone, and who knew what would happen then.

Christian's heart lurched.

'Hello? Hello?' Rhia was saying to him impatiently.

He blinked and stared at his sister. 'Yes?'

'I've decided to pick some flowers for mother, and make her a bracelet. Would you help me?' she asked before swooping down to the ground, and Christian was taken aback. He wasn't aware he ever had a choice with Rhia. She was inspecting a smyrnium bush when he joined her.

'I didn't think mother appreciated this colour,' he said, inspecting the yellow flowers with their dark green leaves. 'Aren't these edible?' He picked one delicately.

'Indeed they are,' Rhia replied, her tone light as she picked her way along the bushes, selecting the best and brightest flowers. 'But I wouldn't eat them like that,' she added. 'They should at least be washed, and then cooked.'

Christian could not understand the way she was talking. It was as if she'd been hiding a whole new personality up her sleeve and was only just showing it. He took this as an opportunity.

'Have you seen anything lately?' He tried to sound casual.

Rhia shot him a look, but followed it with a sigh. 'No, and I don't understand why.'

'Do you think it's possible that I could?'

She tucked another flower into the loose side pocket of her dress. 'I don't see how, Christian. The Elana cursed me not you. You are lucky.' She flopped down onto the grass, deflated. 'There is something getting in the way. It's as though I've become lost in a maze, and whenever I think I should be seeing, there is only a wall. What makes you think you're involved?' she asked him, reverting back to bitterness. 'You always want to be a part of it.'

Christian sat down, twirling the only flower he'd picked between two fingers. He chose to ignore his sister's comment, refusing to give up this conversation.

'The last few nights I've had a recurring dream. I'm searching for the Emerald and end up in the square, and then I hear this horrible laughter behind me and I can't escape it. I practically throw myself into this hut and I see this færie. She's holding the Emerald and when I try to get close an array of colours fills my mind. At that point I wake up,' he said, his words sinking into the silence. A flock of birds squawked as they glided over the valley and he looked up to watch them. The sky was sapphire blue; it was pleasantly warm, and here he sat with his sister shrouded in gloom.

Rhia ran her fingers through the stream. 'I've dreamt only of father.'

Christian let the flower drop from his grip. It hadn't been what he'd expected.

'Rhia, I'm sorry.'

Chapter Eight

He felt his sister's pain when she looked at him, her grey eyes watering.

'Are you?' She'd put up the defence shield once again. This was as far as Christian was going to get, and then it occurred to him.

'It's the Elana! They're trying to reach you.'

Leaning away from him, Rhia appeared horrified by his assertion. 'No. You're wrong.'

'You-'

'What does it even matter anyway? It won't bring him back!' In one swift movement she was in the air, flowers in hand. Christian was losing her.

'I'm going home. I can't bear this.'

'Mother said-' but once again he was interrupted.

'Christian, do you think that I of all færies will be troubled by mother's reaction?'

He jumped up in defiance. 'You can't go back yet, neither of us knows what's going on. You have to trust her.'

Rhia glowered at him. 'As you know I don't trust so easily anymore. I can't sit here any longer. Oh, and with regard to the Elana, they have done nothing to help us and I doubt they'd start now.'

'Don't go back!' Christian said, riled. Riled because he knew she'd already made up her mind and he couldn't stop her as she flew away. At times like this he saw clearly their differences. They both had a temper but Rhia was stubborn, whereas Christian always tried to think things through.

Christian let out an angry exclamation and kicked the grass. He burst into a run alongside the trickling stream, following its path through the glen. He would excel his anger this way. He ran fast, feeling each step like a heartbeat. It felt good to be heading in a direction that led away from disaster. Despite the burning in his lungs Christian pushed on, the air hitting his face brusquely. He ran until he reached the mouth of the valley, where he stumbled to a stop, breathless.

Christian gazed upon a striking landscape. The centrepiece was a lake of deep blue; sunlight licked the surface in little waves. It was surrounded by the rolling hills of Krazonia that became gold in the far distance, as the realms crossed over. He could fly and fly and would at some point reach Gloryn, the Golden realm.

He opened his wings and flew towards the water. He reached its rippling surface, and with an intake of breath, dived straight in.

※

Christian burst through the main doors to see Dill, Rhys and Gayle standing at the stairwell, mumbling to each other. The three of them stopped simultaneously at his arrival, shocked to silence by his appearance. Christian knew he must have looked dishevelled and not at all "like a prince". The guards regained composure and bowed.

'Please return to your base, Gayle,' Christian said.

Gayle bowed again and walked away, his shield clanking against his armour at every step.

'Have they gone?' It was obvious who he meant.

'Yes sir, they have,' Dill responded.

'Where is my mother?'

'She's upstairs in the drawing room with Rhia. I believe they're waiting for you.'

Christian made his way up the spiral stairs to the first floor.

The door was ajar, and he opened it cautiously to see Rhia looking withdrawn, arms folded as she sat in her invisible shell. The Queen of Krazonia sat at the other end of the table, her back straight, wings taut. There were two letters beside her slender hands.

Christian closed the door.

Anya's expression was grave. 'I was tempted to send out a search for you. Sit down.' She said nothing of his crumpled attire, and continued talking while Christian made himself as comfortable as he could. 'As you well know, Zanians have been here. The two meetings have been concerning the Emerald.'

Christian gave an exasperated sigh. Everything revolved around that stone.

'Why won't she just leave it be?'

Chapter Eight

'Tæ has given us options.'

Rhia smacked her hands flat on the table. 'Yes, let us fight and have our færies die for nothing!'

'Rhia!' Anya scolded. 'Do you think I want to do this – to even consider it?'

'Tell me, what are these options you speak of?' Christian asked, his gaze settling on the letters: one weathered, the other freshly written.

'Well, I say options, it's more an ultimatum. The Zanian queen is giving us "one last chance" to give her the Emerald. Or, as she has declared in this letter, she will "take it by force",' Anya explained. 'She knows that we won't simply hand it over to her. We have always fought to keep it safe and out of her hands. This, however, feels different. It feels more final.' She picked up the fragile discoloured paper.

'"You have five days. In that time you may wish to prepare your army. I give you one last chance to bring the stone to me, or Zania will take it from you by force and without mercy. I expect to see you at the border by sunset on the fifth day. The Emerald will be mine..."' Anya fell silent, folding the page up neatly. She slid it into her dress pocket. 'The rest you do not need to know.'

Christian put his head in his hands. 'She won't ever give up, will she?'

'Mother, you can't give the stone to her. Think about father!' said Rhia, on the verge of crying. 'You can't.'

Christian looked at her. He didn't want to talk about father and he was sure mother didn't either.

'Rhia, don't.'

He flinched when she slammed her fists down on the table.

'You will regret it if you agree to this!' she cried, jerking back when Anya reached out to her with a trembling hand. 'Don't touch me.' She pushed her chair back and bolted from the room, leaving Christian and his mother to soak up the silence.

'You know what we must do,' Anya said.

Christian wiped his eyes. 'You've written a letter?' he said hoarsely, sitting up. 'Who will receive it?'

'I've written to Mikæl, Gloryn's king. I will need him on my side for this. Zania's army has doubled in size over the last three years, and we don't stand a chance alone.'

The words hit Christian hard, but he refused to show it. He hated how much power Tæ had over his mother. The prospect of going into battle because of her insane greed for power sent tremors of anger through him, and he had to clench his fists tightly to stop himself overthrowing the table.

'Is there no way of avoiding this?'

'No, if I don't want to have to keep sending my soldiers away to fight an unjust war. I wish I didn't have to get Gloryn involved. Christian, my darling I am sorry.' She covered her mouth, looking down at the table. Then she shook her head slowly.

'It isn't your fault,' Christian said. 'I just wish she would leave us alone. I wish she would die!' he blurted out.

Anya lifted her chin and stared ahead. 'I feel the same.

'Don't think I'm going to allow her to manipulate us in this way, Christian. If she wants a battle then we will fight with everything we have.' She picked up her dress slightly to stand, and taking the other letter in hand kissed Christian on the forehead before turning to leave.

'Won't you use the Emerald against her this time?' he questioned, twisting around in the chair. Christian could see his mother had already considered the possibility; her face muscles relaxed and she pressed a hand on his shoulder.

'The thought has crossed my mind more than once,' she said, drifting from the room.

Chapter Nine

'Sky, please tell me why you think it's okay to be going outside at this time? It's almost midnight. If there's something troubling you, please tell me,' Grace said after shutting the front door. Sky was about to go upstairs.

'I told you I needed some air, I'm really sorry.'

'Hang on a minute,' her mother's stern voice caused Sky to freeze on the third step and turn around sheepishly.

'Sky,' Grace crossed her arms over her dressing gown and looked at her daughter with worry in her eyes. 'I don't mean to be angry, but I would like to know if you have any concerns – about anything. School, boys…'

Sky managed to disguise her laugh with a cough. 'No, no it isn't that,' she said, one hand clutching the banister. 'There's definitely nothing wrong with me, but you could say since coming back to school I've started wondering where I'm going to go in life. Call it a quarter life crisis.'

'You're too young for that, I hope,' Grace replied. 'Let's just talk about this tomorrow, like we agreed, okay?'

Sky nodded, already thinking about the necklace. 'That's fine,' she said in a strained voice. 'See you tomorrow.'

'Goodnight sweetheart,' she heard her mother say as she went up the stairs.

Sky closed her bedroom door and leaned her head against it, her hands still wrapped around the handle for support. Taking a deep breath, she walked tentatively towards the necklace' hiding place hoping Elle had been wrong. Sky hoped with all her heart. Opening the drawer, her knees nearly gave way.

Nestled between jumpers and t-shirts the jewel shone a vibrant green, illuminating the drawer as it had done before she threw it out of the window. Here it sat, as if it hadn't gone anywhere.

Sky stared at it for some time, trying to make sense of Elle's explanation. Time was of the essence apparently, but she couldn't bring herself to touch it just yet. First she had to persuade herself there was no choice in the matter.

Sky paced to the other end of her bedroom. Elle was right when she said it would be back where she first placed it, despite trying to get rid the thing. But the prospect of putting it on and being warped to some alternate dimension quite frankly made her feel queasy. Dreams she could handle, but the reality of becoming something else, a person with wings?

'It was meant to be you.'

'Why me?' she whispered at her shadowy reflection in the mirror.

'The sooner you put it on, the sooner this will all be over...'

For a few minutes Sky sat on her bed, soaking up the silence of the night.

She'd been backed into a corner, and it seemed the only way out was to place that delicate chain around her neck. She didn't want it to take over her life. It was already threatening to.

'Fine,' Sky said, marching across her bedroom to snatch it up. She glared at it as it glowed brilliantly, taunting her, then clicked the clasp together at the back of her neck. For something so small it felt remarkably heavy. She went to her bed, and settling on the edge of it, began twiddling with her hair as a way to remain calm. It wasn't really working. Her heart raced and her stomach seemed to be rolling over and over like waves in a storm. If Elle was telling the truth, Sky would soon be experiencing something she never thought to be physically possible. Did any other person on this earth know there was another world? Who had owned the necklace before Elle?

'That's if Elle isn't telling porkies,' Sky said to herself. She mentally counted the seconds, her eyes focused on the digital clock that sat on her bedside table, and how it changed colour in the pulsating green light.

Chapter Nine

Then it happened: the sensation that cement was being poured into her veins, locking her limbs. She started to panic, a scream rising in her throat like a gasp for air. No, no, she was not ready.

Slipping off the bed, the carpet came up to meet her and Sky landed flat on her face. In an attempt to move she tried lifting her arms. Tried and failed. The room started to spin. Clutching at the carpet Sky squeezed her eyes shut, waiting for it to pass, waiting for...

***

The ground beneath her was hard and cool, and uneven like rock. Drowsy and with her eyes still shut Sky felt around, trying to get a grip on her surroundings before she gave into this new reality, because she knew for a fact this was no longer home.

Opening her eyes she saw nothing but black. Sky lay in darkness and the atmosphere was as cool as a refrigerator. She pushed herself up and stood with quaking knees. Swallowing hard, she rubbed her hands down her –

Dress?

Pinching the material, Sky realised she no longer wore leggings and a hoodie, but a dress. 'Okay Elle, I believe you now,' she said and her quivering voice came back to her in an eerie echo. She took a few deep breaths, scared to move.

'Hello?' The only response was her own voice resonating against the walls of this place. Water dripped onto the rocky floor. The chilly air and echoic atmosphere told Sky she'd landed in a cave, where there was no light and she had no idea how to get out.

'What a great way to start,' she whispered, stepping forward. 'Is anyone here?' she called again, bolder this time. Sky wondered briefly why the rock felt so cold and damp against the soles of her feet.

'I have no shoes on,' she said, astonished. No shoes. She felt a swell of emotion at the back of her throat but was strong enough to hold back the tears, knowing full well they couldn't be transformed into laughter this time. She walked forward, stretching her arms out as a barrier. Slowly there came a luminous light similar to that of the emerald; it floated, small and bright through the gloom until it reached her. Sky shrank back.

Along came another and another until there were half a dozen hovering before her like minute glowing gems. Their movements were sporadic and they began to drift away from her. They would soon be gone and Sky felt she had no choice but to follow the lights, regardless of whether or not they led her in the right direction.

Sky felt helpless in the dark, surrounded by cavernous walls that were cool and wet to the touch. There's something about this place, she thought, glancing around. She felt alone, but something told her she wasn't. It was on the tip of her tongue. What was it Elle had said about fireflies, a cave…

'Bluewater,' she whispered, shivering as she walked through the very caves Elle had told her about. Sky felt lightheaded and wanted to stop, but couldn't because that was only half of what she felt, the other half felt terror and wanted to run as fast as she could to escape.

Water droplets trickled down the walls, translucent in the fireflies glow. Only then did Sky think to check that she still had the necklace.

It hung around her neck, but out of fear she quickly unclasped it, placing it into a pocket of the dress. Elle had said the king and queen threatened her with exile, and Sky didn't want a repeat of those circumstances. It would remain in her pocket until the right time, whenever that would be.

After a while Sky noticed a glimmer of sunlight, just a glimmer, but it was better than nothing. In that same moment the fireflies dispersed, flitting in different directions. She marched on.

She had to battle through foliage before she was out, and for a few seconds was unable to see it was so bright. Once her eyes had adjusted, she shielded them with a hand and looked around, mouth agape. For one, it was hot. The sun blazed in a clear sky the colour of sapphire and everywhere she looked there was

Chapter Nine

greenery: plush grass, blooming flowers. It occurred to her then that she stood in a valley; either side of her rose steep verdant hills and beside her ran a stream. Sky blinked, trying to take it in. It was beautiful.

She glanced left and right, considering her options. She curled her toes in the soft grass.

Right led to a vast expanse of open land that seemed to go on forever until reaching a horizon of gold, but there were no towns and no færies. This helped Sky make a decision. Turning left she began to walk and at the same time make an attempt to put her thoughts into order. She kept her head down, thinking hard. Elle was right. She hadn't been lying after all. But this meant that Sky was walking through another world, a world that to all humans was just a myth. As a matter of fact, færies to human beings were those little creatures at the bottom of the garden. It had never crossed Sky's mind that there was any other "earth". Her mind had officially been blown. Here she was, and there was no going back.

All the while she was faintly aware of a sensation in her spine, as though she had a heavy rucksack strapped to her. Every now and then she felt them, these things that protruded from her back. They were a part of her, but Sky was too terrified to look.

Upon that thought she felt a release of pressure against her back, and her feet no longer touched the ground. She couldn't help the shrill scream that escaped her lips. Twisting and turning Sky landed in a heap on the ground, her whole body trembling though the wings were taut.

'I can't do this,' she whimpered, too afraid to move. Rollercoasters she could do, but flying in the most real sense without a seatbelt or a bar was too much. The thought made her want to laugh as well as cry, yet it was inescapable. Færies had wings. She was one of them.

Sky stood and brushed herself down before continuing. She had to try and keep her feet on the ground. How hard could it be?

There was a village in sight, and it spurred her on.

After what felt like an hour Sky became attuned to the sounds of amicable chatter and laughter. Merged with those were other sounds; clinking and the rhythmic thud-thud of chopping wood. It was busy, this village. Huts were made from wood but built better than any "hut" on human earth, Sky decided. Not that she'd seen many huts.

She walked amongst færies as an unknown but received no inquisitive looks, no questions were asked. Of course, she looked just like any other. The females wore dresses similar to hers – of simple design and colour, though some had camisole styled tops with shorts. The males had either shorts or trousers with plain tops, some with sleeves and some without.

Sky gazed at the færies' wings: almost transparent, they were a sort of pearly white threaded with hairline veins, and slightly curled at the tips. Sky glanced cautiously behind her, just about able to discern the shape of her own. She put a hand on her chest and kept walking, her heart thumping beneath her fingertips. *You're okay*, her conscience told her.

Elle did not describe Christian or Rhia's appearance. How was she going to find them?

Thankfully these færies spoke the same language. In fact, they were very well spoken. Sky found this out by approaching one, a blonde haired female with friendly brown eyes.

'Hello, I'm looking for Christian, or Rhia?'

The færie raised her eyebrows. Perhaps Sky should have said "Prince" or "Princess". A moment later she pointed over Sky's shoulder and smiled.

'To reach the mansion you need to fly through Krazonia square, you will see it then.'

'Thank you,' Sky said, already deciding that she would walk. Turning on her heels, she made her way through the crowds but soon found herself getting hot and flustered. Crowded streets were bad enough, but a crowded village of færies was another matter.

Breathless, Sky searched for somewhere quieter where she could regain self-control. To her right, above and between færies flying around she spotted a place to go. If she ran, it would only take a minute. Clutching the necklace in her pocket Sky darted and dodged until she was in a place much less crowded. It was

Chapter Nine

a place dominated by oak trees, their gnarled trunks thick from age while their leaf covered branches sprawled outwards, offering areas of shade. Sky flopped down in the nearest available shaded spot and heaved a sigh of relief. Licking her lips, she was about to lean back against the trunk when she lurched forward, having temporarily forgotten about certain things that were attached. Cringing, she covered her face. 'Come on, Sky,' she groaned through her trembling fingers.

She was practically in full-blown conversation with herself when she heard someone close by say 'excuse me'. Sky's mouth snapped shut. The same someone cleared their throat, and slowly she pulled her hands away from her face and glanced up.

'Hello,' she said.

'Are you okay? You look confused and a little lost. Can I help?' Whoever it was spoke kindly and without judgement. Færies definitely seemed more courteous than most humans, Sky thought, shielding her eyes to get a better look. Silhouetted against the sun she was able to work out that he was tall, toned, and with short, unkempt dark hair. He wore shorts and an off-white shirt slightly crumpled.

'Yes. Well, um, is this Krazonia?' It was the first question that came to mind and she could have slapped herself for saying it out loud.

The stranger frowned. 'It is.' Sky felt her cheeks flush. This was getting awkward. 'Are you sure you aren't in need of any help?'

'No, no.'

'Okay then. Take care,' and just like that he expanded his wings and took to the air. Mesmerised, Sky watched his wings beating together firmly as he disappeared over the trees, lost to her in the breeze. She could have told the truth there and then. *As a matter of fact I've just come from the human world and I have the necklace and I need to inform Krazonian royalty that the Emerald is in danger although I'm not sure why, yet.*

Sky ran a hand through her hair and managed a laugh. Easier said than done.

Chapter Ten

The sound of forks tapping and scraping plates echoed throughout the dining hall. Christian ate slowly, for he didn't feel much hunger and looking around the table it seemed his mother and sister didn't either. Anya was chewing her food distastefully, and eventually she placed down her fork and knife on either side of the plate and signalled over the butler who'd been standing idle, waiting for an order.

'Please take this away. I'm sorry,' as she said that, the door opened to one of the guards. It was the guard with dark curly hair that reached his shoulders. He peered in with alert, round eyes.

'Your Highness, General Warren has arrived,' said Simian.

'I see. Escort him to my office and I will be there shortly,' the queen replied, dabbing her mouth with a napkin. Christian glanced sideways at Rhia, and she looked back at him with an open expression of perplexity. Always more outspoken, Christian knew his sister would have something to say, and his heart sank. Rhia shuffled in her seat.

'The General is here? Does that mean you're going to have a meeting with him about fighting Tæ?' She took a mouthful of food before sitting back and crossing her arms, chewing deliberately. Christian cringed at his mother's glare, but it was as though Rhia welcomed it.

'Yes, that is what I'm going to do,' Anya responded, leaning back to allow the butler to take away her half-finished meal. Simian bowed before making his escape. Christian knew that it angered his mother when Rhia acted so nonchalant before others. It proved she didn't care what other færies thought of her.

Chapter Ten

Rhia's mouth pulled into a frown. 'I suppose that Christian and I are not allowed to be present?'

The butler glided out of the room.

'Well done,' Christian muttered, but it went unheard for his mother had already started talking back louder than before, her authority on full display.

'Rhia Meldin, you should be thankful you are not required to attend these meetings. I make the decisions, and they are extremely difficult decisions. Your time will come. You needn't think I don't want you involved, but I inform my family and færies only what is needed,' she placed a hand to her heart, 'I carry the heaviest burden. It is all part of being queen.' She picked up her dress and pushed the chair back. 'Ask yourself whether you're ready for that.' With that she walked away, her eyes staring into nothing, lost in thought. Christian watched with alarm Rhia's facial expression change. Her forehead creased and a red flush appeared on her cheeks, as if she were about to burst.

'Well it doesn't feel that way to me!' she exploded. 'Given the fact I'm already connected with the Emerald, is it not better that I know what's happening every step of the way, rather than receiving solely the things you *choose* to tell me? What if I *chose* what to tell you?' She stared at her plate and gripped her knife and fork tightly in each hand.

Christian sunk back in his chair. Why did Rhia have to react this way? Even he wouldn't dare reproach his mother in such a manner, and he was supposed to be the older, more rebellious sibling. His mother stopped at the end of the hall, her dress swaying slightly. For a moment she rested against the doorway, wings twitching. And then she turned and Christian was relieved to see Anya Meldin had reverted back to her calm self despite her daughter's animosity.

'That is why,' she said, her voice echoing around the spacious room. 'You already have that to deal with, and you know full well how important it is for you convey to me all that you see. It isn't a matter to joke or be bitter about, but I can understand why you must feel that way.'

Rhia's breathing slowed and she let go of her cutlery to touch her head. Christian recognised the signs.

'Rhia,' he said hesitantly.

She made no response, screwing her eyes shut.

Anya drifted back across the room. 'What is it?'

Rhia smiled grimly. 'I couldn't tell you.' But before his mother had a chance to snap Christian caught her attention. 'Remember this isn't the first time,' he whispered, and they waited in a pensive silence.

'I don't see anything,' Rhia said eventually, opening her eyes. 'I don't know what's wrong with me.'

'Maybe, maybe it's...' Christian said, scrambling for the right words. 'Maybe it is nothing! Rhia, please don't let it get to you.' Even he didn't believe what he was saying, but he injected as much conviction as he could into his words. 'Try not to worry. It can't be helped. Maybe it really is nothing.'

'Like the Zanian guards arriving is nothing? This doesn't happen without a reason,' Rhia said, her lower lip trembling. 'You know that.' In a moment her expression had moulded into one of anger. 'I hate it!'

Anya kissed her forehead. 'For now we know what is happening, don't we? I need to go. Will one of you please take a message to a family in Hale for me? Or would you go together?' she asked, looking at Christian.

'I'm sure my brother will be more than happy to go,' Rhia snapped, pushing back her chair and storming from the room. 'I'm not going anywhere!' she called out before banging the door shut behind her.

⁓

Christian took the message, and in the main hallway wished his mother luck before they flew their separate ways. Anya went up the spiral stairs to meet the General, whereas Christian headed out into the scorching sun to Hale village.

On his way back to the mansion he recognised Willa, daughter of Simya and Gray Fælin, wandering about, looking very small and very lost amongst other færies. He hoped she'd remember

Chapter Ten

him.

'Willa?' he said, trying to catch her eye. She looked up and gave him a toothy grin. 'You the prince!' she said.

'That's me,' Christian replied, and cast a curious glance around before focusing on her his complete attention. 'Where is your mother, is she here? What about your father?'

'Pap here...' but her face saddened. 'I lost him.'

'Do you want to go home?'

'I want home.'

Christian offered her his hand, and just as she latched on to it he heard a voice bellowing:

'Willa! Willa!'

Christian looked around him. Gray's shoulders sagged with relief and he approached with a grin. He enclosed his wings and lifted his daughter into his arms, releasing Christian.

'Sir, I thank you. We became separated in the crowds. I was in the air looking for her – of all færies to come to her aid.' He bowed. 'Will you walk with us?'

'Of course.'

'May I ask how you are doing?' Gray said politely, while Willa fidgeted in his arms. 'Willa, be calm,' he murmured. Her response to that was to poke his nose, and he chuckled. Christian smiled.

'Yes,' he replied. 'I'm very well.' He was well, but the situation at home certainly wasn't. 'How have you settled in here with us Krazonians?'

Gray looked surprised. 'Good sir. Thank you for asking.'

Sometimes Christian wished færies weren't so concerned about how they spoke to him - he was just like them, a fellow Krazonian. Only because of his prominence did they hesitate and worry about what to say and how to say it. Understandably, no færie wanted to upset anyone of "high rank" but most of the time it didn't bother him. He wanted to be seen as equal, for being prince hadn't been his chosen path. He'd been born into it. Why else would he come to the town square so often?

'Please, go on.'

'Morel village is beautiful. Krazonia is beautiful,' Gray said wistfully. 'Approaching the King of Gloryn with a request to come here was one of the best decisions I've made. I explained that my stall wasn't earning me enough to keep my family going, but I know that here the market place is thriving. The trade in Gloryn is different and has been constantly changing and growing over the years. The true worth of handmade garments and ornaments Simya and I make was lost on bigger dealings. When Mikæl granted me and my family leave, I felt sad, but also hopeful,' he finished with a sigh, and Christian nodded with interest.

'I'm glad. I need to visit this stall of yours.' They walked over a steep grass verge and headed down towards Morel village, where clusters of the delicious morel mushroom sprouted, and large oak trees offered shade for those who wanted to be relieved from the heat of the sun.

'Simya is there at present, with Byron. Perhaps some time you'd come and pick something to take to the queen. Maybe a necklace adorned with yeal stones. I can tell you now that when they catch the light, they glisten like sunrays on water. The yeal stone can help lift a færie's mood.'

Christian flexed his wings. 'I know she would appreciate that very much. Expect to see me soon!' he said a little too joyfully. Gritting his teeth he waved before turning home. He hadn't been in the air long when another sight came to his attention, of a færie in a plain sky-blue dress sitting a short distance away beneath the wavering leaves of an old oak. Christian hovered, watching her with curiosity. She glanced around looking more than a little confused, and she was talking to herself, making wild gestures with her hands.

Maybe he could help, he was prince after all.

'I'm full of good deeds today,' he mumbled, landing easily on the feathery grass.

'...either way, I have no choice, do I?' the young færie murmured before covering her eyes with hands that visibly trembled.

'Excuse me,' Christian said. He retracted his wings and waited for the færie to notice. After a moment he cleared his throat, and the færie slid her hands from her face and peered up at him.

'Hello,' she said, blinking hard as if she were trying to pull herself out of a daze.

Chapter Ten

'Are you okay? You look confused, and a little lost. Can I help?'

'Yes. Well, um, is this Krazonia?' she asked, shielding her eyes from fragmented sun rays that crept through the gaps in the leaves. Christian then noticed how blue her eyes were, and they were piercing.

'It is,' Christian replied with a frown. 'Are you sure you aren't in need of help?' He could only hope she wouldn't take offence to that. Then again, when she asked such questions...

'No, no,' but she sounded unsure. Christian stood there a moment longer. She wasn't hurt, just confused. She didn't ask any more questions.

'Okay then. Take care,' he said, flying away from the scene, aware that her penetrating eyes were locked on him. Never in his eighteen years had he seen eyes so captivatingly blue.

At home, mother was still in discussion with the General. All guards stood at their posts with an air of determination. Dill and Rhys weren't in their customary light hearted debate, Gayle kept an unyielding gaze on the wall opposite and three guards rather than one patrolled the back doors which led to the reservoirs. As he wandered through the living area, Christian noted how quiet it was, how tense. Pulling back a heavy door that blended in expertly with the wall, he went through and closed it quietly behind him.

He walked down the narrow corridor and through the doorway that led to a small library. The walls were lined with book cases embossed with the Krazonian emblem: a set of wings within an emerald. Ebony wood trestle tables carved to perfection by expert carpenters acted as a centre piece. If he wanted to go somewhere spacious to reflect, this was not ideal. Bluewater was best for that. He didn't come here often and for that his mother chastised him.

'Don't you want to read tales of the brave Kings and Queens throughout the years, or the Elana? You need to educate yourself Christian Meldin.'

But over the past few days he'd started thinking about his father, and wanted to hold the one element of him which remained. Knowing it had rested upon his head and touched his hands, Christian wanted to look at it again. He hadn't for a long time.

Weaving in between the tables, his eyes locked onto the chest that rested on top of one of the book cases. He flew up to reach it and brushed off as much dust as he could before drawing it down carefully, his heart thumping hard. It felt like four years hadn't passed, that his father still lived and breathed and was just on a long journey to Gloryn to visit Mikæl, his ally. Sitting at the table, Christian unclicked the gold clasp and raised the lid. The crown sparkled within its bed of silk woven with the colours of Gloryn's gold and Hæthen's rose. Why Christian's heart raced he didn't know. Perhaps because one day it would be placed onto his head and he would become king. Would he ever be as courageous and strong willed as his father? At this point in time, he couldn't ever see that being so. Taking a breath, he lifted it out.

He held the heavy object in his hands; pure gold, with each of the six formed spires encrusted with rubies that gleamed. Thankfully, José hadn't worn the crown when he visited Zania for the last time. If he had, Christian certainly wouldn't have been able to look at it let alone hold it in his hands.

He was placing it back in to its bed of silk when the ground began to tremble. With haste it put the chest back where it was safe, and flew to the single pane window, all the while the tremors were increasing in strength. Christian couldn't recall the last time this had happened. Zania's dormant volcano was so many miles away, yet still Krazonia felt the effects of it. Somehow they felt the reverberations deep in the ground and it caused terror amongst Krazonians every time.

With a struggle Christian squeezed through the window and headed up two floors, flying close to the brick work. The cool breeze blew against him and if he wasn't so thrown by the event that was taking place, he'd have revelled in it. Now he needed to get to his mother whatever the weather. Knocking on the window, he peered through hoping to catch sight of her. It didn't matter whether or not she still had company.

'Damn!' Christian cursed. The drawing room was empty. Rhia would have seen this coming, yet she had told them, hadn't she, that she felt the pain but it was as if something was blocking her view causing her to see nothing but a blank wall. It was impossible to hazard a guess. With a burst of speed, Christian flew upwards

Chapter Ten

until he felt he was floating on top of the world. If he stared hard enough into the distance, he could see the grey clouds of gloom that hung over the dark realm. Meanwhile færies below him scattered like they were being pursued by Zanians. Christian supposed that in some ways they were. Heart still racing, he went to find his mother.

Chapter Eleven

Sky was making her way through Krazonia square when it felt as though she was losing her balance. Glancing down at her feet, she realised it wasn't her moving, but the ground. Deep rumbles seemed to resonate from beneath her. Frozen, Sky could only watch as tiny grains of gravel and earth shivered across the ground by her feet, and suddenly the place was in frenzy.

Trembles became quakes and Sky looked around, eyes wide with panic. It was as though the sky was bleeding; a heavy grey cloud loomed on the horizon, smothering the blue. A bell began to sound and Sky ran into the centre of the furore, where færies were abandoning their market stalls to fly into their homes whether they were on the ground or in trees. Sky shot anxious glances in different directions, searching for somewhere to go.

One stall fell, causing fruit of various shapes and sizes to tumble and roll across the path.

'Help!' she cried, not knowing what else to say. Most færies had made their escape, they certainly knew what was coming. In the corner of her eye she saw someone waving, trying to attract her attention. An elderly færie was beckoning her to safety.

'Here!' he shouted, his voice nearly breaking. Not bothering to ask questions Sky ran over and stumbled into his small abode.

'What's going on?' she shrieked, scrambling onto a hard seat.

'It's the volcano,' the old færie said with a sigh, blowing out the few candles that due to the earthquake threatened to drop off the small carved table. He was calm, and took his time to sit down, his frail wings quivering to keep him balanced. Sky took it as a reassurance, that he wasn't going about yelling 'we're going

Chapter Eleven

to die!'

'Does this happen a lot?' she asked, her voice shaking almost as much as the ground beneath her.

'No. It's Zania's doing.'

Sky was gripping onto the chair as a tremor threatened to throw her from the seat. 'Zania?'

The elder didn't judge her on this. 'Zania is the dark realm, and its queen is our enemy. This hasn't occurred for a long time,' he shot out a hand to stop a bunch of exotic-looking flowers in a pot from crashing to the floor. The færie continued unperturbed. 'We don't know whether it's random, or if Tæ is able to incite it with dark magic. It would not surprise me.'

Sky jumped at the sound of books crashing to floor from the case behind her. She couldn't understand why this man was so calm.

He revealed a pipe and began to smoke it, and Sky watched, her mouth dropping open. She could soon inhale its sweet, musky scent, not like tobacco smoke.

'She doesn't scare me anymore,' the færie said.

Sky latched onto the arm of the seat to stop herself from being thrown off of it. How kind of Elle to bypass such information as Krazonia being threatened by a volcano and an evil queen.

The tremors eased and Sky found she was able breathe normally again, the panic loosening its hold around her throat.

'Are you not from around here?' asked the old færie.

'I...um, I've just arrived,' Sky said faintly, unpeeling herself from the seat. 'My name is Sky.'

'Nice to meet you Sky, my name is Roal. Well, that was interesting. We've had no trouble lately, but it is most certainly back with a vengeance. I wonder why,' Roal said, easing himself up off the chair.

Sky checked the necklace still sat snugly in her dress pocket. Though the beat of her heart slowed, it continued to ache.

'I hope it hasn't caused too much damage,' said Roal.

'Thanks for letting me shelter in here,' Sky said hoarsely. She wandered forward, half blind from tears.

'You are most welcome, Sky. Look after yourself.'

75

She pulled open the door. Færies were returning to inspect the damage done in a quiet, timid manner. Some children were crying. Feeling utterly overwhelmed and unable to stop herself, Sky burst into tears.

When she'd dried the tears and wiped her face clean, she decided to help some of the færies restore the market place to how it was before as some stalls had collapsed, scattering fruit, vegetables, and ornaments across the ground. Sky bent down to retrieve shards of a painted vase, careful not to cut her fingers. The pattern on it was of red and yellow swirls painted unevenly. It was handmade and therefore unique. Sky sighed. It couldn't be mended that was for sure.

'I wouldn't even try,' said a tall, slim færie with eyes the colour of the sea. He had dirty blond hair cut roughly to meet his shoulders.

'It's a shame,' Sky replied, handing over the remains. The færie shrugged as he took them from her.

'It's happened before, but not for a long time. It's taken us by surprise hasn't it?'

Sky nodded. 'It sure has,' she said, brushing her hands together to wipe off dust. 'Um, where's the mansion from here?'

The færie hesitated. He probably thought she was deranged for not knowing. 'It's behind you.'

Sky spun round and lo and behold, there it was. A brick-built structure sat atop a hill that overlooked the square, about a twenty minute walk from where she stood.

'Thanks,' she said vaguely. She couldn't defer it any longer.

Her journey started here.

Sky wandered through the heat only half aware of her surroundings. The sun tinged her skin, the breeze cooled her down. The sounds of life had become white noise.

She'd probably been here for less than two hours and already there'd been an earthquake. An *earthquake*, and she could only hope it wasn't a sign of things to come. Brushing her hair out of her face and with her eyes locked on the Krazonian mansion, Sky began to make her way up the path leading to the entrance. There was one guard beside the double doors, shifting from foot to foot and glancing around anxiously. Before she could approach him one of the doors opened to another guard and they began to converse quietly. Sky almost didn't want to interrupt but alas, she had an important matter to sort out. Preparing her words she advanced towards them. They were both tall and wore metallic armour on their chests, elbows and knees; one had stern features and the way he stood told Sky he was the more dominant. The other guard looked timid in comparison, despite standing at the same height.

'Excuse me..?' Sky began.

They stopped talking and spun to face her, each gripping a shield to their chest.

'Yes?' was the answer from the no-nonsense guard. He stared at her with inquisitive dark eyes.

'I need to speak with the prince or princess,' she said, determined not to be put off.

'This really is not a convenient time.'

'Do you need help?' the other guard asked. Young and fresh-faced, he gazed at her with innocent eyes, forest green.

Sky considered her answer. 'Yes, but I need to speak with Christian or Rhia. It's really important.'

They stood silent for a few seconds, the sun beating down on them. Sky bit the inside of her mouth, the irritation prickling her skin like the heat.

The no-nonsense guard then shook his head. 'This is not a good time. Is your home damaged, are you injured? You can find aid in the village.'

Sky shook her head back at him. 'I'm fine. Are they not available to speak?'

'What is it concerning?'

Her mind went blank. 'I can't say,' she said quietly, unsure of whether it was better to tell the truth or conceal it. What if they arrested and condemned her as a spy? She felt the guard scrutinising her from head to toe.

'Perhaps you should come back in a little while?' suggested the other guard.

Sky was about to blurt out that she had nowhere to go, but

thought better of it. Instead she spoke calmly.

'It's fine. I'll wait here until they can see me,' and with that, she strolled halfway down the hillside and settled herself on the grass. She didn't care what the guards thought. They couldn't escort her from the premises. This was a free world, or at least she got that impression. Sky ran her fingers through the soft grass and took in a view that consisted of an endless azure sky and clusters of trees. It was hard to believe what had just happened. Some færies were cleaning up debris caused by the brief but damaging earthquake.

Taking a deep breath of fragrant summer air, Sky told herself that although the earthquake had thrown her, she couldn't let it affect the rest of her time here.

Only a few minutes had passed when there came the low, rhythmic sound of beating wings. Sky looked up to see one færie, most likely Rhia, making her way from the mansion towards a village. Another færie dutifully followed. Sky did a double take.

It was the same boy who'd approached her beneath the tree. It had to be Christian. Sky stood up and glanced behind at the two guards who were watching with their eyebrows raised, as if to challenge her.

'I'm just going to go this way,' Sky said.

The no-nonsense guard shrugged and resumed his position, keeping his focus ahead of him and his shield by his side. The other guard mirrored his actions.

Sky rushed down the hill, her wings twitching. *No, I am not flying*, she warned them. *I'm not going to make a fool of myself.* With all her might she managed to prevent them from doing what they naturally wanted to do, and continued with haste in the direction of the village.

Out of breath by the time she arrived at the scene, Sky hid herself behind a tree and with one hand against it, peered round it to observe the goings on. She felt the coarse trunk beneath her fingers and for a moment had to close her eyes, overcome with the dizzying realisation once again of where she stood, and of the world that surrounded her.

Catching her breath, she opened her eyes, taking in the sights and sounds. A little way ahead Rhia was helping an injured færie

Chapter Eleven

stand. There was an older male who held the hands of two small children, visibly upset. Planks of wood hung from the tree and some were on the grass, splintered and broken. When Christian walked over to help, Rhia threw a scornful look at him.

'I'm here to help. Simya, Gray, I am so sorry,' he said.

Rhia didn't look impressed. Sky studied her. She had shoulder length brown hair, a straight nose and a moody mouth. Her eyes were sharp. Sky could almost see the chip on her shoulder and it was like she resented the whole world.

'This is your fault,' Rhia said venomously.

'You can't put all the blame on me,' Christian said. 'It was a joint effort, and you were more than a little distracted. Gray, I really am so sorry. Are your children okay?'

Gray, clutching their little hands, nodded. Sky could see Christian staring in dismay at the wooden planks scattered along with the family's belongings. Only half of the tree house remained.

Rhia turned her attention to the færie, Simya, beside her. 'Will you be alright to walk to the square? There is aid there.'

Simya smiled weakly.

'We will send for a carpenter to do this job properly,' the princess added.

Christian backed away. 'Yes,' he said. Surely he couldn't apologise again? Rhia hadn't, not once. He and his sister took to the air once more and Sky started back towards the mansion in hot pursuit. On the outskirts of the village she caught sight of three young færies crouched in a circle.

'No, that isn't how you do it. You grind your fingers into the palm of your hand then the dust will appear.'

Sky couldn't help but wander towards the huddle, eyeing them with curiosity. One noticed and moved aside to give her a better view.

'Look,' said one boy, who Sky presumed was the expert. She was intrigued. The young færie clenched his fists and took a long breath. A smile crept onto his face as he opened his hands and shimmering dust like starlight drifted from his palms and onto the grass. The boy blew on it a little, and continued to sprinkle the dust, like anyone would sprinkle herbs, or salt. Slowly but surely a bud appeared amongst the grass. It began to grow and bit by bit flowered into something red, something so pretty.

'Wow,' Sky said, dumbfounded. She stared at it long and hard: a solitary flower with soft, vibrant petals swaying slightly.

'See? All it takes is a bit of concentration and patience,' the smallest færie said and then jumped into the air. He was joined by the other two, and their pearly wings beat together rapidly, carrying them away.

Snapping out of the daze Sky pushed on, resisting the urge to look back at the blossom that had been brought to life by færie dust.

Rhia was talking loudly at one of the guards, one Sky didn't recognise, beside the main doors of the mansion. She looked angry and jabbed a finger against the guard's armoured chest. From where she was, Sky sensed a bad atmosphere. She stood at the edge of it. The other two guards remained obediently quiet. Christian walked inside, followed by a now sullen Rhia. Her victim, the stunned guard, readjusted his armour before traipsing down the hill. He passed Sky without looking at her as she dashed up the path, only to be halted by the fresh-faced guard. She really needed to have a plan B in these cases. Saying that, she'd never needed a "plan A" before.

'Please!' she said, exasperated. 'I need to talk to them.'

'You mean you haven't already?' he asked, still blocking her entry with a sturdy arm.

Sky released a sigh of relief when Christian emerged. Recognition flashed in his eyes.

'I need to speak to you or your sister – the princess. It's important.'

He was obviously still reeling from his sister's nasty accusation in the village and didn't have much patience.

'Why? What is so important?'

Sky hesitated. 'Please can we talk somewhere more private?' Maybe she could get through to him first.

The other, obnoxious guard sniggered and Sky ignored him. Christian rubbed his face.

'Rhys, lower your arm,' he said, pausing with his mouth open as if a sudden thought occurred to him. Sky linked her fingers

Chapter Eleven

together, clasping her hands in anticipation.

'On second thoughts,' said the prince. 'I will come outside.'

Christian stepped out into the sun and walked forward a few steps before turning to face her, arms folded. His look made Sky want to dig a hole and fall into it. He had intense brown eyes and a moody mouth, like his sister. At this point his lips were pressed together and Sky knew he was sussing her out. Given their first meeting he probably thought she was a complete weirdo.

'What's your name?'

'Sky Francis.'

'Anything you wish to discuss with my sister goes through me first.'

It was a threat. Sky's skin tingled beneath the hot sun and her arms began to itch. So did her scalp, and her ankles. She shifted her weight from one foot to the other. 'I…' the words were ready, waiting to pounce off the tip of her tongue.

'Well?'

'It's about the Emerald. I think it's in danger.'

Christian's arms dropped to his sides and silence fell like a blanket over their heads. Sky thought it best to stay quiet, focusing on settling the nerves in her stomach.

'What do you-' Christian said, faltering. Sky glanced down, conscious of the necklace in her pocket. 'What makes you say that?' she heard him say.

'I've been told. Been warned, you could say.'

'Warned by whom?' Christian snapped. She was mortified to feel tears in her eyes, blurring her vision. She didn't *want* to cry, but she needed someone to believe her. She wiped them away quickly.

'I know something bad is going to happen, I was sent here. I'm-'

'You were sent here?'

'No, I mean,' she lowered her voice, preparing to drop the bombshell.

'I'm from the human world.'

Christian stared at her, his expression unfathomable.

Sky held his gaze, determined not to fall apart.

Chapter Twelve

'I know something bad is going to happen, I was sent here. I'm-'

'You were sent here?' Christian interrupted.

'No, I mean...' the færie said quietly. 'I'm from the human world.'

Christian couldn't understand why she'd say such a thing. This conversation had been ridiculous from the start and clearly she had a few problems - here stood the færie who'd asked him whether or not this was Krazonia. Suspicion crept into his mind and he searched her face for a twitch, for a hint that she was lying, but her jaw was set. Her blue eyes held only tears.

'You can't be from the human world,' he said, unable to accept such a proclamation. Deep down, this was something he hoped he would never have to face again.

'I am.'

Christian stepped back warily.

'You've got to believe what I say,' Sky pleaded in a voice quiet and fearful. 'Please don't exile me.'

To that, Christian could say nothing. This hadn't happened for four years. No færie spoke of the other world where humans ruled. Four years ago everything went wrong. His father was killed, Rhia was cursed because she'd tried to help a færie who claimed to be human...

He had to walk away and think. Looking back, Sky hadn't moved. Her long black hair blew in the breeze and her hands remained clasped tightly together.

Beneath the bright sun, with her ivory skin and black hair, the

Chapter Twelve

girl looked displaced. Suspicion gave way to curiosity. Had she really arrived from the human world? She looked like she could be. Sky Francis didn't quite fit in here.

Approaching her slowly, all the possibilities knocked about in Christian's head. Having been through it first-hand Rhia was the best færie to speak to. If she would listen, she may be able to understand better than Christian what this meant. Another thought struck him. If he let her go she could tell any Krazonian, the news would spread. That was to say she hadn't already. The prospect was enough to make his wings quiver.

'Come this way,' he said, leading her up the path. Dill and Rhys stood firmly at the main doors with their shields.

'Dill, I want you to accompany me.' This had to be taken seriously, and Christian wanted to prove he could handle it himself. Mother needn't know just yet.

Sky followed him inside, shoulders hunched. Did she think the ceiling was going to cave in on her? He directed her through the hallway, past the kitchen and down the corridor to the vast space of the living area.

'Wait here while I find my sister.'

Sky let out a small gasp when she entered the room. Christian could appreciate what she saw: a high ceiling decorated by three hanging, candle-lit chandeliers, lavish furnishings. The far windows displayed Krazonia's reservoirs surrounded by fields, intense green beneath the sun, stretching into the distance.

'This place is beautiful,' she said, sitting down on a long yew wood seat draped with soft Gloryn cotton and cushions. She looked around, entranced.

Christian ruffled his hair and went to pass Dill, who lingered in the doorway. 'Watch her while I fetch my sister.'

Dill caught him on the arm. 'She could be one of Tæ's spies.'

Christian pulled away. 'We don't know that. Just keep an eye on her, will you?' A spy wouldn't come out with "I'm from the human world and the Emerald is in danger" would they? Spies were supposed to be subtle and devious.

'You don't know her,' Dill hissed.

Christian realised the guard didn't trust his decision to bring her in. 'You are stating the obvious, aren't you?' he hissed back. 'Wait here.'

All he had to do was follow the sound of her voice. She was yelling from somewhere on the first floor.

'I didn't feel anything! How could this happen?' Christian stopped short a few feet away from the door to her bedroom, listening intently.

'Rhia, don't be angry. Maybe we were wrong about the Elana. Do not blame yourself for this,' Anya said in her soft, comforting voice. Christian strained to hear his mother's words. 'The only difference is we would have been a little more prepared.'

'That is not the point. We both know I would have felt it or seen something. Okay, so not much could have been changed, but why didn't I *know*? The Elana, they made the message clear, before...I just...'

Christian burst in. There would never be a right time with his sister.

'What do you want, lime leaf?'

Mother rolled her eyes.

'Rhia, there's a færie downstairs, you should talk to her. Well, she certainly needs to talk to you.'

'No one ever *needs* to see me,' she said.

'What about?' asked Anya. Christian wished she'd been somewhere else, not here. With all that was going on he didn't want to add another problem to her list.

'This færie just has some concerns about some things.'

Anya's look was questioning. He'd always been an appalling liar.

'We rarely let Krazonians into our home without knowing their reasons, Christian.' Her forehead creased. 'What are you not telling us?'

He squared his shoulders. 'I'm not hiding anything from you. Rhia, will you come down?'

Anya raised a hand, and held it still. Christian held in his exasperation by biting the inside of his cheek. 'This is not the time to lie,' she said, her almond brown eyes locking onto him. She was serious.

Chapter Twelve

He would have to tell her something – the partial truth. 'Her name is Sky. She has come to the mansion to speak to Rhia because,' he paused, 'she thinks the stone is in danger.'

His mother stepped towards him like she hadn't heard clearly, her face twisting into an expression of bewilderment.

Christian had to speak quickly. 'Mother, please don't be angry. She wants to speak to Rhia. I promise we'll tell you everything once we know it all. Please,' he implored. 'You already have enough to deal with.'

Rhia cut in at this point. 'Why now?' Her tone surprised Christian. Instead of spitting out words with malice to disguise her shock, there was a tremor in her voice that immediately revealed it. 'What makes her think that?'

That had been Christian's exact thought, initially. 'I don't know, which is why you should speak to her, hear her out.' His mother headed for the door and obediently he stepped aside.

'You will tell me everything,' Anya said sternly.

'Of course, mother.'

Christian waited until she was safely out of ear shot. 'Are you coming?' he said to his sister.

'Answer my questions.' She'd regained her wilfulness. 'Or I am not going anywhere.'

There was no point trying to persuade her otherwise. Rhia's mind was made up.

'Did you take pity on her?'

'No I did not,' Christian said, the frustration slipping out. 'I think any concerns about the Emerald should be taken seriously. Will you come and speak to her?'

Rhia's hard expression didn't change. 'So be it.'

Christian lingered in the hallway after Rhia went in to greet Sky. He wanted to hear this conversation, for he didn't doubt it would be an important one, or at least an intriguing one. Dill remained by the open door until Christian ordered him back to his post. With a complacent shrug the guard walked away, his shield knocking against his leg armour.

Making sure he was out of view, Christian leaned against the wall to listen.

85

'So what, may I ask, do you have to say about the Emerald?' said Rhia with amiability that was clearly forced.

'Okay. Whether you choose to believe me or not is up to you, but I've come as a warning. I think it's in danger. I mean, is it safe?'

Rhia's laugh was short and humourless. 'I don't see how any of this is any of your business. Yes, it is safe.'

Christian cringed.

'You say, I quote, that you have "come as a warning". But where have you come from?'

A weighty silence followed. Christian lowered his head, listening intently, his heart hammering against his chest.

'I don't know if you'll believe me.'

'Try me,' Rhia said.

'I'm human! I come from human earth.'

'That is impossible.'

'I can tell you now it isn't because I'm here. I came through the portal.'

Christian rubbed his neck anxiously, feeling the pull of his skin beneath his fingers.

'What was that earthquake about?' Sky asked. 'A færie I spoke to said it hadn't happened in a long time.'

'Enough!' Rhia shouted. 'I want you to leave. You know nothing and have no right to be asking these questions. Christian was a fool to let you in here.'

'No, he did the right thing. I need you to believe me. I'm human!'

'Say that again and I will have you exiled.'

Christian froze. Rhia was certainly taking extreme measures, or was it only extreme because he hadn't the guts to do it himself?

'Rhia, if you would stop and listen-'

'You address me like an acquaintance. I don't know you and I don't care for what you have to say. Get out!' said Rhia angrily. Christian looked around the door in time to see Sky jump up from her seat. A part of Christian admired her determination but it would be tough competition going up against Rhianne Meldin. Neither færie seemed to notice him in the doorway as he watched

Chapter Twelve

the scene unfold.

Sky held up her hands. 'I don't believe that you don't care. I think you're scared. I swear I'm telling the truth and have been sent here to help-'

'You think we need help? Well we do not, and certainly not from a deluded færie like you,' Rhia was breathless with anger. 'You have no right to make these assertions. The Emerald is safe and will remain in its dome of glass until the world ends. I don't want to hear another word from you. If you don't leave now the guards will drag you out,' she said, her wings opening and closing in blunt movements.

'That isn't fair!' Sky exclaimed. The princess glared at her, daring another reproach. Christian moved back as a fuming Sky stormed past him. She burst through the main doors and was soon lost in sunlight. The two guards looked at each other and then to Christian. He couldn't determine their expressions. He shrugged and went in to the living room to see his sister pacing back and forth, tears streaming down her face.

'Rhia?'

'I can't go through it again,' she cried. 'I can't trust anyone. I won't, and definitely not another...human, if what she says is true.'

Christian walked towards her, but before he was able to offer consolation she'd taken the same number of steps away from him.

'You let her in.'

'I know. I thought I was doing the right thing.'

'Did you really?'

Christian clenched his teeth and swallowed down the anger. 'What else could I do? I was faced with her telling me the Emerald is in danger and that she's human, we don't get that every day. I could hardly send her back down the hill. I'm sorry!'

Rhia let out a sob and fled the room. With a heavy heart Christian glided to the large windows, staring out at the landscape. The wind rolled over the hills in silver waves and sunlight glistened on the reservoir's surface. From this side of the mansion no færie would have known an earthquake had shaken the ground not long before, sending Krazonia into disarray. From this side of the mansion, the world looked peaceful. His thoughts overturned, and he began to wonder about Sky Francis.

She'd left the mansion fuming. That was enough to prove to Christian that she wasn't a spy – she'd opened up to Rhia like she had to him, only Rhia had refused outright to listen. Now she was wandering around Krazonia, and who could say whether she would spill the secret - for a secret it would have to be - of where she came from. Christian wasn't sure whether she could be trusted, so he'd have to find her.

As he made his way through the main town he caught sight of his friend Aeron, setting up his vegetable stall. Tall, with hair the colour of Gloryn sand and eyes forest green, many found him charming yet somewhat intimidating. Christian thought it was his hearty laugh that did it. It had a habit of bursting out, usually making those with him jump out of their skin.

Aeron was being helped by his assistant Tomas, who had a handful of carrots and was cleaning them ferociously with a cloth. Aeron turned around to greet the next customer and his eyes brightened.

'Christian! Are you here to survey the damage?' His smile was tight - unusual for him, but not unexpected given recent events.

'You could say that. How are things?'

Aeron stopped work on the stall and rubbed his hands together. 'Things are okay,' he hesitated. 'Can I ask you something?'

With a sense of dread Christian nodded slowly. 'If you must.'

Aeron scratched his chin and glanced around. 'Many of us have seen the Zanians. We just want to know whether or not we should be concerned. Well, we already are concerned but we need some answers and some reassurance. We have had none as of yet.'

Christian's heavy heart now felt heavier. 'Aeron, I want so much to explain what is happening but you know it isn't my place. The queen will come to the square soon enough, I'm sure. With regard to your concerns, you don't need them. At the moment we want things to continue as if nothing has changed.'

'But something has.'

'I've told you it is not my place.'

Aeron pursed his lips. 'Sorry, I'm sorry. It's good to see the

Chapter Twelve

princess is looking even more miserable than usual.'

Christian tried to laugh, but it tailed off. 'Yes that's true, and I have to live with her!' he said with a joviality that was painfully false. He knew his friend wasn't stupid. Aeron gave him a nudge.

'I'm sure it will all be fine.'

'Here's to hoping,' Christian muttered. 'I need to go, but we will speak again soon.'

'Bye for now.'

He got a far better view in the air, and with his wings beating fast and steady he scanned the land below. It didn't take long to spot her trudging east over the hillsides toward the lake. She probably didn't know where she was going and didn't care. Flying down, he felt the wind rushing against him and a fluttering of nerves in his stomach. He couldn't fathom why they appeared so suddenly at the sight of her.

His feet touched grass.

She turned her head to him and jumped in surprise. Then her expression reverted back to that of anger; her eyebrows furrowed and those piercing blue eyes stared hard at the ground. She didn't speak. Christian gazed at her, expecting some sort of verbal response. In a way he was amazed by her audacity to ignore him.

'Sky?' he said after a while. Then more assertively, 'Sky!'

She stopped and looked at him. 'What?'

Christian blinked, startled by her tone. He was beginning to regret chasing after her, if this was how she spoke to Krazonia's heir to the throne.

'Sky, you must tell me what you know,' he said, extracting any emotion from his voice.

'You heard what I said to Rhia, make what you can out of that,' she said. 'Now if you'll excuse me I need to go and have a think, see if I can find a way to escape this place.'

'Then you heard what Rhia said to you,' Christian said, deadpan. 'It's very easy for us to exile faeries to the Arids, and we only need one reason.' He crossed his arms and closed his wings tightly together. 'What shall it be?'

Chapter Thirteen

Sky knew she was being unreasonable, but couldn't help it. She hadn't yet calmed down, and now Christian walked beside her demanding answers. It was difficult to know where to start but there was one thing she was sure of: exile would mean the end. Stopping and closing her eyes momentarily, Sky allowed the breeze to lay its calmness over her.

'I don't mean to be rude, I'm sorry.' She became aware of a flute being played from somewhere on the hillside, birds singing and the hum of insects. Then Christian's voice cut through the serenity.

'I wish to speak with you and believe it or not, I'm willing to hear you out,' he sounded a little less severe. Sky opened her eyes, shielding them against the daylight with one hand on her forehead.

'Were you heading in any particular direction?' Christian asked.

How well did he think she knew this place? 'Not really,' Sky said.

'Well you're walking towards the lake, and that is probably the ideal place to talk.' His curious eyes flickered to her and then the ground.

They walked in silence, but the voice in Sky's head was loud, firing questions in quick succession like bullets. What sort of "talk" were they going to have? What would the prince want to know? Could it be he just wanted as much information as he could get, before sending her to the desert anyway?

He wouldn't know about the necklace in her pocket.

Chapter Thirteen

Upon arriving at the lake, Sky left Christian's side and ambled to the water's edge, observing its surface as the sun rays illuminated the ripples, turning them into liquid gold. A cooling breeze came as a welcome relief from the heat and Sky found it hard to believe how cold and gloomy it was at home. Looking into the water she imagined the two dimensions were split much like the world above water, and the world beneath its surface. So near, yet so far. So different.

Sky eased down onto the feathery grass, sitting on her knees, somewhat nervous. She bound her arms across her stomach, trying to make it look like a casual gesture when inside she could feel the knot of tension forming. Christian settled himself opposite her.

Typically, they both opened their mouths to speak at the same time.

'How did you-'

'Your sister-'

They both went quiet and Christian frowned, averting his attention to a lilac flower that poked out from the grass. Sky watched his wings flex in the same way she'd stretch her arms in a yawn. She was gawping but couldn't help it.

Christian lifted his head.

'What is it?'

'Um, your wings, that's all,' Sky replied, her eyes following the trail of thin veins weaving their way across a translucent skin that curled at the tips. They looked fragile, yet she didn't doubt they were as strong as steel. She couldn't help wondering what they felt like to touch.

'You have them too, if you didn't notice,' said Christian.

Struck with a sudden dizziness Sky looked down at her dress, hoping it would pass. *You're okay*, she told herself, swallowing down the sick feeling.

From the edge of her vision she noted Christian getting comfortable.

'I may have overstepped the mark with your sister,' she murmured. 'But did she really need to bite my head off? I thought she might want help. I was only telling her what I knew.'

Christian sighed.

'Rhia doesn't want help,' he said. 'Or at least she acts like she doesn't. I really think she believes she can handle whatever life throws at her but she isn't that strong. With you claiming to be from...claiming to be a human, it's thrown her,' he paused, and Sky felt him studying her face. 'It's thrown me.

'I'm going to ask you one more time, and it's easy to lie, but remember what I said. Even if you tried to fly away you'd be found, no doubt. Guards will find you and my mother will have you sentenced,' he leant towards her, his dark brown eyes smouldering, a fire blazing behind them. 'Are you from the human world?'

His breathing became shallow. Sky guessed he wanted her to say "no, I was just kidding, I was kidding about everything" and then he'd get up and walk away awash with relief, back to normality.

There were other færies around, lying about and basking in the sunshine. Thankfully, none of them were close enough to clock onto this conversation.

'I'm not lying. I'm from the human world,' Sky told Christian, looking him square in the eye. Let him see the truth - in the way she held his gaze, and the way she'd set her mouth into a determined pucker.

The air between them was taut with tension, Sky could feel it.

'Okay,' Christian said, falling back onto his elbows. He threw a look up at the clouds. 'Okay. Now, you will listen to me.'

He started explaining Rhia's story. The fire behind his eyes faded to embers and he spoke in a way that suggested he felt pity for his sister. Every now and then he clenched his fists and Sky knew those particular events had to be what hurt most.

'Four years ago there was this færie...I can't remember her name...' Sky held back from giving him the answer. 'She came to the mansion, confused and pleading with my parents for help because she was human. I don't know how she got past the guards. Of course my mother and father were shocked, and dismayed. At eleven years of age Rhia was naïve and a little rebellious. With naivety came a kindness she wanted to give to any færie, but she used her kindness *wrongly*.

Chapter Thirteen

'Despite my father's orders, for it was my father who had the discipline, Rhia went to meet this human. Bearing in mind there had been exchanges between our king and Mikæl of Gloryn, who'd received an invite from Zania to join *her* side.

'That was Tæ's distraction. That night Rhia went with this færie to Bluewater Glen in search of the Elana, because my sister really thought they would help. But for a hundred years they *haven't* helped.' Sky heard the sound of his teeth clamping together. He glowered at the lake. She wanted to know more about the "Elana" but thought better of it. He hadn't finished.

'We were ambushed, the Emerald was kept safe but we lost many in the process. Rhia was inconsolable – the færie…human, had left her alone in the caves and she kept saying over and over that the Elana had cursed her. Sometimes it's a blessing, sometimes a curse. At that time it was a curse.'

Sky sat perfectly still, her hands clasped in her lap. There would surely be a reason as to why he was telling her this.

'Tæ murdered my father.'

Sky was stunned. So that's what Elle had planned to say before she'd abruptly cut her off mid-sentence. But it couldn't all have been Elle's fault.

Christian had worked himself up into a trembling fury, and without thinking Sky latched onto his wrist to get his attention, maybe even to bring him out of the past and back to the present. 'You don't have to tell me anymore.' She was surprised he'd told her so much.

At that Christian looked at her with dismay and Sky immediately withdrew her hand. *Bad move.*

'My point,' he said slowly, 'is that Rhia no longer trusts anyone, especially those deluded enough to claim they are human – especially if they really are. After what happened you can see why she reacted in the way she did.'

'Yes.'

Christian ran his hands through his hair. 'I don't even know you and I've just spilled my life story.' He threw her another one of his serious looks, the unspoken threat readable in his eyes. 'You cannot speak of this to anyone else.'

Sky shook her head. 'I won't say anything. I wouldn't be doing myself any favours.'

Christian looked away. 'Tell me about you,' he said.

Sky's mouth went dry and the knot in her stomach returned. 'I, well, in the human world I'm at school studying for my GCSE's.'

At that, Christian arched an eyebrow.

'We take exams. Written tests on lots of different subjects. I live pretty much a normal life. Lived, I *lived* pretty much a normal life. Anyway, so I was walking home and bumped into this lady who dropped a, she dropped…'

'What did she drop?'

Sky's mind went blank as a fearful apprehension shattered any ready thoughts she had. She put her hand into her dress pocket and touched the small chiselled jewel with trembling fingers. The chain was cool against her skin. She had to tell the truth, no matter what the risks. Finally her tenacious streak shone through, barging past any impeding fears.

'The woman dropped an emerald necklace and I have it. It's in my pocket. It brought me here.' It sounded so farfetched when she spoke the words aloud. 'I started having dreams that I was flying. In some I was walking through some sort of village, or should I say town square…' Christian stared blankly ahead and it was hard to tell if he was listening. After a moment Sky went on while the prince remained as still as a statue.

'It started glowing, actually glowing. It terrified me. I met the woman who dropped it, and she told me it's connected to this place,' she proceeded to clear her throat. 'Through the stone you keep here.' With trepidation Sky revealed the necklace from her pocket.

'The "portal" between our worlds is still open, that's how I got here. The woman I spoke to, Elle, she was the one before me.'

Christian's eyes widened and he lurched backwards as if Sky had revealed a poisonous snake. He tried to speak but no words came.

The surge of confidence Sky had felt dissolved into ice cold terror as she waited for him to say something. Christian was staring at the necklace.

Chapter Thirteen

'I can't believe it,' he said quietly. Sky cast a sideways glance to see a group of faeries settling down on the grass a few metres away. They smiled at her and the Krazonian prince. Sky placed the necklace in her lap, unable to return the friendly gesture.

'Do you think Rhia will listen to me now?' she said.

Christian blinked, springing into life. 'I need to tell the queen,' he said, jumping up. 'I need to get back.'

'Please don't!' Sky shrieked. Her limbs were frozen with shock, so she remained sat on the grass even though she'd wanted to jump up. 'I really don't want to be exiled to the desert!'

'My mother needs to know. Heavens, you're...you...'

Christian stared at her like she was an alien, not a human. He must have given the onlookers a scare, because they bowed and quickly went away.

'Christian, what if she thinks I'm a threat? She might blame me for your father-'

He walked away in haste, expanding his wings for flight.

Sky scrambled up and went after him, clutching the necklace like her life depended on it. 'Christian, wait!' Oddly enough no faerie interceded, but simply watched the commotion or ignored it. 'Don't you want this?' she cried.

At that he paused, turned around. Sky found herself blinking back tears. Through the blur she could determine Christian's shape as he advanced towards her.

'Do you think I wanted this?' she asked, wiping away a tear that had escaped. 'I was quite happy with the life I was living and now I'm here in this strange world, with some so called "mission" to complete and I don't even know what it is. You don't know me but I need you on my side. I need someone on my side.' She sniffed hard to rid herself of tears.

Christian had one hand knotted in his hair, and was visibly struggling with his conscience. Sky bit down on her lip and blinked the remaining tears away from her lashes. She had to be strong. Crying would not do.

'Christian, it's scary for you. Well, I am terrified, but I've got no choice. Before you tell your mother everything I wanted you to know that,' slowly she held the necklace out for him but he seemed scared to touch it. 'Have it.'

He studied her. 'What will you do?'

Good question. 'I don't know. Sit around and wait I suppose.'

Christian closed his eyes, shaking his head. 'If you're human you'll have no home here.'

'That's correct,' Sky croaked.

'I know you're terrified, Sky,' he said in a low voice, 'but you must realise what this means to my family and I. The last human brought only disaster.

'You will stay at the mansion, it's better for everyone. We can't take any risks, do you understand?'

It was a chance and a warning all rolled into one. Desperation melted into relief. 'I understand,' Sky said. 'What will you say to the queen?'

"The queen" to Sky was an ominous figure who had yet to become a real, breathing person. The thought dropped into her mind like a stone, causing a ripple of fear through her. At the end of the day even if she'd secured Christian's trust, it was his mother who had the last word. Rhia would be displeased to say the least.

'I will tell her what she needs to know, but if she asks I won't lie. Keep the necklace for the mean time.'

Sky nodded, placing the necklace back into her pocket. Christian stretched open his magnificent wings and began to beat them together, and every time they made a subtle whooshing sound. It was time for Sky to reveal another truth.

'I don't know how to fly.'

Christian lifted into the air. 'You haven't flown yet?'

'No. I can't.'

'I may not be a very good teacher but I can tell you from experience, you must relax.'

'It's alright for you. Okay,' Sky held her breath and tensed. She couldn't help it.

'Don't tense your shoulders.'

'I'm not tensed!' she snapped. 'Sorry, I'm sorry.' She blew the air out of her lungs slowly and glanced up at the sky, and the few strands of white cloud that floated across it. Sky shut her eyes, trying to draw in some positive energy. She could fly just like any

Chapter Thirteen

færie here, couldn't she? Her wings were connected to her body, they had to cooperate.

Soon enough she was eye level with Christian and could hear and feel her own wings beating together to keep her in the air. She flailed helplessly and would have lost balance had Christian not grabbed her arms. He hovered directly in front of her.

'See?' said Christian, as if she was a toddler taking her first steps. 'You'll manage.'

The dizziness returned, making Sky lightheaded. 'I haven't exactly gone anywhere,' she said faintly. She felt like she'd sat up too fast, and had to blink away the stars that twinkled in her periphery vision. Christian still had one hand on her arm, keeping her steady. 'Won't other færies stare?' Sky asked as he helped her manoeuvre so she faced the right direction. 'Sorry if this is embarrassing for you. You are the prince after all.'

'Don't worry, Sky. Let them think what they want. We have more important things to be concerned about.'

After a long, cautious journey she made it to the mansion with Christian's guidance. Sky knew he was struggling with the concept of her being from the "other world" and every now and then he'd glance at her, his forehead creasing with confusion. But at least he had the decency to give her a chance.

Her legs were like jelly when she touched ground again, the adrenalin pulsing through her. Flying was freedom absolute, like a rollercoaster that she wanted to ride again and again. The sun was setting and the wind had dropped, leaving a chill in the air. All merry feelings were lost when Sky stepped over the threshold, past the guards and into the Krazonian mansion. Rhia appeared at the other end of the hallway, giving her a cold stare, cold enough the raise the hairs on her arms. Sky looked away, knowing full well the princess would continue to eye her with contempt.

'Christian!' she barked.

Sky thought it best to linger by the main doors, it made her feel safe. Christian didn't hesitate to approach his sister and he led her out of view. Their discussion started out quiet.

'…nowhere…go.'

'…anything I said?'

'...believe...human...'

'How can you go against your own sister?' Rhia said loudly, making it no secret. Sky began to chew her fingernails. *She hates me.*

'I don't want the same thing to happen again, Christian. I hope you are prepared for mother's reaction when I tell her.'

'You aren't telling her, I am,' he argued.

'Well then you'd better go now!'

'That was my plan.'

Sky sank into the dark corner when Christian reappeared looking hassled. 'I need the necklace.'

With a slight nod, she picked it out of her pocket and as she handed it over the glimmering green stone caught the evening light. Christian snatched it. 'For now, I am on your side,' he whispered, probably because he'd had a spat with his sister.

Sky heard Rhia gasp.

'What is that in your hand?'

Christian turned away as if Sky wasn't there. 'If you come upstairs then I can explain to both of you at the same time.' He went up the spiral staircase with Rhia close behind.

Sky sagged against the wall. This would definitely go down as one of the craziest, most overwhelming experiences of her life.

Gradually colours changed; the warming glow of the evening sun was replaced by candlelight and tiredness replaced the adrenalin in Sky's body. By now she'd made herself at home on the floor. The guards' stayed rooted to their posts and more than once she'd wanted to start a conversation but then decided against it. She wouldn't know what to say, anyway. The younger guard with a friendlier face looked around the door from time to time but said nothing. Understandably, he wouldn't know what to say either. Somewhere in the building Sky knew Christian was talking with his sister and mother.

She could only hope he was fighting her corner.

Chapter Fourteen

They went into the drawing room. Christian waited for his mother and sister to sit down before shutting the door. He knew Rhia had seen the necklace and when he turned around the shock was plain to see. Nervously he took a step forward to address them both.

'I spent some time talking with Sky-'

'Would you please reveal what you have in your hands, Christian?' Rhia interjected. Her mouth twitched as she stared at the object. 'Show it,' she ordered.

Christian placed it onto the table, holding his breath. A shard of history lay glistening before him. He recalled his father telling him about the necklace, lost in the human world. It was frightening yet captivating. Rhia was up and out of her chair. Anya, with both her hands on the table, leaned across to stare at it. Her expression was unreadable; each emotion fleetingly came and went, too quick for Christian to work out how she felt. Her words told him.

'Where is she?'

'Sky is downstairs by the main doors.'

Anya glowered at him. 'Were you sensible enough to have her under guard? Who's down there? This makes her a human. We have a human in our kingdom, again. Is she under guard?' she repeated.

Christian nodded. 'Dill and Rhys are there. I really don't think she means any harm.' He could have kicked himself for being so candid. It made him look naïve, just like his sister had been.

Rhia laughed in disbelief. 'You seem to have conveniently

forgotten what happened four years ago when one came to our lands. That girl to whom I offered help used me. For the sake of the Elana I wish we had had her exiled and for my own sake I wish I'd listened to father!' she said, casting a despairing glance at the ceiling. 'Sky must be the wall. She must be what is blocking my vision.' Rhia's grey eyes focused on Christian. 'You cannot trust her. I'm telling you this from experience.' She curled her lip in abhorrence. 'Never trust a human. They forced our kind away.'

Meanwhile Anya paced in her long, elegant dress, her eyes half closed. Christian watched her move back and forth slowly, no doubt trying to think through the anger.

'Sky told me she found the necklace,' he said. 'She doesn't want to be here. Mother, she fears you will exile her for being from the other world but I ask you to hear what she has to say first.'

Anya hushed Rhia, who had her mouth open to speak.

'I shall make judgement in the morning. She will stay here under guard for it would be a foolish idea to let her run loose. We know that from having learnt the hard way.

'Set up two posts, one outside of her room and the other on the outer grounds. I want her in the room on the third floor, away from me and away from the Emerald,' said Anya. After a few moments of gazing at the necklace she picked it up and held it. 'I will look after this.' Christian thought he'd heard a tremor in his mother's voice.

'Well I certainly don't want it. I don't want to even look at it,' Rhia said, leaving the room.

Panic flashed in Anya's soft brown eyes. She would be confused. Christian felt the same, but he couldn't bring himself to hate Sky Francis. She had nothing to do with the past. He did however dislike how her being human filled him with uncertainty and apprehension.

'Go downstairs and ask Simian to take her to her room. I won't be joining you for the meal,' Anya said, gathering her dress. 'Neither will the human,' she finished indignantly. Christian felt his skin prickle with the familiar sense of irritation usually caused by his sister.

'If that is what you want,' he said before bowing his head. 'One

Chapter Fourteen

thing to think about,' he added, looking up. 'The reason I don't believe her to be a threat is because when I went to see her by the lake she offered the necklace to me, I did not have to take it. And she is one, we are thousands.'

'I don't care. She could cause a huge amount of damage, Christian. A single human is a risk to us.'

He disregarded his mother's hostility with a slight shake of the head. 'Why not speak with her this moment, then?'

'It must wait until morning. I can't think clearly right now. It will also give the human some time to re-evaluate her existence.' Anya pressed a hand on her forehead and shut her eyes. 'Please do as I ask, Christian.'

With an inward sigh, he left the room.

Wandering down the stairs, he wasn't surprised to see Sky hadn't moved. She sat within shadows and silence. The main doors were shut, blocking out any sound from the outside world. Candlelight flickered brightly on the wall.

'You can stay, but will be called on by a guard in the morning to speak to the queen,' Christian said, speaking with little emotion. He had to remember his role in all of this. They were not friends, nor acquaintances. *A single human is a risk to us*, had been his mother's words.

'Wait here.'

'I'm not going anywhere,' he heard her say as he turned to find Simian.

Alongside the guard, he led a wary Sky up the spiral stairs to the third floor. He showed her to a room and without waiting for her to settle, shut the door. The blunt sound caused his heart to lurch. Did he really want to do this? His thoughts led him to glance at the guard. As if he knew what the prince was thinking Simian shrugged. Unsure of how much the guard knew, if anything, Christian mumbled a thank you and went downstairs to the dining room.

Christian ate in silence opposite his sister at the polished oak table. They couldn't be any further apart. Butlers hovered by them, refilling their glasses with distilled water from the reservoirs. Even if they hadn't been present, conversation would have been hard to find. Christian struggled with his sister because he knew they wouldn't be able to discuss the situation amicably. Rhia would unleash her temper on him and in return Christian would get irate so instead they ate in an uncomfortable quiet. Rhia, in her stubborn way, had hardly even glanced at him.

After a time his sister finally spoke up. She timed it well, having just finished her meal. Placing down her cutlery she tilted her head and looked at Christian plaintively.

'I can't help but dislike her, Christian. Færies and humans just do not go together. It isn't natural for us to be friends with them. It might have been a long, long time ago but it isn't anymore. It's wrong. I'm sure you already know all of this.'

'Yes. Say what you really mean, will you?'

'Fine, I don't want you to get attached. I will not allow you to.'

'For the sake of the Elana, I do not even know her. I simply didn't want our mother casting Sky out of Krazonia before she had even a chance to give her side of the story. I'm just trying to be fair. But don't think I've forgotten what happened four years ago.'

Rhia sat back in her seat. 'You're just trying to be fair? I see. Well, I am not going near her.'

'That's your choice.'

'Which side are you on?' she snapped. 'Everything you say leads me to believe that you oppose the true, better side which is your own flesh and blood.'

'No, Rhia. Of course I am on your side. Who said anything about taking sides anyway?'

'You, the moment you allowed that human into our home without consulting your mother – the queen – first!' Rhia pushed her chair back and flattened down her dress with both hands. 'I'm going to see if she needs some support, because she clearly won't get any from you,' and with that, she sauntered out of the room. Christian twisted in his seat to watch her leave. Disbelief left him without words. He then realised the butlers had been standing by the whole time, too shocked to move. Christian stood up.

'Clear this up,' he said. 'Thank you,' he added with a tight smile, but it was lost when he turned away. Heading into the

Chapter Fourteen

living area, he crossed the large room to the back doors. Opening one, he slipped out into the cool evening, his brain so crammed full of thoughts he felt any more would cause him to pass out. The Emerald, Sky Francis, the impending battle he'd almost been able to forget about. Christian looked out across a changing landscape beneath the sun's fading light. On the horizon it had almost disappeared, leaving behind a dim orange glow much like a dying flame.

He slept well, but woke early. He turned over but as he slowly came to an anxious feeling seeped through him, stealing away any chances of falling back to sleep. Pushing back the cover Christian sat up and rested on the edge of the bed, rubbing his eyes and face. Today would be an interesting day. He would find out the fate of his realm and the fate of the human.

'Sky, her name is Sky,' he said to himself. He had taken no food to her which meant she'd probably gone through the day without a single morsel to fill her stomach. He would go to the kitchens and find her something. Itching to relieve himself of this unexpected guilt, Christian got dressed and made his way quietly down to the kitchens which at dawn would be unoccupied. Dusky pink light filtered through each window as he checked cupboards and the cool room. A cup of apple juice would be refreshing, but what did she eat? A drink would have to suffice.

He stopped for a moment, questioning himself.

'I shouldn't be doing this,' he said.

Færies and humans just do not go together. It isn't natural for us to be friends with them...

Chapter Fifteen

It was soon dark. Sky lay on her side, gazing out the window. Thin curtains were tied back revealing a night adorned with stars, like glitter strewn across a black canvas. Her limbs felt heavy and her head throbbed. Sky knew it was due to dehydration and lack of food. She wanted so badly to sleep, but her body refused to give up consciousness. It was torture. The wings on her back clung to her like sap to a tree and she still struggled with the concept that flying was even possible. How many films had there been, books where characters had this power? It was nice for imagination but terrifying for reality.

'This is my reality,' Sky whispered, a coldness running through her. Closing her eyes she felt her restless heart beating, beating through it all.

The night took forever to pass, and after drifting in and out of a dreamless sleep Sky woke to a horizon of lilac and pink, its pastel light flooding the room. She sat up and looked around. The hunger in her stomach had become a sickening cramp.

She sat on a four-poster bed that was soft and cream coloured. The posts at either end were of wood carved to perfection in the shape of a pair of wings: one left, one right. Candleholders clung to each wall, cupping a thick wax candle waiting to be lit. In the far corner sat a chest of drawers and beside it an exotic plant, settled in a stone pot. At least she hadn't been thrown into a cell.

Sky flopped back onto the bed, hoping the queen would take pity on her. By the looks of things humans and færies were not so different, and given the chance, Sky would prove it.

There came the sound of murmurs through the door, followed

Chapter Fifteen

by a hesitant knock. Dragging herself up Sky went to answer it, the cramp in her stomach worsening. Heaven knows what she looked like.

'Not that I care,' she muttered before pulling back the door.

Her eyes met Christian's. He pursed his lips, holding out a drink to her.

'Good morning,' he said.

'Hi. Thank you,' Sky said, accepting it. She took a small sip, fighting the urge to guzzle it like someone who'd been stranded on an island for three days. The juice was sweet and zesty on her tongue.

Christian talked to her in a quiet, serious manner.

'It didn't end so well yesterday. It is difficult for my family, as I said it would be.'

"Difficult" probably meant Anya was against her being here, and hated her as much as Rhia did. Sky placed her free hand on the doorframe, gripped it. 'I understand. It must be difficult for you too.'

Christian's mouth puckered. 'I suppose it is. I wanted to clear things up with you this morning. After you have spoken to my mother a guard will escort you downstairs. I will organise some sort of breakfast if I can.'

Sky rested her head against the doorframe, trying to ignore the pain in her chest that felt like her heart was being squeezed. 'It all depends on the queen's decision doesn't it? I mean, about me.'

Christian's dark brown eyes studied her face, and Sky wanted so badly to look away. His gaze was unsettling and it caused her to blush.

'Mother is not heartless,' Christian said eventually. 'With all that she's been through over the years her view on certain matters has changed. She has a good heart but won't let it get in the way of what she thinks or believes is the right thing to do. I know speaking to the queen is a horrifying prospect. I can see that. Let me advise you on one thing. Do not cover anything up with flustered lies because you're panicking about being…of being exiled,' he practically mouthed the word. 'She is kind, but she is

Krazonia's ruler. It's a balance we all have to work with.'

'I won't lie,' Sky said. 'I wouldn't dare.'

Christian took a step back, ending the conversation. Beckoning the guard over, he walked away with his head down.

Sky shut the door. The prince didn't hang about, did he? She swigged down the remainder of her drink, the cool liquid making its way towards her gurgling stomach. Stifling a yawn, Sky placed the cup down and retreated to the bed. She wouldn't sleep but resting was better than nothing at all.

After some time, she heard another knock. Preparing for what felt like a prison sentence Sky walked slowly to the door, knotting both hands in her hair before running her fingers from root to tip. She took a deep breath.

It appeared to be the nicer one out of the two guards who held posts at the mansion's entrance. He was tall with a slender face and kind green eyes. He even managed a little smile for her.

'You need to come with me, now.'

Sky peered around the door. 'Where did the other guard go?'

'The prince requested I take you and Simian needed a break. How are you feeling?' It sounded as if he actually wanted to know.

'I feel alright, but nervous. Should I be nervous?' They began to make their way down the corridor. The guard deliberated over this for a few seconds and all Sky could hear was the clink, clink of his armour. They were about to venture down the staircase when a butler came drifting up and the guard put an arm out to hold Sky back. The butler completely ignored her as he breezed past.

'I would be nervous too,' said the guard as he started down the stairs with Sky close behind. 'She's the queen. The most powerful færie in this realm. At times she makes me feel on edge, but Dill always manages to calm me down. Dill knows best.' There was a sliver of cynicism in his tone. Dill had to be the other guard at his post.

'My name is Rhys, by the way.'

'Hi Rhys. You probably already know my name is Sky.'

'Yes, I was informed.'

She wasn't going to ask whether Christian had informed Rhys of anything else. All too soon Sky stood facing the door that led

Chapter Fifteen

to the "office".

Her heart made a jump into her throat and she couldn't breathe. Her palms were damp with a nervous sweat. She quickly wiped them on her dress. 'Rhys, I'm scared.'

'You'll be okay, Sky,' he said, rapping on the door and taking a step back.

Sky's heart was beating so fast she thought it might be trying to make an escape, so she pressed a hand on her chest to try and steady it.

The door opened to a stony faced Rhia and with a grimace she pushed past, knocking Sky's shoulder as she went. Sky was too preoccupied to respond. She imagined this is how it would feel to go bungee jumping, and she was standing on the precipice.

Rhys nudged her forward. 'Good luck,' it was almost inaudible, but she heard it.

'Thanks,' she squeaked.

The guard moved away and Sky stepped into the room. The queen, Anya Meldin, was standing behind a large square desk, leafing through papers with a pencil in hand. The pencil was put down.

'Sky Francis,' she affirmed, pointing to a seat. 'Sit down.' Her voice was gentle, as was her temperament. Sky did as she was asked, taking in the færie before her. The queen had light brown hair and it was long, swept around one shoulder. There were streaks of grey in it and she had a few faint lines around her eyes, but overall she'd held her youth well. She wore a long, thin material dress that matched the colour of the clouds Sky had woken to this morning; a rosy pink.

The queen sat down opposite. She seemed the calm, diplomatic type but Sky would not be able to relax until she knew the verdict. Anya Meldin was supposed to hate her.

'Thank you for seeing me,' Sky said, trying to keep her voice level.

Anya looked at her with the same eyes as Christian, dark and intelligent.

'I understand this,' she placed the necklace on the desk, 'was in your possession. You must tell me how and where you acquired it.

You need to tell me how you got here and lastly, if you are alone or have brought assistance.' She narrowed her eyes and lifted her chin in the same way a teacher would, trying to suss out whether their pupil was cheating on their test.

'It's extremely important you tell me the truth,' she said, clasping her hands together, allowing the words to disperse into the atmosphere so Sky could soak up their full meaning. Anya had used the same technique as Christian. It was a threat, but also an opportunity to speak the truth, to justify herself.

There was no way Sky would even be able to conjure a lie under such pressure, so she decided to start from the beginning.

'I was walking home from school. It was pretty much just a normal day for me until I bumped into this woman. We had a bit of an argument because she hurt my shoulder...' Would the queen want such detail? Not likely. Bullet-pointing it in her mind, Sky continued.

'The woman walked away, leaving me to pick up the money I'd dropped. Then I found the necklace and there was no way I could leave it there.'

She went on until her mouth was dry, covering everything: the necklace, the dreams, Elle, and finally her arrival the day before. It was when she'd told Anya about Elle that the atmosphere changed. The explanation had turned the queen's knuckles white and her posture became rigid.

By the time Sky finished she was close to fainting. The edges of her vision were hazy and she had to blink a few times to focus on the queen and understand her.

'For many generations, stories have been passed down about your people,' she said. 'How you live in a frightful, dangerous world. From the day the Elana fled, we never imagined the two worlds would once again coincide. If you met Elle that means you know what happened when she came here.'

Sky swallowed. 'Yes and I'm so, so sorry. But you must see, I'm not the same as Elle. Although it wasn't her fault, I won't run away like she did. I want to know why I'm here too – that's why I asked Rhia if the Emerald was safe. There must be something going on.'

Anya Meldin sat very still in her seat. 'There is a lot going on,

Chapter Fifteen

Sky.'

'I'm not expecting you to trust me, all I ask is that you don't send me away. Please.' She could see how easy it had been for Elle to fall apart, how little time it had taken.

Sky was an iceberg drifting beneath the sun, melting slowly. Seconds passed. *Keep it together.* She closed her eyes and began to count. 7, 8, 9-

'You will not be exiled,' said the queen.

Sky slumped back into her seat, weak with relief.

'It crossed my mind more than once. This is only the second encounter during my lifetime, the first being four years ago. You will stay here because it's safer for my realm. If you say that you're here because something bad is heading our way, then you should be kept close,' she said, gazing down at the necklace. 'Also, I wish to learn from my mistakes from four years ago. I didn't know what to do then, but I believe I do now.'

'Thank you.'

'Thank Christian. He said something that made me think twice. In the shock and anger I felt yesterday I could have sent orders to have you taken away there and then,' she touched the necklace with slender fingers. 'However due to his words I managed to see past the anger and so changed my mind. I'm not ruling you out as a threat, but at the moment you don't seem to be. I can only hope that history will not repeat itself now we have another human in our midst.'

'It won't,' Sky assured her.

Anya's lips turned up into a smile that didn't quite reach her eyes. 'It had better not.'

Sky was led by Rhys downstairs into a lavish dining area. 'Have a seat here and I'll let Christian know.'

Sky released a nervous little laugh. 'I'm not sure he cares all that much, but okay.'

The rest of the morning was a blur. She was served a dish of poached egg with two slices of olive bread, and she relished every bite. Then, a butler led her upstairs to a wash room where she could get herself cleaned up. It was a large space with marble flooring. The bath was deep and round and there was only one tap. When she ran it the gushing sound was sudden and loud, taking her by surprise. She sat on the edge and put her hands in the water flow and then came another surprise. It was perfect temperature.

'How do they do it?' she wondered aloud.

As far as shampoo and conditioner went, there were small containers labelled 'hair conditioning oil' so that would be her best bet.

One thing that frustrated Sky was the lack of clocks. Færies seemed to work by judging the skies: dawn, morning, midday, evening and night. She would have to learn to do the same.

Eventually she reappeared washed and fresh, but still in the same dress. Unsure of what to do and with Christian nowhere to be seen, she decided to venture back to her hiding place. Along her way she collided with Rhia.

'I can see you've made yourself at home.'

'I wouldn't say that.'

Rhia arched an eyebrow. 'So you were given good news?'

'Well I'd say so, but it doesn't seem the case for everyone,' Sky said.

Rhia scowled. 'Mind how you speak. I may not have the authority my mother has but I still have some. I have enough,' she said brusquely. 'Just because the queen and my brother have accepted you, it doesn't mean I will.'

Sky sighed with exasperation. 'I don't think it's a case of acceptance. I'm not like her. It isn't fair for you to tar me with the same brush.'

'Tar you - what did you say?'

'It doesn't matter,' Sky muttered. She didn't particularly want to argue, she just wanted to curl up on the bed, shut the world out for a while and wait for her hair to dry. 'I get what you're saying. Now if you'll excuse me,' she went to pass Rhia but the færie latched onto her wrist, giving her a jolt.

'It matters. Having you under the same roof matters, trust me. I will be looking out for my family so don't you dare try anything.'

'I wouldn't dream of it. Please let go of me.'

The princess did so with an air of disgust and it was Sky's turn

Chapter Fifteen

to scowl before walking away.

Sometime later there was a knock at the door.

Sky sat up. 'Come in.'

'Good afternoon,' said Christian.

'Hello,' she said, consciously fiddling with the tips of her hair, tidying it up. Not that she cared about her appearance *that* much. 'How're you?'

'I'm well, how about you?'

Sky thought about how she felt in that moment as she went over the day's events in her mind. She was in another world, and the realm's queen had saved her from exile. 'I'm managing.'

Christian lingered in the doorway. 'I've decided to show you more of the realm. I know you need to be minded, mother made that clear, but I don't mind taking on that responsibility for a while.'

Sky contemplated being able to explore Krazonia away from Rhia's watchful eye, and found the idea appealing. 'Your sister won't mind?'

'Why would my sister mind? She'd prefer you were out of sight.'

'She despises me.'

Christian shrugged. 'Rhia feels that way about many.'

'But she despises me in particular, with good reason,' Sky said slowly as she slid off the bed. 'Don't you?'

Christian shrugged again, staring past her and out the window. 'No. I don't know you, Sky. Therefore I shouldn't think badly of you, despite,' he paused, cringing a little, 'being from the human world.'

Sky couldn't help herself. 'Give it time.'

Christian lips pressed together in a suppressed smile. 'Do you wish to see Krazonia or not?'

Chapter Sixteen

Christian was waiting for Sky at the main doors when the message arrived. He knew immediately what it would be.

'Thank you,' he said, taking the letter. The messenger bowed.

'Is there anything to be taken, sir?'

'Not today.'

With that, the messenger flew away. Christian held the neatly folded letter in his hands and traced a finger along its seal – a thin trail of glimmering, golden færie dust. He didn't move but remained by the open door, a warm breeze making its way in. Soon enough Sky's voice called him out of his frozen state and he turned to face her. She would see his expression, and though he wasn't sure what exactly it would be, Christian was sure it wasn't a cheerful one.

'Ready when you are,' she said, slowing her steps as she touched the bottom of the stairway. Her hand slipped from the banister. 'What's wrong?'

'Wait here. Don't move,' he managed to say. 'I must speak with the queen.' He raced past her and up the stairs, heading for the office.

'This just arrived. It must be from Mikæl,' he said upon entering the room. His mother sat at the desk, reading. Startled by the sudden intrusion she dropped the book and looked up. Christian held out the letter. She took it without a word, but the fear was spoken in her eyes. For Christian, fear was a snake coiling itself around his heart.

Anya peeled open the letter.

Chapter Sixteen

Christian watched her eyes skimming over the single page. Some of the færie dust had settled on the desk, specks of shimmering gold. 'Mother?'

She sat motionless.

'Mother!' Christian said a little louder. It dawned on him that perhaps this time the Golden realm would stand aside and refuse to risk its færies for a battle that, in truth, was between the Dark and the Light. It had to be bad news.

His mother's lips barely moved. 'Mikæl has confirmed his allegiance. He will gather Gloryn's army and they should be with us in a few days. So it really is happening.' She placed her hands flat on the desk and looked at them. 'I wish we didn't have to get Gloryn involved,' her voice was a strained whisper. 'I can hardly bear it, but I cannot let Tæ win.'

Despite the need to sit down, Christian kept his back straight and his wings taut. He wanted to show strength and resistance.

'You will have mine and Rhia's support as well as that of the General and your army. We can do this.' He had to believe they could, even when there was a high possibility that Tæ would triumph, wearing his mother down in the process. Tæ was so powerful because she was relentless.

Anya snapped out of her daze. 'I know. I just didn't want to fight, but it seems Tæ will have it no other way. I can't stand the thought of so many færie's losing lives for the sake of revenge.'

Christian cocked his head. Had he heard her right? 'Why revenge?'

The queen kept focus on her hands. 'Well, she wants the Emerald, doesn't she? We've managed to keep it thus far despite her attempts to take it from us.'

'But not without sacrifice.'

'I don't need you to tell me that.'

'I know,' Christian whispered. Silence filled the room; his thoughts grew loud, they swamped his brain. Battle was inevitable. Mikæl, a true ally, had confirmed his allegiance, sentencing many of his own færies to a possible death. Tæ had already achieved part of her plan. She would get the fight she wanted. All of these things caused Christian's strength to diminish, leaving a weakness in his bones. He needed to make a quick escape before he hit the floor like a felled tree.

'I'm taking Sky out for a while...I think it would be good. I promise to take responsibility for her. Is that – okay?' he could hardly string a sentence together.

'Christian you're in your eighteenth year. Do what you will. All I ask is that you do not let her out of your sight. She must be kept close, you understand,' his mother said tiredly. 'Do what you will,' she repeated. 'Now there are things I must do.'

Christian met Sky at the main doors and summoned her outside. Having not yet managed to untangle his thoughts from the brief but tense conversation he'd exchanged with his mother, he didn't speak a word until they were away from the mansion. Though he tried to push it out of his mind, it lingered at the edges just enough to become a distraction. Revenge, what did she mean?

'I thought I could show you Bluewater first,' he said, his feet pounding the ground as he went. He felt on edge, battling against the anxiety that threatened to overwhelm him. He focused on the ground, the sun's stifling heat pressing against his wings and back. He sensed Sky casting curious glances his way. With a sigh, he stopped.

'Do you have something to say?' he asked.

Sky moved away from him. 'Do you?' She scooped her black hair around one shoulder before crossing her arms, setting her and Christian further apart.

He'd told her enough about his life already. Until he was calm enough to speak about the latest revelation without wanting to kick something, he would say nothing. With that thought at the forefront of his mind, Christian shook his head resolutely.

'No. Will you be able to fly without my assistance?' He hadn't intended for it to be an insult but Sky's blue eyes darkened in response, telling him otherwise.

'Are you really sure you want to give me a guided tour?' she asked. 'I don't want to be a burden or anything.'

'You aren't a burden Sky.'

'Allow me to rephrase that. A distraction, I don't want to be a

Chapter Sixteen

distraction. Well, I don't want to add to whatever has already got a hold of you.'

That was enough. What made her think she had a right say these things, and without remorse? A spark of anger set off a fiery trail through Christian's veins and in the next blink he found their faces were only inches apart. He was close enough to see Sky's eyes were not only blue but held flecks of indigo that blended inwards, so that there was a dark ring around the pupil.

'I'm giving you a chance, Sky. I asked you a simple question so you need to stop questioning me and *answer it*,' the last two words were a snarl.

She bit down hard on her lower lip and stared back, a flare of defiance in her eyes.

'I really don't think this is going to work,' she said quietly.

The sound of færies getting on with their daily business carried through the air; laughter and chatter, and the faint chop-chop of wood cutters, acting as a reminder of where Christian was. He stepped back and brushed himself down, trying to brush away the anger like creases in his clothes. His behaviour was questionable. He needed to get himself into order.

'Would you like to see Bluewater?'

Sky's arms fell to her sides. 'Look, you don't have to do this,' she said earnestly, and they were back to square one.

'I'm sorry,' she went on, 'here you are, sticking your neck out for me and I'm being a complete eed. I mean, what is there to be angry about? Apart from like, everything?' She released a little laugh. 'What I'm trying to say is that I don't mean to be difficult. I have no right to snap at you. I'm still trying to adapt. I'll get myself sorted.' Her shoulders sagged. 'I have to.'

Christian only just managed to understand what she was saying. She'd apologised, he knew that much, but what was an "eed"?

He couldn't help but ask and when Sky laughed again, Christian laughed too. The laughter was a bubble in his chest, and for a moment the weight lifted, and they were one in the same. He pretended not to notice.

'An "eed" is just an idiot. A fool? I guess you know what a fool is,' Sky said.

'Yes, I know what a fool is. Now I know what an eed is too,' he said, and cleared his throat of any laughter than remained. 'We should go.' At that Sky craned her neck round, tensing her shoulders.

'I'm hoping that if I stare at them they'll do what my brain tells them to do,' she said.

'Remember these wings are a part of you. It will come naturally,' Christian said, beating his strong wings together in a steady rhythm. His feet no longer touched the grass. Meanwhile Sky was jumping up and down, getting flustered. Letting out a huff she blew the hair out of her face, and focused ahead of her with an air of determination. *How could she be a threat to the kingdom?* The thought popped into Christian's mind before he could stop it.

Sky looked at him and smiled sheepishly.

They were both high up in the air and flying at moderate speed towards Bluewater. Every now and then Sky stuck her arms out, nearly punching Christian, but she explained it was just her reflexes seeing as flying was not a natural thing for a human to do.

They reached Bluewater Glen, a green valley where the land either side rose steeply and on which beds of vibrant flowers sprouted. As they walked Christian could see out of the corner of his eye Sky leaning down to gaze into the stream, and it must have been the tiny fish swimming within it that caught her attention. Christian stopped and looked around, inhaling the valley's floral sweetness. Much further along, the grassy hillsides gave way to stone concealed mostly by moss and weaving vines. To his left sat a row of Smyrnium bushes, and it reminded him of the bracelet Rhia had said she was making for mother. The nerves came back and it was as if a hole had opened itself within him, allowing all good feelings to fall through. He wiped his clammy palms together and prepared to keep going, but playing ignorant was proving to be a struggle.

'Sky, let me show you what's at the end of the valley,' he said. Sky straightened up.

'Lead the way,' she said, and as Christian turned away he noticed concern in her expression. He turned back.

Chapter Sixteen

'You look worried, Sky.'

'I'm fine,' she said, her eyes darting around. 'What's at the end of this valley?'

Christian scrutinised her, but he didn't know her well enough to discern whether she was lying or not.

'How about a race?' he suggested. Sky's mouth dropped open. Only her eyes moved, flickering in the direction they were walking. She breathed in sharply as if she was about to dive into the stream, before throwing herself forward and spreading her wings wide. She was off before Christian even had chance to blink. He felt the lash of wind on his face as she flew past him. With a shake of the head he stretched his wings and readied himself. One moment she couldn't even hover, and now she was ahead of him. Taking flight, Christian pushed himself forward and quickly caught up. He flew on the opposite side of the stream and the edges of his vision became a blur of colour as he increased speed. He began to overtake Sky, and stealing a sidelong glance, could see how hard she was trying. He slowed down a little. The end of the valley was drawing near when it struck him that Sky had not yet flown this fast and she might have trouble stopping.

'Sky!' he called. 'Slow down.'

She opened her arms out. 'I feel invigorated!' she shouted into the wind.

The valley opened to a world of hills and lakes. Christian tried to grab Sky but it was difficult when she was flying so fast. He swiped for her one last time before nearly losing balance himself.

He watched horror-struck as she went soaring across the expanse. When was she going to stop? Christian slowed to a hover and tried to follow her sporadic movements as she went upwards, looping in the air and turning this way and that against the backdrop of an azure sky.

There was no point trying to catch her. It would have been like trying to catch a butterfly. Christian slumped onto the grass and waited, squinting against the dazzling sun.

Sky touched down by the lake and started running. A few times she stumbled. When she reached Christian, he could see that she'd been crying. In fact, she still was. Out of breath she collapsed onto the grass beside him and her hands shook as she rubbed her eyes.

'I thought you were going to end up in the lake,' Christian told her, his tone reproving.

'I'm sorry. I just wanted to push myself, really come to grips with what I am. It's weird because I feel like I'm dreaming. Just then I was expecting to wake up. I thought about throwing myself into the lake but that really would have been stupid of me. It's just confusing.' She covered her face.

Christian sat there, unsure of what to say or do. He'd been the one to suggest they race. Now he felt guilty.

'I shouldn't have done that. I was an eed.'

Sky smiled through her tears. 'I'm scared, Christian.'

Christian boldly faced her and placed a hand on her shoulder.

'It looks as though you are here for the duration, of whatever is happening.'

Sky peered at him between trembling fingers.

'You must get yourself together,' he added, with as much kindness as he could to soften the words. 'You can't fall apart. If it means anything you aren't the only one.' He withdrew his hand and averted his gaze. He'd said too much.

Thankfully Sky didn't press the matter, but rather she silently accepted it. They both stood up and Christian led the way back through the glen. They walked slowly. He found he was able to see its beauty but no longer appreciate it. How could he when knew what was coming? The approaching events overshadowed every blossom and every butterfly.

'Our next stop is the Ever-growing Forest,' he said, forcing lightness into his voice.

A large portion of Christian's day was spent showing Sky around his future realm. A part of him wondered if he was doing the right thing, showing a human his world.

From the Ever-growing Forest, to the crops where færies flitted between different fields picking and planting. He showed Sky where the carpenters worked as well as the crèche in Krazonia's main village. Christian then led her back the main Krazonian town and with the two lunes he had in the pocket of his shorts,

Chapter Sixteen

made a purchase of some olive bread.

They ended up at the outskirts of Morel village, and they ate the bread and talked. Sky tried to explain what the human world was like and to Christian it all sounded so severe.

'Everything seems so expensive. You have to pay so much to live. It really is a shame that you can't just fly everywhere. I mean, it can be tiring but at least we don't have to pay to go from one place to another.' He leant back, resting on his elbows. 'And you say you have a government who make decisions for the…country?' So they didn't have realms, but countries, and so many of them.

Sky lay on her stomach, picking at the remaining olive bread. When it was finished she started playing with her hair, plaiting strands of it together.

'Yeah we do, and they don't always make the right decisions. I don't know much really but my dad always rants at the news when it's on, so I presume it's because politicians are being stupid. I don't know.' She looked thoughtful, while Christian turned the word 'po-li-tic-ian' over in his mind.

'I'm only telling you the bad things,' Sky mused. 'There are lots of good things about where I'm from, like music. You have it here too. Where I'm from, there are so many different types of music, and festivals. I've never been to one but when I'm eighteen that's the first thing I'll do.'

Christian sat up.

'I've forgotten about the field festival,' he said aloud, staring ahead.

'The field festival, what's that?' he heard Sky ask so calmly, so unaware.

He jumped up. 'How could I forget?' Anger and guilt flooded through him. He may have forgotten but why had no one said anything? Usually his mother made the announcement. No doubt Rhia had a part in this.

'I must go back to the mansion. Come on.'

Sky looked up at him. 'Now?'

Christian glared at her. 'It isn't your place to question me, come on.' He clenched his fists with frustration. 'As if mother doesn't already have enough to worry about. What kind of son does this make me? A selfish one, that's what.'

Sky stood up. 'You aren't selfish.'

'You say that with such confidence,' Christian retorted. 'What do you know?' He struggled to contain his temper so before he said more he thought it best to walk away, expecting Sky to follow. She didn't.

'Sky you are coming with me,' he said without turning around.

'I think I should keep out the way.'

'I was asked not to let you out of my sight. I won't be able to save you again,' he said over his shoulder.

At that, she followed. Christian picked up the pace, anger surpassing sympathy.

He knocked once and without waiting for an answer, stepped into Rhia's bedroom and slammed the door shut.

'Are preparations being made for the festival?'

She sat on her bed, writing. 'Yes.'

'And you didn't think to tell me?'

'I didn't see the point.'

'Why didn't you see the point?' Christian said, seething. She was obviously not going to stop writing to talk to him.

'You're so wrapped in that human I thought it best not to get you involved. I conferred with mother, aired my concerns. I wasn't sure whether you could handle festival preparations on top of everything else. Mother and I are getting on fine without you.' The words hit him hard.

'I've done more than you ever have,' he said angrily.

Her hand froze on the page. Delicately she placed the pencil beside her and Christian knew he'd hit back with the same strength.

'I'm not the one who forgot!' she snapped. 'You did.'

Rage pulsed through him. 'That is not fair!' he shouted. Rhia didn't flinch. 'You told mother I wouldn't be able to handle it. You didn't give me a chance.'

'This is important,' Rhia said. 'Father always took pride in this annual event. You, brother, have got your priorities very wrong. As of yet that human has done nothing to help. She is an obstruction.'

Chapter Sixteen

'She's here because something is going to happen,' even as it said it, Christian realised how pathetic it sounded. If he stopped to think, if he took a step back to review the situation, Rhia was right.

'You know as well as I do that is was only a matter of time,' he said. 'Tæ will never let it go, and you know what, Rhia? You need to learn to let go of your hate.'

'Go away, Christian.'

'Fine.'

Chapter Seventeen

Sky sat in the living area with her legs curled under her. She wanted nothing more than to be at home with a bowl of curly fries watching TV. She craved the warm, friendly company of her parents. Instead she was in another world with no clue how she was going to get back, and this led her to an overwhelming sense of isolation. She'd never felt so alone and hadn't thought it possible to feel pain as a result, but her chest ached. Her whole body ached. It was as if all her strength had left her.

Sky looked around the large living space. A butler was passing through but he didn't even glance in her direction. Christian had left her here and had not yet returned. It must have been an hour when she finally decided to move. She needed a drink, and then she would leave this mansion and go somewhere. She would seek out the Elana just as Elle had done.

She dragged herself up. Finding her way to the kitchen wasn't too difficult and she walked through the doorway with her hands clasped together, hoping she wouldn't be shouted at. There were two færies cutting and chopping vegetables and speaking quietly to one another.

'Excuse me?' Sky said.

One færie who wore a dull, knee-length dress beneath an apron approached her with a tentative smile.

Sky found herself talking "properly" in hope that it would make her more respectable.

'I am a guest here and was wondering if I could get a drink, if it is not too much to ask?' It sounded funny, but she felt compelled to speak this way. At home, Sky would have joked with Cassie

Chapter Seventeen

and they'd have laughed to themselves, if they ever had a supply teacher who talked in such a manner.

The færie nodded and Sky remembered that the majority of Krazonians were compassionate, and non-judgemental. 'Let me get you some water.'

She drank the water quickly and placed the cup on a counter top. 'Thank you.'

On her way outside, Dill shot his arm out to prevent her passing.

He shook his head. 'You can't leave unaccompanied.'

'So I'm imprisoned here, am I?' Sky said hotly, but under the guard's imposing stare was quick to apologise.

'I am imprisoned, then. Can I at least walk down there?' She pointed at the hillside.

'No.'

'You can watch me go. Christian would allow me this.'

Dill narrowed his eyes. 'You won't let it go, will you?'

Sky lingered, fighting the urge to duck under his arm and escape like a naughty child.

'Fine, but you are to stay nearby,' he added austerely. 'No tricks.'

The late afternoon sun was still going strong and in no time she could feel it heating her scalp. In this weather, black hair was not ideal. Sky sat down and sighed. From where she sat she could see the ancient oak trees of Morel village, and the market. Gazing into the distance she tried to visualise a map of the kingdom in her mind. Somewhere out there was Zania and its tyrant queen; somewhere out there was Gloryn with its golden hills, and the other realm, Hæthen, which Christian had said was larger in size but less populated. It was known for its snow covered mountains and icy rivers that flowed between them.

Nothing had happened yet to make her challenge foreseeable. What if she was trapped in Krazonia? What would she do about her family, friends, and school? Realisation struck again and Sky gripped onto the grass, blades breaking off in her fingers.

Sky squeezed her eyes shut and leaned forward, the cramp in her stomach back with a vengeance. She willed herself not to cry but it was difficult when it was all she wanted to do. And so she gave in, allowing the silent tears to trickle down her cheeks and drip onto her dress, one after another.

She needed guidance. The Elana in the glen would help her. They had to help her.

Someone shuffled onto the grass, and given the clank of armour it was either Dill or Rhys. Sky prised open her sore eyes and there sat Rhys, taking in her fragile state. She didn't want pity but she knew she looked pitiful.

'Hello,' Sky croaked.

'What's the matter?' he asked, shifting awkwardly. Clearly armour wasn't comfortable to sit in.

Here lay an opportunity to pour out her feelings and her fears. Dill was far enough away to be out of ear shot. But was it senseless, confiding in a guard? Rhys rolled a red apple around in his hands.

Do I really care right now? Sky asked herself. She sniffed back tears. 'Rhys, do you know where I'm from?'

She heard the juicy crunch as he took a bite out of the apple. She could easily eat an apple, or three. After chewing and swallowing, the guard shook his head.

'I don't, no. Is your home far from here?'

'You could say that. Please don't scream and run away when I tell you. Do you promise you won't?'

'I promise not to scream or run away.'

'I'm from the human world. To cut a long story short, I came through the portal that separates your home from mine. It should be closed, but it isn't. So here I am.'

Rhys' face had turned a shade paler and his mouth made a little 'O'.

'That's probably all you need to know.'

Rhys blinked. 'You're from the other world? You're human?'

'Yes.'

He stared at the apple in his hand, his eyebrows knitting together.

'I have some sort of task, if you want to call it that,' Sky said. 'Don't ask me what it is. I have yet to find out myself.'

Rhys took another bite of his apple, his look thoughtful. Sky was

Chapter Seventeen

relieved to see he had remained beside her. Either he was good at keeping promises, or he didn't feel threatened. He chewed slowly.

'Wow. So much has happened in so little time. You are here, there's the field festival and on top of that Tæ wants us to fight her, again.'

Sky was startled by this. 'Fight her?'

Rhys began to choke, spluttering as Sky gave him a whack on the back.

'I've already said too much. I should get back to my post,' he said, scrambling up the hill, his shield clanging against his leg armour as he went.

Sky got up and took firm steps after him. They couldn't exile her for asking questions. A simple yes or no answer was all she needed and at that thought she felt a rush of confidence.

'Can I ask you both a question?'

Rhys quickly turned to cough some more. Dill shot him a stern look.

'If you must,' said Dill.

'Is Krazonia going into battle with Zania?'

The guard pressed his lips together and held his shield up so it was level with his chest; sunlight glinted off the metal and Sky noticed tiny indentations on its surface. She couldn't help but wonder where it had been and what it had protected the guard against.

'That is a question we won't be answering,' Dill said sharply. 'If I were you I wouldn't push your luck. I know what you are.' To that, Rhys frowned.

'And is it such a terrible thing?' he asked. Dill inhaled deeply through his nose.

'Were you here four years ago?'

Rhys said nothing, but from then he kept his head down. The half-eaten apple remained in his grasp, but was forgotten.

'Then you wouldn't know. There will be consequences, her being here,' Dill muttered. Sky crossed her arms, determined not to fold under the guard's scrutiny.

'I mean no harm to anyone.'

'That doesn't change your origin.'

'I understand. But maybe you should consider the human to færie ratio, here,' Sky said before heading back inside.

Time passed. She lay in bed, resting on her stomach. Her feet were in the air, moving idly back and forth. It was as though she was in limbo, and all she wanted was for her path to appear. All she wanted was to *know*.

A knock on the door pulled her out of a sombre daydream.

In the corridor all candles had been lit. Had Sky really been lying in bed for hours?

Rhia had one hand on her hip, and her head tilted to the side. Her moody mouth was set in a flat line. She held the expression of someone who'd been forced to go out of their way for somebody they didn't like. Funny that. Sky mirrored her hostility by keeping the door half closed, only poking her head around it. 'Hi,' she said and it was so easy to keep a straight face. Nothing about Rhia made her want to smile.

The princess clicked her tongue. 'Unfortunately, I've been asked to do the honours of requesting that you dine with us tonight. Mother has a few things she wishes to say…but you are not sitting beside me.'

Sky shrugged. *As if you need to tell me that.* 'I won't sit next to you.'

Rhia's grey eyes were cold and impassive, even in warm candlelight.

'Good,' she said tersely before walking away. Sky stepped out into the corridor, pulling the door shut behind her. She rearranged her hair as she went while doing her best to ignore the heavy, aching beat of her heart. She had been hungry, but now she felt sick.

Sky wandered into the room. At the head of the table sat Anya Meldin and beside her sat a tall, hard faced færie with shoulder length hair and a neat beard. Christian was the next one down. He fiddled with a napkin in his lap. Rhia sat down in the last spare seat on his side so Sky placed herself at the other end, next to a guard she didn't recognise. She was surprised to see Dill present. No one seemed to notice her arrival and that came as a relief. Butlers glided around, bringing plates of fish with steamed

Chapter Seventeen

vegetables. When they were gone, the queen began to speak and Sky could hardly breathe.

'Before we eat, I wish to talk to you all. The reason I have gathered you here on this evening is because there are some facts I must share, and the five of you that sit at this table are the closest and most valuable to me.' A few heads turned in Sky's direction and she felt her face flush. After the rush of heat, a sliver of ice ran down her spine and she could only sit there, frozen with terror. What was Anya going to say?

'A few days ago we had to deal with the unexpected arrival of Zanians. One of them was an army lieutenant, Farian. It is clear Tæ has already made up her mind. She wants to fight us, and I have no choice but to fight back if I want to keep my realm and the Emerald protected. General?'

A gruff, unfamiliar voice replaced Anya's and Sky looked up to see the General casting a steady gaze around the table as he spoke. He ran a hand across his jawline, tracing his fingers over his trimmed beard.

'Lieutenant Kore and I have spent the last two days visiting the town and villages, recruiting soldiers. Tæ hasn't given us much time to prepare so we will do what we can in the time we have. Gloryn's army should be with us within two days.'

The queen smiled, but there was sadness in her eyes. 'The field festival is going ahead. I want to give my færies an opportunity to enjoy themselves before the majority set off the following morning.' Her eyebrows knitted together, giving away only a little of the frustration she probably felt, and Sky's stomach rolled over and over with unease.

'There is no going back. I feel this is complete injustice, which only makes me resolute on stopping Tæ Asrai from ever doing this again. I see no other way. I'm giving her the fight she wants, but she will not have the Emerald. I fear what would happen if it ever got into her hands.'

'So there's no possibility of a negotiation?' The suggestion came from Rhia, and Anya didn't look surprised that her daughter had spoken.

'I've learned there is no negotiating with this færie. She is a tyrant.'

Sky didn't know how to respond and she wasn't the only one. Rhia didn't argue. Thankfully the mood was lifted when Anya Meldin raised her glass and tossed her light hair back.

'I have one more thing to say.' Every færie followed suit, lifting their glasses. Sky did the same, keeping her gaze on the queen and ignoring Christian's attempt to catch her eye. 'Krazonia is a strong realm. We are the Light and we all know that sunrise brings promise, eliminating the shadows and their obscurities. No matter what happens, the Dark realm will never overshadow us.'

Murmurs of agreement went around the table. Sky gulped her drink but didn't taste it.

After the meal, the queen was escorted out of the room by the General and his Lieutenant and once again Sky felt isolated. Everyone else had a purpose, and she couldn't help but laugh quietly at the irony of it all. She ran her fingers across the table's polished surface before standing up, and came face to face with a sorrowful Christian.

'How are you?' he said.

'Not bad,' she said at length. 'But how I feel isn't the point, really.' She wanted to ask why he'd left her on her own, but then again, what right did she have? Christian didn't owe her anything, and probably didn't fancy the role of 'babysitter'.

'I can't believe Krazonia and Zania are going into battle,' she said, taking in the strain around Christian's eyes. He couldn't have been much older than eighteen, but no doubt would have had to grow up fast, being prince and all.

Sky felt the need to "grow up" too. No longer was she going to be that impatient and at times fiery-tempered sixteen year old girl.

'Can I help in any way?'

'Sit with me for a while,' he said distractedly, his eyes searching the table. 'We can go to the reservoirs.' He stopped a butler from removing a half empty bottle from the table and took it, along with two glasses. Sky followed him through the dining area, towards the huge expanse of living room and to a set of doors,

Chapter Seventeen

the wood dark and stained. She hadn't taken much notice of the space around her, and only lifted her eyes when she felt the tepid evening air touch her skin.

The view snatched the breath out of her throat.

The sun, a small glowing orb, sat on the horizon surrounded by a spectrum of colour; flaming reds and bright orange stretched out far and wide, lined with rosy clouds. It was as though the sky was on fire. Sky felt her mouth drop open. She couldn't stop staring at it. Towards the edges of the world the colours swept into azure, though streaks of pink cloud remained. There were three birds flying somewhere in the far distance, over hills that seemed to roll on forever. It made Sky feel so small. 'I've never seen a sunset like this,' she murmured.

Christian was walking away from her down a long, gentle slope. Sky hurried after him, trying not to trip over her feet, for the view had stunned her.

She sat down next to him. Christian poured what had to be wine into the two glasses and offered one to her.

'Thanks,' Sky said. Christian nodded and took a swig, his feet tapping the grass. He drank some more wine, which to Sky tasted sour, but she drank it anyway.

'I'm worried, Sky. I'm worried about this battle, but I'm also worried about one day becoming king,' he said. 'It's times like this when I try to pin down exactly how I feel and all I know is that I don't want to do...*this*. Well, I don't think I can.'

'Why do you say that?'

'Ever since my father was murdered his absence has made me see things in other ways. I really admired him for his strength – he was always so strong and under all circumstances he remained level headed. But then when he no longer sat me on his knee to tell me battle stories, or took me flying around Krazonia, I saw the stark reality of it all and without him in the picture, I discovered it is not in me. When I think about his courage in doing what he did I try to imagine doing the same and I know I can't. That makes me a coward and therefore not worthy. When I was with him I thought I could follow in his footsteps, but being without him I know I can't. Truthfully I don't even want to try.'

Sky had never played counsellor before, but Christian needed someone to talk to so she came up with the best she could. Plus, this wine had loosened her tongue, and actually, it didn't taste so bad.

'You're still young Christian, like me. At this age we grow and change,' she hesitated. 'So you can't just rule out being king especially as it would be your duty.' She cringed a little at her words, but Christian appeared unfazed, staring into the distance. His glass was almost empty and Sky glanced down to see all that remained in her own were little ruby-coloured bubbles.

'Why can't you follow in the footsteps of your mother? She's doing pretty well and when you lost your father she lost her husband. Christian, you will never be able to take over ruling this realm if you don't believe in yourself. None of us in fact will get anywhere if we don't believe in ourselves that we can, well, get somewhere.' She silently rejoiced at her choice of words. 'I think your mother is a perfectly good example, and when the time comes for you to become king, I reckon you'll be ready. You need to stop saying you can't, like you aren't capable.'

'I appreciate that,' Christian said, giving Sky a warm smile that caused her heart to jump in her chest. 'I don't mean to speak my troubles to you but no one understands,' he went on, his smile waning. 'I don't want to burden my mother and I don't think Rhia cares. I wouldn't expect my friends to understand. Well, Aeron might. But anyway, I'm the prince. I live the ideal life.'

'You obviously don't.'

'Are all humans as honest as you?' he asked, giving her a sidelong glance. Sky shrugged, and drained her glass. The wine had warmed up her insides and eased her mind. 'I don't know whether I'm being too honest. Like, if I sound harsh. I don't mean to.'

Christian's dark eyes focused on her, spearing her to the spot. Sky could feel her heartbeat in her throat, and she couldn't speak.

'I feel better for speaking my mind,' he said quietly. 'Sky, you say you don't know why you're here but perhaps we're beginning to find out. At least, it could be one reason.'

She swallowed hard. 'What do you mean?'

Chapter Seventeen

'To listen, to advise…to make some sense out of what feels like a completely nonsensical situation to me,' he said, touching her hand like it was the most natural thing to do. Confusion flickered across his features and he recoiled. 'We should go back inside. I'll see what else needs to be done,' he added quickly, standing up. He retrieved the bottle and glasses from the grass.

Sky took one last look at the sunset, trying to ignore the tingling sensation on her right hand. The sun had almost disappeared but the horizon remained a blend of oranges and pinks, and the reservoir water was dark except for a slight rippling across its surface, reflecting the evening glow.

The next morning Sky was brought breakfast consisting of two slices of thick bread covered in elderberry jam, and a cup of juice. Once she'd eaten it she awkwardly handed the empty plate and cup back to the butler who'd been patiently waiting outside her door. In the bathroom Sky was able to freshen up, but she longed for a change of outfit. The dress she wore was becoming crumpled and grubby, but before she could muster the confidence to ask, a guard was escorting her to the queen.

'You will help with festival preparations today.'

Sky curled her feet under the chair and her wings involuntarily twitched. 'Okay.'

'Dill will accompany you as he is my most trusted guard. Go down now and he will take you to the fields,' the queen advised. She was sure to have fun with the guard who resented her. *Great.*

'Yes your highness. May I ask if you have any spare hair ties? I could really do with getting my hair off my neck today and I'd be so grateful.'

Anya rummaged through a drawer in her desk. 'Ah.' She passed over to Sky what looked like a small braid tied at one end to create a loop. 'This should do.'

Sky scooped her hair up into a ponytail and tied it into place. She bowed and left the drawing room and for the first time since her arrival in Krazonia, began to feel a part of it.

Chapter Eighteen

There was a light knock at the door. Christian stirred.

'Who is it?'

'It's Sky.'

The door creaked open and he could hear her feet padding across the floor. Opening his eyes, Christian could gradually work out her shape advancing towards him. The only light came from the moon, white and shining through the window. An eerie silence bled through the atmosphere. Sky's face was ashen, and her blue eyes pierced Christian's heart like two daggers.

'Take me to the Emerald,' she said in a sombre tone.

Without thinking Christian went to push back the covers, but as he did so he found it a struggle. His limbs felt extremely heavy, it was difficult to shift them. He managed to clamber out and led Sky along the corridor to his mother's bedroom. The Emerald sat within its impenetrable glass dome, glowing to the beat of Christian's heart. He stared at is at it went from green to a deep, throbbing red. In a blinding flash of light, it vanished.

Spinning on his heels Christian burst into a run, ignoring the shadows as they danced on the walls, taunting him. The stone shone red at the end of a corridor that seemed never to end. His legs slowed, and it was if he was wading through water. Abruptly he was thrown back and a shadow loomed over him, inching closer and closer. Tæ's face lit up, and her eyes were two black pits. Her blood-red lips twisted into a sly grin.

'It belongs to me,' she whispered, and her words were venom seeping into Christian's veins.

'No!' he shouted, jerking awake. Panting for breath he looked

Chapter Eighteen

around, his fingers digging into the mattress. The light dimmed as a veil of cloud smothered the moon and Christian found himself trying to blink away the image of Tæ's menacing smile, but it had been impressed into his mind. Reluctantly he settled back down beneath the sheets and waited for morning to come, deciding not to fear the face that lingered behind his eyelids but to stare back without mercy, into the eyes of a queen who, when given the opportunity, would show none.

Early in the morning Christian went to Morel village. It had become routine that in preparation for the field festival he would go and help Lyra and her family. He'd started a year before the death of his father, and knew José would want his son to continue helping out his dearest friend, Moran. As he flew across dewy grass that glittered in the sun, he tried to block out his personal feelings. How would he greet Moran and Talaya, knowing how badly they'd wanted their daughter and him to be together, knowing how hard they had tried?

It didn't matter. When he saw Moran picking up empty wooden crates and passing them to his wife, the doubt Christian felt soon dissolved. They seemed content in their little bubble and he didn't want to be the one to burst it. No doubt they were aware that today was the day before the soldiers started their journey towards Zania to fight a pointless battle. It was in the nature of a Krazonian to power through the dark times, swallowing down the anxiety and fear like a bitter medicine and smiling despite its awful taste.

Christian landed before them. Moran opened his arms out to him. 'Christian, it's been too long.'

'I know,' he said, embracing his father's best friend. 'I thought I'd help carry the apples over to the field.'

Talaya placed a hand on his arm. 'It's good to see you.'

Christian forced a smile. 'You too Talaya.' Lyra must not have told them about their 'talk'.

Just then she emerged from the hut, wrapping her hair into a bun that sat loosely atop her head. She stopped in her tracks when she noticed Christian standing there. Before he had time to even raise his hand to wave, Lyra had turned away from him, her expression sour.

Despite her hostility Christian went after her. It wasn't fair her treating him as an unwanted guest, and he felt a yearning for them to be friends again, to be normal. He picked an apple out of the sack, spearing it with a stick before he propped it upright in the crate through a small hole. If they were to work in silence, so be it. At least she hadn't shouted at him to go away.

'Christian, it isn't even,' Lyra said at one point, snatching the fruit out of his grasp. She pulled out the stick. 'Why are you helping anyway?'

'I'm helping because it's what I've done the past five years.'

'I didn't expect to see you again.'

'You were the one who said goodbye, not me.' Christian stopped work, holding the stick tightly in his hand. 'You haven't made things easy for me.' He looked at her then, but she avoided his eye.

'I've tried to be honest with you. Twice, and both times you've panicked and flown away. Either you panic or get angry. We've grown up. Our friendship isn't so simple anymore.'

Christian sighed deeply, his heart aching with sadness. 'I've said sorry. You're making it more difficult than it has to be. It isn't fair.'

'I know it isn't fair, but we don't always get what we want,' Lyra muttered. Christian returned to spearing apples and placed them in the crate, finally accepting the words of his friend. Perhaps after this year he would have to break tradition.

They worked in silence. Every now and then Lyra released a little sigh. Moran and Talaya talked quietly with each other but Christian didn't strain to listen. Instead he fell into the well of his thoughts, tuning out of his surroundings. This time last year he'd felt content. Everything had been different. The sun had been brighter; there was no uneasiness amongst færies. He and Lyra had been cleaning apples, talking and laughing. There had been no pressing matters, no worry.

No human.

With the sun at its highest point in the sky he ventured to the fields behind the mansion, where the main preparations were

Chapter Eighteen

taking place. Amongst the vast groups of færies he searched for the one in the blue dress, with long black hair. Many were gathering stones to create a wide circle for the bonfire; stalls were being set up and instruments were being tuned. It was a jolly atmosphere but Christian wasn't blind to the looks some Krazonian's gave him. The flash of panic in their eyes told him they were scared, scared of what would happen to their soldiers and how the battle would end. It had been thrown upon them so unexpectedly. After a moment they would smile, extinguishing the fear, replacing it with excitement. Christian returned the smile, but inside he was hollow.

He helped where he could and soon found Sky, mallet in hand, hammering with all her might a wooden post into the ground. Dill held the post in place, gazing at her with amusement. His shield lay aside on the grass.

Sky's hair was tied back and her dress had smears of dirt across it. When the post was set in place she stopped to look up and her blue eyes were soft and bright.

'Hi,' she said out of breath. Dill bowed.

'It looks as though you've almost finished here,' Christian noted, his gaze following the widespread trail of posts that was the boundary line. Despite the marks they left in the ground, a sprinkle of færie dust would soon spur the grass to grow again. Christian looked back at Sky as she flicked loose strands of hair out of her face.

'I've never had to work so hard in my life. Actually, I've never had to work.' Christian caught the shrewd look she gave Dill as she said it, but the guard only shrugged it off unconcerned.

'Dill, why don't you have a break?' Christian said. 'I'll help Sky here.'

The guard raised a questioning eyebrow. 'Thank you sir,' he said and picked up his shield before jumping into the air. Sky was looking despondently down at her dress.

'I really need to change this thing,' she said.

'I'll see if Rhia will lend you one,' Christian said. 'In fact, she will lend you one.' He'd probably have to beg his sister to do such a thing, but he'd committed himself to it now. Sky would have a clean dress to wear.

'You have worked hard this morning,' he added, hearing the admiration in his own voice.

Christian watched a look of wonder spread across Sky's face. Her cheeks were pink from working in the sun. She pulled the band out of her hair and sighed, surveying the work done. Christian was taken aback to by the stir in his stomach. It was as if he'd just leaped off the edge of a valley and was falling, adrenalin rushing through him. He'd felt that looking at Sky.

'The past few days have been interesting to say the least,' she said, and Christian snapped out of his daze. 'Dill hates me almost as much as your sister you know.'

'He's extremely loyal,' Christian countered. 'He comes across as insensitive most of the time, but that's just him. I think it's a case of Dill being unsure about you, therefore it's easier for him to be, well, mean.'

Sky chewed her bottom lip. 'I have to expect everyone to dislike me, it comes with being human I guess,' she hesitated. 'I think your mother was right to do this. Although it takes organisation, clearly your people put in everything they've got. I imagine it's a welcome distraction.'

'Yes it is,' Christian replied and in his mind's eye he could see his father's face, dark and alluring. 'It was the king's idea. He wanted to bring færies together. This festival has been an annual event for the past ten years and I think if he'd been given the chance Gloryn would have been involved too.' His wings tensed as a memory hit him full force, of his father standing beside him, hand pressed on his shoulder. Christian could almost feel his presence but knew that if he turned, the king's spirit would be gone.

'That's something you can change when you're king,' said Sky and he flinched, recalling how he'd poured his heart out to her the evening before. What on earth possessed him? He shifted his attention to the festival preparations.

'It won't be much longer now. The band is tuning their instruments and there's wood coming from the forest for the bonfire. There will be stalls selling a variety of juices, fried

Chapter Eighteen

vegetables and a place to make færie lights.' Christian heard her laugh.

'Sorry,' Sky said, covering her mouth. 'We have færie lights too, but they're probably different to yours.'

'You have færie lights?'

'We sure do.'

'I can't imagine how they work,' Christian remarked – something else that baffled him about the human world. He bent down to pick up the mallet. 'We should head back to the mansion.'

Rhia was nowhere to be seen, but in his search for her he passed his flustered mother in the hallway. If Rhia had a problem with this arrangement then she'd have to take it up with him.

'Mother, Sky needs a dress to wear for this evening. Do you think Rhia would object if I give Sky one of hers? She has nothing else.'

Anya didn't stop. 'Go and have a look,' she said dismissively with a wave of the hand, gliding into the kitchen.

A hectic afternoon came and went. The sun began its downward journey while a crescent moon rose from behind the hills. Shimmering stars adorned the blue-black sky above the fields, and the night was alive with colour and sound. Christian stood at the back door to his home looking out at the festivities. The banging drums and joyful calls of Krazonians were a comfort and he could almost forget they were on the eve of battle. It was better if he didn't linger on that thought for too long. He wanted to be wrapped up in all that surrounded him and enjoy this night.

Sky sprung up beside him, bringing with her a sweet berry scent. Her black hair was down but her fringe had been clipped back and she wore one of Rhia's white, knee-length dresses.

'This looks so cool.'

'Cool?'

'Amazing, brilliant, however you want to put it.'

Christian nodded, watching the bonfire's wild flames send plumes of smoke into the air.

'Shall we?' he suggested. His heart lurched with dread when he thought again about what lay ahead for his realm, but when he and Sky ventured across the field, drawing closer to music and warmth, anticipation repressed those dark emotions.

Christian soaked up the sights. Celebrating on the eve of battle may have been an outrageous thing to do, but it was what his mother wanted – for her færies to remain within normality for as long as possible. Where Anya was selfless, Tæ was the opposite. Christian was proud of his mother for making sure her realm didn't turn into a state of frenzy. General Warren had spent the last few days organising his army of Krazonian soldiers, and most were a part of the festival tonight. It was a bittersweet send-off.

'Allow me to get you some fresh carrot juice,' Christian said loudly over the cheerful tunes and chatter. Sky grimaced.

'I can't say I'm a fan of carrot juice. What about grape juice?'

'Grape juice it is,' he said, and resting his hand lightly on her lower wings, Christian led Sky through the throng.

They wandered past stalls selling Triffilian nuts with blueberry sauce, morel mushrooms, melrogan juice and fried fish and vegetable skewers. They had yet to pass Moran's stall. Christian purchased them a skewer each and a cup of grape juice. All the while he had not once seen his mother or sister in the crowd and this bothered him. He wasn't surprised his sister wasn't around, but the queen would always join in with the festivities if only for a short time.

'I wonder where mother is,' he said, at a volume only Sky would be able to hear if she was listening.

'She's probably in the mansion, Christian,' she said reassuringly. A group of færies bowed as he passed.

Surely if there were further battle preparations he'd have been asked to help, or to at least support his family. He felt as though Rhia was purposely excluding him for seeing Sky. The thought irritated him like an itch spreading across his skin. He crossed his arms and focused on the band, trying to ignore it. Someone called his name.

'Christian!' Aeron appeared, all smiles. His hair was a scruffy blond mop on his head and he grasped a cup of juice in one hand, and by the glazed look in his friend's eyes Christian knew what he'd been drinking.

'Aeron, are you having a good night?' Christian asked, amused.

Chapter Eighteen

'Oh yes. Who is your friend here?'

'This is my friend Sky. Sky, meet Aeron.' The band started into a loud, upbeat tune.

Sky held her hand out. 'Hi there,' she said over the music.

Aeron happily took it. 'Hello,' he kept a hold of Sky's hand but turned his head to look at Christian. 'She is very pretty,' he said in what Christian presumed was meant to be a whisper. His friend arched his eyebrows, a twinkle of mischief in his eyes.

'She is,' Christian said, patting his friend hard on the shoulder. 'Don't go embarrassing yourself Aeron.' It was Sky who laughed and pulled her hand away.

'He's fine,' she said.

Is he now? Christian wanted to ask. 'I can guess there's melrogan juice in your cup?'

Aeron drank all that remained and smacked his lips together. 'There was indeed melrogan juice in my cup and it was delicious. You obviously haven't had any!'

'Not yet.'

The laughter in his eyes was gone, it was as if he'd sobered up in record time. 'I'm a soldier now, Christian. We leave tomorrow, as you know.'

'You're a soldier now?' Christian asked, though he'd heard the words clear enough.

'I've signed up, so will be joining all the others when they set off at dawn.'

Christian blinked at the grass; the hanging færie lights by a near stall cast it in a mesmerising blue glow. Every musical note sounded flat in his ears.

Why wouldn't Aeron sign his name on the papers to become a soldier in the Krazonian army? Being friends with royalty didn't protect him.

He'd been too young before, but being one year older than Christian at nineteen there was no longer a barrier to hold him back. Here was an opportunity to fight for his realm.

A hand on his arm brought him round and Christian landed back in the field, festival sounds exploding in his ears. The bubble had burst. Sky stood close to him and it was her hand that rested on his skin.

Christian swallowed the lump of emotion in his throat, giving himself a mental shake.

'I wish I could fight alongside you, I really do,' he said and pulled Aeron into a tight hug.

'You're the prince, remember. You look after the realm and we soldiers fight to keep it protected.'

Christian screwed his eyes shut, fighting the urge to shout at him. Being prince, if anything, had made him feel useless. *I don't look after the realm. I don't do anything*, he wanted to say. 'Well you'd better look after yourself,' he said with ardour, clapping his friend on the back.

'I'll come and find you later so you can meet Maya,' Aeron said.

Christian nodded. 'Good. I will see you later.'

'It was nice to meet you, Sky.'

'It was nice to meet you too,' she replied, giving Aeron a quick hug.

Christian watched his friend disappear into the crowd, wondering whether that would be the last time. The thought caused his lungs to retract and he forced himself to take a deep breath. It couldn't be the last time. He searched desperately for a distraction.

'We should dance,' he declared, and Sky's eyes widened.

'No. I can't dance, Christian.'

He offered her his hand. 'Come on.'

Sky shook her head frantically. 'I look like a headless chicken looking for its head!'

He gave her no choice. Grabbing her hands he jumped up, spreading his wings wide. Joining the færies that danced near the bonfire, Christian could see the panic on Sky's pale face.

He twirled her away before drawing her close. 'You're doing fine,' he said with a small smile. His hands were on Sky's waist, while she gripped onto his shoulders. This was the closest they'd been and Christian began to feel nervous. A strange feeling gripped him and there was a flurry in his chest, as if his heart had grown wings.

Sky lowered her head. 'I don't feel comfortable, Christian.

Chapter Eighteen

Some of them are looking.'

'A Krazonian will never scrutinise. Well,' he paused, 'unless you're Dill. They're curious that's all. They will look on but won't ask questions.' Christian wrapped his hands firmly around hers and they were dancing again.

'That's a relief,' she said. 'They might think we're together or something.'

'Let them think what they want,' Christian said quickly. 'We aren't so it doesn't matter.'

Looking away, he spotted his mother. Through the thin haze of bonfire smoke she walked towards the festival, her dress billowing behind her. Rhia stood with two guards at the back door of the mansion. Christian concentrated on the scene as it changed. Rhia must have shouted something, because the queen spun on her heels and ran back to her. His sister fell to her knees, clutching the sides of her head. Anya bent down and touched her daughter's face, and a moment passed before she rose quickly to go inside, something else having caught her attention. A guard went after her.

'I should go,' Christian whispered, releasing Sky. 'My sister-'

The words jammed in his throat. Færies stopped dancing and the band's song dwindled into silence. The only sound came from the bonfire as it sizzled and sparked.

'Something's wrong,' said Sky in a voice etched with fear.

Through the flames Christian began to count the distorted silhouettes. Twelve...fifteen...twenty...

'Please, no,' was all he could say.

Flying with speed directly towards them were Zanians.

Chapter Nineteen

There was a dumbfounded silence among the færies. Sky couldn't believe her eyes. The enemy flew fast and made no signs of stopping. At this rate they would be on the field in seconds.

Then there was uproar, and Sky'd barely had time to think when someone gripped her hand so hard it made her wince. It was Christian, his deep brown eyes reflecting fire and fear.

We must get to the Emerald, they told her.

The next thing Sky knew she was stumbling along, Christian a few steps ahead. She had to keep blinking from the smoke that hung in the atmosphere and tried waving it away. Zanians were hurtling rocks, kicking down stalls and had visibly made it their aim to destroy every stall in sight, simultaneously ruining as many Krazonian's lives as possible.

Throughout it all they looked to be enjoying themselves and Sky stared, horrified. Some brave Krazonian's attempted to fight the ruthless enemy, but were quickly struck down having no weapon but their hands to defend themselves. Sky's ears were swamped with sounds of terrified screams and crying. Her hand slipped from Christian's grasp when an armoured Zanian swooped between them. In a rash decision Sky tore left to what she thought was safety, but she'd only put herself further into the furore and through the grey haze could see glowing fires raging; there came the sound of creaking wood, and more screams. Færies around her were fleeing in the direction of the square. Her throat felt tight but she managed to call out for Christian.

'Christian? Where are you?'

Chapter Nineteen

All it did was draw attention from two Zanian guards. Sky burst into a run, dodging helpless færies as she went. Something sharp hit her ankle and she tumbled onto the grass.

Choosing to ignore the shooting pain in her foot Sky heaved herself up off the ground. She glanced back to see no færie pursuing her, but clocked three children lost and crying. They stood out amidst the smoke and chaos. The children were latched onto one another searching for help. One had noticed her and she had to make a decision there and then, while Zanians still plagued the skies, whether or not to save these young færies. Her mind ticked away the seconds. She wanted to help, but her feet were rooted to the ground. She released a cry of despair at the situation.

'I want to help you,' she said, knowing they wouldn't hear. 'I can't,' she whimpered, turning around to run into the clear night. Could she hear them crying?

Struggling for breath Sky clambered up the hill that led to the back door of the mansion. She threw a look over her shoulder one last time.

With quivering hands Sky closed the door on a scene she could no longer stand to witness. The door clicked shut and she leaned against it, overcome and still fighting for breath. Panic had snatched it right out of her lungs.

Shutting her eyes, Sky blocked all images of the fighting and tried to focus on what this meant for Krazonia, and for her.

Someone called her name in a hoarse voice. At the end of the hall by the main doors, a færie stood. Sky squinted. All the candles had been put out.

'It's me!' said Christian. It hadn't sounded like him.

Sky rushed through the deserted area and down the hall. She was about to put her arms around him when she froze, recoiling with a cry. Lying in the gloom was Rhys. He could have been unconscious, or worse.

'Is he dead?' Three words she never thought she'd say.

'No. Stay with him while I…' On cue there came the sound of clashing metal and yelling from somewhere above them. Sky couldn't speak. Christian's expression was unfathomable. His lips parted as if he were about to say something, then decided against it. With a slight shake of the head he raced up the staircase, leaving Sky on her own with a half dead guard. Shouting from outside signified the ambush was not yet over. With a forced calm, Sky knelt down to tend to Rhys. She had this feeling that everything was changing, the cogs were turning and soon they'd click into place. She dreaded the outcome.

Rhys' chest armour was dented and he had no shield. A deep cut ran from his chin up to his temple and Sky had to cover her mouth, holding back the urge to heave. She willed herself to get a grip. How could she comfort him? She knew nothing about first aid.

She placed a hand delicately on his forehead.

'Rhys, can you hear me?' Looking closer at his face, Sky noticed what looked like red dust around his eyes. She tried brushing it away and flecks of red clung to her fingertips. Then came more yelling, and Sky braced herself. The cries were followed by a loud smash.

Refusing to let fear immobilise her, Sky continued speaking to Rhys, her whole body trembling.

'Please wake up.' She tried to swallow but her mouth was as dry as desert sand. 'I don't know what to do. I don't know what to *do*. Wake up, Rhys.'

His expression remained passive. In a rush of anger Sky shook him hard by the shoulders but nothing changed, his head lolled to the side and a drop of blood dribbled from the wound on his face.

A Zanian could burst in at any time.

'We're so vulnerable here but I can't move you by myself,' she said hopelessly, glancing around for a place to drag him or for someone to help her do so. The butlers must have gone into hiding to evade the chaos.

Finally Rhys stirred, releasing a long groan through dry lips.

'Who,' he croaked, 'who's there?'

Sky could have cried with relief. 'It's Sky. Tell me what happened?' The image of the three children flashed into her mind and her eyes filled with stinging tears. She brushed them away

Chapter Nineteen

before taking Rhys' hand as he struggled through an explanation.

'The guards and I – Zanians came and we needed to find the queen. Simian went outside. Dill went upstairs. I tried to fight. My whole body hurts, but it's my eyes.' He blinked. 'I can barely see. Zanians have færie dust and that burns,' he winced. 'I think they've blinded me.'

'Sit up, sit up,' Sky said, trying to lift him. He managed to ease himself forward so he half leant against the wall and with stiff movements touched his eyelids, and the cut on his cheek. His unseeing eyes told Sky of the pain he felt not just physically but emotionally too.

'I can hardly see,' he whispered.

'It'll be okay.' Given the circumstances Sky had major doubts on that front. She had to say something not only for Rhys, but for herself. 'I have to find Christian.' She touched the guards shoulder. 'I think you're safe here in the shadows.'

Rhys tried to clear his throat. 'He'll be too late.'

'I'm glad you're still alive, Rhys. You won't be on your own for long,' Sky said, forcing her body into action. With her legs trembling she charged up the staircase, following the sound of Rhia's despairing sobs. *He'll be too late.*

'How could you?' she heard Christian say, his tone scathing. 'How could you let them take her?'

Sky halted in the doorway, surveying the scene. A hundred tiny pieces of gleaming glass lay strewn across the floor, with Rhia slouched against the wall beside two large, shattered windows, crying. Christian, upon meeting her eye, scrambled up from his hands and knees. Opposite him were two guards, out of breath. Nobody seemed to know what to do.

The words fell from Sky's mouth. 'Rhys is conscious. He said something about Zanian færie dust and it's in his eyes. He can't see. But, he's alive.'

Dill adjusted his armour. 'I should go to him.'

The tone in which Christian spoke made certain that the guard would be doing nothing of the sort, and a shiver scuttled across Sky's shoulders as he spoke.

'You are going nowhere. I want you here. Gayle, see to Rhys.

Find another guard to check the butlers and maids are safe.'

'Sir,' the guard bowed, and cradling his arm, headed for the door. Only when he passed did Sky notice streaks of blood on his ripped sleeve, and how the tip of his right wing was bent. His face showed no pain.

Christian continued in the same controlled tone but it was lined with rage. 'You are my mother's most trusted guard,' he said, succumbing Dill to a hard, unwavering gaze. 'Tell me how this happened?' His voice grew louder and more aggressive. 'Tell me why I had to witness my mother being dragged away from me by an assembly of vicious Zanian guards, and then vanish in a flash of light? Tell me!'

'We were, we...' Dill fought to justify his actions and it was clear he rarely lost his composure. Sky chewed her lip as she watched the frustrated guard pace up and down, the shards of glass crunching beneath his booted feet.

'The ambush came over too strong and we were not prepared. Gayle and I got here as fast as we could while we tried to fight some Zanians off. Rogan, Rhys and Simian tried to hold the doors, I-' and he stopped as if struck by lightning. Even in the gloomy light Sky could see realisation seep into his features. His shoulders sagged. 'I'm sorry. We simply had no idea. I should have been at her side. You saw for yourself sir, even when Gayle and I just tried to follow them, she was gone. Gone.'

'We are doomed,' Rhia howled. Christian gazed despondently at the floor.

Dill cleared his throat. 'I ask your permission to find the General, sir.'

'Go,' Christian said and so the guard made haste, shouldering past Sky still standing in the doorway. Her pulse throbbed in the tips of her fingers and as she wandered forward the world around seemed to shrink, as though she was viewing it through the end of a telescope. Everything felt small and insignificant. The soles of Sky's feet pressed onto the shards of glass but she hardly felt it. At the window a chilling breeze teased her skin and she closed her eyes as it swept under her hair like a caress.

'I can hardly believe this has happened. This is your fault,

Chapter Nineteen

Sky Francis.' Sky heard the change in Rhia's voice, her emotions rolling from sadness into panic, and finally resentment. When Sky turned around it was clear to see. The princess stared with stone-grey eyes and her lips were pressed together, lines carved in stone. Sky felt pain like a pin prick in her chest when Rhia pointed with a trembling finger.

'My mother is gone,' she said. 'The Emerald is gone. This is all your fault,' her neat eyebrows crinkled, 'I should just throw you from this window, for you have caused nothing but trouble for me and my family, ruining everything within a matter of days.' She bared her teeth like an animal and jumped up. Sky retreated from the window.

'Please, please don't,' it came out like the pathetic plea it was. Sky felt a twitch of irritation in her neck. It seemed the feisty streak had not yet been completely buried by her fear, so she called on it. Taking a deep breath Sky pointed into the darkness. 'This was Tæ's doing, not mine. You can't blame me for this attack.'

With a shriek Rhia lunged, pushing Sky backwards until she was pinned against the wall.

'Is this not what you wanted?'

'No!' Sky exclaimed, staring into Rhia's fierce eyes. It wasn't anger that had a hold of the princess, but a red-hazed fury and there was no way Sky would be able to twist out of her grasp.

'You're *lying*.'

'I'm not lying to you,' Sky retorted, her own anger rising. This was hardly fair. Rhia dug her nails into her shoulders.

'Rhia, let go of me!'

Thankfully Christian came over to intercede. He yanked his sister backwards and put himself between them.

'Rhia, go downstairs and I will deal with Sky.'

'Do not tell me you're siding with *her*, because if you are then I swear to the Elana I will never speak to you again.'

'I am doing nothing of the sort. In fact, I agree with you. It is her fault.'

Rhia wiped her eyes while Sky slowly peeled herself away from the wall, watching the interaction between the two siblings. After his sister had stormed out of the room Christian turned to her, his

Away with the Færies

look smouldering. Sky could feel the hatred emanating from him.

'Christian, I didn't know this was going to happen. How was I supposed to know? This isn't my fault.' She truly sounded like a whiny sixteen year old, but Sky couldn't find the energy to uphold the brave 'adult' façade.

He looked at her and there was not an ounce of sympathy in his eyes, in fact there was no emotion there at all. His hard expression gave Sky a glimpse of the kind of king he could be if he wanted to.

'I told you the second I got here that the Emerald was in danger,' she whispered. 'No one expected this.'

'This time I'm siding with my sister. She was right about you,' Christian's voice shook with an anger he struggled to control. 'Nothing good has come of you being here, just like the last human. Within what, three days, the stone has been taken and my family has been broken apart. How do you propose we fix this, Sky Francis? Do you know what your task is now?'

Fire flared in her chest and before she knew what was happening, Sky could hear herself shouting:

'It isn't my fault that a psycho queen is so determined to have possession of that stupid stone that she'll continue to threaten and fight and destroy your realm for it. I don't want to be here! Unfortunately I have no choice because the stupid Elana or whatever they're called didn't close the portal properly. If you want someone to blame for this mess, blame Tæ. She is obviously deranged and power hungry. I'm just a human, Christian. Did I run away? No,' she took a deep breath, 'do I know what I must do? Yes,' she only realised it when she said the words. 'I need to go to Zania.'

After a long moment, Christian looked away. 'Don't let me stop you.'

Sky's mouth dropped open. 'Are you for real?'

'Am I what?' he snapped.

'Do you really mean that I should go on my own?' Her voice quietened to a whisper, the anger dissipating. 'I don't know the way.'

Christian shrugged and his lack of concern caused anxiety to

Chapter Nineteen

swirl in Sky's stomach.

His features contorted with anger. 'It doesn't matter anymore,' he spat. Sky pushed past him so she was no longer trapped.

She spun to face Christian, a strand of hair sticking to her bottom lip. She swiped it away. 'How am I supposed to get there when I don't know the way?'

'I don't care!' Christian burst out. Sky looked down at her trembling hands, unsure of how to feel; angry, or upset? 'I think maybe it is better you leave. Wow,' Christian went on, 'my sister was right. An obstruction is all you were. All you are. Rhia and I, along with the General, will figure something out.' Sky lifted her head slowly. His hands were open, fingers spread as if he were clutching an invisible ball. Christian probably wished it was her neck he had between his fingers. He dropped his arms to his sides. 'Without you,' he added coldly.

Breathing slowly, Sky stared straight into his eyes in a fleeting moment of calm.

'I understand.'

If she stayed here any longer she was sure to crumble. In her mind she pictured a book torn to shreds; an explosion of paper drifting to the floor like ribbon. Seeing no way to escape her fate Sky turned to leave when a butler appeared, his face drawn.

'The princess requests to see you urgently,' he said to Christian. Sky was invisible.

'I'm coming down,' Christian replied, walking away without looking back.

༄

Torches had been relit and all the fires had been doused. Feeling numb from the inside out, Sky stumbled through the square. Færies everywhere were rushing from place to place, some still crying, others silent and determined to fix what had been broken. Doors to homes had been kicked down and roofs kicked in. Trails of smoke hung like a low mist, unmoving in the dead air. Sky heard the General's voice loud and authoritative above the disorder.

'All soldiers to gather at the reservoir immediately!'

There were questions being thrown at him:
'Where is our queen?'
'Why is this happening?'
Sky slowed her walk to hear the General's reaction.
'We are organising a hasty response to this attack. The Zanian queen will not get away with this. I need all soldiers to report at the reservoir immediately.'

Above the layer of smoke a steady stream of Krazonian's flew through the night towards the mansion. Sky walked until cobble gave way to grass, the air clearing. She took a deep breath to unclog her throat and continued until the square was behind her. There was still the main town to get through. Her jaw began to ache from holding back tears.

Christian had been the one person she believed had been on her side. Who was she kidding? She'd been in Krazonia for less than a week and they hardly knew each other. It was Sky's misapprehension – she'd needed someone to cling to and Christian had provided the body. He'd provided everything and what had she brought to the table, a part from a tonne of bad luck?

Once again Sky pictured the book only this time she was one side, Christian was the other like shreds of paper fluttering through darkness. She walked with tears in her eyes and her feet scuffing the ground. She wanted her mother's arms around her and her father's jokes that would always make her laugh, no matter how terrible they were. In that moment, it was all she wanted.

Chapter Twenty

Christian couldn't think straight. The Emerald was no longer in its dome of glass; the glass he thought was impenetrable, and his mother who he thought invincible, were gone in a flash of green light. In addition to this there was Sky, and as Christian followed the butler down the dim corridor he struggled with the idea of her going out there alone. He had sent her away with harsh words, but he'd only spoken the truth. It was her fault.

Christian cursed himself through gritted teeth. Sky had been honest from the start.

The chandeliers and wall lamps had been relit. Rhia sat on a seat in the dining room looking forlorn and when Christian walked in she lifted her chin slightly, her way of acknowledging him. Simian along with Rogan, a quiet guard whom he seldom noticed, were standing alert against the opposite wall. Though his sister had stopped crying, her eyes were bloodshot and her cheeks were tearstained and blotchy.

'Gayle and Rhys are with a doctor in the kitchens,' she said. 'Dill is presumably with the General,' her tone led Christian to believe she had no interest in the guard, or anything for that matter. 'The Lieutenant is with soldiers at the reservoir and Simian informed me he's sent a messenger to Gloryn. Let us hope he reaches them in time so they can be redirected.'

Christian nodded once. It was rare for him and his sister to be at the same level of understanding but this time he truly felt her pain, and his heart beat heavily as antipathy bled through him. How dare Tæ uproot all the plans his mother had made? How

Away with the Færies

dare Tæ seize her and the Emerald in one fell swoop, as if father had died for nothing?

The heat of rage bubbled in his veins and Christian sat down, managing to refrain from hitting something, hard. He bounced his knee, trying to remain calm. Rhia's grey eyes studied him.

'You let her go then?' she said. 'With a little luck she will be entrapped within the Dark realm never to return.' She seemed to relish the thought.

It was too much for Christian.

'Will you stop?' he snarled, punching the seat arm with a clenched fist. He barely felt the pain. 'Sky has done no harm. Tæ is to blame for all of this.'

Rhia squinted at him. 'Need I remind you that it is due to her presence I have been unable to see? She messed everything up, thus causing this madness.'

Christian took a deep breath. 'Fine. But remember, Sky did not ask to be sent here in the same way we didn't ask for the Emerald, and you didn't ask for sight.' He wished he'd said these things before.

'I'm going to find Sky and I'm going to bring her back. Then we will establish a plan. Perhaps now we can put her to good use.' It sounded punitive but there was no other way of speaking to his unforgiving sister. He gave her no chance to respond. Christian was out of the door and in the air in a flash, flying down the path only stopping a few times to reassure færies that justice would be done, peace would be restored. In the square he caught sight of the General and Dill with two Krazonian's, one being only a child who was mouthing something and gesticulating wildly.

'General Warren,' Christian said, interrupting. The child's mouth went slack and the older færie beside him, presumably his mother, bowed.

The General scratched his beard and held up a folded letter. 'You need to read this.'

Christian couldn't bring himself to touch it for he knew who it was from. 'Bring them back to the mansion along with that letter. I want to hear the full explanation, there is just one thing I must do first.'

Chapter Twenty

He took to the air, flying fast and fighting guilt as he passed færies trying to mend their damaged roofs under fire light. No one tried to stop him. When he spotted Sky stumbling towards the shadow of a tree with her hands on her stomach he initially held back from following, too ashamed of his previous actions. 'I must deal with this,' he murmured, bracing himself.

She was bent double behind the old tree, coughing, and Christian leaned against it with his foot on a root embedded in the ground. He peered round the trunk.

'It's me,' he said as she straightened up to face him. He could barely see her, just the outline of her features. He imagined them to be pulled into a look of bewilderment.

'What are you doing here?' Sky said with trepidation.

'I spoke out of turn before. I was so angry I didn't know what I was saying,' he paused, 'no, I *did* know what I was saying. I just shouldn't have directed it all at you.' He pinched the bridge of his nose with his thumb and forefinger. 'I resent Tæ. I despise her for what she's done.' He couldn't stress it enough. 'I didn't mean to upset you.'

'It's okay. I'm,' she heaved a sigh, 'okay. But if that's all you have to say I should get going...' her voice disappeared into the night as she turned away.

'Come back to the mansion,' Christian said. 'I shouldn't have sent you away on your own. Besides, we'll be discussing what to do next. Though we already know, don't we? You said it yourself.' He caught the scent of wood smoke on the air; lingering evidence of the calamity that had just occurred. A nervous shiver ran down his spine. 'There's also a letter from Tæ.'

Sky gasped. 'What does it say?'

'I have yet to find out,' he said. 'We must get my mother back, Sky. Tell me we will.' He sagged against the tree, thumping his fists against it. 'I've already lost my father to Tæ Asrai – I can't bear to lose my mother as well.' For the first time anger gave way to grief, creating a well inside of him. He placed a hand against his brow, partly to hide the tears that formed in his eyes. He'd suffered the same feeling of hopelessness on discovering his father no longer lived.

'I should have tried harder,' he said, more to himself. His throat felt tight. 'Why didn't I go after them? I was so busy enjoying the festival I forgot my duty.'

Sky lingered by his side and Christian was grateful for her comfort. She didn't need to embrace him, her presence was enough. He crossed his arms, lowering his head to stare at his feet that were just shapes in shadow. He screwed his eyes shut and held his breath until he could feel the blood pulsing in his temples.

'My mother hardly fought them. Dill and Gayle tried and Rhia was too terrified to move. I caught a look in her eye that said "let me go".' A wave of emotion tore over him. Anya had struggled only briefly before giving in. It was almost as if she'd allowed it to happen. She could have fought harder. Christian had feigned ignorance to this fact but now, standing in darkness with only Sky beside him he was able to admit it.

'She didn't fight back, as if she accepted what was happening. When Dill and Gayle made an attempt of pursuit there was this blinding green light, and then they disappeared.' Christian opened his eyes. His bottom lashes were wet with tears and he hastily wiped them away.

'We should go back,' he pushed away from the tree and Sky grabbed his arm with cold hands, stopping him.

'We will get your mother back Christian,' she said. 'We will. There is no way Tæ's going to get away with this.'

He pressed his hand against hers. 'Yes. We will go to Zania together and face her.'

∽

'So the guard made no threats?' Rhia questioned, receiving a slow nod from the General who, after brushing his hands together, fixed his stern gaze on the two trembling færies.

'Did the guard say anything else?'

'Nothing more, just that we had to get the letter to you or the prince or the p-princess,' the young boy whimpered as he struggled to get the words out. 'So we found the – you, we just want

Chapter Twenty

to – to be safe now.' He started shivering. His mother tightened her grip around his shoulders.

Christian shook his head, disgusted. 'How can one færie cause so much grief? She is bent on destruction. She is clever, I'll give her that. But in the name of Krazon,' he lowered his voice to a steely whisper. 'If I ever get close enough, well…' Resentment rippled through him. He rolled his shoulders and flexed his wings, waiting for the feeling to pass before speaking again.

'Sky and I will fly ahead of the army in an attempt to change our fate, which right now does not look encouraging. Our plan is to meet Tæ face to face, try and reason with her. It will be a challenge but I believe we can do it. Or at least we can attempt to.'

Sky looked at him. 'We can do it.'

Rhia barked a laugh. 'You make it sound so easy,' she said contemptuously.

The General furrowed his heavy brow. 'Before you make any rash decisions let us hear what Tæ has to say.' To that, Christian remained mute. It didn't matter because he'd already made up his mind. Rhia leaned forward to address the two terrified Krazonian's.

'I am sorry. Go back to your home. I'll be out shortly to explain what is happening. Spread the word.'

Rogan escorted the færies out. As they passed Christian gave them a reassuring smile, but he knew they could see the hatred that simmered in his dark eyes, ready to overflow. The Zanian queen will not get away with this, he silently told them. Tæ would be knocked down despite her power. *No matter what happens, the Dark realm will never overshadow us.*

Christian blinked, brought round by the sound of crisp parchment being peeled open. Rhia lowered her gaze, holding the letter firmly in both hands. The room held its breath as she began to read in a clear voice:

'"Soon the Emerald will be within my grasp. After all these years it will be where it belongs. You are so good-natured I knew you wouldn't anticipate this. It wouldn't even cross your minds that I might not want to wait, that I would not simply stand by while you prepare your army, though I fully intended to give you that impression. Has your queen learned nothing these past years?"' Rhia paused. Christian could hardly bear the silence, and so threw something into the disjointed circle consisting of Sky, Rhia, the General, Dill and himself.

'How could she have been so sure?' he said, frustration gripping him. 'It makes me feel so weak!'

'The ambush was a distraction,' Sky murmured. 'I suppose when you think how long she's had to plan this, how could it fail?'

The General began to pace. 'Let us not forget that Anya never wanted to fight. She longs for peace, and Tæ has learnt this, using it to her advantage. Of course the festival would go ahead, and it acted as a perfect diversion,' he said.

Rhia read what was left of Tæ's message, her hands trembling. It caused the page to quiver.

'"This is not just about power, it's about vengeance. It is not my place to tell you about the past, but let me tell you this. Your mother is a murderer—"' Rhia faltered. '"I'm not sorry for what I'm doing to you and your realm and I – I never will be."'

Christian's heart thumped heavily in his chest, weighed down by this revelation. It was as if the sky had fallen, he wanted so much to crouch down and cover his head and pretend that it wasn't happening, that this news wasn't crushing him.

Rhia threw the page to the floor as if it had stung her. 'Tæ is spinning lies,' she said. 'I don't understand what she means about mother.' She hesitated before reaching down to grab the page and letting out a cry of frustration, started to tear it up into tiny pieces. Taken aback, Christian could only watch. She kept going until they were scraps of off-white, drifting lifelessly to the floor.

Rhia slumped forward, her hands on her knees. She looked up at the General. 'General Warren, tell me what to do.'

'I can only give you my advice. You and your brother must come to a decision.'

'That is enough for me. I believe he already knows what *he's* doing.'

Christian licked his dry lips. 'Sky and I will begin our journey to Zania shortly.'

Standing up, Rhia brushed her hair back from her face and

Chapter Twenty

pointed at Sky. 'Do not put yourself in danger for her,' she said, eyeing Sky with contempt. Then she turned to the human, shaking off the General's touch. 'This is your responsibility and I can't believe I'm saying this, if you and my brother are going together then he is your responsibility too. You are travelling with the Krazonian prince. You would do well to remember that,' Rhia said bitterly. 'I want him back in one piece, even if he ends up in one piece, alone.' With that she turned and strode away.

'It is not my wish to send you away, Christian,' said the General. 'But I know you're strong like your father, and I doubt I could stop you doing this if I tried. I only ask you to be careful. And,' he glanced at Sky, 'you too. Both of you need to be careful.' He pursed his lips, bowed, and walked after Rhia who now stood at the far end of the room.

Had that been his sister's way of saying goodbye? Not even a hopeful smile, or an embrace. He had to speak to her before he left with Sky, who in that moment looked miserable.

'I'm pretty sure she doesn't want me to come back,' she muttered.

'I'll speak to her before we go,' Christian said. 'Follow me.'

He ventured up the staircase, Sky following close behind. Eira, a maid, was making her way along the corridor.

She bowed. Her hair, usually twisted into a tight coil atop her head tumbled loose and wild about her shoulders. Her apron was spattered with red færie dust.

Christian stopped her. 'Are you hurt?' Her cheeks were streaked with tears. She shook her head.

'No, I hid with Hanna. We managed to slip away just in time.' At twenty five years old, Eira had been working for the queen since she was Christian's age. 'Will the queen...'

'She will be fine,' Christian said with as much conviction as he could muster. 'She is the queen after all. Eira, would you retrieve two cloaks for me and Sky? Find us in the office.'

In the candlelit room Christian scoured the bookshelves before rummaging through papers and letters, until he found what he was looking for. He unfurled the map and pressed his hands on opposite corners to prevent it coiling. He needed to see it all.

He could hear Sky picking around, and then came the click and creak of her opening the desk drawer. She gasped. Christian shot her a sideways glance.

'What have you found?'

'I've found the necklace,' she said, her shadow contorting on the wall as the candlelight flickered.

His knees nearly buckled. 'The necklace,' he echoed. 'I completely forgot about it.'

Sky delicately lifted it out of its hiding place. The small stone emitted a dull, throbbing glow from its centre. It was mesmerising.

'We should keep it close,' he said. 'This is something Tæ doesn't know about, and she must not. Here,' he tilted his head towards the map. Sky fastened the chain around her neck and tucked it beneath the neckline of her dress. Unhooking the candle from its holder on the wall, she brought it to the desk.

Christian was ready to show Sky the route they would take when something caught his eye. Wedged between two books on the edge of the desk was what looked like another letter, and it led Christian to suspect there was a reason it was there half hidden. The thought caused his stomach to flip.

Reaching forward he tugged the letter out; the parchment was weathered and had so many creases it must have been folded and unfolded many times by a pair of anxious hands – his mother's. He unfolded it, fearing what it would say.

'Is it from Tæ?' Sky whispered.

Christian couldn't answer. He recognised the words. They had been read to him before. Anya's voice echoed in his mind as he scanned the page with wide eyes.

You have five days…I give you one last chance to bring the Emerald to me…The Emerald will be mine…

He fell into the chair still reading, for where his mother had stopped, the letter continued:

The Emerald will be mine and I will have my revenge. You murdered my husband, King Rowan of Zania. You destroyed him

Chapter Twenty

and it is only because of your beloved José that you are not dead today. Your dear, loyal husband stepped forward and I could reach neither you nor the precious stone. Did you feel the same pain as I, knowing your love had been slain? This is the final battle Anya Meldin. Having sought the stone for so long, I'm glad to say I am certain to have it soon. That is a promise. A promise I most certainly will not break.

Christian's breaths came short and fast. Pain seared through him like wildfire, igniting in his chest. He didn't move when Eira opened the door. Sky took the cloaks and the maid left. He couldn't unstick himself from the seat, nor could he let go of the letter. It crumpled in his fist.

'Christian, what's wrong?' said Sky, but he didn't want to hear anyone or anything. In fact he wanted to hear his mother try and deny this horrific proclamation. How could she hide such a thing? In a sudden burst of movement he jumped up, jolting the chair and causing it to tip backwards. It wasn't anger that had a hold of him, but anguish. How could she?

'She lied,' his voice swallowed up the dead silence in the room. His vision blurred and he began to shout, pouring out his pain verbally as he threw pencils, books and trinkets from his mother's desk against the wall. At one point Sky latched onto him but he was strong enough to rip away. Christian grabbed books out of the case began hurling them across the room wishing his mother and father were here together, and there were no secrets.

'She killed the king!' He wasn't quite sure whether he meant Rowan, or his own father. Maybe he meant both.

If any færie came to investigate the noise and shouts, Christian wasn't aware. Perhaps they'd expected a meltdown given all he'd been through.

After a while he ran out of steam and doubled over, his hands on his knees, choking out breaths.

Without a word Sky approached, securing her arms around him so her head rested against his shoulder. She didn't let go when he tried to push her off, angry and ashamed. She clung to him. Eventually Christian found himself on his knees and

Sky remained alongside him, their wings touching. They knelt together in silence.

'I'm sure she was only trying to protect you,' said Sky quietly. She must have read the letter while Christian had been shouting and throwing things. He turned his head away.

'Would it not have been better for her and for us if she'd told the truth?' His voice was husky. He tried to clear it with a cough.

'I don't know.'

Christian closed his eyes briefly. 'To tell you the truth, I don't know either.'

Chapter Twenty-One

Sky disentangled herself from Christian, conscious of how near they were sat to one another. Even when she'd sat back, she was close enough to see the taut muscle of his jaw. His face held a hard expression. His eyebrows were pulled together over half-closed eyes as if he were brooding over a memory, re-evaluating a moment in his life. Sky didn't know whether to speak. She quickly came to the conclusion that she had no choice in the matter. They had to get their butts into gear.

'What now?'

He blinked. 'I...we...' he stammered, standing up. 'Put on your cloak, I'll only be a moment.'

Sky lifted herself up and caught the uneasy look Christian gave the room before leaving. It was a mess, but there were bigger things to worry about. Sky eyed the crumpled cloak in the corner. It took a few goes – there were two breaches in the cloak which her wings were supposed to fit through and they didn't want to cooperate. Sweeping it over her head for the fourth time the cloak finally settled around her shoulders, and she flexed her wings to make sure they weren't caught in the fabric. Leaning against the desk, Sky blew the air out of her lips in a huff. Putting on a cloak had been a challenge, how on earth was she going to make it to Zania?

Christian appeared in the doorway holding two pairs of plain-looking boots.

'Put these on. Zania's terrain is different to ours and we won't be able to fly all the way there.'

Sky brushed down the marked soles of her feet and took the

Away with the Færies

boots from him. Why hadn't he mentioned the fact there was an option to wear shoes? She suppressed a groan as she pulled the boots onto her feet. The material felt like canvas. There was no heel and they had thin soles but it was better than nothing. A slim rope tied around the ankle to secure them.

'They aren't a bad fit,' Sky said in surprise. They were comfortable, but one thing was for sure, she would never complain about her grubby old trainers again.

Christian nodded. 'They will suffice. There will no doubt be times when we must walk,' he hesitated, 'or run.'

Her heart lurched. She had no idea of the obstacles they would face, but a "dark realm" was bound to be accompanied by a few enemies.

Sky tied up the boots and wiggled her toes. Christian had his cloak on in seconds. He stuffed the map into a pocket. They were about to leave when it crossed Sky's mind that despite being in a crumpled ball Tæ's letter could easily be reopened, having been discarded on the desk.

Christian was walking away.

'The letter!' Sky burst out. 'Will you tell Rhia?' He stopped but didn't turn.

'No.'

'Should I rip it up?'

'That would be a good idea,' Christian replied, continuing along the corridor. Case closed. Sky did so quickly and left, acutely aware of the precious piece of stone fastened to a gold chain around her neck. She touched the jewel, feeling its weight. Regardless of its size there was an element of power to it.

To think it hung around her neck, touching her skin. If Tæ could use the Emerald, could it be that a shard of it could be used in the same way? Was there enough power within it to cause a thunderstorm, or death? Sky lifted a hand to her lips. These ideas disturbed her.

Reigning in her composure she began to take firm steps down the staircase, fixing a plain expression onto her face so it gave no inner thoughts away.

Chapter Twenty-One

Sky could feel the pressure of what was to come not only for herself but for the færies around her. She shifted from foot to foot, waiting by the main doors for Christian who at that moment was speaking with his sister somewhere. Armoured guards were in and out of the mansion, butlers and maids busied themselves but it was clear their minds weren't on their work. Sky didn't blame them. Her stomach gurgled as it digested the mammoth amount of Triffilian nuts, dried fruit and water she'd filled herself up with at Christian's orders. When she'd asked if he was having any, he'd washed a few pieces of dried fruit down with water and shrugged. Evidently that was enough for him.

Sky looked out into the night, soaking up the sounds of an army preparing for battle; the scrape of metal, the scuffing of boots and jovial cheers between soldiers, as if they were happy about fighting the enemy and risking their lives. Perhaps they saw it differently. For the damage Zanians had caused this was their chance to return the favour.

She couldn't recall her last words to Rhia. Focusing on the ground, Sky thought hard. It was after the Emerald and Anya had been taken. Oh, yes. Rhia had her pinned to the wall, firing accusations at her.

'I'm not lying – let go of me.'

On that thought she heard footsteps and glanced around to meet a grave-looking Christian, lit torch in hand.

'Rhia will be out shortly. We must go,' he said.

Sky took a steadying breath. 'Okay.'

They flew through the square and Sky kept her focus on the town ahead. She couldn't bear to look at the færies still tidying up the ruins of their homes, piecing them and themselves back together. A few called out well wishes and although their voices were hoarse, the hope broke through.

Having almost reached the end of the main town Sky realised Christian was lengthening the beat-beat rhythm of his wings. He was reducing speed. Then he came to an abrupt landing. Taken aback, Sky met the ground too fast and stumbled, once, twice.

She checked herself over before looking back to see what had stopped him. He held the torch low as if he'd half-forgotten it.

Ah. He'd stopped to face the curious and apprehensive gaze of his onlookers. Fear shot through her like a lightning bolt. Sky imagined their thoughts: why must the prince risk his life? Why is this happening? Who is that færie in the creased and dirtied white dress with hair as dark as night standing beside him?

'The princess has asked me to tell you, head to the square,' Christian's words carried clearly through the night. 'Morel village and Hale are also making their way there. All will be explained by my dear sister. So go, now. I am truly sorry and I promise retribution.' Sky could hear empathy in his voice. 'The queen will return to us, that I promise you.'

With that, Christian turned away from his people. The torch's dancing flame threw light on his features, turning his eyes molten. Sky pursed her lips, feeling the responsibility of the whole realm like a weight on her shoulders. Christian flexed his wings as he walked to her, eyes downcast. He felt it too.

The remaining torchlight from the town was fading and the world around Sky grew strangely quiet. After a while there was only the solitary flame of the torch Christian had brought to guide them. To the west, Sky could just make out the silhouettes of færies from Hale village, flying with speed against the murky horizon, to the square. Past the village rose the valley of Bluewater and in her mind Sky could see its clear, sparkling stream meandering through the grasses, making its way to another realm; a place far away where the fields turn golden beneath the sun.

Sky longed for a conversation to break up the silence that hung between her and Christian, but she struggled to find words. She wanted to know what he'd discussed with Rhia and whether she'd been a part of it, but if Christian wasn't going to tell her she certainly wasn't going to ask. And so they flew on, their wings whooshing together and the fire crackling against the wind.

'The map,' Christian said suddenly. 'I had it in my pocket.'

Sky kept her focus ahead as they flew up and over a hill. It was difficult flying so close to the ground, but Christian had said it was better this way. Nevertheless it took a lot of concentration.

Chapter Twenty-One

Like a dying flower the torchlight was withering, losing strength against the battering wind that hit it, for Sky and Christian were flying fast.

'So you don't have it now?' asked Sky after gasping a breath.

'No. It must have fallen out of my pocket. Damn it!'

'Should we go back?'

'It would have been lost to the breeze,' Christian said.

Sky threw him a worried look. 'I really hope you know the way.'

'I think I do,' he sounded unsure. 'Let's slow down a little.'

The way they flew up and over the rolling hills reminded Sky of a ride she loved at the annual fair at home. She and Cassie would throw their arms up with glee, light-headed from laughter as the Octopus swung them round and round, up and down. She could let herself go. Her skin tingled and her stomach flipped on every drop. This rise and fall was similar, only she was doing all the work, and it wasn't fun. It was scary.

Sky became aware of another pair of sturdy wings beating together and for one sickening moment believed it to be a Zanian guard speeding towards them. She was about to grab Christian's arm when a familiar voice called out. 'Sir, wait!'

The moon emerged from behind a veil of violet clouds, casting its silvery light across the expanse of hills. Ancient willow trees whispered as their drooping leaves caught the breeze. Sky landed beside Christian on the crest of a hill.

Dill stood out of breath before them. 'Don't do this.' He swallowed hard. 'It could be a trap.'

'We must, and this is not the time for a debate,' Christian said sharply.

'What if it is a trap?' Dill said in a raised voice. 'We've already seen what Tæ is capable of. You are risking your life going to Zania so unprepared! There must be another way?'

Christian shook his head. Sky took a step back, glancing around warily while the conversation continued. It would have been better to have this talk beneath a willow tree where at least they'd something shielding them. She crossed her arms and waited, fighting the urgency that plagued her. A few minutes of conversation wouldn't hurt.

'Dill, there is no other way. By taking mother she knows Rhia and I won't stand for it. She is probably expecting us to-'

'Then you should do what she does not expect. Don't go.'

'Sky and I must get there before the armies so at least we can *try* to stop her. Maybe even…' Christian gritted his teeth, 'come to an agreement.'

'Perhaps she will trade,' Dill growled, 'she will exchange the queen for you. What then?'

'She will be expecting someone to tackle her face on.' Sky could tell Christian wasn't even contemplating an answer for Dill. He would do whatever was needed if the time came.

'I want my mother safe again,' he continued. 'You need to go back.'

'And you need some sort of protection. Let me come with you. I failed your mother, I can't bear to fail her son too.'

Sky could almost hear the "snap" as Christian reached the end of his tether.

'No! I'm going, and Sky is accompanying me. Do you hear me, Dill? This is an order: go back and help my sister. She will need you.' Without waiting for a response from the guard, Christian's wings shot open and he took to the air. After a moment Sky stretched open her wings and offered Dill a sympathetic smile. In spite of their differences she wouldn't have minded the guard's protection but Christian opposed it. So *that* idea was out of the window.

She felt she should say something though the words sounded feeble. 'It's for the best.'

Dill looked disgruntled. 'Easy for you to say,' and after giving Christian one final look, he took to the air also, flying back to safety and civilisation.

Clouds encompassed the bright moon once again, a splinter of its light reflecting on Dill's armour as he flew over the hills. Then it was all gloom and only then did Sky realise the torch was no longer lit and lay nestled in the grass by her feet.

'Let's go,' Christian said impatiently.

'Right. I know, yes. We have no torch.'

'That's a good thing. We'll blend in with the darkness better.'

Chapter Twenty-One

The hills rose like waves of earth and went on for what felt like forever. Sky had never truly believed her path could be lit solely by moonlight, but in this case it was, turning the grass ashen whenever it emerged from behind a cloud.

Her wings began to ache. They were flying at a steady pace but she wasn't used to doing so for this length of time. If it was possible to get cramp, they were definitely going to seize up soon.

'Can we walk for a while?' she dared to ask.

'Yes,' Christian said shortly. 'Soon we'll be approaching the Dark Forest. It is better we go on foot.' Sky stole a glance at him. He'd sounded angry, but that could be to disguise the fear. It poked at the edges of her own mind but she forced it back. If she caved, she'd be about as useful as a sieve with no holes.

The hills gave way to level, dry ground, where grass only grew through cracks. The willow trees were behind Sky now, replaced by a different variety altogether: wide trunks and stooping branches, where bunches of leaves sprouted out like tufts of hair. Sky eyed the land around her as she walked; dry plains seemed to stretch out on either side indefinitely. Far in the distance to the east Sky noticed small orbs of yellow-orange light. Signs of life.

Christian's analysing gaze skimmed across the landscape.

'You know we can do this, you and me,' he said. 'We'll get to Tæ, and we will stop her somehow. Or at least find a way to get back the Emerald...' he trailed off, ruffling his hair. Sky knew the enormity of this "task". A part of her wished she could have been a coward. It was odd to imagine what would have happened if she'd chosen to snub Elle's advice. She could have walked away and life would have carried on. Sky's Normal Life would have continued.

No, no it wouldn't. Sky mentally argued with these conflicting thoughts. The moment she selfishly picked up the necklace was the moment her Normal Life had ended.

She was pulled out of this sombre reverie by a movement in the darkness, something whole and agile, possibly another færie trying not to be seen. Christian hadn't noticed. Sky hesitated. Her nerves were so not cut out for this.

'Christian,' she said in no more than a strained whisper. 'I think there's someone behind us.'

He looked at her, and then to the trees. Touching Sky's shoulder he moved so she was behind him. 'Come out!' he said boldly. 'Sky, stay behind me.'

Despite his words she shuffled forward, her heart hammering in her chest. 'Maybe we should ignore it? I could have been seeing things.'

'No,' Christian said firmly. 'There is somebody there.'

Sky squinted at the area beneath the tree, where the fragmented moonlight couldn't reach. A figure emerged from the shadows with slow, tentative steps. The first thing Sky noticed was his bare feet. His hair was ash blond; short and tousled. Ragged clothes clung to a lean body. He stopped a few yards away and Sky was able to see this færie's face clearly and she found it to be an intriguing one. He had a pointed chin, high cheekbones and alert round eyes, his face mirroring that of a frightened animal. A part of Sky knew it would be best to stay guarded but looking at him, the other part wondered what harm he could bring them.

Sky opened her mouth to speak but Christian beat her to it.

'Who are you and what brings you here, to the place between realms?' His tone was accusing.

'I live nowhere in particular, and often travel through these lands,' said the færie.

'I can see by your wings that you are Zanian,' Christian said as he leaned forward, placing an arm in front of Sky. She compared their wings. Where a Krazonian's wings curled, that of a Zanian's ended in a sharp point and the veins were darker.

The Zanian didn't shy away. If anything he was oblivious to Christian's hostility.

'You're right, but I don't belong in Zania.'

Sky pursed her lips. Christian glared at the stranger, his eyes dark and reproachful. After a moment he stepped back. 'Sky, let him be,' and with that he marched off down the slope and in seconds was gone from view.

Sky hurried after him, unable to shake the feeling that the Zanian was staring holes into her wings.

Christian didn't even look at her. 'He wouldn't dare follow.'

Chapter Twenty-One

It was a suspicious scenario. The image of his pale, lithe figure blended with that of the frightful Zanian guards who had ravaged part of Krazonia. Sky staggered her steps, losing herself to the vision of their evil eyes and menacing laughs. The sound echoed through her mind.

A little gasp escaped her lips and for the first time in a while, when Christian looked at her, his expression softened with concern. 'You're okay, Sky,' he said, running a hand down her arm. When their fingers touched he pulled away.

The wind had dwindled to a faint breeze. For a while Sky listened to the sound of her boots scuffing against grainy earth, watching every step as they carried her towards the unknown.

'The Dark Forest is our first obstacle,' said Christian. 'We should follow the outskirts because if we go in too deep, we may get lost.'

Sky nodded, half listening.

'I know you wish you were somewhere else, such as your own world where everything is normal and less formidable.' Their eyes met and Sky's heart did a triple jump up into her throat. She swallowed it back down.

'That might be true, but I'm here aren't I? We have no choice but to face whatever there is to face in Zania. Then I can think about getting home.'

Christian's attention was snatched away then by a sudden and unwanted arrival. Displeasure seeped into his features. Sky looked around to see the Zanian gazing at her. Subconsciously she'd been listening out for footsteps or the soft beat of wings but hadn't heard a thing. He now stood like an innocent child before them.

'If you wish to get into the heart of Zania, I can take you.'

Chapter Twenty-Two

Christian couldn't believe it.

'Why are you following us?'

'I'm alone and I'm curious. Sound carries here.'

'We heard what you said.'

'May I ask what route you plan to take?' The Zanian even dared to smile. Christian shook his head.

'I think you should leave us alone.'

'I know these lands.'

This færie was not going to give up. Christian's wings twitched in frustration. 'Do you know who you are speaking to?'

He cast a thoughtful glance to the night sky. 'I can probably guess.'

Sky's eyebrows were raised. Christian couldn't help wondering if he'd been wrong in refusing Dill's help. Dill could have done a better job at getting rid of this færie than he, for all he had was his temper and what good were fierce words to a færie that seemed so unfazed by them? Then again, if the Zanian angered him enough he was more than capable of throwing a punch.

'I can take you through the caves. Whatever it is that you're doing, I imagine every moment is important.' Christian could hardly believe this færie's impudence.

'What makes you say that?' Sky asked. The Zanian approached them, raising his slender hands as if he were surrendering himself, or his identity.

'My name is Arlo Sæl. I used to be a messenger for the Zanian queen but grew tired-'

'A Zanian messenger!' Christian exploded. 'If you really knew

Chapter Twenty-Two

who I was you would not have the nerve to say such things,' he said, turning to walk away, his booted feet hitting the ground hard. He heard Sky's voice and she sounded frustrated too.

'Christian! We lost the map and how well do you know these lands? He may have been a Zanian messenger but I really think we should,' she paused and Christian knew her forthcoming suggestion and dreaded it.

'I think we should let him take us.' He kept walking and the slope eased out to flat, dry ground. Sky gripped his upper arm and he spun to face her, still seething.

'Would you listen?' she said, tucking her hair behind her ears. Christian felt himself begin to calm as her cool fingers trailed ice across his skin to the wrist. It tingled and he tried to ignore the feeling. Sky was staring at him with her piercing blue eyes. 'I told myself I wasn't going to be a whining teenager, but an adult. So I'm trying to be an adult and I'm looking at this situation from an outsider's view. These are...unique circumstances. You can't begrudge this Arlo guy for something he had no hand in.'

Christian glanced over her shoulder to see the Zanian looking in their direction.

'Admittedly, his timing is a little odd,' Sky went on, 'but I have no idea where we're going, and it isn't like you've wandered these paths before is it?' Looking down, she withdrew her hand. 'We'll just have to be cautious. By accepting his help it doesn't mean you're forgiving the Zanian queen. If anything it shows how strong you are. So?' Her attempted smile wavered. She was scared. Sky Francis knew even less of this world than he did.

Christian waved Arlo over, tight-lipped. He would have to discount his pride for this was, after all, a "unique circumstance" and he wanted Sky to be right.

'How exactly do we reach these caves?' Christian met Arlo's eye with a resolute gaze, folding his arms. 'To clarify, this is not me trusting you. I am simply using the resources available, you understand.'

Arlo clasped his hands together, a smile creeping onto his face. He was oblivious to Christian's hostility.

'The Dark Forest leads to the marshlands, and from there we

head north-west. After crossing the Frazian plain we'll eventually reach the caves entrance. This will lead you to the heart of Zania's palace.'

'You make it sound so straightforward,' Sky remarked.

'It is when you say it is.'

Christian glanced at Sky and her expression of bewilderment reflected his own. Was this færie even sane?

They walked a while longer, the silence around them full of unanswered questions. Christian brooded over his stupidity for not keeping a hold of the map. Even if he'd retraced his flight path the map would have caught the breeze, drifting somewhere in the night.

The Dark Forest came into view. A mass of towering trees spread out before them like a black sea, and Christian's heart almost stopped. There were woodlands, forests, and then this. The trees were bigger than he imagined and they trailed left and right, to what seemed the edges of the earth. He heard Sky mutter something like '…out of a game.'

Christian walked beside Sky and nerves left him feeling unsettled, as if a dozen fireflies had been set free in his stomach. He thought about Rhia and found respite knowing that for only fifteen years old, she had the strength and resolve of their father. She would be okay without her brother for the meantime.

'There should be fireflies to light our way,' said Arlo.

'What if there aren't?' Christian retorted. 'Does that mean we'll be lost in the forest for all eternity?' He clamped his mouth shut before he said anything else. Kindness didn't come easily.

But an alarming question surfaced. 'Am I correct in thinking we are to travel through the forest, instead of following the outskirts?' Christian said to the back of Arlo's head.

'Well,' said Arlo. 'If you seek the quickest path, yes. As I said, fireflies will light our way.'

'It might not be a case of the quickest path, but more the safest,' Christian muttered, gazing around him, drawing courage. It was as if the trees were growing the closer he got to them. The trunks grew wider and rose higher and higher until he had to crane his neck to see the tops. They almost touched the grey clouds that

Chapter Twenty-Two

drifted across a black, star-speckled sky. Only now he noticed the distant stars, twinkling clusters similar to færie dust, frozen in time. They led him to thoughts of his father. *Be brave.*

Swallowing hard Christian walked towards the darkness, leaving the moon and stars behind as the forest slowly drew him into its gloom.

Fireflies drifted around like floating orbs, highlighting shadows of fallen trees and hollow logs on the ground. Christian contemplated the possibility of flying, but as he looked around it became clear that would be impossible. The forest was too dense, the trees packed together like soldiers.

The ground felt mossy and soft and the atmosphere cool; the smell of dank earth and rotting bark stole through the air. Christian strained his eyes but all he could see were shapes. Dark shapes against the dark. Fireflies hovered around them, illuminating Arlo's hair every now and then, and when Sky looked at him her blue eyes were as clear as glacier water.

'I wonder how long this is going to take,' she whispered.

Christian looked around, wary. 'I honestly could not tell you.'

A shrill cry from above stopped the færies in their tracks. It echoed all around them. Then it came again, a high-pitch screech causing Christian's blood to run cold.

'What was that?' he heard Sky whisper.

'Shh!' Arlo hissed. 'Wait.'

'The Malen,' he then murmured.

'Would you like to repeat that?' Christian said nervously.

'The Malen – creatures of the forest. They must sense us, well, you and your friend, as unknowns,' Arlo said, turning around.

'I did not anticipate this,' he went on, his eyes wide and searching. 'We must keep low and move carefully, making no sudden movements.' He hunched his shoulders, cowering from the unknown predator.

Initially Christian felt dread but it was swiftly followed by a rush of anger. He clenched his fists. 'You knew about these creatures and forgot to mention it?' he growled. 'Isn't that convenient?'

Arlo shuffled away. 'I'm sorry. If we move slowly we'll be fine, I'm sure.'

'You don't sound sure.'

'What do these things do?' Sky whispered, tailing after Arlo. Christian grudgingly followed. He kept his focus on Sky's wings, not wanting to look up to see what lurked in the treetops.

'If they become aware of trespassers they grow very defensive. They may chase us out of the forest,' Arlo's voice was barely audible. 'They might leave us alone if we can prove we aren't going to hurt them or take their land.'

'Why would we want this land?' Sky replied quietly. 'When will they leave us alone?'

Christian's breaths were shallow. Between the thick ridged trunks of trees and crooked silhouettes of low hanging branches, he searched for a pair of gleaming eyes. He listened intently for another ear-piercing shriek. Fireflies obediently followed them, unafraid. Sky wandered only a few steps ahead of him, weaving between trunks and stepping over logs, mirroring Arlo's movements.

There came another piercing cry and it sounded closer this time. Too close. Christian reached for Sky, who'd released a shriek of her own. She clapped her hands over her mouth, her eyes focused on something in the tree. His whole body trembling, Christian followed her gaze until he met another set of eyes, glowing red. Three fireflies drifted upwards and past the tree, illuminating the sight he feared. This creature had a small round head and a scrawny body, its skin like that of a beetle; a mixture of iridescent green and black. It had two sets of claws which clung to the branch and when its mouth opened to let out a screech, Christian caught sight of what looked like exceptionally sharp teeth: fangs. Its tongue was black.

Sky screamed and Arlo grabbed her arm, yanking her forward and away from Christian.

'We'd better run!' he cried.

Christian ran as fast as the ground allowed him to, scrambling over and under fallen trees while four screeching creatures pursued him. He kept looking back while fear pushed him forward. Sky was gasping for breath but she didn't slow down. Arlo was still ahead, calling at them to keep going. *But where are we going?* Christian

Chapter Twenty-Two

wanted to shout. He'd lost all sense of direction the moment he'd entered this forest.

The fireflies scattered and Christian was running blind with his arms outstretched.

'Come back! Sky?'

'Christian!'

The Malen cried. Christian knocked into an overhanging branch and it scraped against his arm as he tried to lift it over his head. No matter how many times he blinked, his vision swam with the dark as he stumbled along. A nervous sweat prickled the back of his neck.

Something latched onto his arm and he yelped.

'It's me!' said Sky, and Christian took her hand in his and gripped it tight.

'We must-' another screech and the whooshing sound of wings interrupted him, 'keep going.'

The Malens' cries were unrelenting and they swooped down, their claws nipping at Christian's wings. He tried batting them away to no avail.

'We are harmless!' he said loudly in hope that they would understand.

They didn't.

Arlo was long gone. For a while, in between his own breaths, Christian's ears were filled with high pitched shrieks and the snap and crack of breaking twigs under foot.

~

'We've been,' Sky said between breaths, 'running for ages and, I don't know where we're going.'

Christian swallowed hard. 'I know. They'll have to give up soon.' Abruptly Sky's hand ripped out of his and he heard her tumble onto the mossy ground.

Christian fumbled through the darkness until he reached her.

He helped her up off the ground and they started off again, beating their way through the hanging branches that obstructed their path. A number of fireflies returned to guide them, but

Christian only glared into the darkness ahead, purposefully ignorant. They were no help if they came and went, and it was too late to lead them for they were already lost.

'What if we-' Sky began, but screamed when a Malen swooped for her, and then Christian. He threw his free arm up angrily at it.

'Leave us alone!'

There were beady red eyes everywhere, watching. The screeches reverberated in Christian's ears, tormenting him.

'What if we hide in a log or something?' said Sky.

'Good idea,' Christian said, seeking one out. He should have thought of that. Eventually he found one big enough for them to crawl into and the fireflies hovered by, radiating their green light. Sky scrambled in one side and Christian the other. The log crushed against his wings but he'd rather a little discomfort than to continue being attacked by Malen. Though there was light outside of the log, it didn't quite reach inside. Christian's hands and knees were covered in damp moss and the scoured wood felt rough against his wings. The Malen screeches were already becoming distant. Sky was hunched forward on her knees, and her black hair fell like curtains hiding half of her face. She was shaking.

Cocooned in the log, Christian resisted the urge to slump down and surrender to the ache in his muscles, as the burn of adrenalin began to wear off.

'We lost Arlo,' Sky said after a while.

'It doesn't matter. We can do without the Zanian. Look where we've ended up!'

'I guess. We can also do without these horrible, annoying Malen creatures.'

Christian cocked his head to listen. 'I think they've finally left us alone.'

Sky punched the log with a balled fist. 'They might come after us again.'

'They might not,' he muttered, but he didn't believe it and clearly neither did Sky when she grunted a laugh.

Slowly they eased out of the log and Christian put a finger to his lips, ushering Sky over. He wanted to make sure they stayed

Chapter Twenty-Two

close.

The fireflies danced around aimlessly. Christian dared to close his eyes. He needed to think.

'Which way do you reckon?' said Sky.

They should not have given in to that Zanian so easily.

'I don't know. I'm going with my instincts in this case.'

Sky didn't argue with him and they started walking.

They walked an uneven path of twigs and soggy leaves. Christian regularly checked over his shoulder and above him for signs of the Malen, but for the time being they'd retreated to the trees, watching with their sinister eyes.

'I think I can see a way out,' said Sky.

Christian squinted. 'I can too.' His heartbeat quickened. 'Come on.'

They ran, clambering over and under fallen trees, but they had a focus and nothing was going to stop Christian from reaching that pool of dim light, his and Sky's way out.

Out of nowhere an image flashed into his mind and Christian caught onto the notion that he'd been here before. He'd been running through a forest alongside another, feeling panic and at the same time elation, for the end was in sight.

His eyebrows pulled together in confusion. He threw a half glance at Sky, who was running beside him with her full attention on the way ahead.

This is when I take her hand. This is when we burst into the sunlight...

But he couldn't.

They battled with more branches and beneath Christian's feet the ground turned gritty, like sand. Finally he was out and he heard Sky's sharp intake of breath. They stood at the edge of the Dark Forest and Christian found himself staring at hills of sand.

The Arids.

Christian backtracked. 'This is bad.'

The undulating sand dunes were silhouetted against a dawn horizon. The sun had begun its rise, sending clouds like wisps of fire into a violet sky. Anywhere else it would have been beautiful. Here it was frightening.

'We do not want to be here.'

'I can't go back into that forest, Christian,' said Sky. 'I can't.'

He couldn't tear his eyes away from the view, and in his mind rogue færies were stalking the dunes, driven wild by the barrenness of this place.

'We're in the place of exile,' Christian said, scanning the horizon. He'd never seen it with his own eyes, only heard stories. Somewhere in the Arids stood an ancient tree, the dead heart of this land but a home to its inhabitants. It had become a sacred place amidst a desert.

'You cannot expect me to go back into that forest,' Sky said crossly.

A branch snapped, and Christian turned to see Arlo emerge out of breath from the opening, his hair dishevelled.

'We should be at the marshlands, not the Arids,' he said, stepping onto the sand. 'This is not good at all.'

Christian didn't have the patience.

'This is your fault!'

Arlo had the nerve to look surprised. 'I didn't realise the Malen were going to attack us.'

'How could you not realise that? I thought you knew these lands.'

If Sky hadn't stepped forward Christian would have throttled him.

'This isn't helping!' she exclaimed, putting herself between Christian and the Zanian. 'We are going to trail the outskirts of the forest so we aren't in it, that way avoiding the Arids. It's a win-win situation. Which way are the marshlands from here?'

Arlo shrugged, and then pointed right, 'to the east,' he said.

Sky let out a sigh. 'Then that is where we're going.'

Christian couldn't be bothered to argue. He was the one who had lost the map and he wasn't confident enough to lead. His lip curled with resentment. A prince who couldn't even lead three færies out of danger, how could he ever lead an army or rule a realm?

Arlo led the way, with Christian at the back of the line. As he'd refused Dill's protection he felt a duty to keep an eye on the land behind him as the guard would have done. Christian's boots sunk

Chapter Twenty-Two

into the sand as he walked, and with each step the knot of anxiety within him worked loose, little by little. The Malen inhabited the deep forest and they could reach neither Sky nor himself, but his hope was like a flame against the wind for he sensed this freedom wouldn't last.

Rubbing the dust from his eyelashes Christian glanced behind, only to see two færies in plain, faded clothes treading over a dune in their direction. He narrowed his eyes. The dawn light made it difficult to work out whether or not they had functioning wings. If he could see the tips it meant they were just færies, like him. If the wings were shrivelled and wasted to the point they had no use, it meant they were rogues. Over time, sand and sun would cause the veins to dry and contract, and the wings' muscles ceased to work. Christian remembered these facts from a book his father had read to him.

The two færies burst into a run, and the rags around their faces flailed in the wind.

'Rogues,' he breathed, then with more urgency: 'Rogues!' Simultaneously Sky and Arlo whirled round to face him.

'What?' Sky cried.

'Let's not hang around. We should run,' said Arlo, looking over Christian's shoulder.

Christian had to be quick. 'We need to go back into the forest.' Throwing one last glance behind him it was clear these rogues had only one agenda, and they were catching up fast.

Sky screwed her eyes shut and her wings shot open, taking Christian by surprise. When he spoke, grit crunched between his teeth. 'No, no flying yet. We need to be inconspicuous. Follow me.' The urgency burned in his veins and he seized Sky's hand. Without looking back and without a single concern for Arlo, he pushed back through the undergrowth.

Chapter Twenty-Three

This was never going to be easy. Sky knew that. As Christian led her back into the dark she fought hard against the tears that smarted in her eyes, terror seizing the air in her lungs. Even if she'd wanted to scream, she couldn't have mustered a sound.

This was worse than sitting ten exams, worse than losing her pet chinchilla and it was worse than having a nightmare because this was reality. She was being chased by rogue færies back into a forest filled with creatures that only *belonged* in nightmares. Distracted by these thoughts Sky would have ploughed into a tree had Christian not pulled her sideways. She squeezed the tears out of her eyes and tried to shake herself out of this state, focusing on moving her legs and moving them quickly. The fireflies were frantic.

Hearing the Malen screech from the tree tops caused a chill through her bones.

'Be strong. Don't be a wimp,' Sky told herself, the cool atmosphere caressing her skin like the touch of a ghost.

She slipped over a bed of dead leaves, and more than once collided with hanging branches. All the while her hand was locked tightly in Christian's.

'I'm going this way!' Arlo's voice bounced off the trees and Sky couldn't determine its direction.

'All that's going to do is draw attention to us,' said Christian under his breath. 'Here,' he led her into the deep shadows behind a tree trunk. Sky covered her mouth and tried to control her breathing, peering round the trunk. Christian was quick to

Chapter Twenty-Three

pull her back.

'What are we going to do?' she whispered.

'We wait.'

'What if we fail?' she couldn't help but ask. They hadn't yet overcome their first obstacle and time was getting away. Sky shivered and looked up at the darkness that seemed to her to be edging closer, slowly falling down. It gave her the sensation of something pressing on her shoulders, as if the dark was a physical thing. She blew warm breath softly into her hands and looked at Christian, just able to work out his firm features as a firefly drifted past, casting them in an emerald hue. It irradiated the worry in his eyes and how his mouth was slightly open as he looked steadily around, inspecting the trees.

Christian must not have heard. For a moment Sky wished he would wrap his arms around her, protecting her from what lurked in the shadows. She leaned against the trunk, her stomach rolling over like a boat at sea. How long were they supposed to stay here?

She could treat it like a game as a way to distance herself from reality. *I've got ten lives. Why should I worry about being stuck here, in the eerie Dark Forest? This is only the first level...*

The leaves whispered. Sky held her breath. Christian's presence was the only thing that kept her from falling into hysteria. They were in this together.

They just had to make it out of this place together.

'I can't hear them,' Christian murmured.

'Me neither.'

Silence.

Out of nowhere sprung a big burly shape, causing Christian to exclaim aloud. Sky was too shocked to scream and it was as if she'd jumped out of her own skin.

It definitely wasn't Arlo.

Without needing to be told Sky ducked under the rogue's arm and careened further into the forest, but Christian didn't follow. Soon enough she knew why, hearing him yell out 'let me go!' in a voice that resonated fear. They had him. Sky turned around, only to be forced backwards by the other tall, steel-boned rogue, who managed to lift her up by putting his rough hands around her neck. Sky flailed, struggling against the færies' vice-like grip. She was on her tip toes. Blood pulsed in her temples and the edges of her vision turned to glitter.

'Get – off!' she wheezed, trying to prise his fingers from her skin. She kicked forward but hardly touched him. Angry and desperate, Sky tried to untangle herself but the rogue thrust her against a tree, all the while his growling laughter could be heard through the cloth that disguised his face.

Sky heard Christian yelling and then she saw him, highlighted by the hovering fireflies that had remarkably stayed put, as he ran towards her. In a flash he was on the rogue's back, dragging him backwards. Sky slumped to the ground, her lungs expanding painfully. Her throat burned. She had to get up. *Get. Up.*

'Go on!' she heard Christian say in a strained voice. 'Keep moving! I will follow.'

Slowly the glittery stars at the edges of her vision dissolved into the dark. She scrambled up. If she tried to intercede it would only makes things worse, if that was even possible. Where on earth was Arlo?

'I'm going straight ahead, west facing! Find me!' she cried hoarsely, half hoping the exiled færies would tear themselves away from Christian and pursue her, seeing as it was her fault they wound up being chased by them in the first place. She could only hope he would be okay. He had to be. With that, Sky ran.

The smell of crushed leaves and dank earth lingered in the air as she went; it filled her nose. She slowed for only a moment to catch her breath and her step faltered, where the ground fell into what looked like a pit. Sky squinted. It was hard to tell with the light from a solitary firefly.

Something latched onto her ankle and she fell with a bump onto the ground, too stunned to scream. Whatever had a hold of her was intent on dragging her down into the pit and realisation struck like a slap across the face.

Gritting her teeth Sky caught onto a dry root. It was strong enough to stop her from being dragged down further, but she could still feel the strain of being pulled. Keeping a firm grip, Sky attempted to yank herself up. The rough root dug into the

Chapter Twenty-Three

palms of her hands. Casting a quick glance over her shoulder she let out a scream.

Round yellow eyes stared back at her. The fingers that were wrapped around Sky's ankles were akin to the twisted root she held onto.

'*Please...*' a whispery voice came from the shadows.

'Get away from me!'

'*Help.*'

'I'm the one who needs help,' Sky said, trying to heave herself up.

'*Help,*' the voice droned sadly. '*We are the Wise Ones...*' another voice whispered in the same sombre, despairing tone.

'You are the Wise Ones – the Elana?'

The grip on her ankles weakened.

'You are the Elana,' Sky said. How had they ended up here? At this rate she would be joining them. Her arm muscles ached. Soon she would have to let go, and the thought sent a burst of adrenalin through her. With new found strength Sky reached for another root, praying it wouldn't give, and managed to haul herself up little by little like she was climbing vertical monkey bars. The rough roots chafed her palms but she didn't care.

'*Let us show you.*'

'No I don't want to see, please let me go.' But they pulled her down so fast the roots tore from her grasp and she fell helplessly into the abyss.

Sky squeezed her eyes shut, hearing her own screams loud in her ears.

She went back to the day she bumped into Elle. In her imagination she did not pick up the necklace, she turned away. At home she'd have sat with her parents and watched a film with a bowl of macaroni cheese on her lap, cinnamon scented candles glowing on the mantelpiece.

Opening her eyes, Sky's whole body jumped in a spasm of shock. She was no longer falling, but nor was she dead. The eyes were all she could see.

'*Let us show you,*' the voice drifted towards her; a soulless echo.

In a blink the landscape changed and she was standing in a vast plain, where everything was the colour of wet sand. The glowing sun sat low on the horizon. For a moment Sky felt the world fade as nausea rolled over her. She took a deep breath and steadied herself.

No longer was she alone. Before her stood a færie dressed in a full length robe, a weathered rope tied around the waist. Sky could almost feel his gaze grazing across her skin as he took her in with knowing eyes. His face was lined with wrinkles, and framed by wisps of grey hair. Sky struggled to put the broken, eerie voice to the færie standing before her.

There was only one question she could ask.

'Where am I?'

'This is the Kingdom, how it was and how it will be,' he said in a voice distant and contemplative. If she could place him anywhere it would have been at the chapel in her school, for he had the air and temperament of a priest. He cast his arm out in a sweeping gesture before clasping his hands together, a sad smile on his lips. The sadness reflected in his eyes.

Sky was learning to take things as they appeared. She'd never be able to answer the questions that flooded her mind, about this world she'd been thrown into and how færies could even exist. It was a long list and thinking about it for too long threatened her sanity.

The færie was then accompanied by two others dressed similarly, and they stood behind him in silence with their heads bowed.

'A long, long time ago us and Humans lived and worked together. We helped each other survive, but over time they grew stronger and soon stopped believing in magic, and in us. We could no longer stand beside them and they threatened us with war. Krazon and Bælor searched the lands for the largest emerald they could find, for emerald stone is most precious. The twelve of us poured our magic into its core, and using its power we fled Human earth, creating an alternate dimension.

'We knew we needed to keep the Emerald safe and out of reach because in the wrong hands, it can be used to destroy the world as it was created.'

Chapter Twenty-Three

Sky remained still, digging her heels into the dusty ground.

'Armænon chipped off a tiny shard of the stone and attached it to a chain of pure gold. I should have been more wary of him. He wanted the power for himself, though I admit he wasn't alone. I wanted it too. When the portal was created the necklace was carelessly lost – it remained in the world of Humans which meant the portal could never be closed completely. We banished Armænon and twelve Elana became eleven.'

'Time passed and the Færie Kingdom grew. Not all færies were kind. Some rebelled and wanted things done differently so we created divides – four separate realms. We tried to stay in control but we were separated ourselves, you see. The Elana had agreed to disperse, but we hadn't anticipated Zania's growth and that we would have less power apart. In the end we gave the Emerald to Krazonia which had the kind, compassionate færies. We believed it would be safe there. The truth is we became cowardly, confining ourselves to hidden places amongst caves, forests and mountains. We knew that someday, somebody would come along and it would be their reason for living…to gain power from it, to own it. It seems that time has come.'

'What have I got to do with anything?' Sky asked.

'You have been chosen to destroy it.'

'Destroy it?' she shrieked. 'But after everything that you've told me, surely that is the worst thing? If you used it to create this world then what will happen to Krazonia, Zania…'

'We are connected to the stone but we no longer control its power, therefore I do not know. What I do know is that the time has come when something must be done. Over the years our senses have weakened and although I believe the Kingdom will remain along with its magic, I cannot be sure.'

'You're supposed to be the most powerful færies on earth. You created this place with your magic. What the heck do you mean when you say you "cannot be sure"?' Sky'd had quite enough. 'There was another human, like me, who came to Krazonia with a task. In the end she ran away leaving the Krazonian princess with a curse thanks to you guys. What if I choose to run away now?'

The færie shook his head.

'Where will you go?' His stare seemed to penetrate her soul. 'You are the one.'

Sky, her knees trembling, pointed at herself. 'How? How am I the one?'

'You've already proven that you are. One thing you must know is that we may be hiding, but we know what happens in the world. Our senses may be weak, but deep down the magic is still within us.'

Sky's thoughts became tangled as she tried to work out his riddles. She rubbed her face tiredly. 'Then why won't you stop Tæ yourselves?'

'It's too late for us. You are a Human and hold a different power, one that is immune to the stone. *You* must be the one to break it.'

Sky touched the necklace, hidden by the dress' neckline. There was something else she had to know. 'If I succeed, will I be able to get back home?'

The Elana nodded. 'Now you must go.'

The world around her began to evaporate.

'I'm not done! Wait, which one are you?' Sky called out as the ground dropped from beneath her. The færie had disappeared. Covering her face with her arms she allowed gravity to push her upwards like a blast from a volcano. She just caught his whisper, *'Zian.'*

She was now on solid ground, laying in the darkness of the forest. Blowing the hair out of her face she leaned forward to peer down into the abyss.

'Zian, I need to find Christian. The Prince of Krazonia, he is here and I need to find him. Please,' she pleaded, only half aware of the stinging pain in her hands as she clutched the earth.

The eyes looked at her again, and there was a moment of silence.

'I can't do this without him.'

A ray of sunlight burst through the tree tops, highlighting a patch of ground a few yards away. Mouth agape, she stared as the scene unfolded before her eyes like something heavenly. Another beam of light, and then another, creating a path.

Chapter Twenty-Three

And there he was, a stunned figure beneath the rays. Christian's chest heaved as he looked around with wide eyes. He eased himself up as Sky made her way to him, swamped with relief.

For a while he stared up at the light spilling through the trees.

'Sky?' he drew her name from his lips slowly. 'How am I here? There are lights coming through the trees,' he stated, deadpan.

'The Elana brought you,' Sky said. 'As a matter of fact I just spoke to them, well, one of them.'

Christian simply stared at her, eyebrows raised. His cheek was home to a fresh cut, and a bruise was forming above his eyebrow.

Sky took a shaky breath, wanting to touch the wounds she felt responsible for. 'We've got to follow those beams of light. They should lead us in the right direction.'

Sky started off and soon the two of them were treading the path of light. 'What happened?' asked Christian.

'I think you should go first.'

'Well, I managed to get away from the rogues. They did pursue me but I sense they became bored, and so left me alone. They must have just wanted to have some fun with us,' he said uneasily.

'Well they clearly had some fun at your expense,' Sky said, overcome with guilt. To think of what could have happened, had the rogues decided they would no longer play nice, filled her with horror.

'I'm so sorry,' she said, quick to brush away a single tear that had escaped. 'I shouldn't have left you. It was stupid and cowardly.'

'No. I'd rather that than for you to have been hurt,' Christian said, his gaze fixed on the ground. 'I'm fine, Sky,' he added, his tone serious. 'What happened back there?'

Sky gave herself a mental shake.

'I didn't get all that far when I was dragged down a hole by the Elana. They told me I have to destroy the Emerald before Tæ uses its powers to take over the kingdom, potentially wrecking it in the process.'

Perhaps that had been a bit too "to the point".

'Destroy it?' Christian said aghast.

'Zian told me-'

'Zian as in…'

'One of the Elana,' Sky said carefully and Christian lowered his head, releasing a quiet, humourless laugh into his chest.

'I think from this day I will hold judgement on everything. I've read about the Elana, even dared myself to seek them out in Bluewater, for there are some there,' he mused. 'And you speak to them – the Wise Ones who haven't shown their faces for so many years. But can we trust them? They are telling you to destroy the stone that Krazonia has protected for such a long time, the stone that created this world.'

The Malen's ear-piercing screech resonated through Sky like fingernails on a blackboard, making her wince.

'They must know better than anyone,' she said. Afterwards a strange silence fell upon the forest. Time stopped. Now and then Sky snapped a branch with her boot, but it was mostly silent and Christian wasn't speaking. She allowed herself to think, skimming the thoughts at the surface of her mind.

So the responsibility was on her, sixteen year old Sky Francis, to change the future of a kingdom. She'd been entrusted with this task not knowing whether she would succeed, or fail miserably. Sky had to believe in the former.

When she finally made it home, what state would she be in?

Eventually they emerged into a dull world of marshlands; the sun was a glowing white orb shrouded in grey cloud, nothing like the fiery sunrise Sky had witnessed by the Arids. It felt like a mild February morning. If only the sun would break through, Sky thought, she might feel more of its warmth. Consciously she pulled the cloak around her shoulders.

Christian expanded his wings, scanning the land. Sky took a second to inspect her own situation. Her dress was laughable; ripped at the hem, specked with mud and dirt. The boots on her feet were dirty and since when was her ankle bleeding? Sky leaned forward. The cut wasn't deep and the blood had dried, but now she was aware of it, it hurt. In fact so did her hands, and her throat.

As if he could hear her thoughts Christian glanced at her, his forehead creased with concern.

The bruise above his left eye was turning purple and his hair

Chapter Twenty-Three

was a tangled mess.

Sky straightened up. 'So where do we go from here?'

Across the dreary landscape weeds sprouted from the earth, and kissed edges of murky puddles that reflected the bleak sky above. She had no idea which way led to the heartland of Zania.

'Is this Zanian territory by any chance?'

'Yes,' said Christian. 'You could say the forest acts as a barrier between our realms. Thankfully we are still way out, not yet near civilisation. We should keep west.'

Zanian lands. Sky looked over her shoulder to the Dark Forest, the vast, crooked trees standing silent and sinister. She felt the shadows drawing her back in. With a shiver Sky averted her gaze to Christian who was surveying the horizon, deep in thought.

Sky cleared her throat. 'I think I'd feel better if we flew for a while. Flying is faster than running in case, you know...' She hesitated, tuning into the sound of footsteps. She spun round to see Arlo and was unable to find words to greet him. She could picture Christian behind her with a face like Hades.

'There you are,' Arlo said, settling his pale-eyed gaze on Sky. She stared back at him, dumbfounded. 'I'm glad I found you both. Are you alright?' he said.

Christian jabbed a finger at his lean chest.

'Don't act as if you really care for an answer to that question. You led us into the forest and would you look what happened there? In a short amount of time you have deserted us twice. It's a miracle me and Sky found each other and to be honest I'm shocked that you even have the nerve to approach us,' Christian barked at him. 'What are your motives?'

Arlo frowned, delicately pushing Christian's hand away.

'Nothing is in it for me. You say I've twice deserted you, but given the circumstances it has been difficult to stay together. I have no motives. I'm an outlaw with nothing but my knowledge to give. I want to help.'

Sky was torn between what to say and what to think. It boiled down to whether Christian was going to trust him. She would take a backseat. Arlo clasped his hands behind his back, a small smile on his lips as if he already knew the prince's answer. A frustrated

Christian, who was walking back and forth lost in thought, didn't notice. For the meantime Sky would keep her concerns to herself.

'We will be going without you,' Christian said suddenly. 'I think I can remember the way.' He signalled to Sky with a tilt of the head. 'We'll be fine. Neither Sky nor myself had anticipated having a helper anyway.'

'Do you know the route to the caves?'

'Why don't you tell me?'

'No. We are in dangerous territory, you should let me lead. Besides I might come in handy, if we happen to cross paths with any other.'

Sky pursed her lips, surprised by Arlo's boldness. He seemed to have a calm nature and spoke with such assertion, yet there was an underlying threat in the tone of his voice. She couldn't work him out at all.

Christian threw a look to the heavens, his jaw clenched.

His dark eyes flashed to Sky, and then to Arlo.

'These are unique circumstances. Fate seems to have thrown us together so as I said before, we'll have to use the resources available,' he said pointedly.

Arlo shrugged, unperturbed. 'I understand.'

'Well then. Let's fly.'

The clouds hung heavy and dull over the marshlands. Little birds pecked at the ground, paying no attention to the færies that flew past them.

'Does anyone know what time it is?' Sky asked.

'Ask the expert,' Christian muttered and only a second later Sky had her answer.

'It is late morning, almost noon,' Arlo said. 'The sun has not yet reached its highest point. We should reach the Frazian plain by dusk,' he lowered his voice, 'and what an adventure that will be.'

Had he intended to sound so malicious? Sky touched the necklace without thinking and in the same moment Arlo looked over his shoulder. She quickly moved her hand to fiddle with the cloak instead.

'I regret to say that I think there is a storm brewing,' said Arlo,

Chapter Twenty-Three

and Sky noted the dark clouds expanding across the horizon.
'Great.'
'Yes,' Arlo continued, revealing a crooked smile. 'It's going to rain soon.'

Chapter Twenty-Four

Christian stared coldly at the back of Arlo's head. Hateful thoughts lingered at the edges of his mind, of things he could do and say that would make him feel better, but that would not help the situation. It shocked him, how a Zanian could be so audacious yet so naïve. Then again he hadn't come across many Zanians in his eighteen years.

Christian touched the bruise above his left eye. It ached.

He thought about what good could possibly come from this, and about the future. One day he would be king. Tæ would be gone and the stone would be safe. He'd tell his child or children about his adventures as a young prince. Their little wings would flicker with excitement as he explained the courage of him and a girl named Sky Francis as they had made their way through the Dark Realm.

The daydream ended and Christian blinked hard, returning to the present where he was surrounded by grey light and a dismal landscape; the rocky ground under his feet had been worn smooth by wind and time.

Arlo led him and Sky along an uneven path that curved left and sloped downwards. He recalled the map in his mind, picturing the obscure sketches of the Dark Forest, marshlands, a village to the east and one to the north. The north village belonged to Frazians, a small population of Zanians that preferred life on the outskirts away from the bustle of Zania's main town. They took the village name and gave it to themselves and so despite their Zanian blood, they became 'Frazians.' It was a strange comfort to Christian that he could remember these things, for they were

Chapter Twenty-Four

what his father had taught him.

Christian puffed the air out through his lips. Presumably Arlo would continue steering them in the direction of the valley and they would fly down, passing over the plain to remain unseen. A part of him felt weak for giving in, but he did not want his pride getting in the way of an opportunity to reach Tæ's palace quicker. He would however remain wary of Arlo. He would never be able to trust a Zanian.

Out of nowhere Christian was struck by a searing pain through his wings. He made a quick haphazard landing, stumbling slightly. The pain grew and it felt as though someone was scoring his veins with a knife, drawing them out to the tips. He squeezed his eyes shut, and when he opened them again he was on his hands and knees, his whole body quivering.

He clenched his teeth as the knife tore up his spine, momentarily immobilising him. His wings contracted, and he felt something grip them where they met his spine and there was a hot, biting pain that pinched the muscles in his back and shoulders. His stomach lurched. The pain began to ebb away and he was left with the taste of bile in his mouth. Hanging his head, Christian tried to catch his breath. He heard the scrape of tiny stones under foot as someone got up from the ground but he couldn't bring himself to move just yet.

'What was that all about?' said Sky, sounding rattled. 'I – Christian..?'

'I presume we all felt that horrific pain in our wings,' Arlo said weakly.

Christian managed to push himself up off the ground. His wings were taut and the tips still tingled. They would not open on their own accord, nor would they open under his control. Sky frowned and craned her neck to inspect her own and Arlo was watching her intently. She managed to stretch her wings, albeit with difficulty, as if she were peeling them apart.

Realisation came to Christian like a knock on the head. This was Tæ's doing. She was using the Emerald, but how had she mastered it so quickly?

She wouldn't know about Sky, who by the looks of it was

insusceptible to the stone's powers. A look of surprise passed over Arlo's features when Sky's wings stretched open and his pale eyes lingered on her for a moment too long.

'How can I..?' Sky began.

'May I speak with you quickly?' Christian said, throwing Arlo a threatening glare when he tried to follow. Holding Sky's elbow he led her far enough away that they were out of earshot.

Christian kept his voice low. 'Has Arlo seen the necklace?'

Sky shook her head. 'No, at least I don't think so,' she was hesitant. 'He hasn't said anything about it.'

'This is Tæ's doing.'

'I thought so. Can you move your wings at all?'

Christian tried once more, but they were locked. 'They're completely useless. I think Arlo has the same problem but you, Sky...you must be immune to the stone's powers.' It hadn't occurred to him that due to her origin she wouldn't feel the Emerald's effects in the same way as any other færie. 'This could work in our favour,' he said quietly.

She inched a little closer to him. 'Zian told me I was immune because I'm from the human world, and that I'm the "chosen one", hence why I'm the one who has to break the damn thing, if we ever get there.'

Christian's heart lurched. 'I fear what will happen when you do, but who am I to go against the words of the Elana?'

'Do you think Arlo is suspicious of anything? He hasn't even asked why we're going to Zania.'

Christian purposely did not look at him. 'I'm not sure. I don't quite understand the Zanian, but it isn't about understanding. We just need his guidance, all the while keeping our distance,' he paused, 'you must not let him see the necklace.'

'Give me some credit, Christian, please,' Sky said. 'I'm not an idiot. Anyway, what are we going to tell him? He can probably tell he's the subject of our conversation.'

'Don't worry, I will speak to him.'

Chapter Twenty-Four

Christian walked alongside Arlo, aware of Sky trailing a few steps behind, pretending not to listen.

'Arlo, do you know why our wings are paralysed?' he asked, having decided to give away part of the truth, not all, but enough to tempt Arlo to spill some truths of his own.

'I,' he tilted his head, 'I'm not sure. Whatever the reason, it is very frustrating. I suppose it has something to do with the Zanian queen?' he said before pursing his lips. 'Am I right?'

'Yes. You should know that Krazonia's field festival was ambushed yesterday evening, and my mother,' Christian said at length, 'was taken.' The words were accompanied by an ache that resonated from his chest. 'So was the Emerald.'

Arlo's mouth made a little 'o'. 'The stone that created our world, which was kept under guard in Krazonia? Tæ Asrai has the Emerald and your mother?'

Christian drew breath. 'Yes. I believe Tæ is using the stone's power against us now.'

Arlo's eyes narrowed as if he'd spied something in the distance. 'Sky's wings seem to work.'

Christian had half expected this. 'I have no idea what that's about,' he said, feigning uneasiness. He rubbed the back of his neck. 'I just asked her. But it's happened, so we must deal with it.'

'So you're going to Zania to rescue your mother?'

The question threw Christian. Arlo had gone from one subject to another so seamlessly that it took a moment to find an answer.

'Um, yes, that's the plan,' he said as he shifted his gaze to what lay ahead. 'Have you any family?'

'I have no parents, only a sister and she lives in Zania's main town. We,' the words sounded painful to speak aloud. 'Grace and I do not speak. We haven't for some time.'

The path became gritty underfoot and it led Christian down until he stood on the precipice of a valley, where a low mist hung in the air. Although there was no breeze he felt a chill in his bones. The far side of the valley was indistinguishable through the mist and when Christian glanced down, his heart sank. How much easier it would have been to fly.

Tæ had hindered the chances of that being possible.

Well, he would have to hinder Tæ's chances of living then, wouldn't he? Christian folded his arms tightly across his chest, allowing for just one moment the thoughts he harboured, to surface. For one moment he revelled in the prospect of the Zanian queen's non-existence. There could never be peace while she flew this earth.

Arlo's voice sliced through his thoughts. 'When I told my sister Grace about my plans to quit being the queen's messenger, she didn't like it. There was nothing I could do,' Arlo said miserably. Then he perked up and smiled, pointing at the valley. 'Now we just have to get down without wings, which could be interesting couldn't it?' Christian could only stare back at him, puzzled by his sudden change in temperament. Either discussing his sister was too much, or there were two versions of Arlo and he was capable of switching between the two in the blink of an eye.

Sky approached, looking paler than usual. 'Is there no other way?'

Arlo frowned. 'Your wings seem to work, why don't you just fly?'

'No-no,' she stammered before taking a deep breath. 'There isn't any point in me flying down alone when I'll still have to wait for you guys. Also I can't trust these things on my back. They still feel stiff and I don't particularly want to fall to my doom.'

'We'll follow the path,' Christian said. 'With caution,' he added, eyeing what he had identified as the path; a coarse trail with a wall of nettles on one side and an unpleasant drop on the other. But there was enough room to walk – they would just have to take extra care.

Christian allowed Sky to walk ahead, and Arlo began to lead them with tentative steps.

In the surrounding quiet his thoughts became coherent streams flowing through his mind. Christian's could see his sister's face: her grey eyes like flints, her jaw set. She had father's determination and stoicism, and with the General and Dill at her side had the support she needed. It was hard to believe a battle was imminent and all because of one ruthless, vengeful queen. Tæ's want for power was insatiable.

Chapter Twenty-Four

His mother had been ruthless too, to kill the Zanian king. Christian wanted to know why. He *needed* to know, otherwise his relationship with Anya would be permanently altered and he didn't want that. He loved his mother.

Forgiveness was another matter.

He was brought swiftly round by the sensation that he was falling. Too shocked to yell out, Christian couldn't stop his legs from giving way beneath him and he tumbled. Fear struck him like a bolt of lightning and he struggled to get his arms to work. *Don't fall!* His conscience shouted as he dug his fingers into the earth.

He looked up to see Sky's panic stricken face, and her lips moving as if she was speaking yet there was no sound. He couldn't hear over the thump-thump of his heart in his ears as panic flooded his senses.

The hum in his ears faded and he could hear his feet scuffing against the ground, his fast breaths, and Sky saying his name with both arms outstretched. Taking a chance Christian heaved himself up to grab her hand, and he would have pulled her down with him had Arlo not interceded. He leaped over, grabbing a hold of Christian's left arm in a surprisingly tight grip.

'Sky, hold onto his other arm!'

Christian heart beat wildly in his chest and he wrapped his fingers around Arlo's forearm. With help from Sky, Arlo heaved him up and Christian was back on solid ground. He shut his eyes, waiting for the dizziness to pass.

Arlo shook his head. 'You were the one to say we go with caution,' he said and turned around, continuing along the path. Christian watched him walk away, too shocked to speak.

Sky stood there, open mouthed.

Christian acted on impulse and grabbed her hand. 'Thank you,' he said. 'I wasn't thinking-' he paused, 'I was thinking, that was the problem. I wasn't concentrating.'

Sky squeezed his hand and attempted to smile. 'It's fine. You didn't die.'

They continued along the path in silence and Christian kept his thoughts in line, forbidding them to drift onto anything other than the task at hand. The trail zigzagged down, through patches of mist.

By the time he touched flat ground his calf muscles were burning. Christian relaxed his shoulders and tried to spread his wings once more, to no avail. They remained rigid and inactive. Sky had leant forward to catch her breath, as if she'd been holding it the whole time. Arlo looked around, his face drawn in an expression of deep thought.

Christian rubbed his legs with one hand, propping himself up with the other against the rocky wall. Ivy weaved in and out of the cracks; small dark leaves hung lifelessly and Christian realised he'd not yet seen a single flower or a butterfly. Zania truly was a Dark Realm comprised of stone and dust. The villages and towns had to be different. Christian sighed to himself. How could any place in the kingdom end up this way?

'We're at the edge of the plain,' said Arlo. 'Not far now.'

Christian nodded. Sky half-heartedly threw a fist into the air, her face solemn.

'Let's go,' she said, starting off ahead of him and Arlo.

It was a silly question to ask under the circumstances but Christian couldn't help it.

'What's wrong?' he met Sky's swift pace with a determined stride of his own.

'Everything.'

'Okay, allow me to rephrase it. What is wrong with you?' It must have sounded better in his head because Sky afforded him a questioning stare.

'Me?' she hurled the word at him. 'I just keep thinking about what the Elana said to me, how I'm supposed to be the "right one".' She began to count on her fingers, 'the fact that all of the responsibility is on me, how they told me to destroy-'

'Will you calm down?' Christian said, biting back the anger. He didn't want Sky shouting for the world, well, for Arlo to hear. 'Now is not the time to be saying these things.'

'You asked me what's wrong,' she said.

That was true. 'You could at least lower your tone.'

She scowled. Aggression didn't suit her soft features.

Chapter Twenty-Four

'I'm annoyed, okay? It's just suddenly come over me. I feel annoyed.'

'Yes, I can see that Sky.'

This conversation was going nowhere. Christian settled into a broody silence, fixing his eyes ahead of him. Mist lingered in the air above and he wished he could wrap himself up in it and float away, but the parched ground remained solid beneath his feet.

After a while Arlo scuttled past. 'You will see how the valley has started to change shape,' he said, speaking like an enthusiastic tour guide, but this wasn't the flourishing Ever-growing forest from home, Christian thought begrudgingly.

The valley walls had widened, curving outwards, and to Christian it was as if he were walking through the depths of a huge bowl.

'You may not have noticed the ground beneath you has changed,' Arlo added.

Hairline cracks spread like veins along the ground and Christian suppressed the urge to curse Tæ's name.

'I presume this is a bad thing?' he asked instead through gritted teeth.

'Yes unfortunately,' as Arlo said those two words the ground shifted. It was only slight, but Christian felt it the movement. He swayed a little.

'Ah.' said Sky quietly, glancing down at her feet.

'Will you not fly?' His words came out sharp, as knowing she could avoid this yet chose not to, angered him.

'No,' was her response. 'Not without you.'

Arlo danced around a few feet ahead, and Christian sensed the Zanian knew exactly what he was doing. He would hesitate then make a quick, precise leap. Christian pressed his lips together as the cracks in the parched ground widened, revealing what looked like wet sand in between. With a sharp intake of breath, he jumped. The ground moved beneath him and he froze.

Fear swirled in his stomach.

Christian swallowed hard. As much as he disliked Arlo, he seemed the type who would always know what to do next no matter how spontaneous or outrageous it might be.

Away with the Færies

'Arlo, what can we do? We're only half way across.'

'I can't believe this is even happening,' he heard Sky say before letting out what sounded like a strained laugh.

Arlo turned around, shifting his feet precisely so that they balanced on either side of the broken ground. Christian's eyes widened.

'Surely that isn't a good idea?'

Arlo raised a hand. 'Are you ready?'

'For what?' Sky cut in.

'Make a path in your mind. Plan ahead. Watch how they move.'

'What are you saying?' Christian shouted. 'Stop talking riddles. Tell us what to do!'

'Listen to me,' Arlo said angrily. 'We must now walk, briskly – on second thoughts, run - over the cracks until we're over it. Okay?'

'Yes, yes,' Sky said hurriedly.

Arlo ran ahead.

'He must be mad,' Christian said as he dodged a gap in the rapidly cracking earth. The muscles in his legs burned and it was getting more and more difficult to move them in such haste.

'Maybe,' said Sky breathlessly, leaping ahead. 'Never have I had to deal with so much in such a short space of,' she paused to make another jump, 'time!'

Christian pushed on, hitting the ground hard.

Sky soon fell behind.

'Almost there, come on,' he panted.

Slowly but surely the gap between him and solid ground was closing. For a while Christian could only hear his own laboured breaths, and feel his heart galloping in his chest. It certainly proved a test for his strength. When he could, he threw a look over his shoulder to check Sky was okay. Her fists were clenched and her expression pained, but she ran on.

'Keep going!' Christian called breathlessly, making another jump. He reached behind him but Sky didn't make a grab for his hand.

Arlo was ahead, his lithe figure bounding over the fragmented valley floor.

Chapter Twenty-Four

Christian willed his legs to keep moving for it was the final stretch. Sweat prickled the back of his neck.

He lunged, landing on his right shoulder and rolling over twice. When he closed his eyes, the world revolved behind them. He swallowed gulps of air down his raw throat.

Eventually Christian sat up, light-headed, with the taste of dust on his tongue and grit clinging to his arms. He brushed it off carelessly. When he felt able he stood up, his legs quaking. Sky lay face down on the ground, still as a rock. He scrambled over. Arlo was there simultaneously.

Christian studied her face. 'Sky, Sky can you hear me?'

Arlo shifted her onto her back without effort, and her head lolled to the side. Christian fought the urge to push him away.

Instead he rested his hands on either side of Sky's face, brushing back her black hair to reveal her skin, flushed from exertion, and half open mouth. Her eyes were closed.

'Sky can you hear me?' he asked nervously. 'Wake up.'

'Shake her,' Arlo suggested.

Christian glared at him. 'No. I won't.'

'A good shake should bring her round. If you don't, I will.'

'You wouldn't dare,' Christian shot back, but Arlo proceeded to push him aside. He gave Arlo a hard shove, who then bared his teeth like an animal and Christian clenched his fists, ready to defend himself. As quickly as he was angered, Arlo blinked, sat back, and regained the composure of calm as if nothing had happened.

'What do you propose we do?' he said. 'Sky is barely conscious and neither one of us has the energy to carry her.'

Christian let his anger recede. He rubbed his face, feeling minute grains of dust and dirt pricking his skin. 'I will find the energy.'

Chapter Twenty-Five

Sky wanted to sit up and continue the journey, but her limbs were locked and it was as if there were weights pressing down on her eyes.

Hands touched her face, brushing her hair back, and it was oddly soothing.

She became attuned to Christian's voice close by. 'No, I won't.'

'A good shake should bring her round. If you don't, I will,' said Arlo.

'You wouldn't dare,' Christian sounded angry, and there was a scuffle followed by an under-the-breath growl. What were the two færies doing? It seemed there was a struggle.

Stop!

Zian's face emerged from the darkness that had engulfed Sky, a glowing reminder of why she was here. *'Get up, Sky. Get up,'* his voice was like a whisper in the wind.

'What do you propose we do? Sky is barely conscious and neither of us has the energy to carry her,' Arlo again.

With that came a lengthy pause. 'I'll find the energy,' said Christian.

One hand scooped under her neck, fingers rough and cool touched her skin causing it to tingle. Sky felt another hand under her knees. She didn't want Christian wasting his energy trying to lift her. If she could just get her brain to function, to do what Zian told her to do…

The gloom that shrouded her finally lifted.

'I'm alright,' she muttered, opening her eyes to grey light.

'That's a relief,' Arlo said. 'It looks as though it's about to pour

Chapter Twenty-Five

with rain.'

'Does Zania ever see the sun?' said Christian impatiently. 'Sky, can you stand?' His tone changed, as if it were an order. 'We must keep going.'

'I know,' she said. Christian helped her onto her feet and Sky took a moment to look around with bleary eyes, at the fragmented plain that lay behind her, and the boulder lined path she would soon walk. Her legs trembled and it felt as though someone had shovelled grit onto her tongue which she'd tried to swallow.

She refused to give in to her body's complaints.

To think I used to complain about P.E.

∽

Sky stumbled a few times, but rejected Christian's help. 'Really, I'm fine.' she said, breathing in the damp air. She knew that the dense, charcoal grey clouds that loomed would soon be sending down sheets of rain.

Arlo led the way across the grey landscape of stone and weeds. Sky began to search for animals, flowers, anything that brought life and colour but found no satisfaction. Rain began to fall, lightly at first, and she revelled in the feeling. It enlivened her senses. Christian gazed ahead. He was thinking, and whatever he was thinking about was something he apparently did not wish to share.

Rain began to fall hard, and thunder boomed through the dark clouds. Sky glanced up, blinking raindrops from her eyelashes. She wanted to pull her damp cloak around herself and seek shelter. Thunder made her feel uneasy. To add to it, a flash of lightning lit up the clouds.

The ground became slippery and the rocks gleamed silver as they, like Sky, were pummelled by the rain. Although she kept walking, she would soon have to ask if they could find shelter. She'd walked home from school through a few storms, and it sucked. Being in an alternative world, with wings, didn't make it any better.

There was another flash of light, and a few seconds later roaring thunder resounded from the heavy rainclouds.

'Don't panic,' said Christian, looking as unsure as she felt. Raindrops ran like tears down his face and arms. The rain was soaking through Sky's dress, trailing down her skin, turning her hair to rats' tails.

'Wonderful,' she murmured.

Arlo walked through the wet mist. 'Down there is an alcove,' he said loudly over the rain. 'Make your way and I will follow.'

Without question Sky ran with Christian towards shelter, a cramped space not big enough to stand in but enough for three people to crouch.

Christian bent forward with his hands on his knees. Raindrops dripped from the tips of his dark, wet hair, some of it sticking to his forehead. His clothes clung to him, revealing the toned muscles of his stomach. Sky looked away, wringing out her hair and the bottom of her dress with overt concentration. Then she sank to her knees and closed her eyes, resting her head against cold but dry rock. She tried to fight the shivers and rubbed her arms furiously, hoping it would warm her up. She opened her eyes and watched Christian as he sat down and leant against the rocky wall. It didn't look at all comfortable.

Of course it wasn't going to be comfortable.

The rain created a constant flow of noise, like the sound of someone pouring coffee beans into a machine. From the safety of the alcove Sky looked out, wondering how long the storm would last.

'We won't be able to stay long, will we?' she said. The dewy air reminded her of wet January mornings walking to school. She would meet Cassie at the gates, each of them clutching an umbrella and scowling at the gloomy clouds. Then they would make their way up the path to meet Louis and Hannah. They'd sit together in the foyer laughing about puerile things, wishing away winter, longing for the sunshine days of spring.

'Sky, Sky?'

In a flash of lightning the memory was gone, but the thought of her friends and family left a lingering ache in Sky's chest. Her whole body was trembling from cold. She met Christian's gaze.

Chapter Twenty-Five

'The answer to your question is no, we won't,' he said, studying her. 'We'll give it a little more time. If Arlo isn't back soon we will have to find our way without him, and I'm sure we could. I've no idea where he went.' He looked out at the rain. 'I don't trust him. I can't trust him. Are you feeling okay?'

'I'm managing,' Sky replied, but her body ached, she was wet, cold and actually she felt hungry. Thinking about it, she could have easily devoured a pepperoni pizza. Sky sighed. 'How are you doing?'

'I feel I should say the same,' said Christian. He looked about to continue but stopped, frowning. 'You must be freezing. If you sit this side you might be warmer. You don't have to of course,' he added. 'I can't order you to do so. We aren't in Krazonia anymore,' and for just a moment there was a sheepish smile, and his cheeks dimpled. Sky's heart lurched with a sort of pleasant pain.

If they sat together she would be warmer, no doubt.

So why did she hesitate?

Pull yourself together, Sky. 'You're right,' she said, and crawled across the space between them to nestle into his side. Christian placed his arm around her so naturally, yet it caused a flurry of butterflies in her stomach. She did her best to ignore them.

Another shot of lightning threw white light into the alcove, and for a split second Sky saw hers and Christian's crooked silhouettes cast across the opposite stone wall. Then it was gone, replaced by the sound of deep, grumbling thunder. Christian's arm around her made her feel safe.

'We won't be able to reason with Tæ,' he said. 'I don't see how. If she has gone to these lengths to secure the Emerald why would she care enough to listen to my pleas?' His voice was in Sky's left ear, so close and clear it was hard to believe that when she was home, she would never hear it again.

'Maybe you just need to distract her while I go for the Emerald,' Sky suggested, but despite how simple it sounded, she knew it couldn't be. From what she'd gathered Tæ was obsessive and cruel. The stone wouldn't just be lying around for people to take. 'We should probably come up with a plan. Like, now.'

'The only way I can think of stopping Tæ is to end her life, and

Away with the Færies

I don't think I could. But in the name of the Elana I want to.

'I wonder if it's time to swallow my pride and befriend Arlo a little more,' his tone turned sour. 'He could help us.'

Sky turned her head to look at him. In the overcast light she traced the line of his profile, from his straight nose to his firm jaw. Christian's dark, intelligent eyes were focused on the opposite wall.

Sky realised she was taking mental notes, so when the time came that Christian Meldin and herself inevitably parted she would be able to reach for these images stored in her mind, and she could do so whenever she wanted.

She wanted to remember him.

'I'll talk to Arlo if he comes back,' Sky said faintly, still preoccupied with the idea that she liked Christian more than she should. Liking him was pointless. They were working together on a task that would hopefully save the Færie Kingdom, and return Sky to her home. A week ago she wouldn't have believed this world even existed.

Christian nodded. 'What will you say?'

'I'm thinking about that.'

The storm was subsiding, much to Sky's relief.

'How am I going to forgive my mother?' Christian burst out, his arm tensing around her shoulders.

The question came out of the blue, but Sky could tell it had been playing on his mind for a while.

'There's no denying your mother shouldn't have kept it from you, but you can't blame her for wanting to do right by you and Rhia. Maybe she just didn't want you have it on your conscience? So she kept it to herself.'

'You mean to say she just didn't want to admit it to her children – didn't want to explain why she did it?'

Sky shrugged against his arm. 'Christian, you won't know until you speak to her about it. Just don't let it get to you. I'm sure Anya regrets it. Imagine living with a secret like that.' Sky could hardly conceive doing such a thing. There had been times she'd forgotten to hand in homework, and skived off lessons that led to a detention, but it never stayed on her conscience for more than

Chapter Twenty-Five

a few days.

'That's probably why she didn't struggle when Tæ showed up at the mansion,' Christian said angrily, 'as if taking my father away wasn't enough!' His temper was rapidly rising.

'Christian, don't get worked up about it now. We still need a plan, remember?' Sky touched his fingers with her own. 'We need to teach Tæ a lesson.'

'Yes, we do,' said Christian in a quiet, determined voice. 'We focus on getting my mother out first. We'll find Tæ...she'll be wherever the stone is kept.'

Sky nodded. 'We need Arlo's help.'

A shadow moving against the opposite wall caught her attention and before she knew it, Arlo had reappeared, sodden. He crouched down in front of her, bringing with him the smell of rain and wet earth.

He held a bunch of berries between his fingers. 'I can't remember their name but I've eaten them before. They taste good and are very nutritious,' he said. When Sky didn't take any he knelt down and moved his hand closer to her face.

With a sigh Arlo placed them onto the ground and took two. He peeled them hastily, and even with some of the skin left on, shoved them into his mouth. He chewed and swallowed.

'I think we could all do with some, don't you?' he said. Sky eyed the berries like they were about to come alive, but she couldn't help it. Her first thought was that they weren't full of nutrition as Arlo had said, but something that would have the complete opposite effect. Arguably, he had just eaten two.

'So you aren't trying to poison us?' Christian asked with mock surprise. He picked one up. 'We'll eat these and then go, seeing as the rain is easing off.'

Sky plucked one from its stem and peeled off its rubbery skin. She tipped her head back and dropped it into her mouth.

It tasted like a sour grape, a very sour grape. She swallowed quickly to stop from spitting it out. Christian took a handful and tried one.

'Not bad.'

Sky couldn't respond.

Arlo was watching her with raised eyebrows. 'You don't like them?'

She shook her head. 'Not really.'

'Well, I should eat some anyway,' Arlo chided. 'It's strange that you don't like them. Every færie likes them,' he added, not taking his pale green eyes off of her. Sky stared back.

'How do you know every færie likes them?'

'Well, I haven't met one who doesn't.' He tilted his head to the side, wincing. 'Sorry, ear ache.'

~

The rain had passed, as had the storm. The world was quiet again. Sky's dress and hair remained damp and her feet were cold in her boots. Emerging into the colourless world once more she looked around, readying herself.

'Our next destination will be the caves,' Arlo announced.

Sky pulled Christian back to whisper in his ear.

'I'm going to speak to him.'

He scratched his neck. 'Okay. Well, I hope you make some progress.'

Sky walked quickly to meet Arlo's pace. 'So I feel like I may have come across a bit rude. I've made no effort to talk to you.'

'Not at all,' he said.

'Well, I feel I have. What's it like living on your own out here?'

Arlo smirked. 'I've gotten used to it. It isn't much fun, but you don't really have much choice when your sister deserts you and your mother and father aren't around.' He waved a hand. 'And as I said before, I wanted to get away from it all. I survive.'

Sky nodded slowly, debating how to broach the subject of his "help". She needed to know more about him first.

'Having lived in Krazonia as a normal færie, I wonder what it's like being a messenger for a queen.'

Arlo's smile was taut. He said nothing.

'The Zanian queen has such a bad reputation,' Sky went on. 'Tæ Asrai is feared by us Krazonians. Did you ever meet her or was it a case of dealing with guards?'

Chapter Twenty-Five

Arlo gazed at her studiously. 'You do ask a lot of questions.'

'Yes. I'm curious, that's all.'

'I've met her twice and on both occasions she hardly acknowledged me. She wears a lot of dark colours, her lips are painted red. She's very stern. What you'd expect from a queen of the Dark Realm,' he winced again, and rubbed his temples.

'Do you have earache again, Arlo?' Sky asked, feigning concern.

'My head just hurts a bit,' he said brusquely. 'I think it's because I'm dehydrated.'

Sky considered his words. Her throat was dry and her stomach had digested the food she'd eaten at the mansion the evening before. The handful of berries she'd managed to swallow hadn't made much difference. 'Me too. Is there anywhere we can get water?'

'There is a stream that runs by the caves' entrance.'

'Great,' said Sky. 'Is it much farther?'

'The sun will be making its pass to the opposite horizon by the time we get there.'

Sky's shoulders sagged. It sounded like a long time. Hours and hours. 'How do you know what time of day it is?'

She could only see a grey haze and a glowing white orb almost directly above her head. Did that mean it was afternoon? If so then they had less time than she thought. At this rate the army would overtake them and it would all be for nothing. Sky quickly discarded the thought.

'You learn to live by the sun, from what you can see of it,' said Arlo, and the bitterness had vanished. He spoke with enthusiasm. 'You can also tell by the temperature.' He ran both hands through his damp blond hair, tugging his fingers through the knots.

'Why are you here with the prince?' he asked.

Sky contemplated an answer that would be partly true, to save her inventing a lie.

'He's my friend and it was best that the princess stayed in Krazonia. I'm close to them. It couldn't be left without a ruler, or royal færie, you know.' A trickle of laughter escaped her lips, which she tried to conceal with a cough. Arlo gave her an odd look.

'Don't you think Tæ is wrong in taking the Emerald and the queen?' Sky said.

'My opinion won't make a difference.'

'But you're entitled to have one. Aren't you annoyed at her? She's paralysed your wings!' Arlo's impassiveness frustrated her. 'Christian and I are going to stop Tæ from destroying Krazonia, and maybe even Zania. Does that not bother you? Don't you want to stop her from ruining the world you know? Because that's what's going to happen!' Sky's feet were rooted to the ground, and Arlo stopped to face her. His cheeks were flushed.

'She is the Zanian queen. I am Zanian and you – you are not,' he screwed up his nose and Sky read it as a gesture of distaste. 'You and I will never see eye to eye,' he continued. 'I offered guidance, not my service.'

Sky breathed in sharply, ready for an argument. Her tolerance levels had certainly lowered since arriving in this world.

As she was about to speak she felt Christian at her side and the words were lost, like a sweet dissolving on her tongue. She was becoming nearly as hot-headed as him.

'I agree with you there,' Christian said. 'Lead the way, Arlo, and we will follow.'

Arlo's eyes were sharp and his mouth was set in a flat line. His initial appearance had reminded Sky of a scared animal, like a deer or rabbit. Now he was something sly and furtive, like a fox. Perhaps he had a split personality, or harboured conflicting thoughts that every now and then rose to the surface, and the only way to thwart them was with hostility. He must have preferred keeping people at arm's length and usually when people did that, it was because of a secret or a past incident that had left a scar.

'Thanks for stopping me then,' said Sky, concerned with what she would have said had Christian not intervened. He'd remarkably kept his cool, but, given his expression, rage simmered beneath the self-control.

'The sooner we reach the caves the better,' said Christian.

Sky's feet were once again aching by the time the dark, ominous cave entrance came into view. She saw the stream before she heard it and rushed over, her thirst crying out.

Chapter Twenty-Five

Falling to her knees she looked into the rippling water. 'Finally,' she gasped, taking handfuls of it and taking turns to splash her face and drink out of her cupped hands. She gulped the water down, not caring that it dripped down her chin and onto her dirty dress.

Sky sat back, swiping a hand across her mouth to remove the water droplets.

Christian had knelt down and was drinking from his hands with more reservation than Sky. Of course, as prince he would have better manners.

She approached the cave entrance, Sky could feel a familiar panic in her chest, expanding like a balloon and she forced herself to take a deep breath.

The Dark Forest had been terrifying enough. What would the caves conceal?

Don't think. Just do.

And so, with Christian at her side, Sky strode into the darkness.

Chapter Twenty-Six

Christian could feel the shadows drawing him in, lifting the hairs on his arms. Arlo led them towards the darkness unfazed. Whatever beheld them in these caves they would simply have to face, as they had in the Dark Forest.

A worrying thought niggled at Christian's brain.

What if this was a trap? Could Arlo be leading them here to stop him and Sky from doing what they set out to do?

He touched the small wound on his cheek to find the blood had dried, though it still felt sore. His wings remained stiff against his spine. But Christian would ignore all his deficiencies for his legs still functioned, and they would carry him to his destination.

The caves' entrance swallowed him, the velvet dark encompassing him like a cloak. Arlo could be leading them into a trap but alternatively he could be guiding them in the right direction to the cellars and to his mother. Christian had to believe that. He glanced over his shoulder once, twice, watching the outside world shrink away. Before long there was no light left to guide them, only sound.

'Stay close,' said Arlo, his voice rebounding off the cave walls.

'We don't have much choice,' Sky whispered.

The atmosphere was gradually cooling. Christian's clothes were still damp against his skin.

'How long will this take?'

'Well,' Arlo began. Christian sensed the færie was only a few steps ahead. 'A while, I suppose.'

'We'll have to walk in pitch black the whole time?' Sky interrupted, and right on cue Christian heard her boots scuff the

Chapter Twenty-Six

cave floor. He reached out to grab her arm, only to knock her head. He cringed. 'I'm sorry, Sky.'

She laughed a little. 'It's fine.'

Arlo cleared his throat. 'Once we get deeper into the caves there will be fireflies and they will light our way, as they did in the Forest.'

'What about in the meantime?' Christian pressed.

'In the meantime, we walk a fairly straight path.'

Water droplets fell from the cave ceiling, patting the cool, uneven rock under Christian's feet. One landed on his shoulder.

'Arlo, once we reach the cellars, where are you going to go? What are you going to do?' He felt very smart saying it. He was only voicing what he, and hopefully Sky had been thinking the whole time. What was in it for him?

There came no response, and Christian knew that Arlo was formulating an answer, formulating a lie. He had him.

'I will just go back,' he said finally.

'Back where?' The darkness gave him a strange, smug confidence he hadn't felt before.

'I'll go back to living on the outskirts of Zania, what else?'

'What were you really doing on the land between my realm and yours? What made you want to help us? I cannot believe it is purely goodwill,' he couldn't stop the flow of questions.

'Before you say anything I was not spying,' said Arlo, an edge to his voice. 'You should be grateful I was there,' he included under his breath, but it was easily heard in the echoic atmosphere of the caves.

Christian shook his head, the darkness concealing his wry smile.

'We're just wondering,' said Sky wearily. 'If you imagine from our point of view, you seemed to conveniently appear after Krazonia was ambushed. A lone Zanian offering his guidance.'

'I understand,' Arlo said vaguely. 'In fairness you both accepted it.'

Christian recalled Sky's blue eyes and her fingers touching his wrist as she spoke. *'By accepting his help it doesn't mean you're forgiving the Zanian queen. If anything it shows how strong you are...'*

Walking through pitch black, being unable to see a thing, his other senses were heightened; the cool atmosphere carried the scent of dank stone, and he could hear the echoes of water droplets as they tapped the cave floor, creating shallow pools he frequently stepped in.

'Christian, look,' Sky whispered.

He turned his head to see the necklace around her neck glowing a steady pulse of effervescent green. His heart lurched.

'Your pocket,' he murmured. 'Put in into your dress pocket. Pull your cloak around slightly.'

Meanwhile, Arlo was having a conversation with himself in a low, agitated tone. Christian couldn't work out what he was saying.

It was a relief when fireflies began to emerge, casting them in an ambient green glow reminiscent of the Emerald. Christian's eyes adjusted quickly to the changing light. High above him was a cavernous ceiling and attached to it were spikes of pale rock, pointing downwards like jagged fingers. There were many trails to follow; gaping mouths that led elsewhere further into the caves. Arlo didn't look around. He knew this path too well. Christian pressed his fingers against his clammy palms.

'How many times have you been through this place, Arlo?'

'Often enough. You have a lot of questions.'

'Yes. So?'

'When I was a messenger I made my way through these caves, many times,' he said.

'Why?' Though he was a few steps behind, Christian was aware of the Zanian's growing agitation.

'The messages I carried were not always nice ones. Some Zanians grew to dislike me: Arlo Sæl, the bearer of bad news.'

'Where was your sister in all of this?' His question was met with a charged silence and Christian knew he'd finally found Arlo Sæl's weak point.

'I can't do it,' Arlo hissed.

'Can't do-'

'Listen!' he exploded, his voice like a wave throwing the fireflies off course. Arlo knocked his fist against his head once, twice before turning around, his expression fierce and unrecognisable.

Chapter Twenty-Six

'You want to know the truth? Here it is. I told you I used to be a Zanian messenger. I still am. I know exactly what you two are doing. I know about the Emerald. I know Tæ has plans to kill the Krazonian queen,' he was practically spitting the words. Christian felt the colour drain from his face. 'Sky, I lied about my sister Grace. Tæ had her thrown into a cell and swears if I don't succeed in bringing you to her before nightfall she will either exile or *kill* her. I mean, to be honest we're running perfectly on time,' he said, becoming hysterical.

'But that isn't the point is it!' he arched his eyebrows and pointed to Sky with a stern finger.

'You were not expected. She is so very curious about you,' his tone oozed resentment. He turned his attention to Christian.

'Why did you have to bring her? Sky has changed everything. Part of me wants to beat you unconscious I'm so mad!'

Christian stared at him with clenched fists, angry but at the same time fearful, thus becoming angrier at the fact this scraggy split-personality deceiver could even put the slightest bit of fear in him.

'Arlo?' was all Sky could say, her voice shaking.

Christian's heart beat heavy and fast, the statement about his mother sinking in. Tæ was really going to kill her. He shot a look behind him, contemplating an escape. This place was a labyrinth.

'You can try and run, but for one you may get lost and you don't want to die here do you? Two, Tæ will not be happy if I fail to deliver the goods.'

'Tell me, what's really going to happen?' Christian fired back.

Arlo's smile was playful. 'You'll get to see your mother again,' when he looked at Sky it vanished as quickly as if he'd blown it out like a candle. 'I'm not so sure about you.'

'What?' Christian growled.

Before Arlo could respond, Christian had forced him to the ground.

Fireflies scattered, disappearing behind walls and up towards the ceiling of the caves.

Christian felt the heat of anger rise within him like a wave and he couldn't stop it. His eyes were locked on Arlo as they wrestled against one other on the ground. Sky's yells for him to stop hardly touched the surface.

'Why are you doing this?' Christian shouted in Arlo's face, his echo repeating every word.

'I want my sister alive!' Arlo retorted, struggling to free himself. Christian felt a blow to his stomach and in retaliation shoved Arlo back hard, causing the Zanian's head to connect sharply with stone. His pain-filled cry rang out. Christian had him pinned. His skin was burning and he imagined himself as fire, and Arlo as ice.

'Christian-' Sky started.

He ignored her. 'Is Tæ going to kill my mother?'

His question was met with silence. Christian lowered his head so his face and Arlo's were only inches apart. 'What does Tæ want with Sky?' he hissed.

Arlo wrapped his fingers around Christian's wrists.

'Let go of me and I will tell you,' he said. Seconds later he was gasping for breath as Christian found himself with his right arm across Arlo's chest, and his left hand pressing down on his windpipe. He couldn't recall making the decision to kill him, but he was unable to break away.

'Please stop,' Arlo wheezed.

'Christian, get off!' Sky shrieked. 'You're going to kill him!'

Arlo's mouth opened and closed the way a fish would on dry land, desperately searching for water.

Christian couldn't pull back. All he could feel was fire burning through his blood, and the incessant need to expel his frustration somehow.

Anya's face flashed into his mind before fading like a petal in a stream.

Arlo's eyelids fluttered. He was losing consciousness.

'Christian!' cried Sky, pulling hard at his shoulders. 'He can't breathe!'

Finally he released Arlo and fell back, stunned.

For a short time Christian sat frozen with shock, the fire within him cooling. He looked at Sky, who was silent.

'I don't know what came over me.' He knew he acted reckless at times and easily lost his temper, but this was different. He'd

Chapter Twenty-Six

nearly lost himself, unable to see past a rage that filled his senses, surpassing the logical part of his brain. He pressed a hand to his stomach, his muscles tender from where Arlo had punched him.

'What do we do?' Sky whispered.

Christian leaned forward and could see the rise and fall of Arlo's chest. He was still alive. A mixture of guilt and hatred ran through him as he considered the options.

'We could try finding our way without him.'

Sky bit down on her lip. 'Christian,' she said, patting down her damp hair. 'What if Tæ hurts the queen? We need to get him conscious. We now know about his sister, and it might sound bad but maybe we could use that,' she paused, 'it does sound bad, doesn't it? I just don't want to get lost in this place. I think our only option is for Arlo to lead us the rest of the way. It looks like we'll have to be his prisoners temporarily.'

Arlo had said in his fury that Tæ planned to kill his mother. The thought was a stab of pain in his gut. If she discovered Christian had left her accomplice beaten and unconscious in the caves it could hasten her decision.

'We'll need to get him conscious,' he said. He was taken aback to see Sky bring her hand forward and slap Arlo swiftly across his cheek. It got the required result and shortly afterwards Arlo was coughing, his hands clutching his throat. Sky's lips were pursed, her hands in her lap as if she hadn't done a thing. Christian raised his eyebrows, impressed.

Arlo eyed Christian with contempt as he got up from the ground, his hands trembling as he brushed himself down. Christian stared back at him, fighting against his conscience. Did he apologise, or did he keep his mouth shut?

He would allow Arlo the first word.

The fireflies returned, turning the Zanian's skin deathly white. For a moment Christian wondered whether he had killed Arlo, and he had in fact risen from the dead. His eyes were piercing.

'We should probably keep moving, right?' Sky said quietly. Drip, drip went the droplets as they fell to the ground.

'Yes. Let's,' replied Arlo hoarsely. 'This way.'

They resumed their mission, the atmosphere thick with

tension. Arlo kept stroking his neck, his unsmiling eyes flicking onto Christian often. Christian purposely avoided the steel gaze, keeping his chin up and his focus ahead. He felt a pang of guilt for attacking Arlo, but it wasn't enough for the words "I'm sorry" to fall from his lips. He had too much pride for that.

'How does Tæ know about me?' Sky said suddenly. 'If she didn't know before how on earth does she know if we haven't seen her?'

Arlo didn't look back, nor did he hesitate. 'She is using the Emerald to connect with my thoughts. I'm able to communicate with her. I told her about you.' He coughed. 'Ow.'

Christian felt his fingers twitch but he managed to remain silent, allowing Sky to take the lead, for he was determined not to lose control again.

'I can assure you I'd be no use to her,' said Sky, 'really, I'm nothing special.' Christian felt inclined to disagree, but kept his mouth closed.

'Tæ seems to think otherwise. Even I am a little intrigued,' said Arlo. 'You seem to be immune to the stone's power and despite the berries being renowned for their sugary taste, you clearly found them repugnant.'

'Yeah, I did find them a bit sour but I can't be the only one.'

'You speak differently, too.'

Sky choked a laugh, and Christian knew she was surprised. From their first meeting in Krazonia he had thought the same. It wasn't only her distinct blue eyes and long black hair, but the way she said things, and there were words Christian didn't understand. She was different. Clever Arlo must have caught on.

'Tæ wishes to meet you. She has ordered me to bring you to her,' said Arlo.

Christian glanced sideways at his friend and saw the expression of someone who was concocting a plan.

'If Tæ wants to see me, so be it. I'll talk to her,' Sky said, catching Christian's eye with a subtle smile. Arlo was staring ahead so he was oblivious.

'Maybe we could come to an agreement,' she said. 'Either way I will speak to her, face to face.'

'I don't know what sort of agreement you're talking about, but

Chapter Twenty-Six

I suppose that isn't my business,' Arlo said. 'Although it should be,' he muttered afterwards.

Wherever Tæ was, she'd have the Emerald by her side. If Sky could get close enough she'd stand a chance of destroying it. But Christian could not let her go alone. He would not.

As he walked another thought stole into his mind, one he felt naturally would arise. The Elana told Sky to destroy the stone before Tæ could use it to take over the kingdom. One half of Christian's brain conjured the image of thunderstorms, desolate landscapes and violence under the Zanian queen's rule; the other half saw nothing but a hole, as if all the world had caved in on itself. Without the Emerald that had created this world, what would happen to it and all the færies who inhabited it? He could not imagine what the kingdom would become.

Christian was aware of Sky beside him and of the mad Zanian ahead, with his ash blond hair and sharp-tipped wings. In the green hue they were translucent except for their dark veins. For a while Christian let all emotion dissolve so he was numb, concentrating solely on the winding, cavernous path they walked.

At some point the air began to change, becoming more humid.

The fireflies had vanished, but no longer were the færies in darkness. Christian studied the changing world around him; nailed into the rocky walls were small torches, each emitting a crackling flame. Arlo's silhouette could be seen at the end of what appeared to be a never ending corridor of stone.

'We're here,' said Arlo solemnly when Christian reached him.

'Along here is the entrance to the cellars,' he continued. Christian eyed the crooked stone steps, holding his breath. He had to be ready. What choice did he have?

A cool hand touched his shoulder.

'Arlo, Tæ is probably just using you, you know. She seems the type,' said Sky.

Arlo spun to face her, a sickly grin on his face. 'No, she needs me.

'I achieved what I set out to do so it should be fairly straight forward. She will let my sister go,' the smile faded. 'Besides, it's not like I haven't suffered.'

With that, he began to make his way up the jagged steps that led to a trap door in the cave ceiling.

'I think I'm going to be sick,' Sky whispered.

Arlo let out a satisfactory sigh when the door creaked open.

'What are you waiting for?' he said over his shoulder.

Christian couldn't bring himself to answer. A shiver ran through him.

He clambered up through the door into the warm, dim atmosphere of the Zanian cellars.

The walls and floor were sandstone, candles sat in metal holders, their amber flames wavering. Across the room were four barred cells, two of which were occupied. One held a young færie with hair the same colour as Arlo's. She sat in the corner with her face in her hands, the plait of her hair hooked over one shoulder and trailing down to the floor. In the other cell was the shape of a færie lying still, breathing slowly. Arlo had vanished.

Christian looked around in a daze. This didn't feel real.

Sky jumped in front of him. 'Arlo's gone to alert the queen I think,' she said in a low whisper. Christian steeled himself against the fear that threatened to weave itself around his heart in a serpent-like grip.

Sky pressed her hands against either side of her face. Christian peeled them away and locked his fingers with hers. 'When we reach Tæ, you must distract her and I'll do whatever it takes to get that stone.'

Sky didn't look convinced.

'We'll have my mother on our side too.' It had to be her lying there in the other cell.

Christian rushed over, placing his hands on the thick bars and wishing he could rip them apart. He felt something tearing at his insides: anger, guilt, love and hate were all battling against each other.

Anya Meldin sat up in her crumpled dress. 'Christian,' she said. 'How on earth did you get here?' she could have been relieved, but her tone was angry. Christian could hear Sky scouring the room and its dark corners for keys, or another way of unlocking the cells.

Chapter Twenty-Six

'I'm here to get you out,' he said, ignoring his conscience that demanded to hear her explanation. It would have to wait.

'The keys won't be here,' she said with a sigh, shuffling towards the bars that separated them. Her cold fingers wrapped around his.

'I've failed you, Christian,' her lower lip quivered, and her almond brown eyes were imploring. 'I am so sorry. I've let my realm down as well as my children. There will be a battle, a pointless battle and Krazonia will be ruined. Tæ plans to take over everything,' she fell back, horrified. 'Where is Rhia?'

'She's in Krazonia. She is strong mother, and someone had to stay behind. Do you know where the Emerald is?'

'Tæ was kind enough to taunt me with it, before throwing me in here. She just could not help herself. It's in the Great Hall.'

Sky crouched down beside Christian. 'How do we get there?'

The queen shook her head, glancing down. 'I was blindfolded for the journey. Tæ is not a complete fool.' She narrowed her eyes at the ground as if seeing something within it that she disliked.

'She is cunning,' she said, clenching her fists around the material of her dress.

Christian glanced to the færie in the corner, hoping she wasn't paying too much attention to this conversation. She was looking straight at him. The resemblance to her brother Arlo was undeniable – they had the same round, alert eyes and high cheekbones. They also possessed the same derisive stare. In the end it was Christian who looked away.

He tuned in to Sky's anxious words. 'Apparently if Tæ uses the Emerald to take over each realm it'll all go pear shaped…I mean, she's basically going to destroy everything which is why I must get to it first. She really could ruin everything. Zian warned me.'

Anya's mouth dropped open. 'I – see. I can't believe you've seen the Elana. I can't believe it.'

'She won't let you near it,' Arlo's sister Grace hissed from her corner. Christian looked round.

'It is a nice idea, but I don't see it happening somehow,' she went on. 'She will have me killed, have you-' she pointed a shaky finger at Anya, '-killed, and then she'll just use the Emerald to rule all of the realms.'

The main door was thrown open. A Zanian guard stomped in, meaning business. Christian remained protectively beside his mother. The guard shoved him out of the way and jammed a key into the rusty lock, swinging back the door to his mother's cell.

'Out,' the guard ordered.

Chapter Twenty-Seven

The bang made Sky jump. A broad shouldered guard walked in, heading straight for Anya's cell. He pushed Christian aside and was so close to Sky that if she moved just an inch, her nose would meet with his armoured elbow.

'Out,' the guard said gruffly.

'Who do you think you're talking to?' Christian retorted.

'Not you, now move.'

Another guard lingered by the door, his bulky arms folded across his chest. Anya stepped elegantly out of her cell, expertly disguising her emotion; eyes focused ahead, all facial muscles relaxed. The first guard signalled at Christian to stand. Sky did the same, but the guard laughed cruelly in her face and with one swift movement pushed her back down.

'No. You remain in here. I've been told only to escort Queen Anya and her son.'

Sky could feel the panic rising. 'What?' She couldn't be separated from Christian.

'Tæ's orders, sorry,' the guard said with a complacent shrug. Sky stared at him. He wasn't sorry at all.

'Let's move!' he commanded, grabbing Christian's arms to drag him across the floor.

'Stop!' Christian exclaimed, fighting to stay. 'Let me go!' Sky reached out and had hold of him for a second before the guard shoved her back, her hand ripping from Christian's skin. She stumbled, and despite the pain in her shoulder, tried again.

'Don't take him!' she shouted, balling her fists to pummel the stupid guard.

Arlo walked in, bringing with him an essence of calm and Sky, breathless with anxiety, realised then that he was her only hope.

'I swear if you do anything to Sky...' Christian said, battling with the guard in the doorway.

Arlo arched an eyebrow. 'You'll what?'

Sky met Christian's gaze, her arms dropping to her sides. He struggled but wasn't strong enough to break out of the guard's grasp, which meant their plan was no longer achievable. Overwhelmed momentarily by despair she made a break for the door, but Arlo must have been expecting it because he had her before she'd even taken two steps. He gripped her arms, rooting her in place.

'Let him go won't you?' he hissed in her ear. Sky heard their scuffled footsteps receding and soon it was only the sound of her own laboured breaths. Panic was choking her.

'No,' she said, voicing only one word from a stream of terrified thoughts running through her mind.

Sky was ushered into a cell by Arlo who, she noticed, was pointedly ignoring his sister. She cursed his name and spat at him, saying everything was his fault. He made no signs of retaliating. At a loss Sky sat down on the stone floor of her cell, listening to Grace's rant.

'Arlo Sæl, you disgust me. Tæ told you she would find mother and father and you're so gullible that you believed her. You fell for it. You are no better than the dirt on my grave, because that is where I will end up.'

'I was trying to save you!' Arlo shouted, 'I thought it would be safer for you here. And you are not going to die!'

'Safe? Here? You are nothing to me now, Arlo.'

'You don't mean that.'

'Don't I? I think you'll find that I mean every word.'

'Stop talking,' he groaned. Arlo had his hands on his head and was staring at his sister. In the candlelight desperation glimmered in his wide, pale eyes and his cheeks were wet with tears. Arlo was crying. Sky hadn't thought him capable. He was passionless about most things, but could go from nought to irate in a matter of seconds. This emotion, however, wasn't one he'd used.

Chapter Twenty-Seven

'I. Hate. You,' Grace said, leaving a pause between each word, and to Sky it sounded as though she truly meant it.

Arlo ran his hands down his face. Slowly he began to retreat until he was overshadowed by darkness in a corner where the scope of candlelight didn't reach. Sky frowned at Grace. She imagined those words to be like weights, and they'd pushed Arlo away until he was alone in the shadows, suppressed by the realisation that his only sibling loathed him. She had to say something. Sky shuffled herself around to face Grace's cell.

'I think you may be being a little harsh on your brother. He brought me here with the hope of *saving* you, as he said. I'm the one whose supposed to be "sacrificed" I think you'll find.'

Grace let out a huff. In an unexpected flash of blinding green light, another figure appeared in the room. Sky did a double take.

There was nobody else it could possibly be.

'Grace Almaya Sæl, what pain you are causing your brother,' she sounded menacing, and Sky covered her mouth to suppress the scream. It was like coming face to face with a nightmare.

'Your Highness.'

'Be quiet!' Tæ snapped. The cell door swung open without being touched and hit the wall hard, the metal bars ringing. Grace cowered before the queen of Zania, whose presence was intimidating to say the least.

'Arlo!' she snapped. 'Execution or exile, what shall it be?'

Arlo emerged from the shadows. 'You said you weren't going to kill her.'

'Exile it is.'

'No!'

Tæ smiled at him. 'Your thoughts were distressing, I came to help you, and no one wastes my time. The decision has been made.'

'But not so you could-' Arlo began, but stopped.

Sky felt her way back in her cell until she was as far from Tæ as she could get. Yet there was no getting away. She wanted to shut her eyes but couldn't tear them from the fearful sight of the queen. Sky tried to steady her breathing, while her heart was trying to escape from her chest. *You're okay*, she told herself. *Calm down*.

Arlo jumped up and made a run at Tæ. There was another flash of green light and in that second Sky truly saw her for the first time: black hair scraped back into a painfully perfect bun, black eyes and cherry red lips. Baring her teeth at Arlo he flew back, hitting the wall. He sank to the floor and Sky, horrified, couldn't tell whether he was alive or dead. Tæ licked her lips, her gaze sweeping across the room. Any moment now it would land on her.

Thinking only of finding Christian and the Emerald, Sky clambered out of the cell. *What are you doing?* Her conscience screamed, and she didn't know. She just wanted out.

Tæ shoved Grace to the floor and spun to face Sky as she tried to run past. With speed she hadn't believed possible, Tæ moved to block her way. She attempted to dart past, but in the blink of an eye Tæ was obstructing her path once again.

'Guards!' she bellowed.

'You must be the one,' she continued. Sky stood as straight as a soldier to stop her whole body from quivering. If she remained tense, she couldn't fall apart.

Tæ spread her fingers as if she were cupping an invisible football. A green glow radiated from between her hands and she gazed through it at Sky, her eyes like two black pits that Sky was desperate not to fall into, but she couldn't look away. Concentration overtook Tæ's features, pulling her neat eyebrows together. A moment passed.

'Guards!' The Zanian queen shouted again, before disappearing in a warp of dazzling light, leaving Sky stunned.

Shaking herself out of it, Sky glanced around at Grace, and then at Arlo slumped in the corner. She made to them a silent apology. Once she had the Emerald none of this would matter. She rushed out of the room, heading down the gloomy passageway.

Sky turned the first corner and wham, straight into the cold steely chest armour of a Zanian guard. Without a word he launched at her, picking her up easily and throwing her over his shoulder. Sky punched and kicked to no avail.

'How am I any help to you? I have nothing!' she shrieked,

Chapter Twenty-Seven

hearing only her own desperate voice in the dingy corridor of stone. 'I've done nothing wrong. Tæ's going to ruin everything, not me.' It was desperation that drove her, neither motivation nor determination, but the feeling that her chances were disappearing like sand through her fingers.

'I didn't ask for this you know!' she yelled as the guard jostled her through the doorway. She was pushed onto the stone floor, scraping her knees. She turned around just as the cell was, this time, locked shut. The guard threw the key at the ground by Arlo, who slowly crawled towards it.

'This is your responsibility,' he mumbled before trudging out.

Sky wanted to punch the wall and scream, but what was the point? She sat with her wings against the cool wall, feeling sick with exhaustion.

'Where is Grace?'

'Oh, she's gone,' his voice wavered. 'If they take her to the Arids I will have to go after her. She shouted at me when I told her that. Apparently I belong in these cellars and I am worth nothing, as you heard.'

'Well, that isn't true,' Sky replied, trying to catch his eye. Arlo grabbed the key from off the floor and held it close. It alarmed her that there was blood on his hands. Keeping his head down Arlo stood up uneasily and wandered to the opposite wall. Only when he walked beneath the soft glow of candlelight did Sky notice the blotch of dark red in his hair.

'You're bleeding!'

'I know,' Arlo muttered, sitting down.

And that was the end of that conversation. Sky stared at a candle in its metal holder, watching the creamy wax as it crawled down the wick.

She thought hard about the best way of tackling this situation. Christian and Anya had to be in the Great Hall, and Tæ had probably transported back there with her crazy powers. The Emerald was in the Great Hall. Sky suppressed a groan. Everything was in there.

Questions buzzed around her brain like a swarm of wasps and it was beginning to hurt, all these questions stinging at once.

How could she persuade Arlo to help her?

What if she didn't get to the Emerald? What if what if...

'This sucks,' she said under her breath.

'Excuse me?'

'I'm just thinking out loud,' she said, gazing at Arlo through the bars of the cage in which she was being held captive. His legs were stretched out in front of him, his head tilted to the side. One hand held the back of it while the other was in his lap, squeezing the key as if it was a live eel trying to escape his grasp.

'Arlo, you deserve better,' Sky said, as heartfelt as she could without sounding patronising. 'I don't get why you don't just make your escape now. All Tæ has done is brainwash you and take away the only family that you have. And let's not forget she just threw you against the wall without a second thought.'

Arlo shook his head. 'No. She does what she has to do. My sister was mean to me anyway,' he said feebly. 'Maybe I am better off without her.'

'Tæ is using you.'

'She promised me a better life and she promised me she would find my parents.'

'And you believed her?' Sky could see this was hurting him, but with his guard down there was no better opportunity and she had to take advantage of that. When Arlo didn't respond she opted for a subject change.

'What does Tæ want with me?'

Arlo let out a long-winded sigh. 'She thinks you could become her assistant. You're like a flower bud in a sea of dead roses and thorns and she wants to keep you. She wants to use you,' he simpered. 'Tæ reckons that with the Emerald you would make an extremely powerful team.'

Sky inched forward until she could wrap her fingers around the bars. The smell of metal immediately led to the thought of blood: the battle.

'I can stop this.'

Arlo barked a laugh. 'How?'

It was time to be cruel. 'I trusted you at the beginning. How was I to know you had such a disgusting, selfish ulterior motive?

Chapter Twenty-Seven

stone of the necklace pressing against her palm and whether it was the right decision or not, she lifted it out in all its glowing glory.

Chapter Twenty-Eight

After a time of struggling Christian gave up, allowing the guard to nudge him forward in whichever direction. It was best to save the energy he had. It took them a while, weaving through shadowy passages and up cramped spiral staircases, before they came across anything homely. A door was opened, leading him into a bright corridor. Well, bright compared to the dim cellars he'd previously passed through. Walls were ochre, and the floor was of tiled limestone. Carved sandstone pots lined the length of the corridor. Each pot held a plant with dark leaves; red flower buds poked through the mass. As Christian walked along it occurred to him, disturbingly, that there were no windows. There were plenty of rushes giving off flare, but no way for natural sunlight to get in.

He wasn't sure what to say to Anya. There were many things he could speak of, but it didn't feel right to do so, here. He couldn't mention the letter or the battle, and certainly not father while walking down the very same corridor he had four years ago; the corridor which had led him to his death.

So Christian was left with nothing but his own anguish, as he followed in his father's footsteps.

A guard shoved him forward. He hadn't realised he'd stopped walking. His mother was a few steps ahead and she looked back, her eyes full of regret.

Finally a set of large, carved doors came into view. Christian knew what lay behind them and with every step could feel his heart thumping hard in his chest. He pictured Tæ's face, her piercing dark eyes and wicked smile.

Chapter Twenty-Eight

One guard yanked his arms back while the other pushed against the doors, and they gave way with an ominous creak.

Christian took the first step into the Great Hall.

It was astounding, with a vast high ceiling and walls exhibiting dusty family portraits that ventured through generations. A marble floor spread out before Christian, and he took in the mahogany furniture and ornate rugs like large stepping stones, leading to the throne. Tæ ruled so differently to his compassionate mother. Here every single thing revolved around the queen as if the whole world was beneath her. At the far end was the Emerald encased in a floating glass globe much like the one at home. Christian blinked away the image of it smashed and empty in his mother's bedroom.

In the high throne sat Tæ Asrai, her cold eyes settled on the precious stone that did not belong to her. She sat motionless with her hands in her lap, dressed in a thick black gown. Only her wings moved, slowly, along with her breathing.

'At last,' her voice echoed around the hall, addressing those who'd arrived. She turned her head and raised a hand, beckoning them closer.

'Anya, your son has grown to look so much like the late Krazonian king.'

'I know. He has eighteen years in him now, Tæ,' Anya replied in a quiet, respectful tone.

'Come here,' Tæ commanded, and Christian balked. Guards, who he could have sworn were not there before, appeared from behind and roughly escorted him forward.

He didn't want Tæ to be real, but she sat there breathing and blinking, as alive as he and the guards that had hold of him. Her skin was as pale as the moon on a clear night, and her charcoal black hair was pulled tight into a high bun. Her lips were as red as they were in his dream. At that point they broke into a sinister smile and he felt the queen's eyes eagerly taking him in.

'You do have your father's features,' she said wondrously.

Christian kept his mouth shut, managing to hold back from firing insult after insult at her, which he could have easily done.

'But oh, you seem to have gone through a bit of an ordeal,' Tæ continued. 'I would apologise...' she stopped, tilting her head in a playful manner. 'But it isn't in my nature.'

'No, it's just in your nature to be heartless and evil,' Christian retorted, and having never imagined being in such close proximity to the Zanian queen was fighting the urge to tear her wings off. In an odd way he was relieved he had two tough guards holding him back. His knuckles were turning white his fists were clenched so hard.

'I'm heartless and evil?' Tæ repeated, and she laughed before focusing on Christian with eyes filled with a dark fury. This must have been eating away at her for years, since Rowan had been murdered by his mother.

'Every single thing I have done since my beloved's death has been in preparation for this day. I swore to myself I would get revenge and not rest until it is done,' she was speaking through gritted teeth, her face dangerously close to Christian's.

Christian held his breath, the anger draining out of him.

'Today will be the start of my ruling over the kingdom. Things are going to change, starting with your mother.' She sat back and sighed as if Anya was simply an inconvenience.

'Guards, take Anya Meldin away. I don't actually need her here at the present time. I must speak with her son.'

'Mother!' Christian cried, twisting to try and face her but the guards' firm grip on his arms kept him frontward. They shoved him backwards into a seat, each gripping onto a shoulder. It was hard and uncomfortable, like Tæ's stare. His spine ached.

'Where are you taking her?'

Tæ shook her head. 'I ask the questions.'

Christian knew just who these questions would be concerning.

'Tell me more about your friend.'

'Why?' came out of his mouth before he could stop it. Even though he knew the risks Christian just did not want to give her the satisfaction. It was a foolish thing to do. The Emerald's glow brightened and Tæ's piercing stare moved to his chest. He felt pressure against it, like an iron fist, and yelled out in pain. It pressed harder and he struggled for breath. Then, it stopped.

'Answer me.'

Chapter Twenty-Eight

'Look, Tæ, she's just a færie who-'

'Why did she come with you in the first place? Where is the princess? Through communications with Arlo I know about the fact her wings weren't paralysed, unlike yours. And I tried the Emerald's powers on her to no avail. Tell me.'

'I swear she's just a færie. She is my friend. We're close, and she offered to accompany me while Rhia took care of Krazonia after you ambushed us and abducted our queen,' Christian's voice rose. 'Were you expecting a family visit? You are wasting your time,' his gaze passed Tæ and the Emerald to the vast windows that displayed a bleak landscape. He could see small villages and Zanians within them busying themselves beneath the colourless sky. The main town spread out across the western side of Zania, an immensely crowded place of huts and markets. They had to know about the battle, and they would see it all, yet Tæ didn't care. He wondered how they felt, and how many of them were truly loyal to their queen.

'The way you continue to say "just a færie" suggests to me she is not,' Tæ said.

'Sky accompanied me here that is all.'

'And why did you come?'

Christian felt a searing pain in his chest, distracting him.

'What were you going to do, break into your mother's cell and whisk her away to safety while the battle rages on? At least Arlo did his job, I suppose,' she added and Christian wasn't sure how much more he could take. After what felt like forever, the pain receded and he could breathe easily again.

'Yes I wanted to rescue my mother,' he said. 'But also to try and reason with you about this battle and your absurd plans to take over the kingdom. Tæ, please.' It dented his pride but he had to try. As he had nothing, he would try anything.

'Why do you have to put your færies, and ours, through this? I know about my mother murdering Rowan. I've read the letter. But surely you've had your revenge? My father is dead because you killed him,' he couldn't control the tremor in his voice. 'So aren't you and my mother now even? You are both widowed and resentful,' he hesitated, the tide of anger rising within him. 'Only there is a difference. Anya Meldin didn't let it take over her life. She continued, ever graceful and brave, and the Light realm was restored, whereas you have allowed it to crush you. This led you to feel only rage. You've sought the Emerald stone for so long, believing it could fill the emptiness inside of you. You never accepted it and now look where you are,' he lowered his voice, trying to level out his anger. 'You are an embittered queen who has turned two realms against each other, if not three. This can only lead to disaster.'

Tæ stared down at him pitifully.

'Nice try,' she said and stood up, holding her heavy gown with long, slim fingers. She stepped down and walked over to the floating globe to gaze inside it.

'Isn't it magnificent?' she whispered.

Christian bit his tongue.

Tæ sighed. 'I think it is a beautiful, dangerous thing.'

'It is,' Christian said. The two silent guards lifted him out of the chair and pulled him towards Tæ. He didn't try to fight them.

'Is it magic?' the queen smiled, not taking her eyes off the Emerald. 'Sky could be such a help to me. If she is immune to the Emerald's power, she could accompany me to each realm and we would be unstoppable.'

'You intend to use her as your shield,' Christian said, disgusted.

'I'm giving you one last chance to answer the question.'

'Sky hides nothing. You need to go out there with my mother and stop the battle before it starts.'

'Oh you are foolish. Just like your father.'

Tæ closed her eyes and bowed her head. She held onto the globe and it looked as though she was about to lift it. Instead, the Emerald shone white from within and the space around it filled with a spectrum of colours which quickly dissolved, leaving an image of his mother standing in shackles, surrounded by darkness.

'What is this?' Christian asked urgently, 'what are you going to do?' his voice was on the verge of breaking. Tæ remained still with her head bowed. Looking back in, Christian stared in horror as a guard pushed his mother roughly to the ground. She lay in her

Chapter Twenty-Eight

torn dress as they kicked and taunted her.

'Please stop, please,' Christian pleaded, desperate to look away but being unable to, his eyes glued to the horrific vision that the globe portrayed. If the guards continued to attack her she would be broken. Christian too would be broken.

After a while the guards went away, leaving Anya curled up on the ground, not moving. Christian waited, blinking back tears. He prayed to the Elana his mother would awaken. She didn't.

'You've killed her!' he cried out, twisting his arms and kicking, wanting to wipe what he'd just witnessed out of his mind. 'I hate you!' he yelled in Tæ's face.

'She's not dead,' Tæ replied calmly. Weak from shock Christian fell limp, the guards no longer restraining him but holding him up.

'But that will happen if you do not tell me the truth about your friend.'

Christian gathered his strength and raised his head. He hadn't anticipated such an emotional battering.

'You are insane.'

A door swung shut and the sound of footsteps echoed through the hall.

'…I mean it,' he heard his mother say.

Christian closed his eyes, overcome with relief. The distress he'd felt on discovering his mother's secret was nothing compared to the idea of losing her completely.

'I told you she wasn't dead,' said Tæ, to which Christian couldn't respond. 'However I'm not ruling it out. I think I've made that clear.' She clapped her hands together hard. 'Bring the queen forward.'

Christian watched the glowing Emerald that was the reason for everything moral and everything corrupt. He wondered if the Elana ever knew how their story would end.

Tæ seemed to sense Christian's inner struggle and with cool fingers held his chin, turning his face to hers. She had a firm grip, and Christian looked helplessly into her cruel, black eyes.

'Tell me now,' Tæ said quietly. 'Tell me,' she hissed, her fingers pressing into his jaw, carrying the threat: tell me or your mother will die.

There were so many hands on him that Christian felt he no longer belonged to himself.

'You could just ask her,' he whispered.

'Tæ, release my son,' said Anya.

'Help! Help me!' Arlo came bursting in through some unknown entrance. He slipped down onto his hands and knees. Christian saw the blood, but where was Sky?

Chapter Twenty-Nine

Sky followed Arlo through the narrow, torch-lit labyrinth. Whenever a guard appeared she would lower her head, withdrawing into her shadow against the wall, contorted beneath the firelight. Arlo gave the same explanation every time.

'Tæ didn't want me to alert you but she wishes to see Sky in the Great Hall, so if you will excuse me, she'll be wondering where we are.' Thankfully none of them questioned it. Perhaps they were as gullible as Arlo. Armour and a shield offered no protection to the mind, only the body.

Sky walked briskly, going over the plan in her head. It had to work. She just had to make sure she was brave, after all Tæ was just like any other færie at the end of the day, wasn't she? The Emerald may be in her grasp, but Sky had human fortitude on her side.

Arlo led her up a staircase and straight ahead were a set of large double doors, shut fast.

'That'll lead us straight into the Great Hall. I have a better idea,' said Arlo, taking her arm and leading her back down the steps.

'What's that?' asked Sky, wondering why on earth they were going the opposite way to where they needed to be.

There was in fact another way beneath the stairs: a mahogany door that opened only when Arlo threw himself at it. He rubbed his shoulder afterwards.

Sky offered him a look of sympathy. 'Down here, then?'

'If I'm correct this should lead to a lesser-known entrance.'

'So you aren't taking me somewhere to end my life?' Sky asked, only half joking.

'Of course not,' said Arlo, allowing Sky to walk ahead, and she did so cautiously.

They stumbled through the darkness. Sky should have been used to the dark but still she found herself skimming the walls with her fingers, walking slower than necessary. Arlo nudged her forward. 'Go faster.'

'It isn't like I know the way.'

'You're human, you know everything.'

Sky didn't reply, biting back a snappy comment about how she regretted telling him, but he might have thrown her back into the cell had she not admitted the truth. Arlo was more observant than she thought.

She lifted the necklace out from beneath the neckline of her dress and the immediate space before her illuminated green. She half expected Arlo to make a grab for it, but instead he only stared. Perhaps he was afraid.

Though the stone's glow was intermittent, it was enough light to give her the courage to run.

The passageway led Sky left and then right, Arlo's quick steps echoing behind her. A steep staircase led them into a narrow corridor, at the end of which was a door. She attuned her ears to the voices she could hear, muffled by wood and distance. Arlo was breathing too loud, probably from nerves.

'Be quiet for a moment,' Sky whispered, and Arlo covered his mouth with a bloody hand. 'Are you feeling okay?' Despite his craziness, Arlo had gone through an ordeal too and Sky couldn't ignore that.

A shrug was his answer.

'Please stop, please,' Christian was pleading, and Sky pressed closer to the door, her mouth sapped of moisture. She swallowed hard.

There came a brief moment of silence, and then, 'you've killed her! I hate you!'

His voice was heavy with emotion; fear and rage and ultimately confusion.

'She's not...' Sky strained to hear Tæ, thinking of the only

Chapter Twenty-Nine

possible victim. Christian's mother.

Sky stepped back, lowering her eyes. How easy it would be to find a corner to hide in.

'I can't hear what they're saying,' she said and moved away, allowing Arlo to dutifully take her place. Any minute now he would burst through the door and the act would begin, him as a helpless Zanian, Sky playing the part of "psychotic human". She fiddled with the necklace, trying to round up the confidence that seemed to have deserted her at the last second. Tæ couldn't hurt her.

Christian and Anya were behind that door, and so was the Emerald. Anya…

'Tell me we can do this,' Sky said anxiously, and Arlo smiled. His eyes revealed suffering but his smile said otherwise. Arlo Sæl, the færie with two personalities.

Færies and humans were definitely more alike than they would ever admit. Sky returned the smile.

Someone clapped. Tæ spoke loud enough for Sky to hear. 'Bring the queen forward.' Arlo raised his eyebrows, his hand hovering over the handle.

She cleared her throat, waited. After counting to five she gave him a small push.

'Go,' she whispered, and without hesitation Arlo opened the door, daylight streaming in. In a moment he was gone.

'Help me! Help!' he yelled, and Sky's heart lurched painfully. She flattened herself to the wall. She felt the pressure against her wings, and a similar pressure pounding in her head.

With her eyes screwed shut she took a deep, preparatory breath. There was certainly no going back after this.

Sky peered around the doorway. For a short time Arlo grasped the centre of attention, and Tæ looked angry that someone dared to disturb her cruel interrogation. He fell to the floor but quickly pushed himself up to latch onto a guard next to Christian.

'Arlo!' Tæ bellowed.

'It's the girl! She just tried to kill me!'

Sky found herself walking towards the Emerald within its protective dome of glass, casting a quick glance at Anya, who thankfully was still alive. The Krazonian queen used this momentary distraction to pull out of the guards' grasp. She ran at Tæ, who turned her head and with one sweep of the hand sent her sliding back across the floor. Sky had to stop herself from running to Anya's aid, returning her focus to the tyrant queen who was now glaring at her.

'Mother!' Christian cried, getting up from the chair, only to be yanked back by a guard.

'Tæ, be careful. She might kill you!' Arlo was shouting as two guards seized him.

Sky held back the urge to laugh. It rumbled deep inside of her, making its way up into her throat. She choked it out but managed to keep a straight face. This felt like a dream, one very ridiculous dream.

She was only a few metres away from the Emerald and soon she would have to make a smash and grab, without Christian's help.

Sky locked eyes with Tæ Asrai. *Show no fear.*

'Don't move,' Tæ barked at her, and though her expression was grave and she showed no signs of weakening, her eyes reflected uncertainty. She was as easy to read as an open book.

'I just want to look at it,' Sky said with a shrug. Tæ turned her head to the window.

'It won't be long until the armies collide,' she stated.

'Gloryn is fighting with us!' Christian cut in.

'You think I wouldn't have realised you would get Gloryn involved?' Tæ laughed bitterly. 'You never fight any battles on your own. All of you Krazonians are weak, and you are all cowards.'

Sky dashed forward, but no sooner had she gone two steps a guard charged at her unexpectedly side on, knocking the wind out of her. She landed on the hard floor under his hefty weight. Her bearings were lost.

Sky grappled with the guard but he was ten times stronger, squeezing the air out of her lungs.

Tæ laughed. 'Not fast enough. Lift her up Julian.'

Sky felt weak and vulnerable when she didn't want to be. Tæ sat smugly in her throne with the precious stone in her lap.

Chapter Twenty-Nine

'I have something that might interest you,' Sky said through gritted teeth. Her arms were aching from where the guard had them pulled behind her back, but he clearly didn't care about how much pain he caused her. Tæ had influenced them all with her sadistic ways.

Tæ caressed the Emerald, her mouth pinched.

'What would that be?'

Sky braced herself

'I have a necklace.'

'That is of no interest to me, Sky. How about we discuss what you're really doing here?' Tæ turned her head to look outside, and her lips drew into a menacing smile. 'I wouldn't mind just watching this for a moment. It will give me such pleasure to watch the Krazonian army fall.'

'I'll be more specific. I have *the* emerald necklace.'

Tæ turned back quickly, eyes wide. 'Say that again?'

'The one belonging to the Elana.'

'The necklace that was lost at the Beginning? No, it's impossible. Julian, search her.'

Roughly the guard began to check her pockets, lifting her cloak with one hand, the other locked tightly around her upper arm so she couldn't get away.

Suddenly it came to her. She'd thought it once before – if Tæ could manipulate the Emerald's power, couldn't Sky use the necklace in the same way?

If he managed to get a hold of the necklace she'd have no weapon.

With her free hand Sky pushed against the guard's armoured chest, squeezing her eyes shut to focus on the precious stone. *Leave me alone, leave me alone, LEAVE ME ALONE.*

She felt a surge of energy, heard the guard's yell, and opened her eyes to see him sprawled on the floor. Christian was staring, mouth agape.

Sky glanced down, aware of the buzz that had jolted through her, still lingering in her bloodstream like adrenalin.

'Get her!' shrieked Tæ, but upon seeing the necklace no guard moved, despite the queen's orders.

It was time to experiment. Sky walked towards the glass dome, playing with the necklace that hung around her neck.

'Do not come any closer,' said Tæ. 'I have the Emerald in my hands.'

Sky took another step, flexing her wings. Adrenalin, nerves and shock all mingled in her system. 'But you don't want me dead do you? You *need* me. Don't you want to know what I am?'

Lowering her head Tæ grasped the Emerald, her eyes locked on Sky. Her mouth twitched.

'Should I be in some sort of pain?' Sky asked, flashing a smile. She may as well act mad, that was the plan after all. Take a leaf out of Arlo's book.

Tæ shook her head, holding the Emerald tightly in her thin, pale hands.

The ground began to tremble.

'I'm from the human dimension, Tæ.'

'You can't be.'

Sky sighed. 'It's true. How else do you think I retrieved this necklace? At the Beginning it was lost in my world and has been passed on through generations.

'I know about the Elana. It's been made clear that the Emerald's powers are useless on me – you've learnt that first hand. They warned me about someone who would yearn for its power, a færie filled with greed and resentment. That færie is clearly you.' Sky pointed a finger, copying her teachers: the finger that seemed to work as a freeze gun, fixing the injudicious pupil in their seat. 'I'm here to stop you.'

It was as if she'd announced the death sentence to all færies in the room. No one said a word. Tæ's eyes were wide and she drew the Emerald into her chest, clutching it like it was her favourite teddy bear and Sky was threatening to set it alight.

Sky felt the silence closing in. The adrenalin ebbed away until only reality remained. Looking out at the cloudy horizon she could have cried. She clamped her teeth together. The Krazonian army loomed and it wouldn't be long until they were met by the Zanians. It would be one big show for the færies on ground level. So adding to the list of Tæ's traits, she was not only a merciless,

Chapter Twenty-Nine

tyrant queen, but one who had no regard for her people and how they'd be affected. Unless they'd been conditioned to think bad was good.

Had Tæ announced a battle, and received a cheer?

Sky took another step forward, realising these færies were afraid. 'You should already know the powers are useless on me.'

'You can't have it!' Tæ cried, leaping out of the throne. Her black gown swayed as she spun around to face the window.

'I don't need you after all,' she said, thrusting the stone outwards. It set off a silver-white light so bright Sky had to look away. The ground began to quake, causing family portraits that previously decorated the walls to fall down and the mahogany bookshelves to topple over. Things were smashing and crashing all over the place. Outside a storm was forming; dark clouds gathered in the sky. The guards looked around in horror.

They must not have been expecting this. In turn they ran out, away from the madness that was Tæ.

Hundreds of Krazonian soldiers, now joined by Gloryn, tore through the black clouds towards the Zanian army. In seconds they would clash. The ground was still shaking and Sky struggled to stay balanced. She managed to stagger over to Christian and he grasped her shoulders.

'What happened?' he asked anxiously.

'The, we-' why could she not speak? 'Christian, we have to stop her.' Sky grabbed onto him for support.

'I know. I'll run and-' he breathed in sharply. 'Mother, no!' Sky turned to see Anya jump into the air, throwing herself at Tæ. They collided and the Emerald, having been dashed from Tæ's grip, proceeded to roll across the marble floor. The two queens spun around like dancers, their wings spread wide. Sky watched with horror as they smashed through the huge windows, causing an explosion of glass. Soon they were lost in the fierce storm clouds.

The armies were like locusts plaguing the skies.

The battle had begun.

'Why hasn't the storm ended? Tæ doesn't have the Emerald,' Sky said, hearing the strain in her voice. She couldn't tear her eyes away from the battle, too shocked to move. She could barely feel her feet.

'Tæ must be connected to it somehow. Perhaps it's mirroring her emotions. Come on,' said Christian. The Emerald rested on the floor a few feet away, still glowing, still whole. Sky let Christian pull her by the hand, and her heart was flipping over and over at the sight of it. How could things change so drastically in so little time?

'This is your chance,' said Christian, and a curious doubt entered Sky's mind when she looked at him. Sadness flickered across his features, his shoulders rose and fell with a sigh. His jaw tightened as he pointed at the stone. 'Do it.'

'I can't imagine what this will mean for you,' Sky said quietly, and her conscience chastised her for dillydallying. *Stuff you*, she told her inner self. *This matters*.

She would never see Christian again. It had been what, five days? Not even a week. So why did she feel this way? Tears welled in her eyes and she looked down, the stone a green blur in her vision.

'It can't get much worse,' Christian replied.

'I'll do it now,' she said, wiping her eyes. The battle raged on. Soldiers attacked one another mid-air, some fell, and others fought on with swords and færie dust.

Thunder rumbled across thick storm clouds that had brought with them a strange, eerie gloom, and wind howled through the shattered windows.

Sky reached down to pick up the stone but stopped half way, frozen by the sight of a brawny guard approaching them with speed. Christian's name was on the tip of her tongue, but she wasn't quick enough. The guard lunged at the prince, and Sky saw the flash of shiny metal. She felt a stab in her gut, but after a moment realised it was only a reaction because it wasn't her who'd been wounded.

Christian shouted out before collapsing onto the floor. The guard backed away, bloody knife in hand, his eyes like flints. The sight of Christian's blood was enough for Sky. She could feel the heat rising, prickling her skin.

'No!' Sky yelled, disregarding her own safety to fly at the guard.

Chapter Twenty-Nine

He had to pay for what he'd done. With all the energy she could muster she whacked the guard's armoured chest, but by the way her skin smarted it was causing her more harm. Someone pulled her back hard and she cried out in frustration. Blowing the hair out of her face, she met the calm gaze of Arlo, so out of place in this madness.

'I'll take it from here,' he said, not giving her a chance to respond. He pursued the guard and tackled him to the floor a short distance away. Sky turned her head, not wanting to look.

For that brief moment she'd forgotten about the stone. She couldn't return to it until she'd checked on Christian.

Sky sank to her knees. With trembling hands she helped him manoeuvre onto his back. He released a long gasp of pain.

'Christian?' she didn't sound like herself, her voice was strained and she could feel a lump of emotion building in her throat. 'Christian,' she said again.

Chapter Thirty

One moment he was standing, the next he lay face down on the ground. He must have been hit hard in the back by a guard, and the suddenness had left him paralysed. Or at least that's how it felt.

Christian wanted to stand up but couldn't muster the strength. The muscles in his arms trembled when he tried. Someone turned him over and he opened his eyes to a ceiling that seemed so far away. Sky was next to him.

'Christian?' she said.

He shut his eyes, trying to pinpoint the sensations running through his body. Initially he'd just been thrown into an ice cold lake, and then there was an intense pain in his lower back and he couldn't help the gasp that escaped his lips. He needed to find his mother, for she was out there somewhere in danger, fighting against Tæ.

The ice had turned to molten lava and he could feel it seeping out of him, taking with it his energy. He could recall Sky's look of horror, the way she'd reached out. Something bad had happened, and Christian realised then what it was. It hurt to lie on his back. He needed to be on his side. The pain intensified.

'Sky,' he croaked, feeling the cool floor around him.

'Christian,' she said, gripping his hand. 'I don't know what to do.'

'Move me onto my side,' he whispered, meanwhile the battle continued. He could hear it all; the whistling wind through shattered glass, battle cries of his færies as they fought for their realm and their lives.

Chapter Thirty

'Your sister should be here,' Sky said.

'Destroy that stone, Sky.' This felt very much like an out of body experience. Christian sensed that come any moment the Elana would flood his thoughts, and he would see his father's face, welcoming him into a place where time did not exist.

Rhia. This would ruin his sister that he was sure of, and what of mother? Christian's eyelids grew heavy.

'Christian, don't you dare,' Sky's voice sounded distant.

'Sky, you need to do it now. Færies are dying.'

'You don't need to tell me that,' her tone was prickly, yet it was a comfort to Christian. It was selfish of him, wanting her to stay, but he couldn't help it.

Soon it would all be over.

With his energy fading, he felt for her other hand and took it in his.

'Stop being an eed, and destroy the Emerald.'

Her laugh turned into a sob. 'I'm going to do it.'

Sky's hand left his and Christian was as aware of its absence as much as the searing pain that was spreading through him.

'Sky, is that - what happened?'

'Rhia!' Sky cried.

Christian's senses had begun to fade though his heart soldiered on, continuing a slow, steady march in his chest. A part of him wanted to stay alive for his sister, but it was surpassed by the desperate need to escape this dreadful, heavy pain. It had begun to pull him down into unconsciousness, but if he could hang on a little longer…

༄

'Sky! Is that…what happened?'

Sky turned around and locked eyes with a teary-eyed princess.

'Rhia!' she cried, scrambling up off the ground to envelope her in a hug, to hell with their differences. Rhia's damp hair smelt of wood smoke. When Sky pulled away Rhia grabbed her shoulders, her steel-grey eyes wide and searching.

'You know what you must do,' she ordered, before going to her brother. Sky willed herself to keep moving and before picking up the glowing stone, glanced outside once more. There were no claps of thunder or flashes of lightning, just a silent rain that cast the world in a silver sheen. The ground was still, but the battle went on and somewhere amidst it all were Anya and Tæ, the two widowed rulers, one fighting for power, the other for peace.

Sky thought about the færies she'd met here. Rhia, Christian, Anya, Dill, Rhys and Arlo. It had been an overwhelming, crazy experience and it was time to end.

In a surge of anger at the unfairness of it all, Sky raised her hands above her head and threw the stone down onto the hard marble floor. She watched it almost in slow motion as it smashed, causing a thousand green shards to scatter outwards.

Seconds passed. She stood, waiting for a change.

Nothing happened.

Of course, she had to get rid of the necklace too. Sky ripped it off in disgust, ignoring the burn it left on her skin. She dropped it to the floor and lifted her foot to step on it, hard. She felt it break. For good measure she ground the ball of her foot against it and stood back to inspect the remains. It was definitely ruined. How easy that was.

Arlo had done his usual thing of appearing out of nowhere. His clothes were ripped, his skin stained with blood. They shared a momentary look of despair before Sky rushed back to Christian's side.

'He's still alive, but barely,' said Rhia. She sat on her knees with her hands in her lap, so reserved, so detached from Christian. Sky slumped down next to her and took Christian's hand. It was ice cold. Anger fuelled tears escaped her eyes, and her conscience screamed one question. *Why didn't it work?*

'I don't know what I'm supposed to do,' she said despondently, wiping her face.

'There is nothing you can do,' said Rhia. 'The battle will end when one side falls, or if Tæ comes to her senses and sides with mother, that way they can call a truce.'

'What are the chances?' Sky asked, hope slipping into her voice. She clutched onto the idea even though she knew Tæ would never

Chapter Thirty

admit defeat. She hoped anyway.

'I don't believe we have any.'

'Well that's encouraging. Even now, when Christian is...' she trailed off, words failing. She swallowed down the lump in her throat. Just then Christian opened his eyes.

At the same time Sky was caught by a bout of dizziness and fell sideways, the room revolving like a turntable. She lay uncomfortably on her side, and no matter how many times she tried to sit up she was unable to. She could still see and hear, so why couldn't she move?

Rhia called her name.

The world became a blur, like she was gazing through a misty window. This is how she'd felt before she first awoke in Krazonia.

Rhia called her name once more, but it dissolved into the black oblivion Sky was falling into.

She felt weightless as she drifted along a waterway, and then it covered her completely. Feeling in a way reprieved, Sky let herself go, surrendering to the dark.

∽

Rhia peered down at Sky, alarmed. Just a moment ago she'd been sitting beside her and now she was scarcely breathing.

'Sky!' Rhia exclaimed. 'Sky?' As if this situation wasn't bad enough! She turned back to her dying brother who was trying to lift his head, his eyes searching. It seemed Sky really had an effect on him. Deep down Rhia felt sympathy for what could never be, but there was no way she'd reveal it. As always she kept her emotions at bay.

'Is she – okay?' Christian asked between laboured breaths. Rhia leant forward and touched his wrist, finding it more difficult than usual to repress her emotions. She got angry so easily, and she'd smothered her grief with it. But now it was the opposite and all she wanted was to release the torrent of tears that had welled up inside of her.

'I don't know, Christian.' She wiped her eyes and stood up.

'What is that?' she whispered, shielding her eyes from the light that was moving across the realm.

'Sky may have succeeded after all,' answered a færie in dirtied clothes with scruffy ash blond hair, who Rhia hadn't noticed before. She acknowledged him before averting her gaze to the large, shattered windows.

It could have been a falling sun. The storm ceased and by the looks of it all færies had diverted their attention to the heavenly light that was being cast across the land. The bright white light split, becoming many smaller rays darting around the kingdom like lightning. Rhia's fingertips began to tingle, as did her toes. Shivers ran up and down her spine and through her wings, sparking at the tips.

The light spread. Rhia felt for her brother and placed her arms over him to protect him from whatever was happening.

'We are giving you a choice,' a voice echoed. *'Either to let your brother pass on in this kingdom where he will be remembered as one of the bravest færies who lived, or you can allow him life but on the alternate earth. He will not survive here.'*

Rhia sat up, the light dazzling her. 'Who am I talking to?'

'Soon he will die. You must decide,' it said softly, rekindling a memory she'd kept buried until now. It took her back four years, to Bluewater.

Rhia covered her eyes, hunching forward to fight painful cramps in her stomach. The Elana were contacting her again. 'You choose to appear now?' she whimpered.

'Decide, Rhia.'

She threw her head back. 'You're too late!'

She touched her brother's face to find his skin disturbingly cold. He looked so pale and Rhia knew the wound was draining the life out of him. He had hardly any left. Time went on and soon it would steal Christian away from her forever. *I will lose him either way,* she realised. Conceding Rhia raised her hands, tears trailing down her cheeks.

'Let him live, let him live.'

Chapter Thirty

She sank down onto the floor to lie next to him, savouring their last moments. She pressed her forehead to his, wishing there was another way to rid him of this pain.

Rhia forced herself to smile, even though with his eyes closed Christian wouldn't see it. Not wanting to know what came next she curled into herself on the marble floor, keeping one hand wrapped around her brother's.

She heard her father's voice, reaching her through white light. 'It's over.'

Chapter Thirty-One

Sky lay face down. She gradually lifted a hand to cover her already closed eyes, listening out for battle cries and rolling thunder and hearing only the light hearted whistles of a songbird, a shocking contrast. It meant she was no longer in the other world, but had landed back in her own. The musky scent of old makeup and dust filled her senses. Realisation swamped her and if she hadn't already been lying down, she'd have ended up that way.

Sky wasn't yet ready to move. She processed each connecting thought one by one as she adjusted to her surroundings. Krazonia had been her home for the past five days. She'd travelled to its neighbouring realm that happened to be full of horrors and ruled by a heartless queen. The task Elle had spoken of had been completed. She had succeeded. Sky moaned into the carpet. How could she possibly resume Normal Life?

Inhaling deeply, she braced herself for the reality as she pulled her hand away and opened her eyes, half expecting to see Christian gazing at her, concern drawing his eyebrows together. *'Are you okay?'*

Instead Sky looked at an alternate familiarity: her pine wardrobe. Trying to raise her head was like trying to lift a 2 tonne bowling ball, so she focused on moving one limb at a time until she managed to get onto her hands and knees. Dawn light stole through a gap in the curtains, casting the room in a dreamy pink hue. Sky found her way to the bed and slumped onto it, taking in the space before her with bleary eyes. Pine wardrobe, check. Her wonky standing light with the lace covered shade, check. Then

Chapter Thirty-One

her gaze landed on the chest-of-drawers and without thinking she rushed over to it, her heart bursting into a sprint. Pulling open the middle drawer she began rummaging through her clothes in search of the necklace, sweat prickling on the back of her neck.

The drawer was absent of any jewellery. It really was gone. Done. Finito.

'I destroyed it,' Sky told the wall. Saying it aloud made it all the more real and she waited for the words to sink in. They didn't seem to, rather hitting an invisible shield within which Sky had encompassed herself, so she wouldn't have to face the truth – the truth being that she didn't know how the hell she was going to continue with life after this. This gave Sky insight into how Elle must have felt these past four years. The word "tormented" sprung to mind. With effort she dragged herself back across the room, stopping in front of the full length mirror next to her bed, the mirror she'd brushed her hair and happily applied makeup in front of so many times. Blocking the stream of sunrise behind her, Sky looked into the eyes of someone barely there, a shadow of the person she'd been five days ago. Leaning closer she inspected its face. She could determine the blueness of her eyes and the shape of her nose and mouth. She wore a hoodie with black leggings. Sky Francis looked like Sky Francis.

She didn't feel the same inside. Something had shifted. She'd grown like a tree through the seasons, battling wind and rain, revelling in the comfort of warm sun. Had five days been enough time for that transformation? Silently Sky removed her plimsolls and changed into a long t-shirt before slipping into bed.

Shivering, she pulled the quilt up to her chin, hoping it would seal in some heat. Minutes ticked by and she felt no warmer. It was as if her heart had turned to ice and was pumping it in liquid form through her blood stream. Sinking a little further under the covers, Sky brought her knees up to her chest. She closed her eyes, surrendering herself to a daydream. The scene from a few days ago was still painfully fresh in her mind, of her sweltering under the hot sun, mallet in hand while the cynical Dill looked on. She'd knocked in post after post until her arms ached and her fringe stuck to her forehead. Christian had flown down to see her and Dill. Sky could recall how her cheeks flushed pink when she met Christian's curious gaze, and pictured herself standing there, out of breath and sweaty in a creased dress. His smile had caused her heart to leap, and all she could do was smile back, temporarily forgetting her appearance.

White cotton wool clouds passed through an azure sky. A perfect summer's day. Krazonians were working hard and laughing while they did so. The image began to dissolve and sunlight turned to dusk. Sky found herself back in her room, shaking beneath the bed covers. She felt a tugging in her chest; a physical longing that made her wish there was a magical way to forget everything. At the time she'd looked around thinking, *I want to remember this*, but in hindsight that had been a mistake. It would be easier to move on if she could forget.

She felt sick. Very soon she'd have to get up for school.

Sky laughed quietly at that thought, covering her mouth with her hands to repress the sound. The laugh developed into a sob that rose in her throat and she couldn't fight the sadness that overwhelmed her. She could hardly believe it was sadness, though it mingled with relief and shock. She needed to cry, so she buried her face in the quilt and let the tears come.

She must have fallen asleep. A light was switched on and someone was saying her name, chastising her for sleeping through the alarm. Sky was pulled out of her dreamless slumber when the covers were snatched away, revealing her to a cold world. She was no longer cocooned in the pocket of air under her quilt. Sky stretched her aching limbs and blinked away sleep, opening her eyes slowly. Grace Francis was staring at her, her smile half expectant and half accusing.

'Sky, you don't want to be late for school again do you?'

She tried to sniff but her nose was blocked. Her face felt dry and sore. Sky swallowed and shook her head, secretly relieved when her voice came out as a croak.

'I feel terrible, mum. There's no way I can go in today.' She sniffed again, for good measure.

Grace frowned, sitting herself down on the edge of the bed. 'You don't sound too good.'

Chapter Thirty-One

Sky's eyes stung with fresh tears and she turned her head away. 'I feel awful. I can't face school.' *I can't face life.*

Her mum sighed and patted her arm. 'Okay, I'll let the school know. Perhaps Cassie will bring some revision round later?'

Sky shook her head. 'I don't want to see anyone today, please.' She gazed at the plain lilac wallpaper, refusing to meet her mother's eye. She could sense another conversation looming.

'You have been a bit stressed recently-' Grace began, at which point Sky looked at her with eyes wide, a twitch of irritation in her jaw. She couldn't deal with this. It was too early in the morning.

'Please can we not go there right now? I promise I'll talk to you this evening.' Sky closed her eyes. 'I really just want to sleep.'

Grace delicately lifted the covers back over her. 'Fine, fine.'

Sky managed to avoid school for three days. On the second evening Cassie came over, revision books in hand. Wrapped in a blanket Sky opened the door to her friend.

Cassie in her pink bobble hat and parka, smiled tentatively. 'Hey.'

'Hello.' The cold winter air began to seep in and Sky beckoned her friend inside.

'Come in quick,' she even managed to smile, but with her head down it was hard to tell if Cassie noticed.

Sky shut the door against the frosty night and led Cassie through to the living room, silently craving for feelings of normality to return. Even with her friend here Sky struggled to remain in the present.

She sat opposite Cassie on the sofa, picking up her science book. 'How's your mum, Cass?'

'Um, she's okay. Well she's going in for radiotherapy this week. Thursday. That will be for two weeks.' Cassie took off her hat and held it in her lap, fiddling with the bobble absentmindedly as she spoke. 'The specialist did say she has a good chance of beating the cancer.'

This brought Sky round fast. She was so preoccupied with herself she hadn't thought about her best friend, who was suffering for other reasons that were far more important than her own. Cassie pressed her lips together and smiled. 'She'll be fine,

I know she will.'

Sky nodded and sat forward, giving Cassie her undivided attention. 'Of course she'll be fine,' she said. 'Hilary Harrow is a trooper.'

Cassie smiled weakly. 'She really is.'

'So, is it science or maths?' Sky piped up, willing her friend out of her sombre mood and pushing her own issues aside. 'Let's crack on.'

Cassie sighed and picked up a chunky text book that curled at the edges. 'Maths I'm afraid, but I need more help with this so,' she passed the book to Sky, 'ask me some stuff.'

The evening passed that way. Sky fetched herself and Cassie crisps and cake, they asked each other questions, talked about normal things and Sky felt the weight on her shoulders lift, and the black hole inside of her begin to shrink. When Cassie left she felt different, having forced herself to think of Hilary who would soon be facing radiotherapy.

The stark reality was that Sky had the choice to get on with her life, there was nothing physically wrong with her. But she couldn't stop thinking and wondering about Christian and Rhia, mainly Christian, and it continued to drag her down.

Perhaps school would be the kick start she needed.

The following morning Sky feigned illness again. 'I'll be better for tomorrow,' she said, scrunched tissue in hand. She hadn't slept well so that part was easy. Her parents' looks became more suspicious, but they never questioned it. She sensed that if another day went by, they would.

Putting on her coat and scarf Sky went for a walk, unintentionally starting the route to school. That wasn't such a good idea. Turning swiftly around she headed for home again, cursing.

'What am I, a hermit?' she asked herself. She wandered along the path on which she'd bumped into Elle. Would she be working today?

Even if she was, Sky was not yet ready to face her.

That evening around the table she felt the looks her parents were giving her: looks that led to questions. She chewed on a piece of steak. Her glass was filled with water. *I never did get around*

Chapter Thirty-One

to trying melrogan juice in Krazonia.

'Sky, you are worrying your mother and I a bit,' said James, fork poised by his mouth. Sky sat back in her seat, placing down her cutlery in preparation. *Here we go.*

He was debating whether to eat the steak, or put his fork down. A second later it was in his mouth. Sky saw it as his way of prolonging the conversation.

'You said you'd talk about it the other night,' he said, lowering his eyes. 'We haven't even touched on the subject yet.'

Sky shrugged. 'There really isn't much to say. I haven't felt a hundred per cent for a while. Since I got back to school, really.' She took a swig of water, feeling the cool liquid making its way through her. 'I don't know what you want me to say.'

Grace glared at the table.

'I'm offended,' she said. 'Do you think we're stupid? Blind to the fact you are unhappy?'

'Mum, it isn't that I'm unhappy. I'm just…deciding what I want to do with my life. You must remember doing the same. Maybe you *don't*,' Sky said with more spite than she intended. 'Sorry, sorry. I am revising believe it or not, and I'll be back at school tomorrow. Neither of you have to worry.'

Grace looked dissatisfied with her answer, but it wasn't going to change. Sky looked down at her plate and continued eating, wanting to fill the stupid hole. When would this *go away*?

Her father let out a small, conceding sigh. 'Okay, fine. You are sixteen after all. It must just be teenager syndrome.'

Sky smiled at that. 'That's what it is.'

'Have you still got that necklace by the way?'

Her smile faded and she looked down at her plate. 'Um, yeah. I'm going to drop it into the police station though, really soon.'

Sky had the house to herself that evening. She sat with her feet up on the sofa, watching TV. There were celebrity interviews happening on the red carpet for an awards show, women in dazzling dresses and men in impeccable suits were everywhere. She recognised many of the faces and imagined herself living that life. Who knows, it could be fun. Better than this.

There was a bang on the front door, making her jump. She

clutched at her chest and turned down the volume on the TV, listening out.

Three hesitant knocks this time. It was about half past eight, way too early for her parents to be arriving home. She walked out into the hallway and switched on the light.

Two knocks.

Sky had her hand on the latch, slowly lifting it.

'Who is it?'

'It's me.'

The two words ricocheted around her head. Sky leaned on the door for support, resting her forehead against the cold, painted wood. This was real, he was not. She shut her eyes.

'It's Christian, let me in, Sky? Please.'

She'd got it into her head she would never see him again. It had to be some cruel mind trick.

'I'll just wait here, then,' he said.

Sky opened the door a crack and peered out. Christian Meldin was standing there, not a figment of her imagination but alive and breathing in a jumper and jeans.

'It is you!' she said, gobsmacked. He looked the same: tall, with tousled brown hair and a strong jawline. He was a beautiful being but not one who belonged in her world.

'Yes, it is me,' and his face broke into a smile, softening his features. 'It's rather cold out here.'

Sky opened the door fully, her hands trembling. The hallway light bathed him in its ambient glow.

'Hello,' he said, and his breath clouded like mist in the space between them. Sky wanted to invite him in and hug him and kiss him...yet she stood still, her feet rooted to the spot.

'I-' she started. 'Come in.'

She stepped back in a daze, allowing him to walk into her house.

Christian was here.

Sky gazed at him, full of wonder. This had to be a dream, and it could continue for as long as it liked.

'How did you get here?'

'I don't know. I woke up a few days ago in some place...' He

Chapter Thirty-One

trailed off, crossing his arms. Sky shut the door and the two of them faced each other in the hallway.

'Elle found me.'

Sky's mouth fell open.

'What did she say?' She had to presume Christian knew the truth about Elle. 'I can see she's bought you some clothes,' she added. 'They're nice.'

Shut up Sky.

Christian laughed. 'Thank you. It's been rather overwhelming for me I must say. She told me everything I needed to know.'

The silence became heavy with unspoken thoughts. 'What about Rhia and your mother? They aren't with you?' Sky asked.

'On the day I arrived, my sister spoke to me through some sort of dream. I don't know exactly how, but I think the Elana had something to do with it. I remember being stabbed.'

Sky winced, remembering it well.

'She said she had to make a choice. I wouldn't have survived if I'd stayed in Krazonia, but if I went through the portal then I would be healed and well, become human, like you.'

'Wow,' she said with a heavy heart. 'You must miss them.' She thought about how she'd missed her family and friends in Krazonia, but she'd got them all back.

Christian looked at her and shrugged. The hallway light glittered in his dark brown eyes. 'I do miss them. A lot.'

Ignoring the butterflies fluttering madly her stomach, Sky wrapped her arms tightly around him, resting her head against his shoulder; the fabric of his clothes still held the chill of winter.

Christian's arms moved around her, locking them together. 'I know my family are okay. I will have to be content with that,' he sighed against Sky's hair. 'I'm still getting used to having to walk everywhere. Flying would be so much easier.'

Sky smiled to herself.

'I think walking might be safer, for me anyway.' She kept one arm around him and led him through to the living room. 'We should sit down. I need to sit down.'

Christian sat on the sofa and Sky sat down opposite, even if all she wanted to do was jump around, flailing her arms with happiness. She felt lightheaded with it.

'I keep expecting you to disappear,' she said.

Christian shook his head. 'I don't see that happening somehow.'

It went so quiet Sky could hear the clock ticking in the kitchen. She fell back against the cushions.

'What now?'

Chapter Thirty-Two

Christian was pulled sluggishly out of unconsciousness by the sensation of little stones pressing into his abdomen. He peeled open his eyes to inspect his surroundings, keeping the rest of his body still. There were trees, and birds singing, their songs carrying through the crisp air. It had to be early morning, for the pale haze that shone through between the jagged trees meant the sun would be on the crest of the horizon. No longer did Christian feel the life bleeding out of him, only lethargy remained. He sat up a little too quickly, causing a low buzz to ring in his ears.

Christian groaned. 'Not just yet,' he told himself, slipping down again. Focusing on a bunch of glistening leaves, waiting for the dizziness to pass, he made an attempt to gather his thoughts together. He'd been in Zania. Færies were fighting in the storm. This was not Zania.

The realisation snatched the breath from his lungs. He managed to lift himself up onto his knees and gulped down the cold, damp air. He held his hands to his head, looking around with equal fear and wonder. *Think. What was the last thing that happened?*

He'd been stabbed. Rhia was holding his hand. Sky had to destroy the Emerald.

His head spinning Christian scrambled up, clutching at his clothes and looking around aimlessly for somewhere to go. 'I should be dead,' he said desperately. He could still hear a low hum and knew it wasn't in his head. Where did it come from? His boots were ripped and the ties worn. The cloak still hung about his shoulders but something vital had been lost, as if he were missing half of his heart.

It was when he tried to flex them that Christian understood. His strong wings, the same as his father's, had been taken away from him. For a moment Christian was doubled over, fighting the urge to scream and yell. The temptation clawed at the back of his throat. He clenched his fists and started up a grassy slope sheltered by trees, afraid that if he didn't move he would fall to pieces.

It led Christian to the only possible conclusion: he was on human earth.

The slope ended at a level path of paved stone. He glanced left and right.

'Sky, where are you?' Christian's words trailed into the air and some desperate hope made him wonder whether they would carry, and she would hear them. There was nothing for it. He started walking. The sun had begun its rise into the sky, bringing with it a blush of pink that bled into blue above him. Christian began to shiver. The weather here was so unlike Krazonia.

The path brought him to a wider path and the source of the hum: metal works on wheels, with people inside of them moving along at speed. Sky's voice came to mind. They'd been talking at the edge of Morel village, chewing on olive bread.

'Cars help us get around. We drive them...' she'd said. So these were cars.

Walking slowly along the path he watched the cars with bewilderment. Some other humans were running along in tight black clothes with yellow stripes. They stared at him as they went by. He contemplated removing his cloak, but the frosty air was unappealing and he wanted as much cover as possible. He kept it on and continued walking. It may well have looked odd, but in that moment Christian didn't care.

If he'd been brought here, what would be the point if nobody would help him?

He wandered down a hill, passing small buildings which must have been "shops", made of brick with glass at the front. They reminded him of the shops in Krazonia square. A stab of pain

Chapter Thirty-Two

came from nowhere, hitting him right in the chest. Christian thought of his home, of his moody sister and loving yet dishonest mother, of the butlers and his friends Dill, Rhys, Lyra and Aeron. Would he ever see them again?

'Excuse me?'

Christian was halted by a young woman. She studied him with curiosity. Her brown hair was tied back and she had fine green eyes. Christian felt her gaze probing him and he didn't like it.

'Yes,' he wasn't sure what else to say.

'I know this is going to sound very weird but…are you Christian?'

The question stunned him. He stepped away from the stranger. 'Who are you?'

She covered her mouth with a gloved hand. 'So you are Christian Meldin?' Her voice came out muffled.

He nodded slowly.

The woman gasped. 'You're *here*. Do you know…wait,' she rummaged around her pocket and pulled out a small object. Moments later she was talking into it, while Christian looked on. This world was different indeed and it wasn't safe. At least, he did not feel it. This person knew who he was, he'd have to wait. To walk away now would be a foolish idea.

'Hi, I can't make it in today. Adam I am sorry. I know,' she said, frequently glancing at Christian as if to check he was still standing there. 'Why don't you see if Yvonne can cover, or Alicia. I can't come in,' she added weight to the last four words. 'It's too important. I'm sorry but personal matters come first. Bye,' she said and put the object back into her pocket.

'Christian, I know you must be having a bit of a breakdown right now. Are you on your own?'

He blinked, struggling to get his head around this bizarre situation. 'Yes. Who are you?'

'My name is Elle Harris. Will you walk with me?'

Elle. *Elle.* The name stirred up a memory from the depths of his mind, bringing it to the surface. Christian looked at her face again, harder this time, but still did not recognise it.

'I will walk,' he said. 'If you can explain what has happened to me.'

Away with the Færies

She tilted her head at him and then sighed.

'It's all very strange.'

'Why?'

They walked side by side. 'Basically, four years ago I came to Krazonia to complete a task. I failed. Do you remember,' she hesitated and Christian could see the difficulty she was having in phrasing what she was trying to say. That or she just did not want to say it.

'I pleaded with your parents for help and I was rejected, cast aside. Your sister, however, helped me.'

Christian was filled with dread.

'She believed me and she talked about the Elana, saying that they could offer guidance if we could find them.'

'And you did,' said Christian with contempt, realising he walked alongside a coward. She was the human before Sky.

'Yes. I ran away and left her there to face them alone. But think about this,' she ended the sentence sharply. 'I had no idea where I was. No one told me what to expect and my God, no one on this earth believes in an alternate dimension inhabited by færies. "It's all myth and folklore". The truth has been buried over the centuries or however long your world has existed for. The fact is you can't be angry at me and you cannot blame me for your father's death!' she burst out. Christian had never thought he'd blamed this stranger, but perhaps he had, given the bitterness he felt and the harsh words on his tongue.

Elle grabbed his arm, taking him by surprise. Her eyes were watering.

'For four years I've had it on my conscience,' she said and when she blinked, a tear dribbled down her cheek.

'I'm eighteen years old and I live alone. My friend's think I'm a freak. It's like I've had this burden weighing me down and I just need you to tell me I'm not the one to blame.' She released him and Christian looked into her tired eyes, no longer feeling animosity towards her, only sympathy. It had been tough for him losing the king: his brave, compassionate father. But it seemed almost as bad that someone who hadn't known him at all had felt the weight of his death on their conscience for the same amount

Chapter Thirty-Two

of time. Just like Sky, Elle had not asked to be transported to Krazonia. Fate had simply thrown her into it.

'Of course it's not your fault,' he said softly. 'I'm sorry that it's been four years.'

Elle nodded and rubbed her eyes. 'Thank you. Are you hungry, or thirsty? You could probably do with a hot drink. Come back to mine and we can talk. I want to hear about everything.' Christian struggled to understand her. All her words seemed to roll into one sentence. 'I'm guessing you'll want to see Sky soon? Clearly she succeeded where I failed.' Her look was distant. 'She did it.'

Christian's heart jumped in his chest. 'You know Sky? He asked with a smile, but it faded as realisation crept in. 'If I'm here and Sky accomplished her task, that means I will never be able to get home. The portal is closed.' He balled his fists in his hair, anguish taking hold of him.

'I don't know if it will ever be possible to return,' said Elle, 'and for that I'm sorry.'

Shaken to the core Christian sank to his knees, the gritty path nicking his skin. 'I'll never see my family again,' saying the words made it all the more real, and all the more painful. But just like his father, he'd be brave. He ran his hands through his hair and something dropped onto the ground; a tiny shard of glass. Christian carefully picked it up, and upon closer inspection realised it was a tiny part of the Emerald. He stared at it until a hand touched his shoulder.

'Come on,' said Elle softly.

Christian placed the shard into his pocket for safekeeping, keeping quiet on the matter.

'Do you know where she lives?' he asked Elle.

They started walking again. 'Of course I do. We only spoke last night,' said Elle casually, pushing opening a gate.

Christian felt his heart expand in his chest. 'Is this her house?'

'Unfortunately no, this is mine. To be honest I think Sky will need a few days to readjust. Just give her a few days, and then you can surprise her.'

'How could you have spoken last night? She was in Krazonia for five days.'

There was a jingling of keys and Elle opened the red painted door. Christian followed her inside, immediately catching a waft of herbs, mingled with a sweet fragrance.

Elle peeled off her coat and slung it over a banister. 'I think time works a little differently in our worlds. That's the only explanation I can offer you. Make yourself comfortable, if you can.'

She made a hot drink called "tea" and it tasted like nothing Christian had ever tasted. The sweet, hot liquid warmed him through, and sitting in a soft chair he felt the weariness return to his limbs. But he would not sleep. He drank the tea and spoke to Elle about Sky, and all that had happened. There were many objects he didn't recognise and could only hope in time he would accustom himself to their uses - assuming the portal had closed and he'd never return to his alternate earth. All he could do was take in each surreal moment.

'I can't believe you went through all of that,' Elle stated, shaking her head. 'And Sky managed to do it. She was the right one after all.'

'Sky was very brave. She had to be,' Christian remarked.

A high pitched ringing sound came out of nowhere. Elle rushed out of the room and the sound stopped. 'Hi Adam,' he heard her say.

Christian sank back in the chair, his heart and mind full. What would he do now he was here? He was a prince in Krazonia, but just a human in this world. If he began stating claims he imagined it wouldn't go down well with other people.

Although he'd arrived here on his own he knew he wasn't alone. Sky was somewhere, and Elle had spared him from wandering these unknown paths and for that he was thankful.

Elle reappeared in the doorway. 'I have to go to work, Christian. There is no one else. So, um,' she looked around the room, biting down on her lower lip. 'I hadn't exactly expected any visitors. Will you stay here, today? Don't go outside.' She clasped her hands together. 'I know I shouldn't be bossing you around seeing as in Krazonia you were prince and all but if you could just wait until I come back?'

Chapter Thirty-Two

Christian laughed into his tea. 'I understand. I wouldn't dare venture out without a guide.'

A short while later he was in an empty house.

He lay down on the long sofa and closed his eyes. Time passed.

'Christian can you hear me?'

He was asleep but Rhia's voice was in his head. Christian imagined opening his mouth to respond but he didn't need to. *I can hear you.*

'I'm so sorry,' her voice echoed with sadness. *'The Elana have given me this chance to contact you. I wanted to say that they gave me a choice and I chose to save you...'*

Is that why I'm here? Christian felt calm when he said the words.

'Yes. I could have chosen to let you die here, where you would be buried and hailed as a hero but I thought it better to lose you to another life, than to death. I don't care how selfish that makes me, but I do miss you, so much. The portal is closed, Christian,' her voice became an eerie whisper. *'Mother and I are okay but our world is different now.'*

Why?

'I want to tell you, but I can't. The less you know the better.'

Tell me.

'Christian, I can't.'

It's not fair, Rhia. In spite of himself, Christian lifted his arms. He was stretching them, reaching out for someone who wasn't there. There was only darkness. Grief enveloped him in its embrace, choking him.

Rhia, he said in a restricted voice. *Are you still there?* When he received no response he let his arms drop, grief giving way to emptiness.

A few days passed. Elle bought him some new clothes, a drastic change to his usual plain shirt and shorts. Now he had extra items to think about, like *socks*. Elle explained to him the ways in which this world worked. She showed him the television and he read newspapers to find out about the government and the world's current happenings. It was strange, how much interest

Away with the Færies

these countries had in one another. Everyone knew everyone's business, it seemed. Christian went along with it, baffled by it all.

One evening Elle was washing up in the kitchen and Christian was drying like it was the most natural thing to do, when she stopped and leaned against the counter.

Christian froze, towel in hand.

'You should go tonight,' she said.

'Go where?' he replied, but he knew.

'Enough time has gone by. I'm surprised you haven't said anything, actually. I'll tell you how to get there.'

Christian swallowed and placed the towel on the side. He felt excited and nervous all at once, his stomach teeming with fireflies.

'Okay then,' he agreed.

Elle saw him to the door. 'She will be shocked but I know she'll also be happy, just give her a minute to regain composure.'

Christian stepped out into the cold night air, bracing himself.

'I've known her for so little time,' he said quietly, surprised by his own feelings.

Elle sighed, resting her head against the doorframe. 'Sometimes these things just happen. Fate is strange like that. Have a good evening.' Her smile was mischievous as she closed the door.

Christian walked down the path, recalling the directions. Right, right again, over the hill, left and then left again. It would have been so much quicker had he been able to fly.

He focused on his shoes hitting the pavement at a fast pace, mirroring the beat of his heart. He found the cold wind invigorating. As he walked, Christian glanced up at the winter sky and at the twinkling stars that adorned it.

The past wouldn't be forgotten, and the future was unknown.

With that, Christian burst into a run.

Epilogue

Sky picked up her glass of lemonade, ice cubes clinking against one another as she drank. It was the summer before she and her friends started college, so she had to make every day count. Today was a joint celebration for Cassie's birthday, and her mum's remission. Hilary had been given the all clear after final tests, which was the best birthday present Cassie could have asked for.

Sky breathed in the warm air tinged with honeysuckle, viewing the world from behind her grey tinted sunglasses. She wandered over to Cassie who, alongside Fran, was attempting to set up the barbecue.

'Everything alright here guys?' she asked.

'Totally. As you can see we are pros,' said Fran, poking the charcoal bag with a skewer while Cassie finished screwing in a bolt to one side of the barbecue.

'Where are the boys?' asked Sky. This was a job for one of them.

'They're in the kitchen getting the food ready.'

'This is the wrong way round,' Sky thought aloud, putting down her drink on the nearest plastic table. 'I'll be right back.'

She headed inside, passing Christian and Elle along the way. Christian entwined his fingers with hers and they shared a smile. Sky turned her attention to her friends, keeping a hold of his hand.

Her friends, who were supposedly sorting out the food, were in fact in conversation, drinking their cans of cider.

'Louis, Alex and Simon – get out there and sort out the barbecue.' She raised her eyebrows at them and pointed outside.

'If you want to eat tonight I would go now. Plus it is Cassie's birthday so she shouldn't be doing all the work.'

They had the decency to look guilty. Cans in hand, the three of them headed for the garden.

'Get ready to bring the food out then!' Simon called over his shoulder.

Sky was in the bathroom, washing her hands. In the mirror she observed the slight tan she'd caught from days in the sun, no longer did she sport the 'naturally pasty' look. Her fringe had grown out completely, and she'd had a few inches chopped off. She looked different, and felt better for it.

Only when she'd finished drying her hands on the fluffy towel did she notice, and the sight caused her stomach to lurch.

In February Christian had revealed to her a ring, created from a shard of the Emerald. It signified what they'd been through, and Sky hadn't taken it off since. It had remained a rich green colour.

Sky held her trembling hand up to the light to make sure.

She hadn't been seeing things.

It was glowing again.

Away with the Faeries

Acknowledgements

To my family and friends, thank you for your support. Writing is a lonely task. It's surprising what a few words of encouragement can do.

Mum, my co-editor. I appreciate the time you took, red pen in hand, to read and edit *Away with the Færies* when it was in a raw state.

Paul at *www.extrabold.design*. With your expertise, you've created the ideal book cover for this story. Thank you for the cover design and text setting, helping me bring it all to life!